THE ULTIMATE COLLECTION

Volume Six

WINTER OF CHANGE

and

A WINTER LOVE STORY

Two full-length novels

Harlequin Mills & Boon Limited,
Eton House, 18-24 Paradise Road, Richmond, Surrey TW9 1SR

This compilation: THE ULTIMATE COLLECTION
© Harlequin Enterprises II B.V., 2002

First published in Great Britain as:

WINTER OF CHANGE © Betty Neels 1973

A WINTER LOVE STORY © Betty Neels 1998

ISBN 0 263 83648 7

Set in Times Roman 11¼ on 12½ pt.
141-0103-103658

Printed and bound in Spain
by Litografia Rosés, S.A., Barcelona

BETTY NEELS
THE ULTIMATE COLLECTION

Betty Neels's novels are loved
by millions of readers around the world,
and this very special *12-volume collection*
offers a unique chance to recapture the pleasure
of some of her most popular stories.

Each month we're bringing you a new volume
containing two timeless classics—irresistible love
stories that belong together, whether they share the
same colourful setting, romantic theme, or follow the
same characters in their continuing lives...

As a special treat, each volume also includes an
introductory letter by a different author. Some of the
most popular names in romance fiction are delighted
to pay tribute to Betty Neels; we hope you enjoy
reading their personal thoughts and memories.

We're proud and privileged to bring you
this very special collection, and hope you enjoy
reading—and keeping—these twelve wonderful
volumes over the coming months.

Volume Six

*—with an introduction from international
bestselling author*
Margaret Way

**Enjoy the magic of Christmas
with these two charming novels...**

*WINTER OF CHANGE
A WINTER LOVE STORY*

We'd like to take this opportunity to pay tribute to **Betty Neels**, who sadly passed away last year. Betty was one of our best-loved authors. As well as being a wonderfully warm and thoroughly charming individual, Betty led a fascinating life even before becoming a writer, and her publishing record was impressive.

Betty spent her childhood and youth in Devonshire before training as a nurse and midwife. She was an army nursing sister during the war, married a Dutchman and subsequently lived in Holland for fourteen years. On retirement from nursing Betty started to write, inspired by a lady in a library bemoaning the lack of romantic novels.

Over her thirty-year writing career Betty wrote more than 134 novels and was published in more than one hundred international markets. She continued to write into her ninetieth year, remaining as passionate about her characters and stories then as she was with her very first book.

Betty will be greatly missed, both by her friends at Harlequin Mills & Boon® and by her legions of loyal readers around the world. Betty was a prolific writer and has left a lasting legacy through her heartwarming novels. She will always be remembered as a truly delightful person who brought great happiness to many.

Dear Reader

When my editor asked if I would like to submit a tribute to that very special lady, the late Betty Neels, I didn't have a second's hesitation. Betty Neels's contribution to Harlequin Mills & Boon's enchanting world of romance has been immense. Betty's longevity, both in her lifespan and her wonderfully successful career, must have been due not only to her strong physical constitution and the delightful buoyant spirit that shines through her writing but also to her self-discipline, her sense of commitment and the great sense of accomplishment I know she derived from her writing, knowing the end result would bring joy and comfort into the lives of countless thousands of women all around the world. What more could any writer want? To create love stories to live in the memory. I think it a fine and appropriate thing that Harlequin Mills & Boon® have honoured Betty Neels by bringing out twelve volumes of her work. This is a great opportunity for her devoted readership to secure the enduring works of a much loved and widely collected writer.

Vale, Betty! I know you're happy, wherever you are!

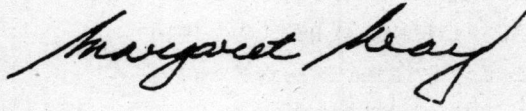

WINTER OF CHANGE

by

Betty Neels

CHAPTER ONE

SISTER THOMPSON made her slow impressive way down Women's Surgical, bidding her patients a majestic good morning as she went, her sharp eyes behind their glasses noticing every small defect in the perfection she demanded on her ward—and that applied not only to the nursing and care of the ladies lying on either side of her, but also to the exact position of the water jugs on the lockers, the correct disposal of dressing gowns, the perfection of the bedspreads and the symmetry of the pillows. The nurses who worked for her held her in hearty dislike, and when posted to her ward quickly learned the habit of melting away out of her sight whenever their duties permitted. Something which Mary Jane Pettigrew, her recently appointed staff nurse, was, at that particular time, quite unable to do. She watched her superior's slow, inevitable progress with a wary eye as she changed the dressing on Miss Blake's septic finger; she had no hope of getting it done before Sister Thompson arrived, for Miss Blake was old and shaky and couldn't keep her hand still for more than ten seconds at a time. Mary Jane, watching Nurse Wells and Nurse Simpson disappear, one into the sluice room, the other into the bathrooms at the end of the ward, wondered how long it would be before they were discovered—in the meantime, perhaps she could sweeten Sister Thompson's temper.

She fastened the dressing neatly and wished her superior a cheerful good morning which that good lady didn't bother to answer, instead she said in an arbitrary manner: 'Staff Nurse Pettigrew, you've been on this ward for two weeks and not only do you fail to maintain discipline amongst the nurses; you seem quite incapable of keeping the ward tidy. There are three pillows—and Miss Trump's top blanket, also Mrs Pratt's water jug is in the wrong place...'

Mary Jane tucked her scissors away in her pocket and picked up the dressing tray. She said with calm, 'Mrs Pratt can't reach it unless we put it on that side of her locker, Sister, and Miss Trump was cold, so I unfolded her blanket. May the nurses go to coffee?'

Sister Thompson cast her a look of dislike. 'Yes—and see that they're back before Mr Cripps' round.' She turned on her heel and went back up the ward and into her office, to appear five minutes later with the information that Mary Jane was to present herself to the Chief Nursing Officer at once, 'and,' added Sister Thompson, 'I suggest that you take your coffee break at the same time, otherwise you will be late for the round.'

Which meant that unless the interview was to be a split-second, monosyllabic affair, there would be no coffee. Mary Jane skimmed down the ward, making a beeline for the staff cloakroom. Whatever Sister Thompson might say, she was going to take a few minutes off in order to tidy her person. The room was small, nothing more than a glorified cupboard, and in order to see her face in the small mirror she was forced to rise on to her toes, for she was a small girl, only a little over five feet, with delicate bones and a tiny waist. She took one look at her reflection now, uttered a sigh and whipped off her cap so that she might smooth her honey-brown hair, fine and straight and worn in an old-fashioned bun on the top of her head. The face which looked back at her was pleasant but by no means pretty; only her eyes, soft and dark, were fine under their thin silky arched brows, but her nose was too short above a wide mouth and although her teeth were excellent they tended to be what she herself described as rabbity. She rearranged her cap to her satisfaction, pinned her apron tidily and started on her journey to the office.

Her way took her through a maze of corridors, dark passages and a variety of staircases, for Pope's Hospital was old, its ancient beginnings circumvented by more modern additions, necessitating a conglomeration of connecting passages. But Mary Jane, her thoughts busy, trod them unhesitatingly, having lived with them for more than three years. She had no idea why she was wanted, but while she was in the office it might be a good idea to mention that she wasn't happy on Women's Surgical. She had been aware, when she took the post, that it would be no bed of roses; Sister Thompson was notorious for her ill-temper and pernickety ways, but Mary Jane, recently State Registered, had felt capable of moving mountains... She would, she decided as she sped down a stone-flagged passage with no apparent ending, give in her notice at the end of the month and in the meantime start looking for another job. The thought of leaving Pope's was vaguely worrying, as she had come to regard it as her home, for indeed she had no home in the accepted sense. She had been an orphan from an early age, brought up, if one could call it that, by her grandfather, a retired Army colonel, who lived in a secluded house near Keswick and seldom left it. She had spent her holidays there all the while she was at the expensive boarding school to which he had sent her, and she had sensed his relief when she had told him, on leaving that admirable institution, that she wished to go to London and train to be a nurse, and in the three years or more in which she had been at Pope's she had gone to see him only once each year, not wishing to upset his way of living, knowing that even during the month of her visit he found her youthful company a little tiresome.

Not that he didn't love her in his own reserved, elderly fashion, just as she loved him, and would have loved him even more had he encouraged her to do so. As it was she accepted their relationship with good sense because she was a sensible girl, aware too that she would probably miss a good deal of the fun of life because she would need to work for the rest of it; even at the youthful age of twenty-two she had discovered that men, for the most part, liked good looks and failing that, a girl with a sound financial background, and she had neither, for although her grandfather lived comfortably enough, she had formed the opinion over the years that his possessions would go to some distant cousin she had never seen, who lived in Canada. True, old Colonel Pettigrew had educated her, and very well too, provided her with the right clothes and given her handsome presents at Christmas and on her birthday, but once she had started her training as a nurse, he had never once offered to help her financially—not that she needed it, for she had the good sense to keep within her salary and although she liked expensive clothes she bought them only when she saved enough to buy them. Her one extravagance was her little car, a present from her grandfather on her twenty-first birthday; it was a Mini and she loved it, and despite her fragile appearance, she drove it well.

The office door was firmly closed when she reached it and when she knocked she was bidden to enter at once the outer room, guarded by two office Sisters, immersed in paper work, one of whom paused long enough to wave Mary Jane to a chair before burying herself in the litter of papers on her desk. Mary Jane perched on the edge of a stool, watching her two companions, feeling sorry for them; they must have started out with a desire to nurse the sick, and look where they were now—stuck behind desks all day, separated from the patients by piles of statistics and forms, something she would avoid at all costs, she told herself, and was interrupted in her thoughts by the buzzer sounding its summons.

The Chief Nursing Officer was quite young, barely forty, with a twinkling pair of eyes, a nice-looking face and beautifully arranged hair under her muslin cap. She smiled at Mary Jane as she went in.

'Sit down, Staff Nurse,' she invited. 'There's something I have to tell you.'

'Oh lord, the sack!' thought Mary Jane. 'Old Thompson's been complaining...' She was deep in speculation as to what she had done wrong when she was recalled to her surroundings by her companion's pleasant voice.

'It concerns your grandfather, Nurse Pettigrew. His housekeeper telephoned a short time ago. He isn't very well and has asked for you to go to his home in order to look after him. Naturally you will wish to do so, although I've been asked to stress the fact that there's no'—she paused—'no cause for alarm, at least for the moment. I believe your grandfather is an old man?'

Mary Jane nodded. 'Eighty-two,' she said in her rather soft voice, 'but he's very tough. May I go at once. please?'

'As soon as you wish. I'll telephone Sister Thompson so that there's no need for you to go back to the ward. Perhaps when you get to your grandfather's, you'll let me know how things are.'

She was dismissed. She made her way rapidly to the Nurses' Home, thankful that she wouldn't have to face Sister Thompson, her mind already busy with the details of her journey. It was full autumn, it would be cold in Cumbria, so she would take warm clothes but as few as possible—she could pack a case in a few minutes. She was busy doing that when her bedroom door was flung open and her dearest friend, Janet Moore, came in. 'There's a rumour,' she began, 'someone overheard that you'd been sent to the Office.' Her eyes lighted on the little pile of clothes on the bed. 'Mary Jane, you've never been...no, of course not, you've never done anything really wicked in your life. What's up?'

Mary Jane told her as she squeezed the last sweater into her case, shut the lid and started to tear off her uniform. She was in slacks and a heavy woolly by the time she had finished, and without bothering to do more than smooth her hair, tied a bright scarf over it, pushed impatient feet into sensible shoes, caught up her handbag and the case and made for the door, begging her friend to see to her laundry for her as she went. 'See you,' she said briefly, and Janet called after her:

'You're not going now—this very minute? It's miles away—it'll be dark...'

'It's ten o'clock,' Mary Jane informed her as she made off down the corridor, 'and it's two hundred and ninety miles—besides, I know the way.'

It seemed to take a long time to get out of London, but once she was clear of the suburbs and had got on to the A1, she put a small, determined foot down on the accelerator, keeping the little car going at a steady fifty-five, and when the opportunity occurred, going a good deal faster than that.

Just south of Newark she stopped for coffee and a sandwich and then again when she turned off the A1 at Leeming to cross the Yorkshire fells to Kendal. The road was a lonely one, but she knew it well, and although the short autumn afternoon was already dimming around her, she welcomed its solitude after the rush and bustle of London. At Kendal she stopped briefly before taking the road which ran through Ambleside and on to Keswick. The day was closing in on her now, the mountains around blotting out the last of a watery sun, but she hardly noticed them. At any other time she would have stopped to admire the view, but now she scarcely noticed them, for her thoughts were wholly of her grandfather. The last few miles of the long journey seemed endless, and she heaved a sigh of relief as she wove the car through Keswick's narrow streets and out again on to the road climbing to Cockermouth. Keswick was quickly left behind; she was back in open country again and once she had gone through Thronthwaite she slowed the car. She was almost there, for now the road ran alongside the lake with the mountains crowding down to it on one side, tree-covered and dark, shutting out the last of the light, and there was only an odd cottage or two now and scattered along the faint gleam of the water, larger houses, well away from each other. The road curved away from the lake and then returned and there, between it and the water, was her grandfather's house.

It stood on a spit of land running out into the lake, its garden merging into the grass alongside the quiet water. It was of a comfortable size, built of grey stone and in a style much favoured at the beginning of the nineteenth century, its arched windows fitted with leaded panes, its wrought-iron work a little too elaborate and a turret or two ornamenting its many-gabled roof. All the same it presented a pleasing enough picture to Mary Jane as she turned the car carefully into the short drive and stopped outside the front porch. Its door stood open and the woman standing there came to meet her with obvious relief.

'Mrs Body, how lovely to see you! I came as quickly as I could—how's Grandfather?'

Mrs Body was pleasant and middle-aged and housekeeper to the old Colonel for the last twenty years or more. She took Mary Jane's hand and said kindly, 'There, Miss Mary Jane, if it isn't good to see you, I must say. Your grandfather's not too bad—a heart attack, as you know, but the doctor's coming this evening and he'll tell you all about it. But now come in and have tea, for you'll be famished, I'll be bound.'

She led the way indoors as she spoke, into the dim, roomy hall. 'You go up and see the Colonel, he's that anxious for you to get here—and I'll get the tea on the table.'

Mary Jane nodded and smiled and ran swiftly up the uncarpeted staircase, past the portraits of her ancestors and on to the landing, to tap on a door in its centre. The room she was bidden to enter was large and rather over-full of ponderous furniture, but cheerful enough by reason of the bright fire burning in the grate and the lamps on either side of the bed.

The Colonel lay propped up with pillows. an old man with a rugged face which, to Mary Jane's discerning eye, had become very thin. He said now in a thin thread of a voice, 'Hullo, child—how long did it take you this time?' and she smiled as she bent to kiss him; ever since he had given her the car, he had made the same joke about the time it took her to drive up from London. She told him now, her head a little on one side as she studied him. She loved him very much and he was an ill old man, but none of her thoughts showed on her calm, unremarkable features. She sat down close to the bed and talked for a little while in her pretty voice, then got up to go to her tea, telling him that she would be back later.

'Yes, my dear, do that. I daresay Morris will be here by then, he knows all about me.' He added wistfully, 'You'll stay, Mary Jane?'

She retraced her steps to his bed. 'Of course, Grandfather. I've no intention of going back until you're well again—I've got unlimited leave from Pope's,' she grinned engagingly at him, 'and you know how much I love being here in the autumn.'

Tea was a substantial meal; a huge plate of bacon and eggs, scones, home-made bread and a large cake, as well as a variety of jams and a dish of cream. Mary Jane, who was hungry, did justice to everything on the table while Mrs Body, convinced that she had been half starved in hospital, hovered round, urging her to make a good meal.

She did her best, asking questions while she ate, but Mrs Body's answers were vague, so it was with thankfulness that she went to meet the doctor when he rang the bell. She had known him since she was a little girl and held him in great affection, as he did her. He gave her an affectionate kiss now, saying, 'I knew you would come at once, my dear. You know your grandfather's very ill?'

They walked back to the sitting room and sat down. 'Yes,' said Mary Jane. 'I'll nurse him, of course.'

'Yes, child, I know you will, but that won't be for long. He'll rally for a few days, perhaps longer, but he's not going to recover. He was most anxious that you should come.'

'I'll stay as long as I can do anything to help, Uncle Bob—who's been looking after him?'

'Mrs Body and the district nurse, but he wanted you—there's something he wishes to talk to you about. I suggest you let him do that tomorrow morning when he's well rested.' He smiled at her. 'How's hospital?'

She told him briefly about Sister Thompson. 'It's not turning out quite as I expected, perhaps I'm not cut out to make a nurse...'

He patted her shoulder. 'Nonsense, there's nothing wrong with you, Mary Jane. I should start looking for another job and leave as soon as you can—at least...' He paused and she waited for him to finish, but he only sat there looking thoughtful and presently said: 'Well, I'll go and take a look—you'll be around when I come downstairs?'

He went away, and Mary Jane went along to the kitchen and spent some time helping Mrs Body and catching up on the local news until Doctor Morris reappeared. In the hall he said briefly: 'He's fighting a losing battle, I'm afraid,' then went on to give her his instructions, 'and I'll be in some time tomorrow morning,' he concluded.

There was a dressing room next to the Colonel's room. Mary Jane, who usually slept in one of the little rooms, moved her things into it, had a brief chat with her grandfather, settled him for the night and went down to the kitchen where the faithful Mrs Body was waiting with cocoa. They sat at the table, drinking it, with Major, the Colonel's middle-aged dog, sitting at their feet, and discussed the small problems confronting them. Mary Jane finished her cocoa and put down her cup. 'Well, now I'm here,' she said in her sensible way, 'you must have some time to yourself—these last few days must have been very tiring for you. If I'd known, I'd have come sooner.'

Mrs Body shook her head. 'Your grandfather wouldn't hear of it, not at first, but when Doctor Morris told him—he couldn't get you here fast enough,' she concluded, and sighed. 'All the same, I'll admit I'll be glad of an hour or so to myself. Lily comes up each morning as she always does, she's a good girl, and now you're here, I could get away for a bit.'

Mary Jane agreed. 'Supposing you take the Mini for a couple of hours each day? You could go to Keswick or Cockermouth if you want to do some shopping. I'll be quite all right here—I can go for a walk when you get back.'

The housekeeper gave her a grateful smile. 'That's kind of you, Miss Mary Jane, I'd like that. I want my hair done and one thing and another—you don't mind me using the Mini?'

'Heavens, no. Now I think I'll go to bed, it's been a long day. Will you be all right? I'll be in the dressing room and I've fixed Grandfather's bell and I shall leave the door open—besides, he's had a sedative. You will sleep? or shall I bring you something?'

'Bless you, child, I've never taken any of those nasty pills yet, and don't intend to. I'll sleep like a baby.'

It was a bright, clear morning when Mary Jane woke the next morning and her grandfather was still sleeping; he had wakened once in the small hours and she had gone and sat with him for an hour until he dozed off again; now he would probably sleep for another hour or more. She put on slacks and a sweater, tied her hair back and went downstairs. Mrs Body was already up, so they drank their early morning tea together and then Mary Jane took Major into the garden and across the grass to the lake's edge. The water was calm and as smooth as silk, the mountains reflected in it so that it took on their colour, grey and green. Across the lake Skiddaw loomed above the other peaks, the sun lending it a bronze covering for its granite slopes.

Mary Jane looked about her with pleasure as she threw sticks for Major, a pleasure tinged with sadness because the Colonel was ill, and although he was an old man, and didn't, she suspected, mind dying, she would miss him very much. He had been all the family she had known; now she would be alone, save for the cousin in Canada. She had never met him and her grandfather seldom mentioned him. She supposed that after her grandfather died, this cousin would inherit the house and whatever went with it. She knew nothing of the Colonel's affairs; he had encouraged her to earn her own living when she had left school and she had always imagined that he had done so because he couldn't afford to keep her idle at home, for although the house was a comfortable one and well furnished and there was no evidence of poverty, common sense told her that the old man and his housekeeper could live economically enough, whereas if she lived with them, she would need clothes and pocket money and holidays... She went back into the house, and after a reassuring peep at the Colonel, went to eat her breakfast.

Mrs Body left soon after Lily arrived and Mary Jane went upstairs to make her grandfather comfortable for the day. He seemed better, even demanding his razor so that he might shave himself, a request which she refused in no uncertain manner. Indeed, she fetched the old-fashioned cut-throat razor which he always used, and wielded it herself without a qualm, an action which caused him to ask her somewhat testily exactly what kind of work she did in hospital. There seemed no point in going too deeply into this; she fetched the post, opened his letters for him, and when he had read them, offered to read *The Times* to him. Perhaps it was her gentle voice, perhaps it was the splendid sports news, one or other of them sent him off into a sound sleep. She put the bell by his hand and went downstairs. It was barely eleven o'clock, Mrs Body wouldn't be back until the afternoon, Lily was bustling around the sitting room—Mary Jane went into the garden, round to the front of the house where she would be able to hear her grandfather's bell; there was a lot of weeding which needed doing in the rose beds which bordered the drive.

She had been hard at it for fifteen minutes or so when she became aware that a car had stopped before the gate, and when she looked round she saw that it was a very splendid car—a Rolls-Royce Corniche convertible, the sober grey of its coachwork gleaming against the green of the firs bordering the road behind it. Its driver allowed the engine to idle silently while he looked at Mary Jane, who, quite unable to recognise the car or its occupant, advanced to the gate, tossing back her mousey hair as she did so. 'Are you lost?' she wanted to know. 'Cockermouth is only...'

'Thank you, but no, I am not lost,' said the man. 'This is Colonel Pettigrew's house.' It was, she realised, a statement, not an enquiry.

She planted her fork in between the roses, dusted off her grubby hands and advanced a few steps. 'Yes, it is.' She eyed him carefully; she had never seen him before and indeed, she wouldn't have forgotten him easily if she had, for he was a handsome man, not so very young any more, but the grey hair at his temple served to emphasise the intense blackness of the rest, and his eyes were as dark as his hair, under thick straight brows. His nose was a commanding one and his mouth was firm above an angular jaw. Oh, most definitely a face to remember.

'I've come to see Colonel Pettigrew.' He didn't smile as he spoke, but looked her up and down in a casual uninterested fashion.

She ignored the look. 'Well, I'm not sure that you should,' she offered calmly. 'He's ill, and at the moment he's asleep. Doctor Morris will be here presently, and I think he should be asked first, but if you like to come in and wait—you'll have to be quiet.'

The eyebrows rose. 'My dear good young woman, you talk as though I were a pop group or a party of schoolchildren! I'm not noisy by nature and I don't take kindly to being told what I may and may not do.'

'Oh, pooh,' said Mary Jane, a little out of patience, 'don't be so touchy! Come in, do.' She added, 'Quietly.'

The car whispered past her and came to a silent halt at the door, and the man got out. There was a great deal of him; more than six foot, she guessed, and largely built too. She wondered who he was, and was on the point of asking when she heard the bell from her grandfather's room. 'There,' she shot at her companion, a little unfairly, 'you've woken him up,' and flew upstairs.

The Colonel looked refreshed after his nap. He said at once, 'I heard a car and voices. I'm expecting someone, but there's hardly been time...'

Mary Jane shook up a pillow and slipped it behind his head. 'It's a man,' she explained unhurriedly. 'He's got beetling eyebrows and he's got rather a super Rolls. He says he wants to see you, but I told him he couldn't until Uncle Bob comes.'

A faint smile lighted up her grandfather's face. 'Did you, now? And did he mind?'

'I didn't ask him.'

Her grandfather chuckled. 'Well, my dear, if it won't undermine your authority too much, I should like to see him—now. We have important business. Morris knows he's coming and I don't suppose he'll object. Tell him to come up.'

'All right, Grandfather, if you say so.'

She found the stranger in the sitting room, sitting in one of the comfortable old-fashioned chairs. He got to his feet as she went in and before she could speak, said: 'All right, I know my way,' and was gone, taking the stairs two at a time. She followed him into the hall just in time to hear the Colonel's door shut quietly on the old man's pleased voice. After a moment she went slowly into the garden again.

She was still there when Doctor Morris arrived, parked his elderly Rover beside the Rolls, greeted her cheerfully and added in a tone of satisfaction, 'Ah, good, so he's arrived—with your grandfather, I suppose?'

Mary Jane pulled a weed with deliberation. 'Yes, he is—and very high-handed, whoever he is, too. I asked him to wait until you came, but Grandfather heard us talking and wanted to see him at once—he said it was business. He seems better this morning, so I hope you don't mind?'

The doctor shook his head. 'No, I'm pleased. You're both here now—your grandfather was worrying. I'll go up now.'

He left her standing there. She stared after him; he hadn't told her who the stranger was, but he obviously knew him. She went indoors, tidied herself and went along to get a tray of coffee ready, to find that Lily had already done so. 'And lunch, miss—I suppose the gentleman will be staying like last time. I'd better do some extra potatoes, hadn't I?'

Mary Jane agreed, desiring at the same time to question Lily about the probable guest, but if her grandfather had wanted to tell her, he could have done so, so too could Uncle Bob. If they wanted to have their little secrets, she told herself a trifle huffily, she for one didn't care. Probably the visitor was a junior partner to her grandfather's solicitor, but surely he wouldn't be able to afford a Rolls-Royce? She went outside again and had a good look at the car—it had a foreign number plate and it came from Holland, a clue which she immediately seized upon; the man was someone from her grandfather's oldest friend, Jonkheer van der Blocq, an elderly gentleman whom she had never met but about whom she knew quite a bit, for her grandfather had often mentioned him. Relieved that she had solved the mystery, she went back indoors in time to meet the doctor coming downstairs.

'There you are,' he remarked for all the world as though he had spent the last hour looking for her. 'Your grandfather wants you upstairs.' He eyed her thoughtfully. 'He's better, but you know what I mean by that, don't you? For the time being. Now run up, like a good girl. I'll be in the sitting room.'

She started up the stairs, remembering to call over her shoulder:

'There's coffee ready for you—would you ask Lily?' and sped on to tap on the Colonel's door and be bidden to enter.

The stranger was standing with his back to the window, his hands in his pockets, and the look he cast her was disconcerting in its speculation; there was faint amusement too and something else which she couldn't place. Mary Jane turned her attention to her elderly relative.

'Yes, Grandfather?' she asked, going up to the bed.

He eyed her lovingly and with some amusement on his tired old face.

'You're not a pretty girl,' he observed, and waited for her to answer.

'No, I know that as well as you—you didn't want me up here just to remind me, did you?' She grinned engagingly. 'I take after you,' she told him.

He smiled faintly. 'Come here, Fabian,' he commanded the man by the window.

And when he had stationed himself by the bed: 'Mary Jane, this is Fabian van der Blocq, the nephew of my old friend. He is to be your guardian after my death.'

Her eyes widened. 'My guardian? But I don't need a guardian, Grandfather! I'm twenty-two and I've never met Mr—Mr van der Blocq in my life before, and—and...'

'You're not sure if you like me?' His voice was bland, the smile he gave her mocking.

'Since you put the words into my mouth, I'm not sure that I do,' Mary Jane said composedly. 'And what do you have to be the guardian of?'

'This house will be yours, my dear,' explained her grandfather, 'and a considerable sum of money. You will be by no means penniless and there must be someone whom I can trust to keep an eye on you and manage your business affairs.'

'But I—' She paused and glanced across the bed to the elegant figure opposite her. 'Oh, you're a lawyer,' she declared. 'I wondered if you might be.'

Mr van der Blocq corrected her, still bland. 'You wondered wrongly. I'm a surgeon.'

She was bewildered. 'Are you? Then why...?' she went on vigorously, 'Anyway, Grandfather isn't going to die.'

The old gentleman in the bed made a derisive sound and Mr van der Blocq curled his lip. 'I am surprised that you, a nurse, should talk in such a fashion—you surely don't think that the Colonel wishes us to smother the truth in a froth of sickly sentiment?'

Mary Jane drew her delicate pale eyebrows together. 'You're horrible!' she told him in her gentle voice. It shook a little with the intensity of her feelings and she gave him the briefest of glances before turning back to her grandfather, whom she discovered to be laughing weakly.

'Don't you mind,' she demanded, 'the way this—this Mr van der Blocq talks?'

Her grandfather stopped laughing. 'Not in the least, my dear, and I daresay that when you know him better you won't mind either.'

She tossed her untidy head. 'That's highly unlikely. And now you're tired, Grandfather—you're going to have another nap before lunch.'

To her surprise he agreed quite meekly. 'But I want you back in the afternoon, Mary Jane—and Fabian.'

She agreed, ignoring the man staring at her while she rearranged blankets, shook up pillows and made her grandfather comfortable. This done to her satisfaction, she made for the door. Mr van der Blocq, beating her to it by a short head, opened it with an ironic little nod of his handsome head, and without looking at him she went through it and down the stairs to where Doctor Morris was waiting.

They drank their coffee in an atmosphere which was a little tense, and when the doctor got up to go, Mary Jane got up too, saying, 'I'll see you to your car, Uncle Bob.' and although he protested, did so. Out of their companion's hearing, however, she stopped.

'Look,' she said urgently, 'I don't understand—why is he to be my guardian? He doesn't even live in England, does he? and I don't know him—besides, guardians are old...'

The doctor's eyes twinkled. 'At a rough guess I should say he was nudging forty.'

'Yes? But he doesn't look...' She didn't finish the sentence. 'Well, it all seems very silly to me, and Grandfather...' She lifted her eyes to her companion. 'He's really not going to get any better? Not even if we do everything we possibly can?'

'No, my dear, and it will be quite soon now. I'll be back this evening. You know where to find me if you want me.'

She went back slowly to the sitting room and Mr Van der Blocq, lounging by the window, turned round to say: 'I don't suppose you got much help from Doctor Morris, did you?' He went on conversationally, 'If it is of any comfort to you, I dislike the idea of being your guardian just as much—probably more—than you dislike being my ward.'

Mary Jane sat down and poured more coffee for them both. 'Then don't. I mean, don't be my guardian, there's no need.'

'You heard your grandfather. You will be the owner of this house and sufficient money to make you an attractive target for any man who wants them.' He came across the room and sat down opposite her. 'I shall find my duties irksome, I dare say, but you can depend upon me not to shirk them.' He sat back comfortably. 'Do you mind if I smoke my pipe?'

She shook her head, and suddenly mindful of her duties as a hostess, asked, 'Where are you staying? Or are you perhaps only here for an hour or two?' She added hastily, 'You'll stay to lunch?'

A muscle twitched at the corner of his mouth. 'Thank you, I will—and I'm not staying anywhere,' his dark eyes twinkled. 'I believe the Colonel expected that I would stay here, but if it's too much trouble I can easily go to a hotel.'

'Oh no, not if Grandfather invited you. I'll go and see about lunch and get a room ready.' She got to her feet. 'There's sherry on the sofa table, please help yourself.'

Lily, she discovered when she got to the kitchen, had surpassed herself with Duchesse potatoes to eke out the cold chicken and salad, and there was a soup to start with; Mary Jane, feverishly opening tins to make a fruit salad, hoped that their guest wouldn't stay too long; she found him oddly disquieting and she wasn't even sure if she liked him, not that that would matter overmuch, for she supposed that she would see very little of him. She wasn't sure what the duties of a guardian were, but if he lived in Holland he was hardly likely to take them too seriously.

Ten minutes later, making up the bed in one of the guest rooms, she began to wonder for how long she was to have a guardian—surely not for the rest of her life? The idea of Mr van der Blocq poking his arrogant nose into her affairs, even from a distance, caused her to shudder strongly. She went downstairs, determined to find out all she could as soon as possible.

CHAPTER TWO

HER INTENTION MET with no success however. At lunch, her questions, put, she imagined, with suitable subtlety, were parried with a faint amusement which annoyed her very much, and when in desperation she tried the direct approach and asked him if, in the event of his becoming her guardian, it was to last a lifetime, he laughed and said with an infuriating calm:

'Now, why couldn't you have asked that in the first place? I have no intention of telling you, however. I imagine that your grandfather will explain everything to you presently.'

Mary Jane looked down her unassuming little nose. 'How long are you staying?' she asked with the icy politeness of an unwilling hostess. A question which met with an instant crack of laughter on the part of her companion. 'That depends entirely upon your grandfather's wishes, and—er—circumstances.'

She eyed him levelly across the table. 'You don't care tuppence, do you?' she declared fiercely. 'If Grandfather dies...'

She was unprepared for the way in which his face changed, and the quietness of his voice. 'Not if, when. And why pretend? Your grandfather knows that he is dying. He told me this morning that his one dread as he got older was that he would be stricken with some lingering complaint which would compel him to lie for months, dependent on other people. We should be glad that he is getting his wish, as he is.' His eyes swept over her. 'Go and do your face up, and look cheerful, he expects us in a short while, and don't waste time arguing that he must have another nap; I happen to know that he won't be happy until he has had the talk he has planned.'

Mary Jane got to her feet. 'You've no right to talk to me like this,' she said crossly, 'and I have every intention of tidying myself.'

She walked out of the room, and presently, having re-done

her face and brushed her hair until it shone, she put it up as
severely as possible, under the impression that it made her look
a good deal older, and went back downstairs, having first
peeped in on the Colonel, to find him dozing. So she cleared
away the lunch dishes and was very surprised when Mr van der
Blocq carried them out to the kitchen, and because Lily had
gone home, washed up, looking quite incongruous standing at
the sink in his beautifully cut suit.

The Colonel was awake when they went upstairs; Mary Jane
sat him up in his bed, arranging him comfortably with deft
hands and no fuss while Mr van der Blocq locked on, his hands
in his pockets, whistling softly under his breath.

'And now,' said the Colonel with some of his old authority,
'you will both listen to me, but first I must thank you, Fabian,
for coming at once without asking a lot of silly questions—it
must have caused you some inconvenience, though I suppose
you are now of sufficient consequence in your profession to be
able to do very much as you wish. Still, the journey is a considerable one—did you stop at all?'

His visitor smiled faintly. 'Once or twice, but I enjoy long
journeys and the roads are quiet at night.'

Mary Jane cast him a surprised look. 'You've been travelling
all night?' she wanted to know. 'You haven't slept?'

He gave her an impatient glance, his 'no' was nonchalant as
he turned back to the old man in the bed. 'Enough that I'm
here, I'm sure that Doctor Morris wouldn't wish us to waste
your strength in idle chatter.' A remark which sent the colour
flaming into Mary Jane's cheeks, for it had been so obviously
directed against herself.

Her grandfather closed his eyes for a moment. 'You're quite
right. Mary Jane, listen to me—this house and land will be
yours when I die, and there is also a considerable amount of
money which you will inherit—that surprises you, doesn't it?
Well, my girl, your mother and father wouldn't have thanked
me if I had reared a feather-brained useless creature, depending
upon me for every penny. As it is, you've done very well for
yourself, and as far as I'm concerned you can go on with your

nursing if you've set your mind on it, though I would rather that you lived here and made it home,' he paused, a little short of breath, 'You're not a very worldly young woman, my dear, and I've decided that you should have a guardian to give you help if you should need it and see to your affairs, and cast an eye over any man who should want to marry you—you will not, in fact, be able to marry without Fabian's consent.' He paused again to look at her. 'You don't like that, do you? but there it is—until you're thirty.'

Mary Jane swallowed the feelings which could easily have choked her. She said, keeping her voice calm and avoiding Mr van der Blocq's eye, 'And your cousin in Canada, Grandfather? I always thought that he was—that he would come and live— I didn't know about the money.'

Her grandparent received this muddled speech with a frown and said with some asperity, 'Dead. His son's dead too, I believe—there was a grandson, I believe, but no one bothered to let me know. Besides, you love the place, don't you, Mary Jane?'

She swallowed the lump in her throat. If he was going to be coolly practical about his death, she would try her best to be the same.

'Yes, Grandfather, you know I do, but I don't need the money—I've my salary...'

'Have you any idea what a house like this costs in upkeep? Mrs Body, Lily, the rates, the lot—besides, you deserve to have some spending money after these last three years living on the pittance you earn.'

He closed his eyes and then opened them again, remembering something.

'You witness what I've said, Fabian? You understand your part in the business, eh? And you're still willing? I would have asked your uncle, but that's not possible any more, is it?'

Mr van der Blocq agreed tranquilly that he was perfectly willing and that no, it was not possible for his uncle to fulfil the duties of a guardian. 'And,' he concluded, and his voice now held a ring of authority and firmness, 'if you have said all you wished to say, may I suggest that you have a rest? We shall remain within call. Rest assured that your wishes shall be carried out when the time comes.'

Mary Jane, without quite knowing how, found herself propelled gently from the room, but halfway down the stairs she paused. 'It's so unnecessary!' she cried. 'Surely I can run this house and look after my own money—and it's miles for you to come,' she gulped. 'And talking about it like this, it's beastly...'

He ignored that, merely saying coolly, 'I hardly think you need to worry about my too frequent visits.' He smiled a small, mocking smile and she felt vaguely insulted so that she flushed and ran on down the stairs and into the kitchen, where she found Mrs Body, unpacking her shopping. She looked up as Mary Jane rushed in and said: 'Hullo, Miss Mary Jane, what's upset you? The Colonel isn't...?'

'He's about the same. It's that man—Mr van der Blocq—we don't seem to get on very well.' She stood in front of the housekeeper, looking rather unhappily into her motherly face. 'Do you know him?'

'Lor', yes, my dear—he's been here twice in the last few months, and a year or two ago he came with that friend of your grandfather's, the nice old gentleman who lives in Holland—he's ill too, so I hear.'

Mary Jane waved this information on one side. 'He's staying,' she said. 'I don't know for how long. I made up a bed in the other turret room. Ought we to do something about dinner?'

'Don't you worry about that, Miss Mary Jane—the Colonel told me that he'd be coming, so I've a nice meal planned. If you'll just set the table later on—but time enough for that. Supposing you go for a little walk just down to the lake and back. You'll hear me call easily enough and a breath of air will do you good before tea.'

Mary Jane made for the door and flung it open. She had a great deal to think about; it was a pity she had no one to confide in; she hadn't got used to the fact that her grandfather was dying, nor his matter-of-fact attitude towards that fact, and the strain of matching his manner with her own was being a little too much for her. She wandered down the garden, resolutely making herself think about the house and the future. She didn't care about the money, just as long as there was enough to keep everything going as her grandfather would wish it to be. She stopped to lean over a low stone wall, built long ago for some purpose or other but now in disuse. The Colonel, a keen gardener, had planted it with a variety of rock plants, but it had no colour now. She leaned her elbows on its uneven surface and gazed out to the lake and Skiddaw beyond, not seeing them very clearly for the tears which blurred her eyes. It was silly to cry; her grandfather disliked crying women, he had told her so on various occasions. She brushed her hand across her face and noted in a detached way that the mountains had a sprinkling of snow on their tops while the rest of them looked grey and misty and sad. She wished, like a child, that time might be turned back, that somehow or other today could have been avoided. Despite herself, her eyes filled with tears again; she wasn't a crying girl, but just for once she made no attempt to stop them.

Major had followed her out of the house, and sat close to her now, pressed against her knee, and when he gave a whispered bark she wiped her eyes hastily and turned round. Mr van der Blocq was close by, just standing there, looking away from her, across the lake. He spoke casually. 'You have had rather a shock, haven't you? You must be a little bewildered. May I venture to offer you a modicum of advice?' He went on without giving her a chance to speak. 'Don't worry about the future for the moment. It's not a bad idea, in circumstances such as these, to live from one day to the next and make the best of each one.'

He was standing beside her now, still not looking at her tear-stained face, and when she didn't reply he went on, still casually:

'Major hasn't had a walk, has he? Supposing we give him a run for a short while?'

Mary Jane, forgetful of the deplorable condition of her face, looked up at him. 'I don't like to go too far away...'

'Nor do I, but Mrs Body has promised to shout if she needs us—she's sitting with your grandfather now, and I imagine we could run fast enough if we needed to.' He smiled at her and just for a moment she felt warmed and comforted.

'All right,' she agreed reluctantly, 'if you say so,' and started off along the edge of the lake, Major at her heels, not bothering to see if Mr van der Blocq was following her.

They walked into the wind, not speaking much and then only about commonplace things, and as they turned to go back again Mary Jane had to admit to herself that she felt better—not, she hastened to remind herself, because of her companion but probably because she had needed the exercise and fresh air. She went straight to her grandfather's room when they got back to the house, but he was still sleeping, so obedient to Mrs Body's advice she went to the sitting room and had tea with her visitor. They spoke almost as seldom as they had done during their walk; indeed, she formed the opinion that her companion found her boring and hardly worthy of his attention, for although his manners were not to be faulted she had the strongest feeling that they were merely the outcome of courtesy; in other circumstances he would probably ignore her altogether. She sighed without knowing it and got up to feed Major.

When she got back to the sitting room, Mr van der Blocq got to his feet and with the excuse that he had telephone calls to make and letters to write, went away to the Colonel's study, which, he was careful to explain, his host had put at his disposal, leaving Mary Jane to wander out to the kitchen to help Mrs Body and presently to lay the table in the roomy, old-fashioned dining room before going up to peep once more at her sleeping grandfather before changing from her slacks and sweater into a grey wool dress she had fortuitously packed, aware as she did so of the murmur of voices from the Colonel's room.

She frowned at her reflection as she smoothed her hair into its neat bun and did her face. If Mr van der Blocq had wakened her grandfather in order to pester him with more papers, then she would have something to say to him! He came out of the adjoining room as she left her own, giving her a wordless nod and standing aside for her to go down the stairs. She waited until they were both in the hall before she said: 'I think you must be tiring Grandfather very much. I don't think he should be disturbed any more today—there's surely no need.'

He paused on his way to the study. 'My dear good girl, may I remind you that I am a qualified physician as well as a surgeon, and as such am aware of your grandfather's condition— better, I must remind you, than you yourself.' He looked down his long nose at her. 'Be good enough not to interfere.'

Mary Jane's bosom heaved, her nice eyes sparkled with temper. 'Well, really it's not your business...'

He interrupted her. 'Oh, but it is, unfortunately. I am here at your grandfather's request to attend to his affairs—at his urgent request, I should remind you, before he should die, and here you are telling me what to do and what not to do. You're a tiresome girl.'

With which parting shot, uttered in his perfect, faintly accented English, he went into the study, closing the door very gently behind him.

Mary Jane, a gentle-natured girl for the most part, flounced into the sitting room, and quite beside herself with temper, poured herself a generous measure of whisky. It was a drink she detested, but now it represented an act of defiance, she tossed off a second glass too. It was unfortunate that Mr van der Blocq chose to return after five minutes, by which time the whisky's effects upon her hungry inside were at their highest; by then her head was feeling decidedly strange and her feet, when she walked to a chair, didn't quite touch the floor. It was unfortunate too that he saw this the moment he entered the room and observed coldly, 'Good God, woman, can't I turn my back for one minute without you reaching for the whisky bottle—you reek of it!' An exaggeration so gross that she instantly suspected that he had been spying upon her.

She said carefully in a resentful voice, 'You're enough to drive anyone to drink,' the whisky urging her to add, 'Are you married? If you are, I'm very sorry for your wife.'

He took her glass from her and set it down and poured himself a drink. 'No, I'm not married,' he said blandly, 'so you may spare your sympathy.' He sat down opposite her, crossed his long legs and asked, 'What did you do before you took up nursing? Were you ever here, living permanently?'

She cleared her fuzzy mind. 'No, I went to a boarding school, although I came here for the holidays, and then when I left school—when I was eighteen—I asked Grandfather if I might take up nursing and I went to Pope's. I've only been home once a year since then.'

'No boy-friends?' She hesitated and he added, 'I shall be your guardian, you know, I have to know a little about you.'

'Well, no.' Her head was clearer now. 'I never had much chance to meet any—only medical students, you know, and the housemen, and of course they always went for the pretty girls.' She spoke without self-pity and he offered no sympathy, nor did he utter some empty phrase about mythical good looks she knew she hadn't got, anyway. He said merely, 'Well, of course—I did myself, but one doesn't always marry them, you know.'

She agreed, adding in a matter-of-fact voice, 'Oh, I know that, I imagine young doctors usually marry where there's some money—unless they're brilliant with an assured future, and you can't blame them—how else are they to get on?'

'A sensible opinion with which I will not argue,' he assured her, his tone so dry that her slightly flushed face went slowly scarlet. It was fortunate that Mrs Body created a diversion at that moment by telling them that dinner would be ready in fifteen minutes and would Mary Jane like to take a quick peep at the Colonel first?

She was up in his room, pottering around because she sensed that he wanted company for a few minutes. When Doctor Morris arrived she waited while he examined his patient, adjusted his treatment, asked if he was through with his business, nodded his satisfaction at the answer and wished him a good night. Downstairs again, he accepted the drink offered him, muttered something to Mr van der Blocq and turned to Mary Jane.

'Your grandfather's happy; he's put his affairs in order, it's just a question of keeping him content and comfortable. You'll do that, I know, Mary Jane.' He stood up. 'I must be off, I've a couple more visits. Fabian, come to the car with me, will you?'

They talked very little over their meal and anything which they said had very little to do with the Colonel or what he had told them that day—indeed, Mr van der Blocq kept the conversation very much in his own hands, seeming not to notice her long silences and monosyllabic replies. She went to bed early, leaving him sitting by the fire, looking quite at home, with Major at his feet and still more papers on the table before him.

Once ready for bed, she went through to her grandfather's room, to find him awake, so she pulled up a chair to the dim lamp and made herself comfortable, declaring that she wasn't sleepy either. After a while he dozed off and so did she, to waken much later to find Mr van der Blocq standing looking down at her. She wasn't sure of the expression on his face, but what ever it was it changed to faint annoyance as she got silently to her feet. He said briefly, 'Go to bed,' and sat down in the chair she had vacated.

She was awakened by his hand on her shoulder. She sat up at once with an urgent whispered 'Grandfather?' and when he nodded and handed her dressing gown from a chair, she jumped out of bed, thrust her arms into its sleeves anyhow and was half way to the door in her bare feet when he reminded her, 'Your slippers—it's cold.' Before she quite reached the door he caught her by the arm. 'Your grandfather wants to say something to you—don't try and stop him; he's quite conscious and as comfortable as he can be. I've sent for Morris.'

The Colonel was wide awake and she went straight to the bed and took his hand with a steady smile. He squeezed her fingers weakly.

'Plenty of guts—like me,' he whispered with satisfaction. 'Can't abide moaning women. Something I want you to do. Always wanted you to meet my friend—Fabian's uncle—he's

ill too. Go and look after him—bad-tempered fellow, can't find
a nurse who'll stay. Promised Fabian you'd go.' He looked at
her. 'Promise?'

She said instantly, 'Yes, Grandfather, I promise. I'll look
after him.'

'Won't be for long—Fabian will see to everything.'

She glanced across at the man standing on the other side of
the bed, looking, despite pyjamas and dressing gown, as impassive and withdrawn as he always did. She wondered, very
briefly, if he had any feelings at all; if so, they were buried
deep. He returned her look with one of his own, unsmiling and
thoughtful, and then went to the door. 'That's Morris's car—
I'll let him in and wake Mrs Body.'

The Colonel died a couple of hours later, in his sleep, a
satisfied little smile on his old face so that Mary Jane felt that
to cry would be almost an insult—besides, had he not told her
that she had guts? She did all the things she had to do with a
white set face, drank the tea Mrs Body gave her, then had a
bath and dressed to join Mr van der Blocq at the breakfast table,
where she ate nothing at all but talked brightly about the
weather. Afterwards, thinking about it, she had to admit that he
had been a veritable tower of strength, organising a tearful Mrs
Body and a still more tearful Lily, arranging everything without
fuss and a minimum of discussion, telephoning the newspapers,
old friends, the rector...

She came downstairs from making the beds just as he came
out of the study and Mrs Body was coming from the kitchen
with the coffee tray. He poured her a cup, told her to drink it
in a no-nonsense voice, and when she had, marched her off for
a walk, Major at their heels. It was a fine morning but cold,
and Mary Jane, in her sweater and slacks and an old jacket
snatched from the back porch, was aware that she looked
plainer than even she thought possible—not that she cared. She
walked unwillingly beside her companion, not speaking, but
presently the soft air and the quiet peace of the countryside
soothed her; she even began to feel grateful to him for arranging
her day and making it as easy as he could for her. She felt

impelled to tell him this, to be told in a brisk impersonal way
that as her guardian it was his moral obligation to do so.

He went on: 'We need to talk; there is a good deal to be
arranged. You will have to leave Pope's—you realised that already, I imagine. I think it may be best if I wrote to your Matron
or whatever she is called nowadays, and explain your circumstances. Your grandfather's solicitor will come here to see
you—and me, but there should be no difficulties there, as everything was left in good order. I think it may be best if you
return to Holland with me on the day after the funeral; there's
no point in glooming around the house on your own, and I can
assure you that my uncle needs a nurse as soon as possible—
his condition is rapidly worsening and extremely difficult.' He
paused to throw a stone for Major. 'He was a good and clever
man, and I am fond of him.'

Mary Jane stood still and looked at him. 'You've thought of
everything,' she stated, and missed the gleam in his eyes. 'I
only hope I'll be able to manage him and that he'll like me,
because I promised Grandfather...'

Her voice petered out and although she gulped and sniffed
she was quite unable to stop bursting into tears. She was hardly
aware of Mr van der Blocq whisking her into his arms, only of
the nice solid feel of his shoulder and his silent sympathy. Presently she raised a ruined face to his. 'So sorry,' she said politely. 'I don't cry as a general rule—I daresay I'm tired.'

'I daresay you are. We'll walk back now, and after lunch,
which you will eat, you shall lie on the sofa in the study and
have a nap while I finish off a few odd jobs.'

He let her go and strolled down to the water's edge while
she wiped her eyes and blew her nose and re-tied her hair, and
when they started back, he took her arm, talking, deliberately,
of the Colonel.

Under his eye she ate her lunch, and still under it, tucked
herself up in front of the study fire and fell instantly asleep.
She awoke to the clatter of the tea tray as Mrs Body set it on
the table beside the sofa and a moment later Doctor Morris
came in.

The two men began at once to talk, and gradually, as she poured the tea and passed the cake, Mary Jane joined in. Before the doctor got up to go she realised with surprise that she had laughed several times. The surprise must have shown on her face, for Mr van der Blocq said with uncanny insight: 'That's better—your grandfather liked you to laugh, didn't he? Now, if you feel up to it, tell me how you stand at Pope's. A month's notice is normal, I suppose—have you any holidays due? Any commitments in London?'

'I've a week's holiday before Christmas, that's all, and I'm supposed to give a month's notice. There's nothing to keep me in London, but all my clothes and things are at Pope's.'

'We will pick them up as we go. What is the name of your matron?'

'Miss Shepherd—she's called the Principal Nursing Officer now.'

'Presumably in the name of progress, but what a pity. I shall telephone her now.' Which he did, with a masterly mixture of authority and charm. Mary Jane listened with interest to his exact explanations, which he delivered unembellished by sentiment and without any effort to enlist sympathy. It didn't surprise her in the least that within five minutes he had secured her resignation as from that moment.

When he had replaced the receiver, she remarked admiringly, 'My goodness, however did you manage it? I thought I would have to go back.'

'Manage what?' he asked coolly. 'I made a reasonable request and received a reasonable reply to it—I fail to see anything extraordinary in that.'

He returned to his writing, leaving her feeling snubbed, so that her manner towards him, which had begun to warm a little, cooled. It made her feel cold too, as though he had shut a door that had been ajar and left her outside. She went to the kitchen presently on some excuse or other, and sat talking to Mrs Body, who was glad of the company anyway.

'You've not had time to make any plans, Miss Mary Jane?' she hazarded.

'No, Mrs Body. You know that Grandfather left me this house, don't you? You will go on living here, won't you? I don't think I could bear it if you and Lily went away.'

The housekeeper gave her a warm smile. 'Bless you, my dear, of course we'll stay—it would break my heart to go after all these years, and Lily wouldn't go, I'm sure. But didn't I hear Doctor van der Blocq say that you would be going back to Holland with him?'

Mary Jane explained. 'It won't be for long, I imagine—if you wouldn't mind being here—do you suppose Lily would come and live in so that you've got company? I'm not sure about the money yet, but I'm sure there'll be enough to pay her. Shall I ask her?'

'A good idea, Miss Mary Jane. Supposing I mention it to her first, once everything's seen to? I must say the doctor gets things done—everything's going as smooth as silk and he thinks of everything. That reminds me, he told me to move your things back to your old room.

Mary Jane looked surprised. 'Oh, did he? How thoughtful of him,' and then because she was young and healthy even though she was sad: 'What's for dinner—I'm hungry.'

Mrs Body beamed. 'A nice bit of beef. For a foreign gentleman the doctor isn't finicky about his food, is he? and I always say there's nothing to beat a nice roast. There's baked apples and cream for afters.'

'I'll lay the table,' Mary Jane volunteered, and kept herself busy with that until Mr van der Blocq came out of the study, when she offered him a drink, prudently declining one herself before going upstairs to put on the grey dress once more. The sight of her face, puffy with tears and tense with her stored-up feelings, did little to reassure her, and when she joined Mr van der Blocq in the sitting room, the brief careless glance he accorded her deflated what little ego she had left. Sitting at table, watching him carving the beef with a nicety which augured well for his skill at his profession, she found herself wishing that he didn't regard her with such indifference—not, she told herself sensibly, that his opinion of her mattered one jot. He wasn't at all the sort of man she... He interrupted her thoughts.

'It seems to me a good idea if you were to call me Fabian. I do not like being addressed as Mr van der Blocq—inaccurately, as it happens. Even Mrs Body manages to address me, erroneously, as Doctor dear.' He smiled faintly as he looked at her, his eyebrows raised.

She studied his face. 'Well, if you want me to,' her voice was unenthusiastic, 'only I don't know you very well, and you're...'

'A great deal older than you? Indeed I am.'

It annoyed her that he didn't tell her how much older, but she went on, 'I was going to say that I find it a little difficult, because Grandfather told me that you were an important surgeon and I wouldn't dream of calling a consultant at Pope's by his first name.'

The preposterous idea made her smile, but he remained unamused, only saying in a bored fashion. 'Well, you are no longer a nurse at Pope's—you are Miss Pettigrew with a pleasant little property of your own and sufficient income with which to live in comfort.'

She served him a baked apple and passed the cream. 'What's a sufficient income?' she wanted to know.

He waved a careless, well kept hand, before telling her.

She had been on the point of sampling her own apple, but now she laid down her spoon and said sharply, 'That's nonsense—that's a fortune!'

'Not in these days, it will be barely enough. There's your capital, of course, but I shall be in charge of that.' His tone implied that he was discussing something not worthy of his full attention, and this nettled her.

'You talk as though it were chicken feed!'

'That was not my intention. I'm sure you are a competent young woman and well able to enjoy life on such a sum. The solicitor will inform you as to the exact money.'

'Then why do I have to have you for a guardian?'

He put down his fork and said patiently, 'You heard your

grandfather—I shall attend to any business to do with investments and so forth and have complete control of your capital. I shall of course see that your income is paid into your bank until you assume full control over your affairs when you are thirty. It will also be necessary for me to give my consent to your marriage should you wish to marry.'

She was bereft of words. 'Your consent—if I should choose' She almost choked. 'It's not true!'

'I am not in the habit of lying. It is perfectly true, set down in black and white by your grandfather, and I intend to carry out his wishes to the letter.'

'You mean that if anyone wants to marry me he'll have to ask you?'

He nodded his handsome head.

'But that's absurd! I never heard such nonsense…how could you possibly know—have any idea…?'

His voice had been cool, now it was downright cold. 'My dear good girl, let me assure you that I find my duties just as irksome as you find them unnecessary.'

This shook her. 'Oh, will you? I suppose they'll take up some of your time. I'll try not to bother you, then—I daresay there'll be no need for us to see much of each other.'

His lips twitched. 'Probably not, although I'm afraid that while you are at my uncle's house you will see me from time to time—he's too old to manage his own affairs, and my cousin, who lives with him, isn't allowed to do more than run the house.'

They were in the sitting room drinking their coffee when she ventured: 'Will you tell me a little about your uncle? I don't know where he lives or anything about him, and since I am to stay there…'

Mr van der Blocq frowned. 'Why should I object?' he wanted to know testily. 'But I must be brief; I'm expecting one or two telephone calls presently. He lives in Friesland, a small village called Midwoude. It is in fact on the border between Friesland and Groningen. The country is charming and there is a lake close by. The city of Groningen is only a few miles away;

Leeuwarden is less than an hour by car. You may find it a little
lonely, but I think not, for you are happy here. aren't you? My
uncle, I have already told you, is difficult, but my cousin Emma
will be only too glad to make a friend of you.'

'And you—you live somewhere else?'

'I live and work in Groningen.' He spoke pleasantly and with
the quite obvious intention of saying nothing more. She had to
be content with that, and shortly after that, when he went to
answer his telephone call, Mary Jane went into the kitchen,
helped Mrs Body around the place, laid the table for breakfast
and went up to bed.

Now if I were a gorgeous creature with golden hair and long
eyelashes, she mused as she wandered up the staircase, we
might be spending the evening together—probably he had some
flaxen-haired beauty waiting for him in Groningen. For lack of
anything better to do and to keep her thoughts in a cheerful
channel, she concocted a tale about Mr van der Blocq in which
the blonde played a leading part, and he for once smiled frequently and never once addressed the creature as 'my dear good
girl'.

The next few days passed quickly; there was a good deal to
attend to and Major had to be taken for his walk, and time had
to be spent with the Colonel's friends who called in unexpected
numbers. The lawyer came too and spent long hours in the
study with her guardian, although he had very little to say to
her.

It wasn't until after the funeral, when the last of the neigh-
bours and friends had gone, that old Mr North asked her to join
him in the study and bring Mrs Body and Lily with her. Mary
Jane half listened while he read the legacies which had been
left to them both, it wasn't until they had gone and she was
sitting by the fire with Fabian at the other end of the room that
Mr North gave her the details of her own inheritance. The
money seemed a vast sum to her; she had had no idea that her
grandfather had had so much, even the income she was to receive seemed a lot of money. Mr North rambled on rather,

talking about stocks and shares and securities and ended by saying:

'But you won't need to worry your head about this, Mary Jane, Mr van der Blocq will see to everything for you. I understand that you will be travelling to Holland tomorrow. That will make a nice change and you will return here ready to take your place in local society. I take it that Mrs Body will remain?'

She told him that yes, she would, and moreover Lily had agreed to live in as well, so that the problem of having someone to look after the house and Major was solved.

'You have no idea how long you will be away?' asked Mr North.

'None,' she glanced at Fabian, who took no notice at all, 'but I'm sure that Mrs Body will look after everything beautifully.'

The old gentleman nodded. 'And you? You will be sorry to leave your work at the hospital, I expect.'

She remembered Sister Thompson. 'Yes, though I was thinking of changing to another hospital.' She smiled at him. 'Now I shan't need to.'

He went shortly afterwards and she spent the rest of the day packing what clothes she had with her and making final arrangements with Mrs Body before taking Major for a walk by the lake. It was a clear evening with the moon shining. Mary Jane shivered a little despite her coat, not so much with cold as the knowledge that she would miss the peace and quiet even though she had it to come back to.

She went indoors presently and into the study to wish Fabian good night. He stood by her grandfather's desk while she made a few remarks about their journey and then said a little shyly, 'You've been very kind and—and efficient. I don't know what we should have done without your help. I'm very grateful.'

He rustled the papers in his hand and thanked her stiffly, and she went to her room, wondering if he would ever unbend, or was he going to remain coldly polite and a little scornful of her for the rest of their relationship? Eight years, she told herself as she got into bed, seemed a long time. She would be thirty and quite old, and Fabian would be...she started to guess and fell asleep, still guessing.

CHAPTER THREE

MARY JANE HAD never travelled in a Rolls-Royce—she found it quite an experience. Fabian was a good driver and although he spoke seldom he was quite relaxed, she sat silently beside him, thinking about the last two weeks—such a lot had happened and there had been so much to plan and arrange; she hoped she had forgotten nothing—not that it would matter very much, for her companion would not have overlooked the smallest detail. He had told her very little about the journey, beyond asking her to be ready to start at eight o'clock in the morning.

They were on the motorway now, doing a steady seventy, and would be in London by early afternoon, giving her ample time in which to pack her things at the hospital before they left for the midnight ferry.

'Anything you haven't time to see to you can leave,' he had told her, 'and arrange to send on the things you don't want— Mrs Body can sort them out later. You can buy all you need when we get to Holland.'

'Oh no, I can't, I've only a few pounds.'

'I will advance you any reasonable sum—do you need any money now?'

'No, thank you, but what about my fare?'

'Mr North and I will take care of such details.'

They had settled into silence after that. Mary Jane stared through the window as the Rolls crept up behind each car in turn and passed it. Presently she closed her eyes against the boredom of the road, the better to think. But her thoughts were muddled and hazy; she hadn't slept very well the night before, and fought a desire to doze off, induced by the extreme comfort of the car, and had just succeeded in reducing her mind to tolerable clarity when her efforts were shattered by her companion's laconic, 'We'll stop for coffee.'

She glanced at her watch; they had been on the road for just two hours and Stafford wasn't far away. 'That would be nice,' she agreed pleasantly, and was a little surprised when he left the motorway, taking the car unhurriedly down side roads which led at last to a small village.

'Stableford,' read Mary Jane from the signpost. 'Why do we come here?'

'To get away from the motorway for half an hour. There's a place called The Cocks—ah, there it is.' He pulled up as he spoke.

The coffee was excellent and hot, and Mary Jane ate a bun because breakfast seemed a long time ago, indeed, a meal in another life.

'What time shall we get to London?' she wanted to know.

'A couple of hours, I suppose. We will have a late lunch before I take you to Pope's. I'll call for you there at seven o'clock.'

'The boat doesn't go until midnight, does it?'

'We shall dine on the way.'

'Oh.' She felt somehow deflated; if he had said something nice about dining together, or even asked her—obviously he was performing a courteous duty with due regard to her comfort and absolutely no pleasure on his part. She followed him meekly out to the car and for the remainder of the journey only spoke when she was spoken to and that not very often. Only when they were driving through London's northern suburbs did he remark: 'We'll go to Carrier's, it's an easy run to Pope's from there.'

The restaurant was down a passage, double-fronted and modern, and Mary Jane, by now famished, chose fillet of beef in shirtsleeves, because it sounded quaint and filling at the same time. She was given a dry sherry to drink before they ate; she would have preferred a sweet one, but somehow Fabian looked the kind of man who would wish to order the drinks himself and she felt certain that he knew a great deal more about them than she ever would; she might be a splendid nurse, a tolerable cook and handy in the garden, but the more sophisticated talents had so far eluded her. It surprised her when he suggested, after she had disposed of the beef in its shirtsleeves and he had eaten his carpet bag steak, that she might like to sample Robert's Chocolate Fancy.

'Women like sweet things,' he told her tolerantly, and asked for the cheese board for himself.

Pope's looked greyer, more old-fashioned and more hedged in by the towering blocks of flats around it than ever before. 'You'll have to see the Matron—you had better do that first,' said Fabian as he helped her out of the car. 'Do you want me to come with you?'

She declined politely and with secret regret; it would have been a pleasure to have walked through the hospital with Fabian beside her; she could just imagine the curious and envious glances that would have been cast at her.

He nodded. 'Good. I've one or two things to do. I'll be here at seven exactly.'

There was a great deal for her to do too. After the interview with Miss Shepherd, which was unexpectedly pleasant, there was a brief visit to Women's Surgical, where Sister Thompson wasn't pleasant at all, and then a long session of packing in her room. It was amazing what she had collected over the years! After due thought she packed a trunk with everything she judged might be unsuitable in a Dutch winter, which left her with some thick tweeds in a pleasing shade of brown, a variety of sweaters, a couple of jersey dresses and a rather nice evening dress she couldn't resist taking, although she saw no chance of wearing it. It was pale blue and green organza with long tight sleeves and a pie-frill collar, and it suited her admirably.

When she had finished packing she went along to the sitting room, where most of her friends were having tea, and found so much to talk about that she had to hurry to complete the tiresome chores of handing in her uniform to the linen room and waiting while it was checked, and then running all over the home to hand in the key of her room, both tasks requiring patience while the appropriate persons were found, the right forms filled in and signed and the farewells made, but she was at the hospital entrance by seven o'clock, wearing the brown tweeds and a felt hat which did nothing for her at all. All the same, she looked nice; her handbag and gloves and shoes were good and the tweed suit and coat suited her small slender person.

She reached the door just as Fabian drew up and got out of the car. He gave her a laconic 'Hullo', put her case in the boot and enquired about the rest of the luggage.

'It's in my trunk—one of my friends will send it on to Mrs Body.'

'Good. And Miss Shepherd—any difficulties?'

'No, thank you. None.'

'Get in, then.'

She didn't much like being ordered about, she was on the point of saying so when those of her closer friends who were off duty or who had been able to escape from their wards for a few minutes arrived in a chattering bunch to see her off. They embraced her in turn and with some warmth, at the same time taking a good look at Mr van der Blocq, who bore their scrutiny with a faint smile and complete equanimity, even when Penny Martin, the prettiest and giddiest of the lot of them, darted forward and caught him by the arm.

'Take care of Mary Jane,' she begged him with the faint lisp which most of the housemen found irresistible, 'and if you want another nurse at any time, I'd love to come.'

He smiled down at her, and Mary Jane, glimpsing the charm of it, felt quite shaken by some feeling she had no time to consider. He had never smiled at her like that; he must dislike her very much. The supposition caused her to be very quiet as they drove away from the cheerful little group on the steps, in fact, she didn't speak at all until they had crossed the river, gone through Southwark and joined the A2.

'You'll miss your friends,' commented her companion, slowing down for the traffic lights, 'and hospital life.' The car swept ahead again. 'There's no reason why you shouldn't go back to work there later on—you could spend your holidays in Cumbria.'

'Oh, I wouldn't do that,' declared Mary Jane, startled out of her silence. 'I shall like living in Grandfather's house and I shall find plenty to do. I shall miss Pope's, of course, but not the ward I was on.'

He shot her a brief, amused glance. 'Oh? Tell me about it.'

She did, rather haltingly at first, but he seemed interested and she found herself saying more than she intended.

'There is certainly no point in you going back to Women's Surgical,' he agreed. 'It sounds a joyless place, and your Sister Thompson needs to go on the retirement list.'

'But she's quite young, only forty.'

'You think that forty is quite young?'

'Heavens, yes.' She broke off as he turned the car down a side road. 'Where are we going? I thought this led to the M2.'

'There's a good place at Hollingbourne, and we have plenty of time.'

The restaurant was pleasantly quiet and the food exceptional. Mary Jane was beginning to think that Fabian wouldn't go anywhere unless the food and the service were near perfection. She remembered the simple meals she and Mrs Body had cooked and wondered, as she ate her Kentish roast duckling, if he had enjoyed them. Probably not.

They kept up a desultory conversation as they ate—the kind of conversation, she told herself hopelessly, that one sustained with fellow patients in a dentist's waiting room. Before she could stop the words, they popped out of her mouth. 'What a pity we don't get on.'

If she had hoped to take him by surprise, she had failed. His expression didn't change as he answered in the pleasantest of voices.

'Yes, it is. Probably as we get to know each other better, our—er—incompatibility will lessen.' He smiled briefly and changed the subject abruptly. 'Tell me, do you ride? If so, there is a good stables near my uncle's house—they could let you have a mount.'

'Oh, could they? I should like that. I'm not awfully good, but I enjoy it.'

'In that case you had better not go out alone.'

Which remark compelled her to say, 'Oh, I can ride well enough, you needn't worry about that—it's just that I'm not a first-class horsewoman.'

They sipped coffee in silence until she said defiantly, 'I shall buy a horse when I get back home,' and waited to see what he would say. She was disappointed when he replied blandly, 'Why not? Shall we go?'

They were at Dover with time to spare. They left the car in the small queue and had coffee in the restaurant and Fabian bought her an armful of magazines. Once on board he suggested that she should go to her cabin. 'We berth very early,' he warned her, 'half past four or thereabouts. We'll stop for breakfast on the way to Friesland.'

His advice was sound. Mary Jane slept for a few hours, and fortified by tea, joined him on deck as the boat docked, and then followed him down to the car deck. There was no delay at all as they landed; they were away in a few minutes, tearing down the cobbled street towards the Dutch border.

The Rolls bored through the motorway from Antwerp towards the frontier and Breda, going through the town without stopping. It was quiet and dark, although a slow dawn was beginning to lighten the sky; by the time they reached Utrecht there was a dim, chilly daylight struggling through the clouds. Mary Jane shivered in the warm car and Fabian spoke after miles of silence. 'We'll stop here and have breakfast.'

It seemed a little early for there to be anywhere open, but he stopped the car outside Smits Hotel, said, 'Stay where you are,' and went inside to return very quickly and invite her inside, where she was welcomed by the hall porter with a courtesy she would have found pleasant in broad daylight, let alone at that early hour of the morning, but Fabian seemed to take it all very much for granted, as he did the breakfast which was presently set before them. They ate at leisure, lingering over a final cup of coffee while he explained the route they were to follow. 'Less than a hundred miles,' he told her. 'We shall be at my uncle's house for coffee.'

And they were, after a drive during which Mary Jane, after several efforts at polite conversation, had become progressively more and more silent, staring out at the flat, frost-covered fields on either side of the road, observing with interest the cows in their coats, the large churches and the small villages so unlike her own home, and wishing with all her heart that she was back there—she even wished she was back at Pope's, coping with Sister Thompson's petty tyranny, but when her companion said, 'Only a few more miles now,' she pulled herself together; self-pity got one nowhere, and if Grandfather could know what she was thinking now he would be heartily ashamed of her show—even to herself—of weakness.

She sat up straight, rammed the unbecoming hat firmly upon her head and said, 'I'm glad, and I'm sure you must be too—travelling with someone you dislike can be very tiresome.'

Mr van der Blocq allowed a short sharp exclamation to leave his lips. 'Does that remark refer to myself or to you?' he queried silkily.

'Both of us.' She spoke without heat and lapsed into silence, a silence she would have liked to break as he took the car gently through a very small village—cluster of one-storied cottages, a shop and an over-sized church—and turned off the road through massive iron gates and a tree-lined drive, and pulled up before his uncle's house. She would have liked to exclaim over it, for it was worthy of comment; built of rose brick with a steep slate roof and an iron balcony above its massive front door. It had two stories, their windows exactly matching, and all with shutters. It reminded her of some fairy tale, standing there silent, within the semicircle of sheltering trees, most of them bare now. She was impressed and longed to say so.

Fabian got out, came round to help her out too and walked beside her up the shallow steps to the opening door. A white-haired man stood there, neatly dressed in a dark suit and looking so pleased to see them that she deduced, quite rightly, that this wasn't Jonkheer van der Blocq. Fabian quickly put her right, explaining as he shook the old man's hand, 'This is Jaap, he has been in the family for forty years—he sees to everything and will be of great help to you.'

Mary Jane put out a hand and had it gently wrung while Jaap made her welcome—presumably—in his own language. She nodded and smiled and followed him into a handsome lobby and through its inner glass doors to the hall, an imposing place, its walls hung with dark, gilt-framed portraits, vicious-looking weapons and a variety of coats of arms. It needed flowers, she decided as she glanced about her, something vivid to offset the noble plastered ceiling and marble floor with its dim Persian rugs. She was arranging them in her mind's eye when Fabian said: 'The sitting room, I suppose—the first door on the left.'

She followed Jaap through a double door into a room whose proportions rivalled those of the hall—the ceiling was high, the walls, painted white and ornamented at their corners with a good deal of carved fruit and flowers, carried a further selection of paintings. The furniture was massive and she had the feeling that excepting for the easy chairs flanking the large open fire, and the Chesterfield drawn up before it, the seating accommodation would be uncomfortable—an opinion which Fabian probably shared, for he advised her to take a chair by the fire, taking her coat and tossing it to Jaap.

'My cousin will be here in a moment,' he told her, and went to look out of the windows, while Mary Jane, left to herself, rearranged the furniture in her mind, set a few floral arrangements on the various tables and regarded with awe a large cabinet on the opposite wall; it was inlaid, with a good deal of strapwork, and she considered it hideous.

'German?' she asked herself aloud.

'You're right,' agreed Fabian from the window. 'The Thirty Years' War or thereabouts, I believe, and frankly appalling.'

She turned to look at him. 'Now isn't that nice, we actually agree about something!' She added hastily, 'I don't mean to be rude—I have no business to pass an opinion...'

He shrugged his wide shoulders. 'I'm flattered that we should share even an opinion.'

'Now that's a...' She was saved from finishing the forceful

remark she was about to make by the entry of a lady into the room. The cousin, without doubt—fortyish, tall and thin and good-looking, her face marred by the anxious frown between her brows and the look of harassment she wore. Indeed, she appeared to be so hunted that Mary Jane expected to see her followed by Fabian's uncle in one of his more difficult moods. But no one else appeared; the lady trod across the room to Fabian, crying his name in a melodramatic fashion, and flung her arms around him. He received her embrace with a good-humoured tolerance, patted her on the shoulder and said in English: 'Now, Emma, you can stop behaving like a wet hen. Here is Mary Jane come to nurse Oom Georgius.'

He turned round and went to Mary Jane's side. 'This is my cousin Emma van der Blocq—I'm sure you will be good friends, and I know she is delighted to have you here to lighten her burden.'

'Indeed yes,' his cousin joined in, shaking Mary Jane's hand in an agitated way. 'I'm quite worn out, for my father thinks I am a very poor nurse and I daresay I am—I'm sure you will be able to manage him far better than I.' She sighed deeply. 'The nurses never stay.'

It sounded as though the old gentleman was going to be a handful, Mary Jane thought gloomily, but she had promised her grandfather, and in a way she was glad, because she would be too occupied to brood over his death. She said in her pleasant voice, 'I'll do my best. Perhaps when you have the time, you will tell me what you would like me to do.'

Cousin Emma became more agitated than ever. 'Oh yes, of course, but first you shall see your room and we will have lunch.' She looked at Fabian. 'You will go and see Father?'

He nodded and followed them out of the room and up the elegant staircase at one side of the hall, but on the landing they parted, he going to the front of the house while Mary Jane and her hostess entered a room at the head of the stairs. It was a large room, but not, she was relieved to see, nearly as large as the sitting room. It was furnished with a quantity of heavy Mid-Victorian furniture, all very ornate, carved and inlaid. The bed was a ponderous affair too, but the curtains and coverlet were pretty and the carpet was richly thick under her feet.

Here she was left alone to tidy herself before going downstairs again, something she was about to do when she was halted by a thunderous voice from behind a pair of handsome doors across the landing, bellowing something in Dutch, and a moment later Fabian appeared, to lean over the balustrade as she went down the stairs and ask if she would be good enough to visit his uncle.

The room they entered was vast, with a fourposter bed dwarfed against one wall and a great many chests and tallboys and massive cupboards. In the centre of this splendour sat Jonkheer van der Blocq, facing a roaring fire. And a handsome old man he was too, with white hair, a little thin on top, and Fabian's features. He didn't wait for his nephew to speak but began at once in a stentorian voice.

'Hah—so my good old friend died, and you are the Mary Jane he wrote so much of.' He produced a pair of spectacles and planted them upon his nose and stared at her. 'A dab of a girl, too. He promised me that if I should outlive him, he would send you to me. Nurses,' he went on in a triumphant voice, 'don't stay. Do you suppose you will?'

Mary Jane walked up to his chair, not in the least put out. 'I don't see why not,' she said in a reasonable voice, 'and anyway, I promised Grandfather I would. I'm not easily upset, you know.' She gave him a kind smile and he croaked with laughter. 'We'll see about that! At any rate you will be a change from that fool daughter of mine, always fussing around.'

'I daresay she wants to help you, but some people—and you, I suspect, aren't easy to do things for; they find fault all the time.'

He sat back against his cushions and she thought that he might explode; instead he burst out laughing. 'Dammit, if you're not like your grandfather!' he declared. 'No looks but plenty of spirit. I shall come down to lunch.' He turned to Fabian. 'And you, what do you think of her, eh?'

'I have no doubt that Mary Jane is an excellent nurse.'

'That wasn't what I meant. However, you may give me an arm and we'll go down. I rather fancy a glass of *Genever* before we lunch.'

'You'll not get it,' observed his nephew good-humouredly. 'A glass of white wine is all that Trouw allows you, and that's what you will have.'

The old man, far from being annoyed at this arbitrary remark, chuckled, and the three of them went down to the dining room in the friendliest possible way. The old gentleman's good humour lasted throughout the meal, and when Fabian got up to go, saying that he had an appointment that afternoon in Groningen, begged him to come again as soon as he could. 'Though I daresay you have a good deal of work to catch up on. How long have you been away?'

And when Fabian told him he continued: 'It will take you a week or two to work everything off, I daresay. Well, come when you can, Fabian.'

His thunderous voice sounded wistful and Mary Jane guessed that he was fond of his nephew, though probably nothing on earth would make him admit to it. Bidden by her host to see Fabian into his car, she walked a little self-consciously to the door and stood in the lobby while he spoke to Jaap, but presently he turned to her and said:

'Doctor Trouw will be here this evening, I believe. He speaks English and will explain all there is to know about my uncle. I hope it has been made clear to you that you are a guest here as well as a nurse, although you will doubtless find yourself called upon frequently enough if my uncle becomes particularly difficult.'

She raised surprised eyes to his. 'A guest? But I understood Grandfather to say that I was to take care of your uncle, I know he's not in bed, but he needs someone, and he's a lot more ill than he allows, isn't he? And he said himself that nurses don't stay. Does he really dislike your cousin looking after him?'

He gave a short laugh. 'I assure you that he does, nor does she like looking after him. Do as you think fit, but I for one shall not hold you to your promise, for you had no idea what it might entail when you gave it, and nor, I believe, did your grandfather. Uncle Georgius is going to get worse very soon now, and he will be what you so aptly describe in your language as a handful.'

'Look,' said Mary Jane patiently, 'you came over to Grandfather when he sent for you and it must have been inconvenient, but I don't think you would have refused, would you? Well, neither shall I.'

She gave him a determined little nod and the corner of his mouth twitched a little. 'Very well,' he said blandly, and turned to go.

'Just a minute,' she was self-conscious again, 'I want to thank you for making my journey so comfortable and for doing so much for us.' She looked at him earnestly. 'You didn't know any of us well, you could so easily have refused—you had every right. I—I heard what your uncle said about your backlog of patients.'

'Like you, I keep my word,' he told her. 'Goodbye.'

She watched the Rolls slip away between the trees and told herself that she was well rid of such a cold, disagreeable man, and the feeling which she ascribed to relief at his going was so strong that she very nearly burst into tears.

Mary Jane slipped into the life of the big, silent house quite easily. She was an adaptable girl and her training had made her more so. In only a few days she had taken over all the tiresome chores which Emma van der Blocq disliked so much; the persuading of the old gentleman to rise in the morning when he flatly refused, the coaxing of him to go to bed at a reasonable hour—more, the battle of wills which was fought daily over the vexed question as to whether his pills were to be taken or not. But at least he slept well once he was in his bed and she had turned out the lights save for one small lamp, turned his radio to a thread of sound, arranged the variety of odds and ends he insisted upon having on his bedside table and wished him a cheerful goodnight, however grumpy he was. She was free then, but too tired to do anything other than write an odd letter or so or leaf through a magazine. She was free during the day too, as she was frequently told, both by Jonkheer van der Blocq and his daughter, but somehow it was difficult to get away, for if the old gentleman didn't want her, Emma van der Blocq did, even if only for a gossip. It wasn't until several days after her arrival that Mary Jane, during the course of one of these chats, asked her hostess why Jaap always referred to her as Freule—a question which kept Emma van der Blocq happy for an entire afternoon, explaining the intricacies of the Dutch nobility. She added a wealth of information regarding their titles, their houses and lands to a fascinated Mary Jane, who at the end of this dissertation, asked, 'So what do I call Fabian? He's a surgeon—is he Mister or Doctor?'

Cousin Emma looked slightly taken aback. 'But of course you have not fully understood. He is also Jonkheer, he is also a professor of surgery, you comprehend? Therefore he is addressed as Professor Jonkheer van der Blocq.'

'My goodness,' observed Mary Jane, 'what a mouthful!' Now she knew why he had looked so amused when she had addressed him as Mister. It had been nice of him not to say anything, though it surprised her that he hadn't taken the opportunity of discomfiting her. Her companion went on earnestly, 'I am old-fashioned enough to set great store upon these things, but I believe that the young people do not. Fabian may not be young any more, but he does not care in the least about his position, he...' She was interrupted by the entry of Corrie, the maid, begging her to ask Miss to go at once to the master of the house, and as Mary Jane got obediently to her feet, she said: 'What a blessing you are to us all. You do not know the relief I feel at not having to answer every call from Papa's room.'

And Mary Jane, skipping up the stairs for the tenth time that day, could well believe her. She was a little puzzled that nobody had offered to relieve her of her duties from time to time—it would be all right for a week or so, but she began to feel the need for a little relaxation and exercise and for some other distraction other than card games and Cousin Emma's rather theatrical conversation.

It was the next afternoon, when after a fruitless effort on her part to escape for a walk, she was playing cards with her patient, that he wanted to know what she thought of Fabian.

'I don't know him well enough to form an opinion,' she told him in a matter-of-fact way. 'He saw to every thing very nicely—we couldn't have managed without him, and Grandfather liked him.' She paused and searched her memory. 'Everyone liked him,' she said in surprise.

'But not you?'

Until that moment she hadn't realised that she had never analysed her feelings towards Fabian. 'I've not thought about it.'

The old gentleman persisted, 'Perhaps he doesn't like you?'

She shuffled the cards and dealt them. 'Probably not. One gets on better with some people than others.'

'You're not much to look at.'

'No—it's your turn.'

He slammed down a card. 'Men fall for a pretty face.'

'So I should imagine.' She smiled at him across the card table and he glowered back.

Presently he went on, 'A pretty face isn't everything. You're delightful company, Mary Jane; it was good of your grandfather to let me share you. You don't mind staying a little while?'

She shook her head. 'Not in the least. I'll stay as long as you want me to.'

He snorted. 'Don't let us wrap up our words. You know as well as I do that I shall probably be dead in a week or so. You're not bored?'

It was difficult to answer that, because she was, just a little. She longed to get away for an hour or so each day; she had known that she would spend some time with Jonkheer van der Blocq each day, but even private nurses were entitled to their free periods, and she wasn't a private nurse—Fabian had told her that. He had spoken of trips to Groningen and getting a mount from the nearby stables; so far she had had no time for either, indeed she had no idea where the stables were, and when, on the previous day, she had mentioned going for a walk to Freule van der Blocq, that good lady had reacted quite violently to the suggestion; it seemed that the idea of being left with her father was more than she could bear, so Mary Jane had said no more about it. When Doctor Trouw paid his next visit, she would have a little talk with him and see what could be done.

She had hoped that Fabian would have come, even for half an hour to see how she was managing, but although the telephone rang frequently, she had no means of knowing if any of the calls were from him; it was really rather mean of him, and she decided that she liked him even less than she had supposed, and told herself forcefully that she didn't care if she never saw him again.

He came the very next morning, while Mary Jane, after a protracted argument between her host and his daughter, was in church. Emma went to church each Sunday, driven by Jaap in the Mercedes Benz which was housed, along with a Mini, in the garage at the back of the house, and she had seen no reason why Mary Jane shouldn't accompany her. 'Jaap will be here,' she had pointed out to her enraged parent, 'he can help you dress and we shall be back very shortly.'

Her father pointed out testily that if Jaap drove them to church, there would be no one to dress him, and he certainly wasn't going to wait while Jaap drove around the countryside just because she wanted to go to church.

Mary Jane, feeling a little like a bone between two dogs, felt her patience wearing thin round the edges. 'Look,' she offered when she could make herself heard 'can't I drive the Mini? It's no distance, and that would leave Jaap free.'

So they had gone to church and on the return journey when she turned the little car carefully into the drive once more, it was to find a silver-grey pre-war Jaguar SS 100 parked before the door. She got out and went to inspect it with a good deal of interest; it wasn't an original but a modern version of it, she discovered as she prowled around its chassis, wondering to whom it belonged, and when Cousin Emma cried happily: 'Oh, good, Fabian's here—this is his car,' Mary Jane, her inquisitive person bent double over the dashboard, remarked:

'I don't believe it.'

'Why not?' It was Fabian who spoke and startled her so much that she turned round in a kind of jump, and when she didn't speak, he repeated impatiently, 'Why not?'

'Well,' she said slowly, 'it's unexpected—I hardly thought that you...'

'I'm too old for it?' His voice was suave.

'What nonsense, of course not, it's just that...' She gave up, staring at him silently. After a moment he laughed and turned to his cousin.

'Well, Emma, how are you? I've been with Oom Georgius. He seems in fine shape, considering all things, though a little annoyed because Mary Jane wasn't at home.'

He looked at Mary Jane as he spoke, and she, aware of his faintly accusing tone, went red, just as though, she thought crossly, she were in the habit of tearing off for hours at a time, whereas the morning's outing, if it could be called that, had been the first since she had arrived. She turned on her heel and walked into the house as Cousin Emma burst into voluble speech.

She was in Jonkheer van de Blocq's room fighting her usual battle over his pills when Fabian came in. He sat down by the fire without speaking, watching her while, with cunning and guile, she persuaded the old man to swallow them down. He still said nothing as she prepared to leave them, only walking to the door to open it for her. She barely glanced at him as she passed through.

They all lunched together in the dining room, and Jonkheer van der Blocq, a little excited at Fabian's visit, talked a great deal, repeating himself frequently and forgetting his words and showing little flashes of splendid rage when he did. The meal took some time and when it was at last finished he was tired, so that for once, when Mary Jane suggested that he might like to lie down for half an hour, he agreed meekly. She accompanied him upstairs again, tucked him up on the chaise-longue in his room, thoughtfully provided him with a book, his spectacles, the bell and the tin of fruit drops he liked to suck, bade him be a good boy in a motherly voice, and went downstairs.

She was crossing the hall when she heard Fabian's voice, usually so quiet and measured in its tones, raised in anger and as she reached the door she could hear Cousin Emma doing what she described to herself as a real Sarah Bernhardt. Her hand on the heavy brass knob, she wondered if she should go in, and had her mind made up for her by a particularly loud squawk. At any moment, she thought to herself vexedly, she would have strong hysterics to deal with, thanks to Fabian. She flung open the door to find Freule van der Blocq standing in a tragic pose in the middle of the room, and Fabian lounging against one of the Corinthian pillars which supported the vast fireplace. He spoke sharply.

'There you are! Perhaps you can answer my questions without weeping and wailing. Have you been out at all since you arrived here?'

'Oh yes—to church.'

'Don't infuriate me, I beg of you, you know very well what I mean. Have you had time to yourself each day, to go out, to ride, to visit Groningen?'

'Well I...'

'Yes or no?' he ground out.

'You see...'

'I see nothing, largely owing to your inability to answer my questions.' He frowned at her. 'There seems to be some gross misunderstanding; you are here as a guest, to give some time and company to Uncle Georgius at your grandfather's request. That does not mean that you have to spend each day cooped up in the house at everyone's beck and call.'

'Don't exaggerate,' Mary Jane told him calmly, 'just because you're annoyed. It's your fault anyway. You should have explained exactly what I was supposed to do—you didn't tell me much, did you, and I dare say you didn't tell Freule van der Blocq anything either. I refuse to be blamed, and I won't allow you to blame her either.'

He gave her a hard stare. 'Oh? Am I supposed to apologise to you, then?' his voice was silky and very quiet.

'No, I don't suppose any such thing, because I can't imagine you apologising to anyone, though you could at least say you're sorry to your cousin. It's unkind of you to make her cry.'

His eyes had become black, he was still staring at her, rather as though he had never seen her before, she thought uneasily. She shook off the feeling and prompted him, 'Well, go on—or perhaps you would rather not do with me here.'

She whisked out of the room before he could reply and crossed the hall to the long drawing room, a very much gilded apartment, with a wealth of grand furniture and huge display cabinets full of silver and porcelain. Not at all to her taste; she hurried over the vast carpeted floor and into the verandah room beyond where there was a piano. With the doors shut she was sure no one could hear her playing, and really, she had to do something to take her mind off things. It was a beautiful instrument. She sat down on the stool before it and tried a scale with the soft pedal down and then went on to a rambling mixture of tunes, just as they came into her head. She played tolerably well, disregarding wrong notes and forgetting about the soft pedal but putting in a good deal of feeling. Halfway through a half remembered bit of *Eine Kleine Nachtmusik,* Fabian stalked in, taking her by surprise because he entered by the garden door behind her. She stopped at once, folded her hands tidily in her lap and waited to hear what he had to say.

'You are the most infuriating girl!' he began in a pleasantly conversational tone. 'I have apologised to my cousin; if I apologise to you will you be kind enough to listen to what I have to say?'

'Of course—though why...'

'Just listen. I apologise for a start, and now to other matter. It seems that Cousin Emma was so glad to have someone in the house who could handle my uncle that she took advantage of that fact. Unintentionally, I should add. In future you are to take what time you wish for yourself. I know that I can depend upon you to do what you can for Uncle Georgius if and when he becomes worse—I imagine Trouw will give you good warning of that, if it is possible. You are free to go where you wish, is that understood? Have you any money?'

'Not much.'

'I will arrange for you to have sufficient for your needs. I will also see Uncle Georgius and explain to him.'

Mary Jane got up and closed the piano. 'You won't upset him? He's such a dear, I like him.'

He gave her a considering look. 'So do I. If you care to do so, I will drive you over to the riding stables in half an hour and arrange for you to hire a mount.'

'I should like that—are we going in that Jag?'

Fabian looked surprised. 'Of course.' He opened the door and they went through together. 'You play well.'

'Thank you—I hope no one minds.'

'No one will mind.' They were in the hall again, where he left her to go to his uncle's room, and she went into the sitting room where his cousin greeted her in a melodramatic manner and a fresh flood of tears. She was still eulogising Fabian, Mary Jane and then Fabian again when the object of her praise walked in, bidding Mary Jane to fetch her coat and go with him—something she was glad to do, for much as she liked Cousin Emma, a little of her went a long way, especially when she was upset.

It was cold in the car, but she had tied her head in a scarf and Fabian had tucked a rug around her. She sat, exhilarated by the fresh air and their progress through the narrow country roads. The stables were a mile or so away; the journey seemed too short; for once Fabian was being pleasant—she allowed him to choose a quiet mare for her use with the secret resolve to pick out something a little more lively once he was safely back in Groningen—there was no use in annoying him over such a small matter, especially as he seemed disposed to be friendly, indeed he seemed in such a good frame of mind that she was emboldened to ask him how his work was going and whether he was still busy.

'Yes, just at the moment, but I shall be able to come over

from time to time—in any case, there will be some papers for you to sign in a few days—some stocks I am transferring.' She looked a little blank and he went on smoothly, 'It seems to me to be somewhat of a paradox that you should trust me without question to attend to your affairs while at the same time you dislike me.'

She bit her lip and wished he wouldn't say things she couldn't answer. After a little thought, she said carefully, 'Well, I haven't much choice, have I?' and was annoyed when he laughed.

He went away after tea and she spent most of the evening trying to convince Jonkheer van der Blocq that just because she wanted to go out sometimes it didn't mean that she didn't like his company. She played three games of Racing Demon with him to prove her point.

The best time to go riding was in the morning. Mary Jane had an early breakfast and took the Mini over to the stables and rode for an hour. By the time she got back to the house, her host was awake and clamouring for her and his daughter was wanting her company. It worked very well, for they hardly noticed her absence, and she, refreshed by her morning exercise, felt prepared to be at their disposal for the rest of the day. And Fabian had telephoned each day too, to make sure that she was doing as he had asked, and she had answered truthfully enough that she was riding each day. Time enough to go to Groningen—at present the old gentleman needed her company, so did his daughter. She had no great opinion of herself, but she could see that the two of them rubbed each other up the wrong way, and a third party was necessary for peaceful living.

It was on her third morning's ride that she decided to ask for another horse; the mare was a nice beast, but a little slow. Without actually telling any fibs she managed to imply that Fabian had told her that she might make another choice if she wasn't quite pleased with the mare, and chose a bay, a spirited animal with a rolling eye and a little too big for her. But he went well and now that she had got the lie of the country she knew just where to take him—along the shore of the Leekstermeer, where there were trees and a good deal of undergrowth on either side of the unmade road. It was a dull morning, with the threat of rain—she had put on two sweaters and plaited her hair so that it would be out of the way, not caring at all if she should get wet. She reached the road to the lake and began to pick a way along the path she saw running beside it, looking about her as she did so. It was pretty there—not a patch on her own lake at home, but still charming and peaceful, even though the trees were bare of leaves and the grass was rough. She and the bay ambled along, for there was time enough; she could canter back along the road presently, there would be no traffic to speak of and there was an ample grass verge if he should get restive.

They were on the point of turning to go back when she became aware of horse's hooves behind her and when she turned to look it was to see Fabian astride a great roan, coming towards her at a canter. He rode well, she noted. He also looked very angry, she noted that too, and pulled in the bay with a resigned sigh.

His 'good morning' was icy, so she merely nodded in reply and waited silently for him to speak.

'I picked out a good little mare for you. Why aren't you riding her?' Mary Jane considered him thoughtfully. 'Well, I'm capable of choosing a mount, for one thing. I'm sick to death of you treating me as though I were a half-witted old maid you can barely bring yourself to be civil to!' She drew a swelling breath. 'And another thing, you may be my guardian, but you don't own me. I've a mind of my own.'

'And a temper, I see,' he observed dampingly. 'You forget that I had no notion of how you rode. If I had allowed you to choose for yourself and you could barely sit the beast and had taken a tumble, I should have done less than my duty to you as your guardian.'

'Oh, pooh!' she tossed her head and the pigtail swung over her shoulder.

'You look about ten years old,' he said unexpectedly, and smiled at her, 'Shall we cry a temporary truce? I came out to see you; I have those papers ready for you to sign and I wondered if you would like to come to Groningen for an hour or so.'

She eyed him with surprise. 'You mean you actually want me to go with you to Groningen?'

His voice was tinged with impatience. 'Yes. You see I'm being civil. We might even manage not to quarrel for a couple of hours.' He spoke without smiling now, his face turned away.

'Oh, very well,' she told him, knowing that her voice sounded ungracious, 'then I'd better go back.'

They rode back in silence. Only when they reached the stables did Fabian tell her quietly, 'I was mistaken, Mary Jane. You ride well.'

FABIAN HAD COME in the Jaguar, so that Mary Jane, with an eye to the weather, tied a silk scarf over her head in place of the unbecoming hat, wishing she had had the sense to bring her sheepskin jacket with her. It was barely November but already cold, and an open car, although great fun, needed suitable clothes, but once they were on their way, she didn't feel cold at all; she glowed with excitement and pleasure. An outing would be delightful, especially if they could remain friends for an hour.

Her patient, in a mellow mood, had agreed to his daughter keeping him company for a short time, only begging Mary Jane to return at the earliest possible moment. His daughter had been rather more urgent in her request not to be left for longer than was absolutely necessary with her irascible parent; she had also given Mary Jane a shopping list of things which she declared she urgently needed. It was a miscellany of knitting wool, embroidery silks, Gentlemen's Relish, chocolate biscuits and a particular brand of bottled peach which could only be obtained at a certain shop in the city. Mary Jane accepted it obligingly, to have it taken from her at once by Fabian, who put it in his pocket with a brisk 'I'll see to these,' and an injunction to hurry herself up. So here she was, sitting snugly beside Fabian, who was making short work of the few miles to Groningen.

She found the city very fine, with its two big squares and its old buildings. Fabian, going slowly through the traffic, pointed out the imposing, towering spire of St Martin's church before he turned off the main street and into a tree-lined one, bisected by a canal. The houses here were patrician, flat-faced and massive, each of them with its great front door reached by a double flight of steps. The sound of the traffic came faintly down its length so that it was easy to hear the rustle of the wind in the trees' bare branches.

'This is beautiful,' declared Mary Jane with satisfaction.

Fabian stopped before one of the houses. 'Yes, I think so too. I'm glad you like it.'

'Is this the lawyer's house?' she asked him.

'No, it's mine. We'll go inside and get those papers dealt with.'

She hadn't thought much about where he lived and when she had, it had been a vague picture of some smallish town house. This mansion took her by surprise, and she was still more surprised when they went inside. The hall was long and narrow and panelled waist high, with rich red carpeting on its floor to cover the black and white of its marble. The wall chandeliers were exquisite and there were flowers on the wall table. She wanted to take a more leisurely look, but an elderly woman appeared from the back of the house, was introduced as Mevrouw Hol and swept her away to an elegantly appointed cloakroom, where she tidied her hair, did things to her face and left her outdoor things before being led to a room close by where Fabian was waiting for her.

She took it to be a study, as it was lined with bookshelves and its main furniture was a massive desk and an equally massive chair, but the chairs by the fire were of a comfortably normal size. Mary Jane took the one offered her and sighed with content; the room was warm and light and airy and quite, quite different from the over-furnished house in which Fabian's uncle lived.

He sat down at the desk now, saying: 'You won't mind having coffee here? We can see to these papers at the same time, they'll not take long.'

She drank her coffee and then, under his direction, signed the papers, each one of which he carefully explained to her before asking her to do so. When she had finished she said with faint apology, 'I'm sorry you've had all this extra work, but I suppose once it's seen to, you won't need to bother, any more.'

'On the contrary.' He didn't smile as he spoke and she felt

chilled. 'If you have finished your coffee perhaps you would like to come with me and get Emma's shopping—and by the way, I believe that I promised you some money for your own use.' He opened a drawer in the desk and handed her a little bundle of notes. 'There are a thousand gulden there. If you need more, please ask me.'

She looked at him round-eyed. 'Whatever should I want with all that money?'

He smiled faintly. 'I imagine that you will find things to buy with it.'

She became thoughtful. 'Well, yes—there are one or two things...'

He went back to his desk and silently handed her a pad and pencil. A few minutes later she looked up. 'You know,' she informed him in surprise, 'I've made quite a list.'

'I thought maybe you would. Would a store suit you or do you want a boutique?'

She shot him a suspicious glance which he countered with a grave detachment. How did he know about boutiques? she wondered, and assured him that a large store would be much easier. 'I'll be as quick as I can,' she assured him.

'No need—I told Cousin Emma that we shouldn't be back until after tea. We'll lunch out and you will have hours of time.'

Mary Jane had forgotten how pleasant it was to go shopping with plenty of money to spend. By the time Fabian had worked his way through the list Emma had given them, it was burning a hole in her purse, and when Fabian left her outside a large store, assuring her that most of the assistants spoke English and she had nothing to worry about and that he would be waiting for her in an hour's time, she could hardly wait to start on a tour of inspection. Fabian had been right, there was no difficulty in making herself understood; everyone seemed to speak English. She bought everything which she had written on her list and a good deal besides, and when, strolling through the hat department, she saw a velvet beret which would go very well with her coat, she bought that too and, a little drunk with the success of her shopping, put it on.

She was only ten minutes late at the store entrance and when she would have apologised to Fabian for keeping him waiting he said to surprise her, 'Late? Are you? I never expected you back within the hour and a half—we agreed upon an hour, if you remember. We'll have lunch and if you have anything else to buy you can get it later.'

They lunched at the Hotel Baulig, and as they were both hungry they started the meal with *erwtensoep*—a thick pea soup enriched with morsels of bacon and ham and sausage, went on to a dish of salmon with asparagus tips and quenelles of sole, and having finished this delicacy, agreed upon fresh fruit salad to round off their lunch. They sat a considerable time over their coffee, for rather to Mary Jane's surprise, they found plenty to talk about, and although she thought Fabian rather reserved in his manner, at least he was agreeable.

They did a little more shopping after they left the hotel, for it seemed sense to her to buy one or two presents while she had the opportunity. It was when she had declared herself satisfied with her purchases that Fabian remarked, 'But you have bought nothing for yourself.'

'Yes, I have, lots of things—and a hat.' She waited for him to notice the beret and was deeply mortified when he said: 'Oh, did you? why don't you wear it, then?' He glanced at their parcels. 'It must be a very small one, there's nothing here which looks like a hat bag.'

She boiled, but silently. She wasn't sure if he was teasing her or if he took so little notice of her that he hadn't even noticed what she was wearing. Neither of these ideas were very complimentary to herself. She answered with a sweetness which any of her closer friends would have suspected, 'I know where it is. I think I've finished, thank you. I expect you would like to be getting back to Midwoude.'

He gave her a searching look. 'Why?'

'Well, you've done your good deed for today, haven't you?' Her voice was light despite his look.

'Indeed yes, and it's made me thirsty. Shall we have tea somewhere?'

She kept her voice light. 'No, thank you. I think I should like to go back now. I'm most grateful to you...'

His tone was curt. 'Spare the thanks,' he begged her coldly, and thereafter sustained an ultra-polite conversation during their short journey back to Midwoude where he handed her and her packages over to Jaap, wished her a distant good evening, got back into his car and drove away, a great deal too fast.

Emma van der Blocq, pouring a late tea in the small room at the back of the house where the two of them sometimes sat, professed surprise as Mary Jane joined her. 'I didn't expect you back until much later,' she declared happily, 'but surely Fabian could have stayed for tea—even for dinner?' She interrupted herself. 'No, perhaps not for dinner—he goes out a good deal, you know. Where did you have lunch, Mary Jane?'

She remembered the name of the hotel and felt rather pleased with herself about it, and Cousin Emma nodded, her interest aroused.

'A very nice place. Of course he really prefers the Hotel at Warffrum—Borg de Breedenburg—but that is for his more romantic outings.' She smiled at Mary Jane. 'He has girl-friends, as you can imagine—I wonder why he didn't take you there?'

'I imagine,' said Mary Jane in a dry little voice, 'that I don't qualify for a romantic background.'

'No, perhaps not,' agreed her companion with disconcerting directness. 'Fabian only takes out very pretty girls, you know—and always beautifully dressed, as you can imagine.' She smiled again, quite oblivious of any feelings Mary Jane might possess. 'He's a most observant man.'

'You surprise me,' said Mary Jane waspishly, thinking of the lovely velvet beret he hadn't even noticed. 'And now I'll just go up and see how Jonkheer van der Blocq is. Did he have a quiet day?'

Her companion's face crumpled ominously. 'Oh, my dear, however did I manage before you came? He was so cross, and he refused to take his pills. Doctor Trouw will be here presently and he will be so annoyed.' She sounded so upset that Mary Jane paused on her way to the door.

'He's far too nice to get cross with you,' she assured her, 'and he knows that it isn't always easy...'

Emma's face broke into a simper. 'Oh yes, he is so good... I've known him for years, you know, long before he married. His wife died last year. She was a quiet little thing—no looks at all. You remind me of her.'

To which remark Mary Jane could think of no answer at all. She escaped through the door and spent the rest of the evening with the old gentleman, who seemed delighted to see her again and to her great relief made no remarks at all about her face or her lack of looks.

It turned a great deal colder the next day, but Mary Jane went riding just the same, bundled in several sweaters against the wind, and returning to the house with glowing cheeks and a sparkle in her eyes. Of Fabian there was no sign, but that didn't surprise her—why should he come anyway? He had only visited the house because he needed some papers signed—it certainly wasn't for her company. Let him use his leisure escorting the beauties of Groningen to romantic dinners, she thought, her lip curling, and then her mood changed and she fell to thinking how very satisfactory it would be if she could be escorted to this hotel Emma had been so enthusiastic about, wearing the organza dress. She sighed and prodded her mount to quicken his pace. Chance was a fine thing, she told him, as they turned for home.

She had her chance the very next day, as it turned out, for when Doctor Trouw called he brought his son with him. A pleasant young man in his twenties, he had recently qualified and was about to join his father's practice. Over coffee he remarked, 'You are stranger here, I don't suppose you go out very much. I should like to take you out to dinner one evening.'

Mary Jane accepted with alacrity, and when, to her delight, he suggested that he should take her to Hotel Borg de Breedenborg on the following evening, she agreed with flattering speed.

She spent the intervening time imagining herself sweeping into the restaurant while Fabian, already there with some girl, would be bowled over by the sight of her in the organza, prettied up for the evening. The urge to shake him out of his cool, casual attitude towards herself was growing very strong, it caused her to take twice as long as usual in her preparations for the evening, which were so effective that when she went along to see her patient before they left, he was constrained to remark upon her changed appearance, as indeed was Cousin Emma, who rather tactlessly remarked that she hardly recognised Mary Jane in her finery.

Willem was rather nice and she was determined to have a pleasant evening. As they drove to the hotel she set herself to draw him out with a few well-chosen questions about his work. It wasn't until they reached the hotel that she was struck by the thought that her chance of seeing Fabian was small indeed. Even if he had a host of girl-friends, he surely didn't dine there every evening. He had his work—presumably that kept him busy, and surely he must spend some of his evenings at home, catching up on his reading, writing, even operating when it was necessary. She left her coat, patted the hair which had taken so long to put up and determinedly dismissed him from her head as she rejoined Willem.

The restaurant was full and she realized with something of a shock that it was already Saturday again—a whole week since she had seen Fabian. She sat down opposite her companion, gave him a brilliant smile and glanced around her. Fabian was sitting quite near their table, and the girl he was with was just as lovely as she had imagined she would be. Mary Jane turned the brilliance of her smile into a polite, tight-lipped one as she caught his eye and turned her attention to Willem, who, once they had ordered, launched into an earnest description of his days, hour by hour, almost minute by minute. She strove to keep an interested expression on her face, and when it was possible, laughed gaily, so that Fabian, whom she hadn't looked at again, would see how much she was enjoying herself. It was a pity that Fabian and his companion should go while they themselves were only half way through dinner. He paused as they passed the table, his hand on the girl's arm. He said austerely, 'I'm glad to see that you are enjoying yourself, Mary Jane,' nodded briefly to Willem and went on his way. Mary Jane watched him smile down at the girl as they went through the door and then wondered briefly where they were going, and then concentrated on Willem, who had started to tell her at great length about a girl he had met at his hospital. She obviously occupied his thoughts to a large extent; by the time he had finished, Mary Jane even knew the size of her shoes.

They went back to the house at a reasonable hour because, as Willem reminded her, his father, who was dining with Cousin Emma and keeping an eye on her father at the same time, needed a good night's sleep. He took his farewell of her half an hour later with the hope that they might spend another evening together before she returned to England, and Mary Jane, thanking him nicely, wondered how she could possibly have been interested in him, even for such a short time; he was so very worthy, and looking back on their evening she could remember no conversation at all on her part, merely a succession of 'really's' and 'fancy that's' and 'you don't say so's'. When he and his father had gone she gave Cousin Emma a potted version of her evening because she could see that the lady had no intention of allowing her to go to bed until she had done so, and then she went to Jonkheer van der Blocq's room to see if he had settled for the night. Somehow or other, he had contrived not to take his sleeping tablet, which necessitated her arguing gently with him for the best part of ten minutes, but when he had finally consented to do as she asked and she had turned his pillows and settled him nicely, he enquired after her evening, observing in no uncertain manner that he found Willem a dull fellow, which naturally had the effect of her replying that he had been a very interesting companion, that the dinner had been delicious, and that he had asked her out again.

'What did you talk about?' growled the old man.

'Oh, his work, naturally. And a girl he met while he was in hospital—he's very taken with her. He—talked a lot about her.'

Jonkheer van der Blocq laughed until he had no breath. Mary Jane gave him a drink, told him severely that there was nothing to laugh about, wished him good night and presently went to bed herself. She hadn't mentioned to anyone that Fabian had been at the hotel too, and she didn't think she would.

He came the next morning while they were in church, and this time it was the Rolls parked outside the door when they returned. As they went in he came downstairs, wished them a pleasant good morning, agreed that a cup of coffee would be welcome and when Emma had disappeared kitchenwards to find someone to make it, turned to Mary Jane and invited her to enter the sitting room.

'I'll take my things upstairs first,' she told him coldly, and was frustrated by his instant offer to take her coat, which he tossed on to a chair.

'It can stay there for a moment,' he told her rather impatiently. 'I see you are wearing the new hat. It's pretty—so you found it.'

She gave him a frosty look and said witheringly, 'It wasn't difficult, it was on my head.'

The dark wings of his brows soared. 'Oh dear—I can see that I must apologise, my dear girl, and I do. I could make a flowery speech, but you would make mincemeat of it, so I'll just say that I'm sorry.'

She walked away from him into the sitting room, where she sat down, telling herself indignantly that she didn't care if he followed her or not. He took the chair opposite hers and stretched his long legs and studied her carefully.

'You wouldn't believe me if I say how charming you looked yesterday evening?' he asked mildly.

'No.' She added nastily, 'You haven't a clue as to what I was wearing.'

His smile mocked her. 'Sea green, or would you call it sea blue, something thin and silky. It had long sleeves with frills over your wrists and a frill under your chin and a row of buttons down the back of the bodice.'

She was astounded, but she managed to say with a tinge of sarcasm:

'A photographic eye, I see,' and then because her female

curiosity had got the better of her good sense. 'The girl you were with was lovely.'

He picked a tiny thread from a well-tailored sleeve. 'Delightfully so. She wears a different wig every day of the week and the longest false eyelashes I have ever seen.'

Mary Jane turned a chuckle into a cough. 'And why not? It's the fashion. Besides, she would look gorgeous in anything she chose to put on.'

He agreed placidly. 'And you found William Trouw entertaining?' he asked suavely.

'We had a very pleasant evening,' she told him guardedly.

'A worthy young man,' went on her companion ruminatively. 'He would make a good husband—do you fancy him?'

She choked. 'Well, of all the things to say! I've been out with him once, and here you are, talking as though...'

He went on just as though she had never interrupted him. 'He has a good practice with his father, so he wouldn't be after your money, and I imagine he has all the attributes of a good husband—good-natured, no interest in drinking or betting, or girls, for that matter—a calm disposition, he...'

She ground her teeth. 'Be quiet! You may be my guardian, but you shan't talk like that. I'll marry whom I please and when I want to, and until then you can mind your own business!'

'From which outburst I conclude that Willem hasn't won your heart?'

She wanted to laugh, but she choked it back. 'No, he hasn't. As a matter of fact he spent quite a long time telling me about a girl he knew in hospital. I think he intends to marry her.'

'Ah, I wondered what it was that you found so interesting, though surely it was unkind of you to laugh so much during the recital?'

'I didn't...' she began, and stopped, because of course she had, so that Fabian should think she was having a lovely time. 'I enjoyed myself very much,' she muttered peevishly, and was glad to see Cousin Emma and Jaap with the coffee tray, coming into the room.

Fabian stayed for lunch, and his uncle insisted upon coming

down to join them, contributing to the conversation with such
gusto that Mary Jane feared for his blood pressure. But at least
he was so tired after his meal that she had no difficulty in
persuading him to take his customary nap, and when she had
tucked him up and come downstairs again it was to find that
Emma had allowed herself to be driven over to Doctor Trouw's
house for tea. Which left her and Fabian. He was waiting for
her in the hall and he sounded impatient.

'Shall we have a walk before tea?'

Mary Jane paused at the bottom of the staircase. 'Thank you,
no. I have letters to write.'

'Which you can write at any time.' He came towards her.
'It's not often I'm here.'

'Oh—should I mind?'

'Don't be an impudent girl, and don't imagine it is because
I want your company,' he added quite violently. 'I had a letter
from Mr North asking me to explain certain aspects of your
inheritance to you, so I might just as well do it and take some
exercise at the same time.'

'Charming!' observed Mary Jane, her eyes snapping with
temper, 'and so good of you to fit me in with one of your more
healthy activities.'

'And what,' he asked awfully, 'exactly do you mean by that
remark?'

'Just exactly what I say. I'll come for half an hour—in that
time you should be able to tell me whatever I'm supposed to
know.'

She crossed the hall and picked up her coat, caught up her
gloves and went to the pillow cupboard, rummaged around in
its depths until she found a scarf which she tied carelessly over
her hair. 'Ready,' she said with a distinct snap.

They walked away from the village, into the teeth of a mean
wind, while Fabian talked about stocks and shares and gilt-
edged securities and capital gains tax to all of which she lent
only half an ear. As far as she could see she would have a
perfectly adequate income whatever he and Mr North decided
to do with her money. As long as she had sufficient to run the

house and pay for Mrs Body and Lily and have some over to
run the car and buy clothes... She stopped suddenly and told
him so.

'You are not only a tiresome girl, you are also a very ungrateful one,' Fabian informed her bitterly.

'I'm sorry—about being ungrateful, I mean, but I can't remember being tiresome—was it on any particular occasion?'

He sounded quite weary. 'You are tiresome all the time,' he
told her, which surprised her so much that she walked in silence
until he observed that since she wished to return to Midwoude
within half an hour, they had better go back. They didn't speak
at all, and in the hall they parted. When Mary Jane came downstairs ten minutes later, it was to find that he had gone. She
told herself with a little surge of rage that it was a good thing
too, for when they were together they did nothing but disagree.
She wandered across to the sitting room, telling herself again,
this time out loud, that she was delighted, and added the hope
that she wouldn't see him for simply ages.

But it wasn't simply ages, it was the following Wednesday,
or rather three o'clock on Thursday morning. Jonkheer van der
Blocq had had, for him, a very good day. They had played their
usual game of cards, and she had helped him to bed, just a little
worried because his colour was bad. But Doctor Trouw had
called that afternoon, and although the old gentleman was failing rapidly now, he had seen no cause for immediate alarm.
Mary Jane went to bed early, first taking another look at her
patient. He was asleep, and there was nothing to justify her
unease.

The peal of the bell wakened her. She bundled on her dressing gown, and not waiting to put her feet in slippers, ran across
the dim landing. The old man was lying very much as she had
left him, but now his colour was livid, although he said with
his usual irascibility, 'I feel most peculiar—I want Fabian here
at once.'

She murmured soothingly while she took a frighteningly
weak pulse and studied his tired old face before she went to
the telephone. It was quite wrong to ring up in front of the

patient, but she didn't dare leave him. She rang Doctor Trouw
first, with a suitably guarded request for him to come, and then
dialled Fabian's number. His voice, calm and clear over the
line, gave her the instant feeling that she didn't need to worry
about anything because he was there—she forgot that they
weren't on speaking terms, that he was arrogant and treated her
like a tiresome child. She said simply, 'Oh, Fabian—will you
come at once? Your uncle'—she paused, aware that the bed's
occupant was listening—'would like to speak to you,' she finished.

'He's listening?'

'Yes.'

'I'll be with you in fifteen minutes. Get Trouw.'

'I have.'

'Good girl! Get Jaap up and tell him to open the gates and
the door. Get Emma up too—no, wait—tell Jaap to do that.
You stay with my uncle.'

She said, 'Yes, Fabian,' and put down the receiver. 'Fabian's
on his way,' she told Jonkheer van der Blocq in a calm, reassuring voice. 'I'm to wake Jaap so that he can open the gates.
Stay just as you are—I'll only be few moments.'

Doctor Trouw came a few minutes later, and in response to
the old gentleman's demand to be given something to keep him
going, gave him an injection, told him to save his breath in the
understanding voice of an old friend and went to Emma's room,
where she could be heard crying very loudly.

Mary Jane pulled up a chair to the bedside, tucked her cold
feet under her and took Jonkheer van der Blocq's hand in hers.
'Fabian won't be long,' she told him again, because she sensed
that was what he wanted above anything else. She certainly was
justified, because a moment later she heard the soft, powerful
murmur of the Rolls' engine and the faint crunch of its tyres
as Fabian stopped outside the front door.

He entered the room without haste, wearing a thick sweater
and slacks and looking very wide awake. He said: 'Hullo, Uncle
Georgius,' and nodded to Mary Jane, his dark, bright gaze taking in the dressing-gown, the plaited hair and her bare feet. He

said kindly, 'What a girl you are for forgetting your slippers!
Go and put them on, it's cold, and tell Trouw I'm here, will
you. I don't suppose he heard me come, with the row Emma's
making.'

His uncle made a weak, explosive sound. 'Silly woman,' he
said, in a voice suddenly small, 'always crying—you'll keep an
eye on her, Fabian?'

'Of course.' He lapsed into Dutch as Mary Jane reached the
door.

Emma was in no state to be left alone; Mary Jane stayed
with her as Doctor Trouw hurried across the landing, and was
still with her when he came back to tell them that his patient
was dead. It wasn't until poor Emma had had something to
send her to sleep, and Mary Jane had tucked her up in bed, that
she felt free to leave her.

The old house was very quiet; there was a murmur of voices
coming from the kitchen, and still more voices behind the
closed door of the small sitting room. She stood in the hall,
wondering if she should go back to bed, a little uncertain as to
what Doctor Trouw might expect of her. It was chilly in the
hall and the tick-tock of the over-elaborate French grandfather
dripped into the stillness with an oily sloth which she found
intensely irritating. A cup of tea would have been nice, she
thought despondently, and turned to go back upstairs just as the
sitting room door opened and Fabian said: 'Ah, there you are.
Come in—Jaap's bringing tea.' He glanced at her pale face.
'You look as though you need it. Cousin Emma's asleep?'

She nodded, then sat down in a chair by the still burning fire
and drank her tea, listening to the two men talking and saying
very little herself. When she had finished she got to her feet.
'Is there anything you would like me to do?' she asked.

Doctor Trouw shook his head. 'The district nurse will be here
very shortly. Go to bed, Mary Jane, and get some sleep. I am
most grateful to you for all you have done and I will ask you
to do something else. Would you look after Emma for a few
days? She has very sensitive nature and I am afraid this will
be too much for her—I will leave something for her, if you

will give it when she wakes, and be round about lunch time to see how she is.'

She nodded, thinking that Cousin Emma would be even more difficult than her father, and went to the door which Fabian had opened for her. He followed her into the hall, shutting the door behind him, and she turned round tiredly to see what he wanted.

His voice was quiet. 'I know what you are thinking. We have imposed upon you and we have no right but I too would be grateful if you would stay just for little while and help Emma— she likes you and she needs you.'

She said shortly, 'Oh, that's all right. Of course I'll stay.

He came nearer. 'You have had a lot to bear in the last few weeks, Mary Jane. Once I called you a tiresome girl. I apologise.' He bent and kissed her cheek with a gentleness which disturbed her more than any of the harsh words he had uttered in the past. She went upstairs, not answering his good night.

The next few days were a peculiar medley of intense activity, doing all the things Cousin Emma insisted should be done; receiving visitors, whose hushed voices and platitudes caused her to sit in floods of tears for hours after they had gone; going to Groningen to buy the black garments she considered essential and relating, seemingly endlessly, her father's perfections to Mary Jane, while crying herself sick again.

Mary Jane found it all a little difficult to stomach—father and daughter had hardly had a happy relationship while he was alive, now that he was dead he had somehow become a kind of saint. But she liked Emma, although she found her histrionics a little trying, and she did what she could to keep her as calm as possible, addressed countless envelopes and kept out of Fabian's way as much as possible.

He came frequently, but her quick ears, tuned to the gentle hum of the Rolls-Royce or the exuberant roar of the Jaguar, gave her warning enough to slip away while he was in the house. But one evening she had made the mistake of supposing that he had left the house; it was almost dinner time and there was no sound of voices from either of the sitting rooms. He must have gone, she decided, while she had been up in the attic, packing away Jonkheer van der Blocq's clothes until such time as his daughter found herself capable of deciding what to do with them. The small sitting room was dimly lit by the firelight and one lamp, and Freule van der Blocq was lying asleep on the sofa. Fabian was on one of the easy chairs, his legs thrust out before him, contemplating the ceiling, but he got up as Mary Jane started to leave the room as silently and quickly as she had entered it. Outside in the hall he demanded: 'Where have you been?'

'Upstairs in the attics, sorting your uncle's clothes.'

'Have you, by God? Surely there's someone else to such work? And that was not what I meant. Where have you been? Whenever I come, I am conscious of your disappearing footsteps. Do you dislike me so much?'

She eyed him thoughtfully. 'I never think about it,' she said at length, not quite truthfully.

His expressive eyebrows rose. 'No? You thought I had gone?'

'Yes.'

He grinned. 'I'm staying to dinner, and now you're here there's no point in retreating, is there? We'll have a glass of sherry.'

She accompanied him to the big sitting room and sat down composedly while he poured their drinks. When he had settled himself near her he asked, 'When do you want to go home?'

'I should like to go as soon as the funeral is over. I understand that Emma is going away the day after—I could leave at the same time.' She sipped her sherry. 'If you would be kind enough to let me have some more money, I can see about getting my ticket.'

'No need. I shall take you with the car.'

She kept her voice reasonable. 'I don't want to go in your car. I'm quite capable of looking after myself, you know. Besides, you have your work.' She looked at him, saw his smouldering gaze bent upon her and added hastily, 'I'm very grateful, but I can't let you waste any more time on me.'

'Have I ever complained that I was wasting my time on you?'

'No—but one senses these things.'

He gave a crack of laughter. 'One might be mistaken. Would you feel better about it if I told you that I have to go over to England anyway within the next few days—I'm only offering you a lift.'

She said doubtfully, 'Really? Well, that's different, I'll be glad to go with you.'

She missed the gleam in his eyes. 'Tuesday, then. Cousin Emma will be fetched by her friends after breakfast. I'll come for you about four o'clock. I've a ward round to do in the morning and a couple of patients to see after that. We'll go from Rotterdam, I think straight to Hull.' He thought for a minute. 'If we leave here after tea we shall have plenty of time to catch the ferry at Europort. If I'm not here by half past four, have tea and be ready to leave, will you?'

'Certainly.'

'You'll want to telephone Mrs Body.' He strolled across the room and picked up the receiver from the telephone on the delicate serpentine table between the windows. 'What is the number?'

It was nice to hear Mrs Body's motherly voice again. Mary Jane listened to her comfortable comments and felt a wave of homesickness sweep over her. It would be lovely to be home again. She told Mrs Body her news and heard that lady's voice asking if the dear doctor would be staying. Mary Jane hadn't thought about that. She repeated the enquiry and he turned to look at her. 'I began to think you weren't going to ask me,' he remarked mildly. 'A day or so, if I may.'

Mrs Body sighed in a satisfied manner when Mary Jane told her. 'That will be nice,' she said as she rang off, leaving Mary Jane wondering how much truth there was in that remark. Probably they would quarrel again before his visit was over, and there was nothing nice about that.

But at least they didn't quarrel that evening, tacit consent, they allied to keep Cousin Emma interested and amused, and succeeded so well that she didn't cry once and went to bed quite cheerful. Mary Jane, quite tired herself, went to bed early too and closed her eyes on the thought that when Fabian wished, he could be a most agreeable companion.

She saw little of him until Tuesday, when Cousin Emma, vowing eternal thanks, was packed off to stay with her friends and Mary Jane found herself alone in the house except for Jaap and the cook. The morning passed slowly enough because she had nothing much to do but go for a walk, but after her solitary lunch she settled down with a book until four o'clock, when she did her face and hair once more, got Jaap to bring down her case and went to the window to watch for the car. It didn't come; it hadn't come by half past four either. She had her tea, punctuated by frequent visits to the window, and when she had finished, put on her outdoor things, made sure that she had every thing with her, and sat down to wait. It was a quarter to six when the car's headlights lighted up the drive. She went into the hall to meet him, saying without any hint of the impatience she felt: 'You'd like a cup of tea, wouldn't you? I asked Jaap to be ready with one.'

'Good girl. I missed lunch—an emergency—I was called back to theatre.'

She was already on her way to the kitchen. 'I'll get some sandwiches.' She paused. 'I hope it was a success.'

'I think so—we shan't be certain for a couple of days.'

She nodded understandingly as she went, to return very soon with a tray of tea and buttered toast, sandwiches and cake. She poured the tea, gave him his toast and sat down again. Presently he said:

'You're very restful—not one reproach for being late, or missing the boat or where have I been.'

'Well, it wouldn't help much if I did, would it?' she wanted to know in a matter-of-fact voice. 'Besides, there's time enough, isn't there? The Rolls goes like a bomb, doesn't she, and the ferry doesn't leave until about midnight.'

'Sensible Miss Pettigrew! But I had planned a leisurely dinner on the way. Now it will have to be a hurried one.'

She smiled at him without malice. 'That won't matter much,

will it? Now if I'd been the girl you were with the other night, that would be quite a different kettle of fish...'

He put down his cup slowly. 'You're a great one for the unvarnished truth, aren't you?'

She got up and went over to the big gilt-framed mirror at the opposite end of the room and twitched the beret to a more becoming angle.

'Seeing that we have to deal with each other until I'm thirty,' she said in a tranquil voice, 'we might as well be truthful with each other, even if nothing else.'

'Nothing else what?' He spoke sharply.

She went to pour him a second cup. 'Nothing,' she told him.

They set out shortly afterwards. It was a cold dark evening and the road was almost free of traffic and Fabian sent the car tearing along on the first stage of their journey. He showed no signs of tiredness but sat relaxed behind the wheel—it was a pity it wasn't light, he told her, for they were going to Rotterdam down the other side of the Ijsselmeer, and she would have been able to see a little more of Holland. Mary Jane agreed with him and they sat in silence as they ripped through the flat landscape. Only when they reached Alkmaar and slowed to go through its narrow streets did he say, 'I'm poor company. I'm sorry.'

'The case this afternoon?' she ventured, to be rewarded by his surprised, 'How did you guess? Would it bore you if I told you about it?'

She wasn't bored; she listened with interest and intelligence and asked the right questions in the right places. They were approaching Rotterdam when he said finally, 'Thank you for listening so well—I can't think of any other girl to whom I would have talked like that.'

She felt a little pang of pure pleasure and tried to think of something to say, but couldn't.

They had their dinner in haste at the Old Dutch restaurant, and Mary Jane, seeing how tired Fabian looked, did her utmost to keep the conversation of a nature which could provoke no difference of opinion between them, and succeeded so well that they boarded the ferry on the friendliest of terms.

The journey was uneventful but rough, but they were both too tired to bother about the weather. They met at breakfast and she was delighted to find that his humour was still a good one. Perhaps now that they wouldn't be seeing much of each other, he was prepared to unbend a little. She accompanied him down to the car deck, hoping that this pleasant state of affairs would last.

It didn't, at least only until they reached the Lakes to receive a rapturous welcome from Mrs Body and sit down to one of her excellent teas. They barely begun the meal when Mary Jane stated, 'I intend to buy a horse tomorrow.'

'No, you won't.' Fabian spoke unhurriedly and with old finality.

She opened her eyes wide. 'Haven't I enough money?' she demanded.

'Don't make ridiculous statements like that—you have plenty of money. If you want a mount, I'll come with you, and you will allow me to choose the animal.' 'No, I won't! I can ride, you know I can.'

'Nevertheless, you will do as I ask, but before you start spending your money there are one or two details to attend to, I must ask you to come with me to the bank at Keswick, and Mr North will be coming here tomorrow morning. He will bring the last of the papers for you to sign, and as from then your income will be paid into your account each quarter. Should you need more money, you will have to advise me and I will advance it from the estate, should I consider it necessary.'

She boiled with rage. 'Consider it? It's ridiculous—it's like being a child, having to ask you for everything I want!'

He remained unmoved by her outburst. 'How inaccurate you are! You have more than sufficient to live on in comfort, and as long as you keep within your income, you will have no need to apply to me.'

She snorted, 'I should hope not—I'd rather be a pauper!'

'Even more inaccurate.'

There seemed no more to be said; she wasn't disposed to say that she was sorry and she could see that such an intention on his part hadn't even crossed his mind. He excused himself presently and she saw him cleaning the Rolls at the back of the house. From a distance he looked nice. He was a handsome man, she had to admit, and amusing when he wished to be, and kind; only, she told herself darkly, when one got to know him better did one discover what an ill-tempered, arrogant, unsympathetic... She ran out of adjectives.

He stayed two more days, coldly polite, unfailingly courteous and as withdrawn as though they were complete strangers forced to share a small slice of life together. She told herself that she was glad to see him go as the Rolls went through the gate and disappeared down the road to Keswick. He hadn't turned round to wave, either, and he must have known that she was standing in the porch. His goodbye had been casual in the extreme and he had made no mention of their future meeting. Mary Jane stormed back into the house, very put out and banged the door behind her, telling Major in a loud angry voice that life would be heaven without him.

CHAPTER FIVE

IT WAS HEAVEN for three or four days, during which Mary Jane explored the house from attic to cellar, examining with affection the small treasures her grandfather had possessed and which were now hers. She worked in the garden too, sweeping the leaves from the frosty ground, and went walking each day beside the lake with Major. It was cold now, and the snow had crept further down the mountains, but the sun still shone. She drove to Keswick, and to Carlisle to see Mr North, reflecting that it would have been marvelous weather for riding. But she had stubbornly refused to allow Fabian to choose a horse for her, and only after he had pressed the matter had she said that she wouldn't buy one at all if she couldn't have her own way; a decision she was regretting, for she had cut off her nose to spite her face, and a lot of good it had done her.

He hadn't even bothered to write to her—out of sight, out of mind, she muttered bitterly to herself, quite forgetting that she had hardly contributed to increase any desire on his part to have any more to do with her other than businesswise. It was that night, as she lay in bed very much awake, that she made the astonishing discovery that she actually missed him. She examined this from all angles and decided finally that it was because his extreme bossiness had imposed itself far too firmly upon her mind. Well, she was free of him now. She had a house of her own and what seemed to her to be quite a fortune—she could do exactly what she liked, whether he liked it or not—and she would too. She fell asleep making rather wild plans.

She found herself, as the days passed, filling them rather feverishly, quite often doing things which didn't need doing at all, taking walks which became increasingly longer, making excuses to get out the Mini and drive into Cockermouth or Keswick, and although she was happy she was lonely too, missing the rush and bustle of hospital life. In a few short weeks it would be Christmas and she wondered what to do about it. She hadn't a relation in the world whom she knew of and her friends were miles away in London, and what was more, they wouldn't be free over Christmas—nurses seldom were. She wondered what her grandfather and Mrs Body had done in previous years and went to ask that good lady, who chuckled gently and said:

'Well, Miss Mary Jane, not a great deal—your grand-father liked his turkey and his Christmas pudding and his friends came in for a drink. When he was younger, he used to give a dinner party—even have a few of his closer friends to stay, but they've died or gone away. The last few years have been a bit quiet.' She looked a little wistful. 'I suppose you haven't any friends who could come—a few jolly young people?'

Mary Jane explained about nurses not getting holidays at Christmas and Mrs Body said: 'Well, there's Doctor Morris, and there's Commander Willis—he's a very old friend of your grandfather's, but Lily was telling me that he's not been so well lately...'

They stared at each other, empty of ideas and a little depressed. The sound of a car turning into the drive sent them both into the hall to peer out of the small window beside the front door. 'It'll be that nice Doctor van der Blocq,' breathed Mrs Body happily, 'Oh, how lovely if it is!'

Mary Jane was looking out of the window; if it was keen disappointment she felt when she saw that the car was an Alfa Romeo and the man getting out of it wasn't Fabian, she was quite unaware of it. The man was a stranger, young, fair and not very tall. He seemed to be in no hurry to ring the bell but stood staring at the house and then turned his attention to the garden. Only when he had looked his fill did he advance towards the door. As he rang the bell Mary Jane retreated to the sitting room, waving an urgent hand at Mrs Body. She just had time to sit down in her grandfather's chair and take up the morning paper before the housekeeper, after the shortest of colloquies, put her head round the door. She looked surprised and excited.

'A young gentleman to see you, Miss Mary Jane. Mr Pettigrew from Canada.'

Mary Jane cast down the paper and goggled at her. 'Mr Pettigrew?' Enlightenment struck her. 'Do you suppose he's the cousin—the Canadian cousin—did he say?'

Mrs Body shook her head. 'He wants to see you.'

Mary Jane went into the hall. The young man was standing by the wall table, one of the Georgian candlesticks which rested upon it in his hands, examining it carefully.

She frowned. Even if he were a relation, it was hardly good manners to examine the silver for hallmarks the moment he entered the house. She said coolly, a question in her voice: 'Good morning?'

He put the candlestick down without any trace of embarrassment and crossed the hall, smiling at her, and she found herself smiling back at him, although her first impression of him hadn't been a good one. When he spoke it was with a rich Canadian accent.

'You must think I've got an infernal cheek...' He paused and widened his smile, and Mary Jane, a little on her guard now, allowed her own to fade, but this didn't deter him from continuing: 'I'm a Pettigrew—Mervyn John Pettigrew. My grandfather was your grandfather's cousin—he talked a lot about him when he was alive.' He put a hand into his pocket and withdrew a passport. 'I don't expect you to take me on trust—take a look at this.' And as she stretched out a hand to take it, 'You're Mary Jane, aren't you? I know all about you too.'

She glanced at the passport and gave it back, studying his face. She could see no family likeness, but probably there wouldn't be any; his mother had been a Canadian; he might take after her side of the family. She said quietly, 'How do you do? Why are you here?'

'We get the English papers—I saw a notice of my great-uncle's death. I had a holiday owing to me, so I decided to fly over and look you up.' He smiled again—he smiled too much, she thought irritably. 'My old man's dead—died two years ago. Mother died when I was a boy, and I'm the only Pettigrew left at home, so I thought I'd look you up.' He gave her a searching glance. 'I don't blame you for not quite believing me, despite the passport. If you'd give me ten minutes, though, I could tell you enough about the family to convince you.'

He had light eyes, a little too close together, but his look was direct enough. Mary Jane said on an impulse. 'Come in— I was just going to have coffee. Will you have a cup with me?'

She was bound to admit, at the end of ten minutes, that he must be a genuine cousin. After all, her grandfather had told her often enough that the nephew in Canada had a son—this would be he; he knew too much about the family to be anything else. And when he produced some letters written by her grandfather to his own father, there could be no further doubt. True, he didn't give them to her to read, but he showed her the address and the signature at the end, explaining. 'Great-uncle was very fond of my grandfather, you know—he was always making plans to visit him. He never did, of course, but he had a real affection for him—Dad was always talking about him too. Have you still got Major?'

Her last misgivings left her. She said with cautious friendliness:

'Yes—he's eleven, though, and getting a bit slow. He's in the kitchen with Mrs Body. Would you like to stay to lunch? Are you passing through or staying somewhere here?'

He accepted the invitation with an open pleasure which won her over completely. 'I'm touring around, having a look at all the places the old man told me about. I'm staying at Keswick and very comfortable.'

'Did you bring your car?' She corrected herself. 'No, of course you couldn't if you flew.'

'I've rented one.' And when he added nothing further she suggested that they should walk down to the lake. Their stroll was an unqualified success, partly because Mary Jane, who wasn't used to men—younger men, at any rate—taking any notice of her, found that not only did her companion listen to her when she spoke, but implied in his replies that she was worth listening to as well, and the glances he gave her along with the replies gave her the pleasant feeling that perhaps she wasn't quite as plain a girl as she had believed. It was a pity, she reflected, while the young man waxed enthusiastic over the scenery, that Fabian wasn't with them so that he could see for himself that not everyone shared his opinion of her. The horrid word tiresome flashed through her mind; it was amazing how it still rankled. A vivid picture of his face—austere, faintly mocking and handsome—floated before her mind's eye. She dismissed it and turned to answer Mervyn Pettigrew's eager questions about the house and its history.

She told him all she knew, studying him anew as she did so. He had good looks, she conceded, spoiled a little by the eyes and a mouth too small—and perhaps his chin lacked determination, although, as she quickly reminded herself, after several weeks of Fabian's resolute features, she was probably unfairly influenced, but these were small faults in an otherwise pleasing countenance. She judged him to be twenty-five or six, thick-set for his height and age. His clothes were right—country tweeds and well-polished shoes. On the whole she was prepared to reverse her first hasty impression of him, and admit that he might be rather nice. It was certainly pleasant to have someone of her own age to talk to; over lunch he told her about his home in Canada, volunteering the information that he was an executive in a vast business complex somewhere near Winnipeg, that he was a bachelor and lived in the house where he had been born—an oldish, comfortable house, by all accounts, with plenty of ground around it. He rode each day, he told her, getting up early so that he could take some exercise before breakfast and going to the office. 'Do you ride?' he wanted to know.

Mary Jane frowned. 'Yes. I haven't a mount, thought. I— I've a guardian who wouldn't allow me to choose a horse for myself, otherwise I would have had one days ago.'

Her cousin looked sympathetic. 'Don't think I'm interfering,' he begged her, 'but why not tell me about it? Perhaps there's some way...surely he can't stop you...' He waved a hand. 'This is all yours, isn't it? and I suppose Great-uncle left you enough to live on in plenty of comfort, and you're over twenty-one.' He added hastily, 'At least, I suppose you are.'

He was very well informed, she thought vaguely; he knew so much. 'I'm twenty-two.' She hesitated; the temptation to confide in someone was very great, and he was family. 'It's a little complicated,' she went on, and proceeded to tell him a little about Fabian and the conditions of her grandfather's will. She was strictly fair about Fabian. He was, she supposed, a good guardian and quite to be trusted with her money, she didn't want her companion to be in any doubt about that, and she was careful not to go into any details about her inheritance—indeed, when she had finished she wasn't sure if she should have mentioned it at all, but Mervyn had seemed very sympathetic and she was further reassured by his brief, vague reply before he changed the subject completely.

He left soon after that and when she asked him if he would like to come again, agreed that he would. 'But not for a few days,' he told her. 'I have some business to do, in Carlisle— friends I promised to look up for someone back home, but I'll call and see you again when I get back.'

She watched him go with some regret; he had helped to pass the day, it had been pleasant to talk to someone and have company for lunch. She went along to the kitchen where Mrs Body was sitting in the shabby, comfortable armchair she had used ever since Mary Jane could remember, and asked that lady what she thought of their visitor.

'He seems nice enough,' said Mrs Body, 'very friendly too. Is he coming again?'

'He said he would.' Mary Jane picked up one of the jam tarts the housekeeper had put to cool on the kitchen table and ate it.

'You'll get fat,' declared Mrs Body, 'picking and stealing between meals. Where's he from?'

Mary Jane ate another tart and told her.

'Why did he come?'

Mary Jane explained that too and then asked a little worriedly, 'Don't you like him, Mrs Body?'

'I've no reason to dislike him, but I don't know him, do I? I'm not quick to take a fancy to anyone.'

'You liked Mr van der Blocq...'

'That's different. Now if you take Major for a quick walk, I'll have tea ready by the time you get back.'

'Let's have it here,' begged Mary Jane, and went off obediently with the dog.

Mervyn didn't came for five days, during which time Mary Jane thought of him quite a lot while she busied herself about the house and the garden, writing letters to her friends at Pope's and answering a long dramatic letter from Cousin Emma, who, it seemed, had quite recovered from her father's death and was engaged in refurbishing her wardrobe—several pages were devoted to the outfits she had bought and intended to buy, to the exclusion of all other news. Fabian wasn't mentioned, nor had he written. That he was a busy man, Mary Jane was well aware, but he could surely have telephoned? But that took time, especially if he needed every free minute he had in order to take pretty girls out...she was aware that she was being unfair to him, but he could have taken some notice. When she wrote her Christmas cards, she sent him one too, and although sorely tempted to put a note in with it, she didn't do so.

She was in the kitchen helping Mrs Body and Lily with the Christmas puddings when Mervyn arrived. He apologised for disturbing her, offered her a box of chocolates with disarming diffidence and invited her out to lunch. 'There's a place in Cockermouth,' he told her, 'where we could eat, and I wondered if you would help me choose one or two things to take home with me—presents, you know.'

She felt faint dismay. 'You're not going back to Canada before Christmas?'

'I haven't any reason for staying longer.'

'What a pity! I was going to invite you to spend Christmas Day here.'

He didn't answer at once and he had turned his head away as he replied:

'That's a sufficiently good reason for me to cancel my flight,

Mary Jane.' He turned and gave her a long, steady look. 'I've thought of you a good deal. When I came to England I decided to come and look you up, because you were family—but now I keep thinking of all kinds of excuses to keep me here.'

Mary Jane listened to him, enchanted. No one—no young man, that was—had ever talked like that to her before. All of a sudden she felt beautiful, sought after, and dripping with charm; it was a pleasant sensation. She smiled widely at him and said a little breathlessly, 'Well, don't go until after Christmas—it's only ten days.' They stared at each other in silence and then she said, 'I'll go and put on my coat—there's a fire in the sitting room, I won't be a minute.'

It was the first of several such expeditions. They would return after their shopping and have tea, and then, later, dinner, to return to the sitting room fire and talk until Mervyn got up to go about ten o'clock. He was an amusing talker, preferring to tell her about his own life than ask her questions about her own, although sometimes she would find that, almost without knowing it, she was answering questions she had hardly noticed about the house and its contents and whether she had enough to run it properly and if her capital was in safe hands. She told him about Mr North, assuring him that he had been the family solicitor for years and was very much to be depended upon.

'Oh, is that the North who lives in Keswick?' he asked carelessly.

'Is there one in Keswick? No, Carlisle—Lowther Street. The firm's been there for ever.'

He had made no comment and had gone on to talk about something else.

He got up to go soon after and she walked with him to the door. As he put on his coat he said, 'I've some business to see to in the morning—a call to Winnipeg. May I come after lunch and take you out to tea?'

She nodded happily and he kissed her lightly on the cheek as she opened the door. It took her a long while to go to sleep that night; it was a pity that her excited thoughts of Mervyn were interlarded with unsolicited ones of Fabian.

She felt a little shy when he arrived the next afternoon, but it seemed that he felt no such thing; he kissed her again, a good deal more thoroughly this time, and told her gaily to get her coat and drove her into Keswick, where they had tea, bought a few things Mrs Body had need of, and drove home again. It was dark already, although it was barely four o'clock, for the mountains had swallowed up what light there had been, only the water of the lake gave back a dim reflection. It would be cold later on, but they didn't care. They roasted chestnuts by a blazing fire and ate their dinner together, and after Mervyn had gone, with yet another kiss, Mary Jane had skipped into the kitchen, her plain face alight. Mrs Body looked up as she went in, asked Lily to take some more logs to the sitting room and when she had gone, observed, 'You're happy, Miss Mary Jane.' Her kind eyes were sharp. 'Has he proposed?'

Mary Jane flung her arms round Mrs Body's ample waist. 'Oh, Mrs Body, do you think he's going to? No one has ever proposed to me before.'

'Which is no good reason for accepting him,' counselled her companion shrewdly.

Mary Jane knitted her fine pale brows. Mrs Body's remark was a sensible one, but it didn't fit in with her own reckless mood. 'Oh, I know that,' she declared gaily, 'but we get on so well and he's such a dear—you know, thoughtful and interested in the house and careful of me—making sure that my future's secure and all the rest of it.' She laughed. 'He actually wanted me to take out an insurance policy!'

Mrs Body said quickly, 'You didn't take any notice of that?'

'Well, I couldn't even if I'd wanted to, Mr van der Blocq sees to all that, but I didn't bother to tell Mervyn... What shall I give him for Christmas?'

Mrs Body made one or two uninspired suggestions, adding, 'And that nice Doctor van der Blocq, what are you sending him?'

'Why, nothing,' said Mary Jane. 'He's got everything in the world, you know.' She danced off again to take Major for his bedtime trot around the garden.

It was several days later, when they were out walking on the hills, heavily wrapped against the cold, that Mervyn let fall that he had met someone who had a roan for sale, sixteen hands, with plenty of spirit but good-tempered with it. 'I know you promised this guardian of yours not to buy a horse, but if you gave me an open cheque, I could buy it for you. I'm not a bad judge and I dare say I could strike a good bargain.'

Mary Jane paused on the slope they were working their way down. 'Well, I'm not sure—I should love it, but Fabian did say that I wasn't to buy one...'

'Yes, but don't you think that he said that because he wasn't here to give you his advice? Probably he was afraid that you might be tricked out of your money—you know how unscrupulous some people are—but surely if I picked out a good mount for you, he wouldn't raise any objection?'

Put like that, it had a ring of reasonableness. Besides, Fabian probably wouldn't come again for months—she would never get a horse of her own. She said thoughtfully: 'All right, I'll give you a cheque. Will you see to it for me, please? I'm sure Fabian won't mind.'

The words sounded curiously false in her own ears, Fabian would mind. He would mind on principle, because he was her guardian and considered that she shouldn't do anything at all without first asking his permission. Indignation swelled her bosom and gave way to a feeling of sneaking relief because he wouldn't know anyway.

The horse arrived two days later, a nice beast who went to his stable quietly enough, although he had a rolling eye. Mervyn explained that the animal was little nervous but would settle down in a day or so. He told her what he had paid for him too, a price which rather shocked her, but when she ventured: 'Isn't that rather a lot?' she was met with a chilly surprise.

'I had to haggle to get him at that price, but if you could have done better...' He left the rest of the sentence in mid-air, where it hung between them like a small, disturbing cloud. It evaporated during the day, but she made a mental note that

Mervyn was touchy about money and she would have to remember that.

It was Christmas Eve the following day, and Mervyn had said that he wouldn't be out until the afternoon, but he had kissed her warmly as he had said it and she hadn't really minded because she had planned to go riding—just a short canter across the fields by the lake, to see how Prince went. The morning was bright and clear and still very cold as she saddled him and led him out of the stable. He was still nervous, dancing along beside her, shying at every stone, and although she wasn't nervous herself, she could see that she would have to go carefully; he was a great deal more spirited than Mervyn had led her to believe. Perhaps in Canada they were used to horses that bucked and shied at every blade of grass. She had him away from the house by now, walking him across the meadow towards the water, she coaxed him to a standstill with some difficulty and was preparing to mount when Fabian spoke very quietly somewhere behind her.

'Don't, Mary Jane, I beg of you.' He was beside her now and had taken the reins into his own hands while she stared up at him speechlessly, a little pale in the face and with a most peculiar tumult of feeling inside her. He was pale too, but all he said was: 'He's not the horse for you—I told you to wait until I could find you something suitable. You broke your promise...'

'I didn't,' she said quickly, 'Mervyn bought him.'

She missed the sudden fire in his dark eyes. 'Mervyn?' repeated Fabian softly. 'Let us go back to the house and you shall tell me about—er—Mervyn!'

He began to lead Prince back to his stable and she perforce, walked with him and waited while he saw to the animal, and then accompanied him into the house to find Mrs Body, beaming with delight, hurrying with coffee and some of her mince pies.

'I knew you would come, Doctor dear,' she told him happily, 'with Christmas tomorrow.' She put down the tray and went to the door. 'I've the nicest piece of beef in the oven ready for your lunch.'

She went out of the room and Mary Jane said with polite haste, 'I hope you'll stay to lunch.' She busied herself with pouring coffee and didn't look at him. His clipped 'thank you' sounded coldly on her ears.

After a lengthening silence during which she sought for and discarded a number of conversational openings, Fabian said, 'And now if you would be good enough to explain about this horse.' He spoke in tones which brooked no hindrance; she explained at some length and in a muddled fashion which in the end left her with no alternative but to tell him about Mervyn too. He heard her out, no expression upon his calm, handsome features, and saying nothing, so that when she had finished she was forced to ask: 'Well?'

He raised his eyebrows. 'My dear Mary Jane, what am I expected to say? I haven't met this cousin yet, although I shall be delighted to do so, even if only to point out to him that I find his taste in horseflesh a little on the inexperienced side.'

Her gentle eyes flashed. 'Pooh! You only say that because you didn't pick Prince yourself.'

He ignored this. 'And what did you pay for him?'

She was a truthful girl, so she told him, waiting for his expected comment on the excessive price, but he said nothing, staring at her with narrowed eyes. Presently he said, 'Not a local animal, I fancy.' He sounded so casual that she let out a sigh of relief. 'No, Mervyn told me he had heard of him from someone he knew in Keswick.'

'Is that all you know?' She sensed the mockery in his voice and bristled as he continued, 'Surely you have the receipt and the bill of sale?'

'Mervyn will let me have them,' she protested, feeling guilty because she hadn't given the matter a thought. 'How is your cousin?'

If she had hoped to change the conversation she was unlucky. 'Very well, thank you. And when is Mervyn coming to see you again?'

She muttered, 'This afternoon,' and fidgeted under his look. 'Excellent. I shall enjoy meeting him. Had you planned anything? I shan't be inconveniencing you in any way?' His cold politeness chilled her. He got up. 'By the way, Prince has a slight limp in his left hind leg—you will agree with me that it should be attended to at once? I know it's Christmas Eve, but I'll see what I can do.'

He went out of the room, leaving Mary Jane with her mouth open in surprise. She hadn't noticed any limp, though now that she came to think about it, Prince had stumbled once or twice. She wouldn't be riding for a day or two; it might be a good idea to get it looked at.

Fabian came back presently and she asked, 'Did you find a vet?'

He strolled over to the window and stood half turned away from her, looking out on to the wintry morning. He said at length, 'Yes—he'll see what he can do some time today.'

'It's not serious?'

He turned to look at her across the pleasant room. 'No, but I don't think you should ride him, though. Now tell me, how are you managing? Have you sufficient money?'

They spent the remainder of the morning in a businesslike fashion, and over lunch they kept to common places while she wondered silently why he was so abstracted in his manner. Once or twice she found him staring at her in an odd fashion, with an expression which she couldn't understand, and indeed, he was so unlike his usual cool, arrogant self that she began to feel quite uncomfortable. And asking questions hadn't helped either, for she had tried that with singularly little success, in fact he had remarked after one such probe into what he had been doing: 'I have never known you take such an interest in my life—should I feel flattered?'

She felt as uncomfortable as she knew she looked. 'No, of course not, but I haven't seen you for several weeks. I just wanted to—to hear what you've been doing.'

His eyes held a gleam in their depths. 'Then I am flattered. Tell me, what are your plans for Christmas?'

'Well, nothing much. Mervyn's coming for Christmas Day—after church, you know, and I expect he'll stay until after dinner, and on Boxing Day some of Grandfather's friends are coming for a drink. Mervyn will be coming to lunch again, but he says he can't stay to meet Doctor Morris, he's got some people to see. It's a pity, because Doctor Morris knew his father, I believe.'

Fabian leaned back in his chair. 'A great pity,' he commented in a dry voice. 'It sounds very pleasant.'

'And you?' she asked politely, and then struck by a sudden thought, added in tones of the utmost apprehension, 'You're not staying for Christmas, are you?'

Somehow the thought of Mervyn and Fabian together filled her with an uneasiness she knew was quite unjustified; she closed her eyes on the vivid picture her mind had conjured up of Fabian blighting Mervyn's cheerful talk with his damping politeness.

His companion's face remained unaltered in its blandness. 'I wasn't aware that I had been asked. Set your mind at ease, Mary Jane, I shall be leaving within an hour or so.'

'Oh well, that's all right,' she exclaimed, so relieved that she hardly realised what she had said. 'Do you mind sitting here while I see if lunch is ready? There's some sherry on the window table, do help yourself.'

She went out of the room, humming cheerfully. If Fabian was going so soon, he and Mervyn would only have to meet for a very short time, perhaps not at all.

Her optimism was ill-founded. They had barely finished Mrs Body's excellent lunch when Mervyn drove up, parked the car in front of the door, and walked in. To say that he was surprised was too mild a way of putting it—Fabian had put his car in the garage; there had been no hint of anyone else being in the house, so Mervyn came breezing into the sitting room, to stop short just inside the door, looking so disconcerted at the sight of Fabian lounging in a chair by the fire that he could say nothing. It was Mary Jane who plunged into speech.

'Mervyn—hullo. Fabian, this is Mervyn Pettigrew, my—my cousin from Winnipeg. Jonkheer van der Blocq, my guardian.'

Fabian had risen and advanced to meet Mervyn, saying in a suave voice which somehow disturbed Mary Jane: 'Ah, Mr Pettigrew, Mary Jane has been telling me about you. I'm glad to have this opportunity of meeting you.'

He smiled, but his eyes were cold, and before Mervyn could say anything he went on: 'You must tell me about your home—Canada is a place I have often wished to visit. Your home is in Winnipeg? In the city itself or outside?' He waved Mervyn to a chair. 'Sit down, my dear fellow, and tell me about it.'

The conversation was in his hands; Mary Jane sat helplessly listening to Mervyn answering her guardian's questions, and even when she made attempts to change the conversation, she was frustrated by Fabian's blandly polite pause while she did so, only to have him resume his remorseless cross-examination again. Quite fed up, she suggested an early cup of tea because then Fabian might remember that he was leaving shortly… She was half way to the door when she heard a car, voices and some sort of commotion; she got to the window in time to see a horse-box and a Land-Rover disappearing down the drive. Prince's head was just visible.

She cut ruthlessly into Mervyn's description of the grain harvest. 'They've taken Prince!' she uttered, and turned to look at Fabian, who returned her startled gaze with a placid unsurprised face. 'I mentioned it,' he reminded her mildly.

'Yes, I know—but I didn't know he was going. Where is he going to?'

'The vet has taken him into his stables. A very good man, I believe.'

'Prince? The horse I bought for Mary Jane?' Mervyn's voice sounded strained. 'What's wrong with him?'

'A limp—the near hind leg, my dear fellow. Nothing much, probably he did it after you saw him. A splendid animal, I must congratulate you on your choice. Which reminds me, Mary Jane couldn't remember from whom she had bought him—you have the papers on you, I daresay.'

Mervyn searched his pockets. His face was a little pale, he looked harassed. 'I've left them at the hotel,' he muttered. 'I quite intended to bring them—I must remember tomorrow.'

'Of no consequence.' Fabian's voice had a silkiness which struck unpleasantly upon Mary Jane's ears as she came back into the room. 'What did you pay?'

Mervyn answered before she had a chance to remind Fabian that she had already told him, and rather to her surprise, Fabian merely nodded his head, remarked that the price of horseflesh had risen out of all bounds, and went on to say that doubtless such a splendid beast would be well known in the district. 'I must go along and see his owner,' he observed casually, 'and see if he has anything as good. Where did you say he lived?'

Mary Jane watched the hunted look on Mervyn's face and wondered about it, and when he said at length that he couldn't exactly remember, helpfully suggested the names of some of the local breeders, to all of which Mervyn answered rather shortly that none of them was correct. At last, goaded by her excessive helpfulness, he said, 'It wasn't a breeder—just someone selling privately.'

'Ah,' Fabian's voice was still hatefully silky. 'Doubtless one of the small estates around here—I should have no difficulty in finding him.'

There was no knowing what Mervyn would have replied to this if Mrs Body hadn't come in at that minute with the tea tray. Mary Jane poured tea and oil upon what she felt might be troubled waters if she allowed the two men to go on long enough, but she need not have bothered, for Fabian seemed to have lost interest in Prince and his former owner. He was talking, much more freely than he usually did, she thought, uneasily, about the house and it contents, which, he assured Mervyn in a manner quite unlike his own somewhat reserved one, were by no means without value and likely to become more so. 'A very nice little property,' he said as he got up to go, 'worth quite a considerable sum in the market today.'

He was about to shake hands with Mary Jane when Mervyn spoke.

'I may not see you again—I hadn't intended to say anything just yet, but as you are here…I want to marry Mary Jane—I understand from her that she needs permission from you before she can marry. Well, I should like it now.'

This speech, uttered in urgent tones, had the effect of silencing Mary Jane completely, although it had no such effect upon her guardian, who remarked airily, 'My dear chap, why didn't you mention this earlier? Now I am forced to leave on most urgent business, and you can quite understand that I'm not prepared to give my consent until we have had a little talk about your prospects and so on. But I imagine that you will be here for another week or so? I'll endeavour to come and see you at the earliest opportunity.'

He glanced at Mary Jane, his face empty of expression. 'I'm sure that you both have a great deal to talk about. Goodbye, Mary Jane. I have no need to wish you a happy Christmas, have I—but I do, just the same.'

He took her hand, and she stared up into his face, completely out of her depth, filled with the ridiculous wish that he wouldn't go away, but stay for Christmas. She whispered some sort of reply and stayed in the middle of the room, watching him walk away.

Mervyn talked a lot after Fabian had gone. He talked about their future together and how he had been wanting to tell her that he loved her for several days. 'We'll get married after Christmas,' he urged her. 'There's no reason why we should wait, is there? I can move in here…'

She was surprised at that. 'But won't you have to go back to Winnipeg? What about your work? Do you want to give up your job there? and if you come here to live you'll have to get something else. Wouldn't it be better if I came to Winnipeg?'

He was adamant that that wouldn't do. 'You would be homesick,' he told her, 'and this will be a marvellous home for us both—we'll get another car, and a boat—something fast.'

She agreed happily, in a rose-coloured future, not quite real. She asked him, 'And your income? Is it enough for us to live on?'

'Oh, don't worry your little head about that,' he assured her, and kissed her. 'We'll go into all that when we're married.'

'But I don't suppose Fabian will let me get married until all that's sorted out. He takes his duties very seriously.'

Mervyn caught her hands in his. 'Look, darling, why do we wait for him? If we get married he can't do anything about it, can he? He's far too busy a man to get involved in our business—besides, he'll be glad to be rid of this guardianship—that is, unless he's feathering his own nest with your money.'

Mary Jane felt a sudden fierce rush of sheer rage. 'That's a beastly thing to say!' she said loudly. 'Fabian is the most honest man alive, he wouldn't touch a penny that wasn't his—besides, he's frightfully rich.'

Mervyn apologised at once, turning it into a joke, but the sour taste of it stayed with her for the rest of the evening, despite his gay talk, although she found it hard to resist his charm. He would be a delightful husband, she assured herself, and how lucky she was that he had appeared out of the blue to fall in love with her and want to marry her. She wished him a warm good night, all her small qualms forgotten, and went along to find Mrs Body making last-minute preparations for the following day while Lily stood at the sink cleaning the vegetables. Mary Jane drew up a chair to the table and began to blanch a bowl of almonds standing on it.

'He's gone,' said Mrs Body sadly.

'Just this minute, but he'll be back for lunch tomorrow.'

Mrs Body thumped the stuffing she was making with quite unnecessary vigour. 'Not him,' she sounded aggrieved, 'Doctor van der Blocq, and I'd like to know where he's going to spend his Christmas.'

Mary Jane, her mouth full of almonds, said indistinctly, 'Holland, I suppose.'

The housekeeper gave her an impatient look. 'Now, Miss Mary Jane, you know as well as I do that he can't get back all that way by tomorrow morning—not with the car, he can't. What are you about not to think of that? It fair bothered me to see him driving off alone this afternoon—didn't you give him a thought?'

'Yes—no—I had something else to think about. Mrs Body, darling Mrs Body, I'm going to be married!'

'To that Mr Pettigrew? Well, I suppose it was to be expected, though how he could allow you to ride that wild animal I can't think. I never was so pleased to see the animal go again—he should have known better. Good thing dear Doctor van der Blocq came along like he did.'

'Oh, Mrs Body, aren't you pleased?' Mary Jane sounded as forlorn as she suddenly felt. 'I thought you would be—I'm not going to be an old maid after all.'

Mrs Body rallied. 'Of course I'm pleased, my dear, there's nothing I'd like better than to see you wed. But Canada's a long way off.'

Mary Jane reached over the table and kissed her housekeeper and friend on the cheek. 'But I'm not going there—Mervyn suggested that he should move in here just as soon as we're married.'

'And Doctor van der Blocq—does he know?'

'Oh yes, Mervyn told him this afternoon, and Fabian said he'd come back very shortly and they'd have a talk—about money and things.' She got up. 'I'm going to get something to drink—we'll toast Christmas before we go to bed.'

She went to sleep almost at once, thinking about the perfect future she was going to have with Mervyn, but she didn't dream of him, she dreamed of Fabian, driving his car endlessly through a lonely Christmas. She remembered it when she wakened in the morning and it became real somehow when Mrs Body brought her early tea and laid a small package on the bed.

'A Happy Christmas, Miss Mary Jane,' she said, 'and the dear doctor asked me to be sure and give you this first thing in the morning.'

There was a velvet box inside the wrapping paper, and in the box was a brooch, a true lovers' knot in rose diamonds, exquisitely beautiful. Mary Jane stared at it for a long time because it somehow seemed to be part and parcel of her dreams, its sparkle, a little blurred because of the sudden tears in her eyes, tears because she hadn't given him anything at all—she hadn't even invited him for Christmas. She remembered with shame that she had let him see her relief when he had told her that he was going away again. He must have said that because he was too proud a man to say anything else. She wondered forlornly where he had gone.

CHAPTER SIX

DOWNSTAIRS, Mary Jane found a delicately painted porcelain bowl on the breakfast table, filled with a gorgeous medley of tulips, hyacinths and dwarf iris. She sniffed their perfume delightedly and looked for a card. They would be from Mervyn, of course. She wandered into the kitchen to wish the others the compliments of the season, exclaiming: 'Those heavenly flowers—I wonder where he got them this time of year?'

Mrs Body dished bacon and eggs before replying. 'Brought them all the way from Holland, he did—made me promise to look after them and put them on the table first thing in the morning. It's a lovely bowl—ever so old. He gave us presents too, but we haven't opened them yet.'

Mary Jane remembered her remorse before she had gone to sleep, and it came crowding back into her head now—even if the flowers and the brooch had only been a gesture from a guardian to his ward, they had been gifts, and she had been horribly unkind. Once more she wondered where he had gone and if he had expected to stay. She pushed the thought away and with it the faint regret that the flowers hadn't been Mervyn, even the brooch, although possibly he couldn't have afforded that. It struck her anew that he had never talked about money to her at all, only sketched in a vague background, leaving her to suppose that he was comfortably off. She sighed, for she was a romantic girl and had always cherished the idea that a man in love went to any lengths to please his girl-friend, and yet it had been Fabian, not Mervyn who was so in love with her, who had taken care that there would be presents waiting for her when she got up on Christmas morning. She ate her breakfast thoughtfully and then went, with Mrs Body and Lily, to church. Mrs Body and Lily wore the new leather gloves Fabian had given them, and Mary Jane wore the brooch.

They had a drink when they got back and then got the lunch ready together. Mrs Body and Lily had friends to share theirs, so Mary Jane laid the table in the dining room for herself and Mervyn. By the time he arrived she was feeling gay and light-hearted, having spent a good deal of the morning persuading herself that Fabian had only called in on his way to somewhere and wouldn't have stayed even if she had asked him.

She had bought Mervyn a picture, a landscape by a local artist of some repute. She gave it to him when he arrived and watched while he unwrapped it, admired it and then laid it on the table in the window. There was an awkward pause until he said, 'I had no idea what to get you—we'll go together and find something later on.'

She made excuses for him—perhaps in Canada they didn't set much store by Christmas—but surely he could have brought a few flowers? She wasn't a greedy girl, only hurt because she had expected that because he loved her, he would have wanted to express that love with some small gift. She stifled the hurt and smiled at him. 'That will be nice,' she agreed. 'And now what about a drink before lunch?'

The bowl of flowers was on the table; he couldn't help but see it. He commented idly upon it, remarking that it looked a valuable piece.

'I don't know about that,' she said uncertainly. 'Fabian sent it.'

He frowned. 'Now that we're going to be married,' he stated categorically, 'I'm not sure that I like you receiving valuable gifts from him, even if he is your guardian.'

She flushed a little and said with a spurt of temper, 'Why ever not? As you said, he is my guardian, and what harm is there in giving a girl flowers? We do it a lot in England—for birthdays and Christmas.'

It was his turn to get angry. 'I don't like it,' he reiterated stubbornly. 'Before you know where you are he'll be giving you something really valuable—jewellery—bought with your money, no doubt.'

'I hope you'll apologize for that.' Mary Jane's voice was

quiet, but it shook a little. 'I thought I had made it plain to you that Fabian wouldn't touch a penny of my money—he's my guardian, not a thief,' she added defiantly. 'He gave me this brooch.'

Mervyn stared at it across the table. Presently he said sullenly:

'Oh, all right, I'm sorry I said it—I didn't mean it, you have to make allowances for a man being jealous when he's in love.' His eyes were still glued to the brooch. 'It looks very expensive—I thought it was something you had inherited from your grandfather.'

He smiled at her. 'I'm a brute behaving like this on Christmas Day, darling. I'm sorry—I suppose I'm a bit on edge. I want to marry you, you see, as soon as possible, and I can't think of anything else but that. I promise I'll make it up to you when we're married.'

He was charming for the rest of the day; she basked in his admiration and listened happily to the delightful things he said, knowing right at the back of her mind that most of them were grossly exaggerated if not completely untrue. No one had ever told her before that she was pretty, nor had they spared more than one glance upon her eyes, which Mervyn declared were quite remarkably lovely; her common sense, buried in a haze of wishful thinking, told her that. But no one had ever been in love with her before, she had no yardstick by which to measure him. She allowed herself to believe every word and squashed her common sense, almost squashing her resolve to wait for Fabian's permission before they married. It was tempting, especially when Mervyn showed her the special licence he had bought, sure that she would give in when she saw it. But she still refused and put his sulky silence down to disappointment on his part.

During the following few days he had become a little difficult, and once or twice, when she was alone and quiet, a small voice deep inside her wanted to know if she really loved him or was she just being swept off her feet because she had never been in love or loved before. She buried the thought under a host of more pleasant ones and scoffed at her doubts.

But they stayed; she asked Mrs Body about them, and that dear soul looked troubled even while she spoke reassuringly. 'And wait until the dear doctor comes,' she counselled. 'It can't be long now.'

It was Old Year's Day when Fabian came. Mary Jane had expected Mervyn to lunch; she had spent most of the morning helping Mrs Body in the kitchen because Lily had gone home for the day and now she sat at the desk in one of the sitting room windows, writing thank-you letters, and keeping an eye on the drive and the road beyond. It had turned cold once more, there were a few snowflakes falling and the frost had been heavy the night before. She had put on a new dress, a dark green pinafore with a matching crêpe blouse under it, and had pinned the diamond brooch into it. She had done her hair with more patience than usual too, but it was getting a little untidy again, for she had a habit of running her hand through it while she was writing and it was two hours since she had done it. She was shocked when she saw the time; it was past one o'clock—something must have delayed Mervyn, and she couldn't think what. She resolved to wait another half an hour and applied herself to her letters again, but only for a few minutes, for a car turned into the drive and she got to her feet and ran to the door without bothering to look out of the window.

It was the Rolls, and Fabian who got out of it. He came in slowly, looking tired, and the sight of his shadowed face stirred a desire deep inside her to help him. But Fabian wasn't a man to accept help or admit tiredness, so she said instead, 'Hullo, how nice to see you, and just in time for lunch—it's a bit late, because I'm expecting Mervyn. You'll be able to talk to him.'

'We have had our talk, and he won't be coming.'

He stood in the open doorway, towering over her, his face expressionless, staring down at her, making no effort to move or take off his coat.

Mary Jane gave him a puzzled look. 'Why isn't he coming?

He particularly wanted to see you—he's got a special licence.'
She bit her lip and went on in a cold little voice, 'Where did
you see him?'

'In Keswick.' He paused. 'I have to talk to you, Mary Jane.'

'He's ill—hurt? Oh, Fabian, do tell me quickly!'

'It's neither. If we could go somewhere?'

'Yes, of course, and you must have something, you look tired
to death.'

He smiled grimly. 'When I have finished what I have to say
and you still want me to remain perhaps you will ask me then.'
He sounded suddenly impatient. 'The sitting room?'

He didn't sit down, but walked over to the window and then
turned to face her. 'Mervyn isn't coming. He won't be coming
again. He has left Keswick and is already on his way to catch
his plane, back to Canada.'

She felt the blood leave her cheeks. 'I don't believe you—
he loves me.'

'I wouldn't lie to you, Mary Jane. He was no good, my dear
girl—you are such an innocent.' He sighed. 'Oh, he was your
cousin all right, always borrowing money from your grandfather, like his father before him, an undischarged bankrupt with
not a penny to his name, who came to hear of your grandfather's death and saw a chance of easy money. And how much
easier could it have been?' His voice took on a mocking, angry
note. 'You, a little bored already, with a house of your own
and money—quite a lot of money...'

She interrupted him, almost stammering. 'He had no idea—
I never told him.'

'No? But he tricked old Mr North into telling him how much
the estate was worth. I suppose you told him where North
lived?' And when she nodded miserably: 'I thought so. And
Prince—how could you have been so feather-witted, Mary
Jane? Did you not wonder why he never showed you the papers
connected with the sale, or the receipt? Why, I smelled a rat
the moment you said—or were you so infatuated with him that
you couldn't be sensible any more? Do you know what he paid
for Prince? Exactly half the amount he told you. He had the

rest; he hired a car in your name too—I paid the bill just now, and the hotel—he owed several weeks' bills and told them that you would pay.' He thrust an impatient hand into a pocket and tossed some papers at her. 'There, see for yourself.'

She left them to drift to the floor. 'How—how did you find out all this?' She tried to speak in a normal voice, but it came out in a miserable whisper.

'I asked around—it wasn't difficult—and then I flew to Winnipeg and made some enquiries.'

'You went to all that trouble?' She had her voice nicely under control now, but the effort to hold back the tears was getting beyond her. She said in a sudden burst: 'Did it matter? He's the only man who has ever asked me to marry him, do you know that? He said he loved me and now you've spoiled it all—I believe you want me to go on living here for ever and ever—I hate you, I hate you, I wish I'd never set eyes on you!' She hiccoughed and choked, then took a breath, for she had by no means finished. Her heart, she most truly believed at that moment, was broken, and nothing mattered any more. All she wanted to do was to hurt the man standing so silently before her; his very quiet made her feelings all the hotter. But the words tumbling off her tongue were stilled by the entrance of Mrs Body with a loaded tray, who after one sharp glance at Mary Jane addressed herself to Fabian.

'I saw the car, Doctor dear, and I said to myself, "He'll be cold and hungry, I'll be bound," so here's coffee and sandwiches, and a Happy New Year to you.' She poured the coffee. 'And where did you spend Christmas, if I might ask?'

'Oh, in Keswick, Mrs Body. I had business there.'

'But why didn't you stay here? If Miss Mary Jane had known...'

'That had been my hope.' He smiled at her with great charm, and Mrs Body, quite overcome, exclaimed, 'You mean to say you came for Christmas and we never even gave you a good Christmas dinner?'

'It didn't matter. As it turned out I had a good deal to do. Thank you for the coffee.'

'Well, you look as though you need it, and no mistake, Doctor dear—worn out, you are. Have you come from Holland?'

He shook his head. 'Canada.'

Mrs Body was no fool. She said, 'Lor' bless my soul! I always knew...' She shot another look at Mary Jane, standing like a statue, taking no part in the conversation, and went out of the room, shutting the door very gently.

Fabian had made no attempt to drink his coffee, and when Mary Jane turned her back upon him he watched her for a few moments and then said softly: 'Mary Jane,' and when she didn't answer: 'I'm sorry, but I had to do it. I couldn't see you throw yourself away on a wastrel and ruin your whole life.' He paused. 'Do you want me to stay?'

She didn't turn round, only shook her head. She heard him cross the room and then the hall, and presently the front door was opened and shut again, and the Rolls murmured its way down the drive. By straining her ears Mary Jane could hear it going down the road, back to Keswick and, she guessed miserably, Holland. He wouldn't come again. There was no need to hold the tears back any longer; she flopped into the nearest chair and cried her eyes out, and when Mrs Body came back, sobbed out the whole sorry story to her, to be comforted and scolded a little and comforted again. 'And that poor man,' said Mrs Body, 'gone again without a bite to eat inside him, and him such a great man.'

'He can starve!' said Mary Jane savagely into Mrs Body's ample bosom.

'Now, now, dearie, that's no way to talk. I never said so, but I didn't fancy you marrying that Mr Pettigrew—far too glib, I found him. I know your heart's broken, but it'll mend, my dear, and you'll think differently later on, and when Mr Right pops the question you'll have forgotten all this.'

'But there isn't a Mr Right!' wailed Mary Jane.

'I'm not so sure about that,' said Mrs Body bracingly, and smiled to herself over the tousled brown head on her shoulder.

But despite Mrs Body's comforting words, Mary Jane found the days which followed hard to live through; she walked herself into a state of exhaustion, going over and over in her mind all that had happened, forcing herself to face the truth—that Mervyn hadn't loved her at all, only her money and her home, seeing her as an easy way to live in comfort for the rest of his life. Just as Fabian had said. She told herself that she would get over it, just as Mrs Body had told her, but in the meantime she was utterly miserable, not least of all because Mervyn hadn't written. He could have at least wished her goodbye— but then she hadn't said goodbye to Fabian either, had she? She had let him walk out of the house, cold and tired and hungry; even if she hated him—and of course she did—she had been pretty mean herself.

By the end of the week she wasn't eating much, nor was she sleeping; her mood was ripe for the letter from Pope's which arrived after a particularly bad night. It was from Miss Shepherd, telling her that there was a severe 'flu epidemic in London, the hospital was halfstaffed and overflowing with patients, and how did Mary Jane feel like helping out on a temporary basis for a week or so?

Mary Jane went straight to the telephone, packed a bag, hugged Mrs Body and Lily goodbye and got into the Mini. She would only be gone for a week or so, but the prospect of having some hard work before her was just what she needed. She drove down the motorway, still unhappy, it was true, but finding life bearable once more.

It was amazing to her that she could slip back into life at Pope's with such ease, and still more amazing that it should be Women's Surgical to which she was sent, because the regular staff nurse was herself down with 'flu. Mary Jane went on duty a few hours after her arrival to find Sister Thompson sitting in her office, drumming impatient fingers on the desk while she harangued a part-time staff nurse whom she obviously didn't like; she didn't like Mary Jane either, but at least they knew each other, a fact she pointed out somewhat acidly before giving her a dozen and one things to do. Mary Jane, impervious to her bad temper, and relieved to have so much on her hands that she had no time to think, went into the ward, to be greeted happily by several nurses she had known. The ward was heavy and full with beds down the centre and cases going to theatre, to return requiring expert care and nursing. Sister Thompson sailed up and down between the beds, giving orders to anyone who was within earshot, complaining bitterly that there were no good nurses any more, and what was the world coming to— a purely rhetorical question which none of her harassed staff had neither the time nor the inclination to answer, at least not out loud.

Mary Jane, worn out after her hard day, slept as she hadn't slept for nights, and what was more, ate her breakfast the next morning. Despite her hard work, a faint colour had crept into her white face and the hollows under her eyes, while still there, weren't quite so noticeable. She was off duty in the afternoon, the day was cold and grey and the staff nurses' sitting room in the Home looked bleak—there were several of her friends off duty too, so she rounded them up and they went in a cheerful bunch to Fortnum and Mason's where they had tea before embarking on a quick inspection of the January sales. She went back to the ward refreshed, and because Sister Thompson was off duty that evening, the work went better than it usually did. She went off duty that evening with the pleasant feeling that at least she had done a good day's work and slept soundly in consequence.

The days slid by, each one packed with work and the small petty annoyances which went with it. Mary Jane found little time to think of anything but drips, pre-meds, closed drainage and the preparation of emergency cases for theatre, and at night she fell into bed and was asleep before she had time to shed one single tear over her broken romance with Mervyn. Just once or twice, when she was in theatre with a patient, she was reminded of Fabian, because the operating theatre was his world; it surprised her that in place of the rage which had possessed her against him, there was now only a dull feeling, almost a numbness. Beneath the mass of bewildered thoughts and memories she had expected him to write to her despite the manner of his going, but nothing came, only letters from Mrs Body, detailing carefully the day-to-day life at home. She had hoped for a letter from Mervyn too, against all her better judgement, but as the days went by and she realised that he wasn't going to write, she knew that that was the best thing. He had never loved her, and she had been a fool to have imagined he did. He would never have left in that craven fashion if he had had even a spark of feeling for her, and certainly nothing Fabian could have said would have deterred him from at least explaining to her. She sighed; it was a pity she didn't like Fabian, for quite obviously he had done his best for her, though in an arrogant fashion and with a total disregard of her feelings for which she would never forgive him.

With each day she found that she was recovering slowly. It was no good moaning over the past, and she had much to be thankful for; a home, enough money, kind Mrs Body and the willing Lily. She would go back to them soon and pick up the threads of her life where Fabian had so ruthlessly broken them off. She would have to find something to do, of course; Red Cross, part-time nursing, something of that sort. And she could sail and ride—only she hadn't a horse, and unless Fabian came to see her again, she was unlikely to have one. Perhaps she would have to wait until she was thirty and free to do as she wished. Her thoughts were interrupted by Sister Thompson's sour voice, enquiring of her if she intended to be all day making up that operation bed and how about Mrs Daw's pre-med? And Mary Jane, who had already given it, said 'Yes, Sister,' in a mechanical way and went to see how the last case back from theatre was doing.

Op days were always extra busy. Sister Thompson went off duty after lunch and the atmosphere of the ward brightened perceptively even though an emergency appendix was admitted, followed by a severely lacerated hand. Mary Jane slogged up and down the ward, a little untidy now but still cheerful though a thought tired. She was going out that evening with some of her friends; there was a film which was supposed to be marvellous, but the way she felt by teatime, she didn't really care if she saw it or not, though probably once she was there she would enjoy it, and anything was better than sitting and thinking.

She was almost through giving the report to Sister Thompson before she went off duty when she was interrupted by the telephone. Sister Thompson lifted a pompous hand for silence and addressed the instrument with her usual severity, although this softened slightly when she discovered that the speaker was Miss Shepherd. She put down the receiver with a strong air of disapproval, observed: 'Matron'—she still called Miss Shepherd Matron because she didn't agree with all the new-fangled titles everyone had been given by the Salmon Scheme—'Matron,' she repeated, 'wishes to see you in her office as soon as possible. First, however, you will finish the report.'

Mary Jane, luckily at the tail end of her recital, made short work of the rest of it, wished her superior good night, waved to such of the patients who were in a fit state to notice, and started off down the corridors and staircases which separated her from Miss Shepherd's office. The hospital was fairly quiet except for the distant clatter of dishes denoting the advent of patients' suppers. She met no one and paused only long enough to fling open the door of Men's Medical where one of her friends worked, acquaint that young lady with the tidings that she might be late and they had better go on without her, and then tear on once more. The office was at the end of a short passage. Mary Jane knocked on the door, watched the red light above it turn to green, and went in.

Miss Shepherd was sitting at her desk and Fabian was standing in the middle of the room with his hands in his pockets, contemplating a very bad portrait of the first governor of Pope's. He took his eyes from it, however, as Mary Jane entered and met her startled gaze. She went red and then white, opened her mouth to speak, clamped it shut and turned for the door, quite forgetful of Miss Shepherd. It was that lady's calm voice which recalled her to her senses.

'Ah, there you are, Staff Nurse. Your guardian is most anxious to speak to you,' she smiled across the room at him as she spoke. 'I'm sure you will want to hear what he has to say.'

'No,' said Mary Jane baldly, 'I wouldn't.' She looked at Fabian. 'Why should you want to see me? I can't imagine any good reason...' She stopped because he was looking at her so oddly, and Miss Shepherd said smoothly:

'All the same, I think you might like a little talk.' She got up and went to the door and Fabian opened it for her with a smile. 'I have a short round to make, ten minutes or so. I daresay that will be long enough.'

She had gone. Fabian leaned against the door, watching Mary Jane, who, very conscious of his gaze, stared in her turn at the portrait on the wall.

'I had no intention of seeing you for some time,' Fabian began coolly, 'this is purely to oblige Cousin Emma. I did a thyroidectomy on her a week ago—she is doing very well, but now she insists that she won't return home unless you are there to look after her. I telephoned you, of course, but Mrs Body, although she knew you were here, had no idea how long you would be staying. Miss Shepherd tells me that she can let you go immediately.'

'There are plenty of nurses in Holland,' said Mary Jane flatly, while she thought with sudden longing of the old house in Midwoude and even more longingly of Fabian's great house by the canal. 'I don't want to go,' she added for good measure.

He chose to ignore this. 'Emma likes you—more, she has an affection for you, she feels that she will never make a complete recovery unless you are there to help her. And it is important that she recovers completely, for Trouw has asked her to marry him and although she longs to do so, she says that she will refuse him unless she is quite well again. And I think that you are the one to convince her.'

Womanlike, Mary Jane had fastened on the piece of news which aroused her interest most. 'Married? How marvellous! Oh, I am glad, and of course she must marry Doctor Trouw. I always thought...she must be very happy.'

Her voice died away because she herself should have been feeling very happy too, married by now, surely—instead of which, she was standing here in Miss Shepherd's office listening to Fabian's calm demands on her time and energy. She said in a husky little voice, à propos of nothing at all:

'I haven't a horse—what happened to Prince?'

Fabian made a sudden movement and then was still again. 'I know. Prince is now owned by the vet. I believe he's very content and they suit each other very well.' He began to walk towards her. 'Mary Jane, I told you that I had no intention of coming to see you, for I am only too well aware of your feelings towards me—you made them abundantly clear—but I am fond of Cousin Emma and I want her to be happy; she has spent a great deal of her life looking after Uncle Georgius—very inadequately, I must admit, but she did her best. And now happiness is within her reach and unless we help her, her stubbornness is likely to ruin everything.' His voice roughened. 'And you need entertain no fears that I shall be under your feet. When I come to see Cousin Emma it will be as her surgeon, not as your guardian. In future any meetings we may have shall be strictly on a business footing, I promise you that.'

For some unaccountable reason her heart sank at his words, for despite his indifference towards her, she had come reluctantly to regard him as someone to whom she could turn. She knew now, standing so close to him in the austere little room, that she had always been aware of him somewhere in the background, ready to help her if she needed help, and despite their dislike of each other he never had and never would let her down.

She was horrified to find her eyes filling with tears. They spilled down her cheeks and she wiped them away quickly, miserably aware that she looked quite hideous when she wept. But she was too proud to turn her face away. 'I'll come because Cousin Emma wants me,' she told him, 'not because you asked me.'

'I hardly expected that.' His voice was remote, as was his expression. They stared at each other in silence for a few seconds and Mary Jane, watching his calm face felt a keen urge to talk to him, to tell him how she felt. She blew her nose and wiped away the last tear and would have embarked on heaven

knew what kind of speech, only she was interrupted by the
return of Miss Shepherd, who sat down at her desk and asked
pleasantly, 'Well, all settled, I hope?'

'Indeed yes, Miss Shepherd. You did say that my ward could
leave immediately?'

'Of course. We are very grateful to the girls who came back
to help us, but we wouldn't dream of keeping them a moment
longer than necessary—Staff Nurse Pettigrew would have been
going in a day or two, in any case.'

'Splendid!' He turned to Mary Jane. 'I'll send your tickets
to the front lodge, shall I? Could you be ready to leave tomorrow evening?'

She was surprised. She had taken it for granted that she
would be with him; that he would take her back to Holland.
She was on the point of saying so and prevented herself from
doing so just in time, for of course he would have no wish for
her company and she had no wish for his. Her voice was as
cool as his own had been. 'Yes, I can.'

'You have enough money?'

'Yes.'

There was a little pause until Miss Shepherd said briskly,
'Well, that seems to be settled, doesn't it? I won't keep you,
Staff Nurse—you are off duty, I believe.'

Mary Jane said that yes, she was. She thanked Miss Shepherd, said goodbye in a cold voice to Fabian and went through
the door he was holding open for her. It shut behind her, a fact
which disappointed her; she had half expected him to follow
her out. She even loitered down the corridor, so that, if he
wished, he would have ample time to catch her up. He did no
such thing, so rather put out, she went off to the Home.

Her friends had gone, leaving a note saying that they would
wait outside the cinema until seven o'clock and after that it
would be just too bad. Her watch said twenty minutes to the
hour; to bath, change, catch a bus to Leicester Square and arrive
at seven o'clock was an impossibility. She would spend the
evening writing to Mrs Body and packing her few things. She
tore off her cap and flung it on the bed, flung off her apron and

belt too and was about to give her uniform dress the same rough treatment when there was a knock on the door.

'Oh, come in,' she called crossly, ripping pins out of her hair, and turned to see Fabian standing in the doorway. She forgot that they were barely on speaking terms, that she hated him, that he was arrogant and always had his own way. 'For heaven's sake,' she breathed, 'you can't be here! This is the Nurses' Home—it's private...' She waved an agitated hand at him. 'Men don't come upstairs—there's a little room by the front door...'

'For boy-friends?' he wanted to know. 'But I'm not a boy-friend, Mary Jane.' He sounded serious, but she could have sworn that he was laughing. 'There was no one downstairs, you see, so I looked in the Warder's office and found your room number.'

'You've got a nerve!' she told him fiercely, still whispering. 'Go away!'

'Of course, if you'll have dinner with me.'

She tossed a curtain of honey-brown hair over her shoulders. 'No, I won't,' she said tersely, then gasped as he came in. 'Supposing the Warden comes along?' she begged him. 'Do go—I'll get into trouble and—and you'll lose your reputation.'

She gave a small shriek at the great roar of laughter he gave. 'Oh, please, Fabian,' she said, quite humbly.

He went to the door at once. 'Half an hour,' he told her. 'I'll be in the—er—boy-friends' room, and don't try and give me the slip. Possibly you will find the situation easier if I assure you that I'm not asking you out for any other reason than that of expediency. I'm leaving England in a few hours and I should like to tell you about Emma before I go, it will be easier for you when you arrive.'

She joined him in half an hour exactly, wearing new clothes she had bought for herself because she had wanted to look nice for Mervyn—a burgundy red coat with its matching dress, a red velvet cap on her pale brown hair, expensive gloves and handbag and suede boots with leather cuffs. She was thankful that she had found time to pack them when she left home to go to Pope's, for she had nothing much else with her—a skirt, a handful of sweaters and her sheepskin jacket which she had flung into the back of the Mini.

They dined at a nearby restaurant, and it wasn't until he had ordered and they were sipping their drinks that he abandoned the polite, meaningless conversation with which he had engaged her during their drive from Pope's. She had answered him in monosyllables, fighting a feeling of security and content, induced, she had no doubt, by the comfort of the Rolls and the anticipation of a delicious meal.

'You are sure that you have enough money?' he wanted to know again.

She mentioned the amount she had and he raised his eyebrows in surprise. 'My dear girl, you will be with Emma for at least two weeks, that's barely enough to keep you in tights.'

'How do you know I wear tights?' she demanded.

His lips twitched. 'I don't live in a monastery. I'll see that there's some money with your ticket. You had better travel to the Hoek by the night boat from Harwich. Someone will meet you there and drive you up to Midwoude. Emma is still in hospital, I should like you to be there when she is fetched home—that will be arranged. You'll need some overalls or something similar for a few days. What size are you?'

'Twelve,' she told him. She had no idea that he was such a practical man.

He eyed her thoughtfully. 'Twelve what?' His voice was bland.

'Well, that's my size—the number of inches I am.'

'Vital statistics?' and she saw the twinkle in his eyes and said severely: 'Yes.'

He made a note. 'Must I guess?' he asked mildly. 'Thirty-four, twenty-two, thirty-five or six—inches, of course. Is that near enough?' and when she nodded, speechless, he went on pleasantly: 'Now, as to Emma—I did a sub-total on her. She has needed it for a year or more, but she always refused—you know how thyroidtoxicosis cases refuse treatment. Besides, I think she felt that she would be letting Uncle Georgius down in some way, but now the way seemed clear for an operation; it was Trouw who persuaded her. It is all very successful, but she doesn't believe it yet—I think you will be of great help in convincing her. Besides, you can encourage her to make plans for her wedding.' He stopped, staring at her, his eyes hooded and she felt her cheeks go white.

'That was unpardonable of me, Mary Jane, I'm sorry.' He looked away from her strained face and continued in an impersonal voice, 'She has made a satisfactory recovery—a sore throat and hoarseness, of course. She's on digitalin and Lugol's iodine, and there are several more days to go with her antibiotic.' He added, 'She's a terrible patient. If you decide to change your mind, I shall quite understand.'

'I haven't changed my mind.'

'I didn't think you would.' He smiled at her and beckoned the waiter. 'The chocolate gateau is delicious here, would you care to try it?'

They were halfway through it before he spoke again. 'Mary Jane, you shall have your horse. I'll go over to the Lakes as soon as I can spare the time and find a good mount for you.' He shot her a lightning glance. 'You need not worry, I won't expect an invitation to stay.'

She didn't look at him. 'That sounds like a bribe.'

She wished she hadn't said it, for he at once became remote and haughty and faintly impatient. 'Don't talk nonsense,' he told her sharply. 'And now if you will listen carefully, I will finish telling you about Emma's treatment.'

The rest of the evening was businesslike in the extreme, for the talk was of such a professional nature that they might have been on a ward round at Pope's. He took her back without loss of time after dinner and wished her goodbye at the hospital gate with the air of a man who had concluded a satisfactory deal and now wanted to forget about it for pleasanter things.

'He's so unpredictable,' said Mary Jane, talking to herself as she went through the hospital to the Home, and a harassed night nurse hurrying in the opposite direction flung over her shoulder, 'They all are, ducky.'

Mary Jane left the following evening, her ticket and more money than she could possibly spend safely in her handbag, what clothes she had stowed in her case. She had wished Sister Thompson goodbye and had been told, to her surprise, that she was no worse than all the other girls who thought they were staff nurses, and if she chose to return at any future date, she, Sister Thompson, would personally ask Miss Shepherd if she could be posted to Women's Surgical ward. Mary Jane, overwhelmed by this treat for the future, thanked her nicely, took a brief farewell of such of her friends as were about and climbed into her taxi, reflecting that even if life wasn't treating her as kindly as it might, at least she had no time to sit and repine. When the friendly taxi-driver asked her if she was going on holiday she told him, 'Work,' adding to puzzle him, 'Work is the great cure of all the maladies and miseries that ever beset mankind.'

He grinned at her. 'Have it your own way, miss.'

CHAPTER SEVEN

IT WAS Doctor Trouw who met the boat at the Hoek van Holland, and Mary Jane, a little wan after a rough crossing, was delighted to see him, although the delight was tinged with disappointment—probably she told herself bracingly as she responded to the doctor's friendly greeting, because she was tired and for some reason, lonely. She would feel better when she reached Midwoude, where she had no doubt her days would be filled.

Doctor Trouw had a Citroën, large and beautifully kept. She sat beside him responding suitably to his pleased speculation upon his hoped-for marriage to Cousin Emma. 'We have always been fond of each other,' he told her gruffly, 'and now that my wife is dead...' He paused. 'I feel that life still has much to offer.' He coughed. 'Of course, we are neither of us in the first flush of youth.'

'I don't see that that matters at all,' said Mary Jane with sincerity. 'There's not much point in getting married unless you're sure that you're going to be happy, and that could happen at any age. I'd rather wait for years and be certain.'

Her companion looked pleased and plunged into plans for the future; she suspected that he was really thinking aloud for the pure pleasure of it—which left her free to consider what she had just said. If she had married Mervyn would he have been the right man? Unbidden, the thought that she hadn't liked him when she had first seen him crossed her mind, to be instantly dismissed—he might have treated her badly, but that was no reason for her feelings to change, or was it? If she had loved him, surely her feelings wouldn't have changed. What did she feel for him now, anyway? Dislike—indifference? She wasn't sure any more, she wasn't even sure now that she had ever loved him. It was all very bewildering and a relief when Doctor Trouw stopped for coffee.

They reached Midwoude just before noon, to be welcomed by Jaap, and Doctor Trouw didn't wait—he had some cases to see, he explained, but he would be back at two o'clock, if she could manage in the meantime.

She and Jaap managed very well, each speaking their own language and understanding the other very well in spite of it. She had the same room as she had had previously and he took her case up for her, telling her that lunch would be in half an hour and leaving her to unpack, do her face and tidy her hair. She did this slowly, savouring the peace and quiet and comfort around her. After that afternoon, when Cousin Emma was home again, she wouldn't be quite so free, so she might as well make the most of her leisure now.

The hospital at Groningen was large and imposing with a medical school attached. Doctor Trouw skirted the main building, and halfway down a side turning ran the car under a stone archway and into an inner courtyard, where he parked the car. Mary Jane, getting out, guessed it to be the sanctum of the senior staff of the hospital and knew she was right when she saw the Rolls in a far corner. They entered the hospital through a small door which led to a short dark passage which spilled into a wide corridor with splendid doors lining its walls, and scented with the faint unmistakable smell of hospital cleanliness. It was also very quiet. The consultants would gather someone behind these richly sombre walls, as would the hospital board, and VIPs visiting the hospital would, no doubt drink their coffee, cocooned in its hushed affluence. All hospitals are alike, Mary Jane decided, treating carefully in Doctor Trouw's wake.

He opened a door almost at the end of the corridor and gave her a kindly prod. The room was large, it's centre taken up by an oblong table hedged in by a symposium of straight-backed chairs. There were other chairs in the room, easy ones, grouped round small tables, and the air was thick with cigar smoke. It seemed to her that the room was full of men—large, well-groomed men, every single one of whom turned to look at her. In actual fact there were a bare dozen, senior members of the hospital medical staff who had just risen after a meeting.

'Over in the far corner,' said Doctor Trouw in her ear, and began to steer her to where Fabian was standing. He had his back to them, talking to two other men, but he turned and saw them and came to meet them. He looked, thought Mary Jane a trifle wildly, exactly what he was; a highly successful surgeon with plenty of money, plenty of brains and so much self-confidence that he could afford to look as though he had neither. She felt depressed and a little shy of him, for he seemed a stranger, and her reply to his pleasant 'Hullo, Mary Jane' was stiff and brief. But he seemed not to notice that; enquiring after her journey, whether she had slept and if she felt herself capable of undertaking the care of Emma within the hour. She told him yes, checking an impulse to address him as sir, and with a perception which took her by surprise he remarked:

'We all look rather—er—stuffy, I suspect. Whatever you do, don't address me as sir.'

She smiled at that. 'Not stuffy,' she assured him. 'It's just that you all look so exactly like consultants, and so many of you together is a bit overpowering.'

The two men laughed as they ushered her to the door again, pausing on the way to introduce her to various gentlemen who would have gone on talking for some time if Fabian hadn't reminded them that they were expected elsewhere. They traversed the corridor once more, this time to a lift. It was a small lift, and with Doctor Trouw's bulk beside her and Fabian taking up what space there remained, she felt somewhat crowded, and more so, for the two men carried on a conversation above her head, only ceasing as the lift purred to a halt, to smile down at her for all the world as though they had just remembered that she was there.

They stepped out into another wide corridor, this time lighted from the windows running its whole length and lined on one side by doors, each numbered, each with its red warning light above the glass peephole in its centre. They entered the first of

these to find Cousin Emma sitting in a chair, dressed and waiting, and if Mary Jane had been in any doubt as to Fabian's
sincerity when he had told her how much his cousin needed
her, it could now be squashed. Cousin Emma uttered a welcoming cry, enfolded her against a fur-clad, scented bosom and
began a eulogy upon Mary Jane's virtues which caused her face
to go very red indeed.

'I knew you would come!' breathed Emma. 'I said to Fabian,
"If Mary Jane doesn't come, I shall make no effort to recover
from this dreadful operation."'' She paused, allowed Mary Jane
to assume the upright and swept aside her mink coat.

'The scar,' she invited dramatically. 'Look at the scar—is it
not dreadful? How can a maimed woman accept an offer of
marriage with such a blemish?'

Mary Jane considered the hair-fine red line drawn so exactly
across the base of her patient's throat. 'You won't be able to
see it in three months' time,' she pronounced. 'Even now it's
hard to see unless one stares—and who's going to stare? All
you need to do is to get a handful of necklaces which will fit
over it exactly—we'll do that, one for each outfit.'

She smiled at Cousin Emma, her eyes kind, unheedful of the
two men standing close by.

'I feel better already,' declaimed Emma, and smiled with all
the graciousness of some famous film star. 'I'm ready.'

Fabian drove her back in the Rolls and Mary Jane followed
behind with Doctor Trouw in the Citroën, giving all the right
answers to her companion's happy soliloquising. He would be,
she considered, exactly right for Cousin Emma, for he obviously worshipped the ground she trod upon, while being under
no illusion regarding her tendency to dramatise every situation.
She asked: 'When do you hope to get married, Doctor Trouw?'

'Well, there is no reason why we shouldn't marry within a
week or so. All the preliminaries are attended to—I persuaded
her to become *ondertrouwt* before she went into hospital. Perhaps you could persuade her?' He looked at her hopefully. 'She
is a sensitive woman,' he explained, just as though Mary Jane

wasn't already aware of it, 'and prone to a good deal of dejection. Once we are married, I believed that can be cured.'

He turned the car in through the open gates and pulled up beside the Rolls. 'Willem is home,' he told Mary Jane as they got out. 'I daresay he will be over one day to see you.'

'How nice,' said Mary Jane, not meaning it—she foresaw a busy time ahead, acting as confidante to father and son while each confided their romantic problems to her. She sighed soundlessly and followed him into the house.

She had said almost nothing to Fabian, nor he to her, nor did he attempt to speak to her before he left very shortly afterwards. He had told her, she recalled, that he would be his cousin's surgeon when he called and not her guardian, now it seemed he had every intention of keeping his word. She answered his brief nod as he went with something of a pang and went to make Cousin Emma comfortable.

It proved an easier task than she had supposed. For one thing the operation had been a success; in place of the emotional, overwrought woman she had been, Cousin Emma had become quieter; her feverish gaiety and sudden outbursts of tears had been most effectively banished. She was still rather tearful, but that was post-operative weakness and would disappear with time. In the meanwhile, Mary Jane kept her company, saw to her pills and tablets, cared for her tenderly, talked clothes, reassured her at least twice a day that the scar was almost invisible, and coaxed her to eat her meals. And when Fabian came, as he did each day, she met him with a politely friendly face, answered his questions with the right amount of professional exactitude, commented upon the weather, which was bitterly cold once more, listened carefully to any instructions he chose to give her, and then retired to a corner of the room, to resume her knitting. Only when he got up to go did she put it down— thankfully, as it happened, because she wasn't all that good at it, and walk to the door with him and see him out of the house. It was on the fifth day after her arrival that he paused on the steps and turned round to face her.

'Have you recovered?' he wanted to know coolly. 'Though

perhaps I'm foolish to ask such a question, for you're not likely to tell me, are you?'

'No, I'm not,' she replied in an outraged voice, her eyes no higher than his waistcoat. She spoilt this by adding: 'It's not your business, anyway.'

He grinned. 'Who said it was? Willem Trouw was asking about you yesterday. He doesn't know about your broken romance and he's having difficulties with his own love life. I believe you might console each other.'

Mary Jane was furious, so furious that for a moment the words she wanted to say couldn't be said. At last: 'You're abominable—how dare you say such things? You're cruel and heartless!' She tried to shut the door in his face, but he took it from her and held it open.

'Probably I am,' he agreed, 'but only when I consider it necessary.' He bent suddenly and before she could turn her head, kissed her mouth. Then he shut the door gently in her surprised face.

Willem came over that very afternoon, and remembering Fabian's words, she was hard put to it to be civil to him; supposing Fabian had said the same sort of thing to Willem? Perhaps men didn't confide in each other, but to be on the safe side she refused Willem's invitation to go out with him that evening, doing it so nicely that he could always ask again if he wanted to.

She had been there more than a week when Fabian, on one of his daily visits, mentioned casually that the continuous frost had made it possible to skate on the lake. 'Do you skate?' he wanted to know.

They were in the little sitting room, Cousin Emma in an easy chair, leafing through a pile of fashion magazines, Mary Jane determinedly knitting. She bent her head over it now, rather crossly picking up the stitches she had dropped, and became even crosser when Fabian remarked:

'I think you are not a good knitter, for you are always unpicking or dropping stitches or tangling your wool.'

He was right, of course; she had been working away at the

same few inches for days, for the pattern always came wrong. Probably she would tear it off the needles and jump on it one day. Now she left the dropped stitches and knitted the rest of the row, briskly and quite wrongly, just to let him see how mistaken he was. It was a pity that he laughed.

'There are skates in the attic,' Cousin Emma informed anyone who cared to listen. 'I shall not skate, naturally, but you, Mary Jane, must do so if you wish. It is a splendid exercise and Willem could come over and teach you if you aren't good at it.' She added complacently, 'I'm very good, myself.' She glanced at her cousin. 'What do you think, Fabian?'

Mary Jane wasn't sure how it happened. All she knew was that within minutes she had agreed—or had she?—to spend the following afternoon skating with Willem. It would be so convenient, said Emma, because Doctor Trouw was coming over to discuss wedding plans with her, and Willem could come with him. They would stay to tea, of course, and Mary Jane might like to make that delicious cake they had had a few days ago— Cook wouldn't mind.

Mary Jane replied suitably, doggedly knitting. But in the hall she said to Fabian: 'I don't particularly wish to skate with Willem, and I should be much obliged if you would mind your own business when it comes to my free time...'

He put on his car coat and caught up his gloves. 'My dear girl, have I annoyed you?' His voice was bland, he was smiling a little. 'Perhaps you have other plans—other young men you prefer to skate with?'

He was still smiling, but his eyes were curiously intent.

'Don't be ridiculous, you know I haven't.' She went on gruffly: 'When can I go home? Emma is almost well.'

He was pulling on his gloves and didn't look at her. 'No one would wish to keep you here against your will, Mary Jane, but I think that Emma would be broken-hearted if you should wish to go home before her wedding.'

'Will they marry soon?'

'I imagine so. Are you homesick?'

She raised puzzled eyes to his. 'No—at least, I don't think so. I—I don't know. I feel unsettled.'

He put a compelling finger under her chin. 'Unhappy?' His voice was gentle. And when she shook her head, 'The truth is that you are still in a mist of dreams, are you not? But they will go, and you will find that reality is a great deal better.'

He went away and she stood in the lobby watching the Rolls being expertly driven down the frozen drive and away down the road. Sometimes he was so nice, she thought wistfully, wondering what exactly he had meant.

She went skating with Willem when he came because there was nothing she could do about it—he arrived with his father, his plans laid for an afternoon on the ice with her. He had even borrowed some skates, and despite everything, she enjoyed herself. The lake was crowded, the bright colours of the children's anoraks lent the scene colour under the grey sky, their shrill, excited voices sounding clearly on the thin winter air. Willem was a good skater, if unspectacular. They went up and down sedately while he told her about the girl he wanted to marry and who didn't seem to want to marry him. 'I can't think why,' he told her unhappily. 'We're such good friends.'

'Sweep her off her feet,' advised Mary Jane. 'I don't know much about it, but I think girls like that. You could try—you know what I mean, be a bit bossy.'

'But I couldn't—she's so sure of what she wants, at least she seems to be.'

Mary Jane executed a rather clumsy turn. 'There, you see? Probably she doesn't know her own mind. Where is she now?'

They were going down the length of the lake again. 'As a matter of fact she's in Groningen.'

'Today? This afternoon?' Mary Jane came to such an abrupt halt that she almost lost her balance. 'What could be better? Go and fetch her here, make her put on skates and rush up and down with her until she's worn out—show her who's master.' She gave him a push. 'Go on, Willem—she'll be thrilled!'

'You think so?' He sounded undecided and she reiterated: 'Oh, go on, do!'

'But what about you?'

'I'm all right here. If I'm not back by dark you can come and fetch me.'

'Really? You don't think I'm being—being not friendly towards you, Mary Jane?'

'No, Willem. It's because we're friends that we can make this plan.' She started off, waving gaily. 'Have fun!'

She didn't look round, but when she turned and came back, he had gone.

The afternoon darkened early and became colder, but she, skating with more enthusiasm than skill, glowed with warmth; she had on her sheepskin jacket and a scarf tied tightly over her bun of hair, and she had stuffed her slacks into a pair of Cousin Emma's boots—they were too big, but they did well enough, as did the thick knitted mitts Jaap had found for her. Her ordinary little face was pink with pleasure and exercise, her eyes sparkled; that she was alone didn't matter at all, because there were so many people around her, enjoying themselves too. She skated to the end of the lake and then, the wind behind her, came belting back. There were fewer people now; the children were leaving, and there was more room. She was almost at the end when she saw Fabian some way ahead, right in her path. Even in the gathering dusk there was no mistaking his tall, solid figure. She began to slow down, for, most annoyingly, he hadn't moved. She was still going quite fast when she reached him, but he stayed where he was, putting out a large arm to bring her to a standstill.

'Whoops!' said Mary Jane, breathless. 'I thought I was going to knock you over—you should have moved.'

He was still holding her. 'No need. I weigh fifteen stone or thereabouts, and I doubt if you're much more than eight.' He laughed down at her. 'You show a fine turn of speed, though I don't think much of your style.'

'Oh, style—I enjoy myself.'

He had turned her round and they were skating, hands linked, back down the lake. Presently he asked, 'Where is Willem?'

'He's gone to Groningen to meet his girl-friend.'

'I thought he was spending the afternoon with you?'

'Oh, we started off together, then he started telling me about her and really, he was so fainthearted, I thought I'd better encourage him to go after her.'

'So you gave him some advice?'

'That's right. Have you the afternoon off?'

'More or less, but I must go home shortly. Will you come and have tea with me? Willem is presumably occupied with his girl, and Cousin Emma and Trouw will be engrossed with each other. That leaves us.'

She considered. 'Well, tea would be nice—but won't they wonder where I am?'

'I'll let them know. Shall we race to the end—you can have twenty yards' start.'

She did her best, but he overtook her halfway there, and then dropped back to skate beside her until they reached the bank, where they took off their skates and walked through the bare trees to where he had parked the car.

His house was warm and inviting, just as she had remembered it. They had tea in a small, cosily furnished room with a bright fire burning and lamps casting a soft glow over the well-polished tables which held them. And the tea was delicious—anchovy toast, sandwiches and miniature cream puffs. Mary Jane, with a healthy appetite from her skating, ate with the pleasure of a hungry child. She was halfway through the sandwiches when she exclaimed, 'We haven't telephoned Midwoude—do you think we should?'

Fabian got up at once. 'I suppose I can't persuade you to stay to dinner?'

She refused at once very nicely and was at once sorry that she had done so, because she would very much have liked to spend the evening with him. She told herself urgently that it was foolish to be charmed by him just because he was being such good company—besides, there was Mervyn. She pulled herself up with the reflection that there wasn't Mervyn; she owed nothing to him, neither loyalty to his memory or anything else; not, said her heart, even love, for it hadn't been love, only a plain girl's reaction to being admired...

'You're looking very thoughtful,' remarked Fabian and sat down again. 'You said you wanted to go home—will you agree to stay until Emma is married as I asked you? I think the wedding will be very soon, probably we shall hear something when we go back presently.'

She spoke at random to fill the silence between them: 'This is a lovely house.'

'You like it? It needs a family—children—in it. You like children, Mary Jane?'

'Yes.' She was unconsciously wistful as they lapsed into silence once more. She had abandoned her confused thinking, and it seemed a good thing; she needed peace and quiet to sort herself out, and Fabian's presence had the effect of confusing her still further. She wasn't even sure what she wanted any more—only one thing was clear, he didn't mind if she returned home; she had watched his face when she had told him that she wanted to go and its expression hadn't changed at all. Not meaning to say it, she asked: 'When I go home, will you need to visit me again?'

His casual, 'Oh, I think not; everything is arranged very satisfactorily. If you should need my services you can always write or telephone,' daunted her, but she tried again.

'But what about the horse?'

'I asked the vet to keep an eye open—he'll let me know when he finds something worth while.'

She said, 'Oh, how nice,' in a small forlorn voice, aware that she had been using the horse as a line of communication, as it were, and Fabian had cut the line. She got to her feet. 'I think I should be getting back,' and when he got to his feet with unflattering speed, 'You said we wouldn't meet—that you would only be Emma's surgeon—I forgot that this afternoon. Did you?'

His dark eyes rested briefly on hers. 'No, I hadn't forgotten, Mary Jane, but there is such a thing as a truce, is there not?'

He fetched her outdoor things and they went out to the car.

A good thing, she thought savagely as she got in, that she hadn't accepted his invitation to dinner—uttered out of politeness, no doubt, for he was obviously longing to be rid of her. Telling herself that it didn't matter in the least, she kept up a steady flow of chat as he drove her back to Midwoude, her voice a little high and brittle.

But he seemed in no hurry to be rid of her company or anyone else's when they reached the house. Cousin Emma and Doctor Trouw were in the sitting room, the tea things still spread around them, deep in wedding plans. They would be married, declared Emma, with a suitable touch of the dramatic, in four days' time—the *burgermeester* of Midwoude had promised to perform the ceremony in the early afternoon at the Gemeentehuis, and afterwards they would cross the street for a short ceremony in church. 'And you will come, Mary Jane, because you have been so kind and good...' the ready tears sprang to her eyes, 'and when you marry I shall come to your wedding.'

'How nice,' said Mary Jane briefly. 'Tell me, what will you wear?'

Her companion was instantly diverted and the two ladies became absorbed in the bridal outfit. They were still engrossed in this interesting topic when the gentlemen wandered off to the other side of the room to have a drink, and when after a few minutes Fabian said that he must go, he did no more than pass a careless remark about their pleasant afternoon before he took himself off.

There was no time for anything but the wedding preparations during the next day or so. Cousin Emma, fully recovered from her operation, plunged into a maelstrom of activity with Mary Jane doing her best to hold her back a little. Recovered she might be and in the happy position of having others to attend to her every want, she still needed to rest. Mary Jane gently bullied her on to the chaise-longue in her bedroom each afternoon and by dint of guile and cunning, kept her there until Doctor Trouw called at tea-time. Fabian came too, but only for a few minutes, to check his cousin's progress, although on the day previous to the wedding he remained long enough to tell Mary Jane that should she wish, he would arrange for her to travel home on the day after the wedding. 'But time enough to let me know,' he assured her carelessly. 'There are few people travelling at this time of year, it will only be a question of a few telephone calls.' He had nodded cheerfully at her and added, 'I shall see you at the wedding, no doubt.'

Getting Cousin Emma to the Gemeentehuis proved a nerve-shattering business. Not only was she excited and happy, she was tearful too, and when almost dressed declared that she looked a complete guy, that her shoes pinched and that her scar was so conspicuous that she really hadn't the courage to go through with the ceremony. It was fortunate that her bride-groom—come, as Dutch custom dictated, to fetch his bride to their wedding—had brought with him his wedding gift, a string of pearls which exactly covered the offending blemish. Mary Jane, rather pink and excited herself, left them thankfully together and hurried to the front door. Jaap was to drive her to the village and she was already a little late. He wasn't there, but Fabian was, strolling up and down the hall in morning clothes whose elegance quite dazzled her.

'There you are,' he remarked. 'I sent Jaap on, you're coming with me.' He stood looking at her. 'Now that is a new hat,' he decided, 'and a very pretty one.'

Mary Jane gave him a doubtful look. The hat had taken a good deal of thought and she hadn't had all that time to escape from Cousin Emma. It matched her coat exactly, a melusine with a sideways-tilted brim ending in a frou-frou of chiffon. Not at all her sort of hat, but after all, it was a wedding and one was allowed some licence. It added elegance to her ordinary face too and gave it a glow which almost amounted to prettiness.

'Someone told you,' she accused him.

'No, indeed not,' he laughed at her, 'and it really is pretty.'

She wished that he would say that she was pretty too, although that would be nonsense, but he didn't say anything else, but tucked her into the Rolls beside him and drove off to the

Gemeentehuis, a small, very old building, ringed around now with a number of cars and little groups of people from the village. Inside, Fabian found her a seat at the back before he went to take his place with his family in the front row. The ceremony was short and quite incomprehensible to her, but the service in the church was more to her taste, for she was able to follow it easily. And when it was over she watched the bride and groom and their families, correctly paired, walk down the aisle to the door of the church. She knew none of them, save for Fabian and Willem. They looked, she considered, a little haughty, very well dressed and faintly awe-inspiring, although the younger members of the party were gay and smiling and enjoying themselves. Willem, she was glad to see, had his girl with him—at least, she hoped it was his girl. He certainly looked happy enough, and Fabian—Fabian was escorting a truly formidable lady of advanced years, just behind the bridal pair.

She waited until almost everyone had gone and made her way to the door, looking for Jaap. He was nowhere to be seen. There were still several groups of people lingering around the porch, but they were all strangers to her. She supposed she would have to walk. She frowned—how like Fabian to forget all about her; she wished she hadn't come, he was horrible, thoughtless, thoroughly beastly... He touched her arm, smiling at her, so that she felt guilty, and felt even more so when he said, 'I knew you would have the sense to wait until I came for you—Great-aunt Corina isn't to be hurried. Come on.'

She travelled back sitting with the old lady, who wasn't haughty at all, while a large young man, whom Fabian introduced as Dirk—a cousin—squeezed in beside them. Fabian introduced the girl sitting beside him too—a blue-eyed creature wrapped in furs. Her name was Monique, and even though he said she was a cousin, Mary Jane didn't take to her. She was still pondering the strength of her feelings about this when they arrived at the house.

The vast drawing room had been got ready for the reception, with a long table and a number of smaller ones grouped around it. Mary Jane, seated between Dirk and an elderly uncle of the bride, found that she was expected to make a good meal. She went from champagne cocktails to lobster meuniere, from venison steaks to chocolate profiteroles, each with its accompanying wine. It was a relief to hear from Dirk that a wedding cake wasn't customary, for what with the wine and champagne and the warmth of the room, she began to feel a little lightheaded. Even the haughty members of the family didn't seem haughty any more, indeed, those she had spoken to had been charming to her. She glanced round her. Everyone looked very happy, but then marriages were happy occasions, although if she married she would want a quiet one with just a few friends. The corners of her gentle mouth turned down; the sooner she stopped thinking that romantic nonsense, the better. She turned to Dirk, who was quite amusing although a little young, she considered, and when he asked her if he might take her out to supper that evening, she refused with a charm which drew from him a regretful smile and a promise to ask her again the very next time they met. It seemed pointless to tell him that she was going back to England the next day, she laughingly agreed and listened with all her attention while he told her about his ambition to be as good a surgeon as his cousin Fabian.

The guests began to leave as soon as the bridal pair had gone; car after car slid away into the winter darkness until there were only a very few left, their owners delaying their departure for a last-minute chat or waiting for each other. Mary Jane felt rather lost; the drawing room was in the hands of the caterers, under the sharp eye of Jaap, being returned to its usual stately perfection. Sientje was in the kitchen, the daily maid had gone long ago. Mary Jane stood in the hall, remembering how cheerfully Fabian had asked 'Tomorrow?' when she had asked him on the way to the wedding if he would arrange for her to travel home. 'I'll send the tickets here to you,' he had told her casually, 'in plenty of time for you to catch the boat train from Groningen. Jaap will drive you to the station.'

Now she wondered if that was to be his goodbye. She had helped him when he had asked her to; her own affairs were in

order, there was nothing more for him to do; did he intend to
drop their uneasy acquaintance completely? Just as well, perhaps, she mused, they had never got on well. She wandered
into the empty sitting room and sat down by the window, staring out into the dark evening, her mind full of useless regrets,
her fingers playing with the diamond brooch Fabian had given
her and which she had pinned to her coat. She had written and
thanked him for it. It had been a long letter and she had tried
very hard to show her gratitude, but he had never answered it,
or mentioned it—she wasn't sure if he had even noticed that
she was wearing it today. She got up and strolled back into the
hall, empty now. Not quite empty, though, for Fabian was there,
sitting in the padded porter's chair by the door. He walked over
to meet her and said easily, 'Hullo—I'm just off. You're fixed
up for the evening, I hear. Dirk told me earlier that he intended
taking you out to supper.' He smiled. 'He's good company,
you'll enjoy yourself.'

'Oh, indeed I shall,' she assured him, her voice bright. How
pleased he must feel, thinking that she was settled for the evening and that he need not bother... 'I hope you have a pleasant
evening too,' she assured him untruthfully, 'and thank you for
seeing about the tickets. I'll say goodbye.'

She held out her hand and had it engulfed in his, and it
became for an amazing few seconds of time the only tangible
thing there; the hall was whirling around her head, her heart
was beating itself into a frenzy because she had at that moment
become aware of something—she didn't want to say goodbye
to Fabian, she didn't want him to go, never again. She wanted
him to stay for ever, because she was in love with him—she
always had been. But why had she only just discovered it? And
what was the use of knowing it now? For even as the knowledge hit her he had dropped her hand and was at the door. He
went through it without looking back.

CHAPTER EIGHT

MARY JANE STOOD staring at the door for a few seconds, hoping that he might come back; that he had forgotten something; that he would ask her to go out with him that evening, Dirk or no Dirk. Anything, she cried soundlessly; a violent snowstorm which would make it impossible for him to drive away, something wrong with the Rolls, an urgent message so that she could run after him with good reason... Nothing happened, the hall was empty and silent, there was a murmur of voices from the drawing room where there was still a good deal of activity, and from outside the crunch of the Rolls' wheels on the frozen ground. They sounded remote and final; she waited until she couldn't hear them any more and then went in search of Jaap.

If the old man was surprised at her decision to go to bed immediately, he didn't show it. They had become used to each other by now, so it wasn't too difficult to let him suppose that she had a headache and wanted nothing for the night. He wished her good night and went back to the caterers.

She slept badly and got up early, which she realized later had been a silly thing to do, for the morning stretched endlessly before her. She wouldn't be leaving until the late afternoon, and somehow the time had to be helped along. She spent some of it with Jaap and Sientje, but conversation was difficult anyway, and they had their work to do—they were to go on a short holiday and return to make the house ready for Cousin Emma and her husband, who had agreed to the happy arrangement of leaving his own house for his son's use and carrying on his practice from Midwoude. Mary Jane, sensing that much as Jaap and Sientje liked her, they wanted to get on with their chores, offered to clear away the silver and glass which had been got out for the wedding, and then went around freshening up the floral arrangements; probably Jaap would throw them out before he closed the house, but it gave her something to do. But even these self-imposed tasks came to an end, and she ate her lonely lunch as slowly as possible, hoping that Fabian would telephone; surely he would say goodbye? But as the minutes ticked by she was forced to the conclusion that he had no intention of doing so. Perhaps he would be at the station—if she could see him just once more before she went away... She told herself it was foolish to build her hopes on flimsy wishes, a good walk would do her good and she had plenty of time. She went and got her coat, tied a scarf over her head, snatched up her gloves, and went in search of Jaap. He seemed a little uncertain about her desire to go out, but she could understand but little of what he said and she wasn't listening very hard; she wanted to get out and walk—as fast as possible, so that she might be too tired to think about Fabian. She made the old man understand that she would be back in good time for him to drive her to the station, and fled from the house before he could detain her longer.

The afternoon was bleak and frozen into stillness; the ground was of iron and she quickly discovered that it was slippery as well. She walked fast into an icy wind, down to the village, and when she looked at her watch and saw that she still had time to kill, she walked on, towards the path which led eventually to the lake. Here the bare trees gave some pretence of shelter even though the ground under her feet was rough and treacherously slithery, something she hardly noticed, trying as she was to outstrip her unhappiness, forcing herself to think only of her future in the house her grandfather had left her. She came in sight of the frozen water presently and paused to look at her watch again. She would have to return quite soon and she decided not to go any further.

There were people skating on the lake, turning the greyness of its surroundings into a gay carnival of sound and colour. Mary Jane drew a sighing breath, the memory of her afternoon with Fabian very vivid, then turned on her heel and started to retrace her steps along the path, and after a short distance, lured by the cheerful sight of a robin sitting in a thicket, turned off it and wandered a little way, absurdly anxious to get a closer view of the bird. But he flew just ahead of her so that when she finally retraced her steps the path was hidden. She hurried a little, anxious to find it again because it would never do to lose the boat train. She didn't notice the upended root under her foot—she tripped, lost her balance on the smooth ice, and fell, aware of the searing pain in the back of her head as it struck a nearby tree.

It was like coming up through layers of grey smoke; she was almost through them when she heard Fabian's voice saying 'God almighty!' and it sounded like a prayer. With a tremendous effort she opened her eyes and focused them upon him. He looked strange, for he was in his theatre gown and cap and a mask, pulled down under his chin.

'You sound as though you're praying,' she mumbled at him.

'I am,' and before she could say more: 'Don't talk.' His voice was kind and firm, she obeyed it instantly and closed her tired eyes, listening to him talking to someone close by. He had taken her hand in his and the firm, cool grip was very reassuring; she allowed the soft grey smoke to envelop her once more.

When she wakened for the second time, the room was dimly lit by a shaded lamp in whose glow a nurse was sitting, her head bowed over a book. But when Mary Jane whispered, 'Hullo there,' she came over to the bed and said in English, 'You are awake, that is good.'

Mary Jane suffered her pulse to be taken, and in a voice which wasn't as strong as she could have wished said, 'I'll get up,' and was instantly hushed by the nurse's horrified face.

'No—it is four o'clock in the morning,' she remonstrated, 'and I must immediately call the Professor—he wishes to know when you wake, you understand? Therefore you will lie still, yes?'

Mary Jane started to sit up, thought better of it because of the pain at the back of her head and said weakly, 'Yes—but no one is to get up out of his bed just to come and look at me. I'm quite all right.'

'But the Professor is not in his bed,' explained the nurse

gently. 'He is here, Miss Pettigrew, in the hospital, waiting for you to wake.'

She went to the telephone as she spoke and said something quietly into it, then came back to the bed. 'He comes,' she volunteered, 'and you will please lie still.'

He was there within a few minutes, this time in slacks and a sweater. To Mary Jane's still confused eyes he looked vast and forbidding and singularly remote, and the fact disappointed her so that when she spoke it was in a somewhat pettish voice. 'You stayed up all night—there was no need. I'm perfectly all right.' She frowned because her headache was quite bad. 'It was quite unnecessary.'

He said tolerantly, 'It's of no matter,' and took her wrist between his finger and thumb, taking her pulse. 'You feel better? Well enough to talk a little and tell me what happened?'

She blinked up at him. His face looked drawn and haggard in the dim light and she felt tender pity welling up inside her so that she could hardly speak. 'I'm sorry,' she managed, 'I mean I'm sorry you've had all this trouble.'

'I said it didn't matter. What happened?' His voice was quiet, impassive and very professional. He would expect sensible answers; she frowned in her efforts to be coherent and not waste his time.

'I went for a walk,' she explained at last. 'You see, I hadn't anything to do until it was time to leave. I went to the village and there was still lots of time—I went down the path between the trees to the lake. There was a robin, I went to look at him and I slipped and hit my head—I can remember the pain.' She stopped, thankful to have got it all out properly for him. 'I don't know how long I was there. Did I dream that I saw Jaap and it was very cold?'

Fabian had pulled up a chair to the side of the bed. 'No— you were cold, and it was Jaap who found you when he went to look for you because you hadn't gone back to the house and he was worried, only he didn't find you straight away because you were a little way from the path. You have a slight concussion—nothing serious, but you will stay here, lying quietly in bed, until I say otherwise. And you will do nothing, you understand?'

She muttered 'Um' because she was drowsy again, but she remembered to ask, 'Where's here?'

'The hospital in Groningen.' And she muttered again, 'Thank you very much,' because she was grateful to be there and wanted him to know it, but somehow her thoughts weren't easy to put into the right words. Forgetting that she had already said it once, she thanked him again. 'I'm such a nuisance and I am sorry.' A thought streaked through the fog of sleep which was engulfing her. 'I'm going home today,' she offered in a groggy voice.

'Yesterday—no, Mary Jane, you are not going home, not just yet. You will stay here until your headache has gone.'

She managed to open her heavy lids once more. 'I don't want...' she began, and met his dark eyes.

'You'll stay here,' he repeated quietly. 'Nurse will give you a drink and make you comfortable and you will go to sleep again.'

She was in no state to argue; she closed her eyes and listened to his voice as he spoke to the nurse, but he hadn't finished what he was saying before she was asleep again.

It was afternoon when next she woke, feeling almost herself, and this time there was a different nurse, a big, plump girl with a jolly face, whose English, while adequate, was peppered with peculiar grammar. She turned Mary Jane's pillow, gave her a drink of tea and went to the telephone.

Fabian was in his theatre gown again. He nodded briefly with a faint smile, took her pulse and, satisfied, said: 'Hullo, you're better. How about something to eat?'

She didn't answer him. 'You're busy in theatre,' she observed in a voice which still wasn't quite hers. 'What's the time?'

'Three o'clock in the afternoon.'

'Have you a long list?' She hadn't meant to ask, but she had to say something just to keep him there a little longer.

'Yes, but we're nearly through. How about tea and toast?'

She nodded and started to thank him, but sneezed instead. 'I've a cold,' she discovered.

'That's to be expected. The temperature was well below zero and you were half frozen. I'll see that you get something for it.'

She sneezed again and winced at the pain in her head. 'That's very kind of you,' she said meekly. 'I'm quite well excepting for a bit of a headache.'

He gave her a smile which he might have given to a child. 'I know. All the same, you will stay where you are until I say that you may get up.'

Mary Jane nodded and closed her eyes, not because she was sleepy any more, but because to look at him when she loved him so much was more than she could bear. When she opened them he had gone and the large cheerful nurse was standing by the bed with tea and toast on a tray.

It took two more days for her headache to go, and even though she felt better, the cold dragged on. Two days in which Fabian came and went, his visits brief and impersonal and kindly, during which he conferred with the nurse, made polite conversation with herself, read her notes and went away again. On the morning of the third day he was accompanied by a young man whom he introduced as his registrar, a good-looking, merry-faced young man, trying his hardest to copy his chief's every mannerism; something which might have amused Mary Jane ordinarily, but which struck her now as rather touching. He listened attentively while Fabian explained what had happened to her and agreed immediately when Fabian suggested that she might be ready to leave hospital. He stayed a little longer, talking to Mary Jane, and then at a word from Fabian, took himself off.

She had got up and dressed that morning and had been sitting by the window watching the busy courtyard below, but she turned round now to face Fabian. She had had a few minutes to pull herself together; she said in a matter-of-fact voice, 'I should like to go home tomorrow if you will allow it and it isn't too much trouble to arrange. I'm perfectly well again. Thank you for looking after me so well...'

He made a small, impatient sound. 'You will do nothing of the kind, that would be foolish, at least for the next few days. As soon as I consider you fit for travelling I will arrange your journey. In the meantime you will come to my house—my housekeeper will look after you.'

She sat up very straight in her chair, which caused her to cough, sneeze and give herself a headache all at the same moment. Her voice was still a little thick with her cold when she spoke. 'I don't think I want to do that—it's very kind of you, but...'

'Why not?' he sounded amused.

'I've been quite enough trouble to you as it is.'

His ready agreement disconcerted her. 'Oh, indeed you have—you will be even more trouble if you don't do as I ask now. I shall be in Utrecht, and Mevrouw Hol will be delighted to have someone to fuss over while I am away. You shall go back to England when I return.'

Her reply was polite and wooden. If ever she had needed to convince herself of his indifference to her, she had the answer now. His obvious anxiety to get her off his hands even while he was treating her with such care and courtesy and arranging for her comfort, told her that, and he didn't care a rap for her...

'What are you thinking?' he demanded.

'Oh, nothing, just—just that it will be nice to be home again. Are you going to Utrecht straight away?'

He was leaning against the wall, staring at her. 'Tonight. You will be taken to my house tomorrow morning, Mevrouw Hol is expecting you. Her English is as fragmental as your Dutch; it will be good for both of you. She is a very kind woman, you will be happy with her. She has the same good qualities as your Mrs Body—to whom, by the way, I have written.'

Mary Jane was startled to think that she had quite forgotten to do that.

'Oh, I forgot—how stupid of me, I'm sorry.'

'You have had concussion,' he reminded her, and added with

a little smile, 'And you have no reason to be apologetic about everything.'

She coloured painfully and just stopped herself in time from saying that she was sorry for that too. Instead she wished him a pleasant time in Utrecht, her quiet voice giving no clue to her imagination, already vividly at work on beautiful girls, dinners for two…perhaps he had another house there. He strolled to the door, his eyes on her still.

'But of course I shall,' he told her. 'I always do.' He opened the door and turned round to say, 'We shall see each other before you go, I have no doubt.' With a careless nod he was gone, and presently, by craning her neck, she was able to see him crossing the courtyard below, Klaus Vliet, his registrar, beside him. She couldn't see them very clearly because she was crying.

She left the hospital the following day, just before noon, and was driven to Fabian's house by Klaus, who called to fetch her from her room in the private wing of the hospital, explaining that his chief had told him to do so—furthermore, he was to see her safely installed with Mevrouw Hol and call daily until such time as her guardian told him not to. Mary Jane, now she was up and about, was disappointed to find that she still had a headache, it made her irritable and she would have liked to have disputed this high-handed measure on Fabian's part, but she couldn't be bothered. She accepted the news without comment and closed her eyes against the dullness of the city streets.

But inside Fabian's house it wasn't dull at all, but gay with flowers and warm and welcoming. Mevrouw Hol was a dear; round and cosy and middle-aged with kind blue eyes and a motherly face. Mary Jane, whose headache had reached splitting point, took one look at her and burst into tears, to be instantly comforted, led to a chair by the fire in the sitting room where she had tea with Fabian, divested of her outdoor things, told not to worry, and given coffee while Klaus tactfully left them to fetch her case and carry it upstairs. He joined her for coffee presently, ignoring her blotched face, and when they had finished it, ordered her to lie down the minute she had eaten the lunch Mevrouw Hol was even then bringing to her on a tray. He gave her some tablets too, with strict instructions to take them as directed. 'And mind you do,' he warned her kindly, 'or the chief will have my head.' He got up. 'I'm going now, but I shall be here tomorrow morning to see how you are. Mevrouw has instructions to telephone if you feel at all under the weather.'

Mary Jane smiled shakily at him. 'You make me feel as though I were gold bullion at the very least!'

'Better than that,' he grinned, 'above rubies.' He lifted a hand. 'Be seeing you!'

She ate her lunch under Mevrouw Hol's watchful eye and went upstairs to lie down. Her room was at the back of the house, overlooking a very small paved courtyard, set around with tubs full of Algerian irises and wintersweet. The room was delightful, not very large and most daintily furnished in the Chippendale style with *Toile de Jouy* curtains in pink and a thick white carpet underfoot. She looked round her with some interest, for it didn't seem at all the kind of room Fabian would wish for in his home. She had always imagined that above stairs, the rooms would be furnished with spartan simplicity. She didn't know why she had thought that, perhaps because he was a bachelor, but of course, the house would have been furnished years ago, for everything was old and beautiful. As she closed her eyes she thought how nice it would be to live in the old house, nicer than her grandfather's even.

She felt much better the following morning. She had done nothing for the rest of the previous day, only rested and eaten her supper under Mevrouw Hol's kindly eye and gone to bed again, and now after a long night's rest she felt quite herself again, even her headache had gone.

Perhaps it was her peaceful surroundings, she thought, as she accompanied the housekeeper on a gentle tour of the kitchen regions, for it was peaceful back in the hall she stood still, listening to the rich ticktock of the elaborate wall clock before wandering into the sitting room to sit, quite content, in one of the comfortable chairs, doing nothing. The sound of the great knocker on the front door roused her though and she got up to greet Klaus, who, after carrying out a conscientious questioning as to her state of health, joined her for coffee. He stayed for half an hour, talking gently about nothing in particular, and when he got up to go, promised to return the next day. When she assured him that this was quite unnecessary, he looked shocked and told her that he had been asked to do so by the chief and would on no account go against his wishes. Nor would he allow her to go out, not that day, at any rate.

'Well,' said Mary Jane, a little pettish, 'anyone would think that I had a subdural or a CVA or something equally horrid. I only bumped my head...'

'And caught a cold,' he told her, laughing.

Two more days passed and she felt quite well again. Even her cold had cleared up and Klaus, looking her over carefully each morning, had to admit at last that he could find nothing wrong with her, a remark which caused her to ask: 'Well, when's Professor van der Blocq coming back?'

Klaus put down his coffee cup and looked at her in bewilderment. 'Coming back? But he has never been away.' His pleasant face cleared. 'Ah, you mean when does he come back to his house? Very soon, I should suppose, for I am able to give him a good account of you today, so surely he will not allow you to return to your home.' He grinned at her disarmingly. 'He is not of our generation, the chief—he holds old-fashioned views about things which we younger men think nothing of.'

She went a bright, angry pink. 'Don't talk as though he were an old man!' she said sharply. 'And I share his views.'

Klaus smiled ruefully. 'I see that I must beg your pardon, and I do so most sincerely. You must not think that I mock at the chief—he is a mighty man in surgery and a good man in his life and much liked and respected—I myself would wish to be like him.' He looked at her with curiosity. 'You knew, then, that he was living in the hospital until you are well enough to leave his house?'

'Of course.' Her voice, even to her own ears, sounded satisfyingly convincing. 'I am his ward, you know. It's like having a father...'

The absurdity of the remark struck her even as she made it. Fabian was no more like a father than the young man sitting opposite her. 'Well, not quite,' she conceded, 'but you know what I mean.'

He agreed politely, although she could see that he had little idea of what she meant; she wasn't certain herself. He got up to go presently, wishing her goodbye because he didn't expect to see her again, 'Although I daresay that you will visit your guardian from time to time,' he hazarded, 'and I expect to be here for some years.'

She gave him a smiling reply, longing for him to go so that she could have time to herself to think. To learn that Fabian had been in Groningen all the time she had been at his house, and had made no effort to come and see her, had been a shock she was just beginning to realize. Maybe he was old-fashioned in his views, she was herself, and she could respect him for them, but not even the most strait-laced member of the community could have seen any objection to him going to see her in his own house—or telephoning, for that matter—and surely he could have said something to her? There was only one possible explanation, he was quite indifferent to her; considered her a nuisance he felt obliged to suffer until she was fit to return home. It would have been nice to have confronted him with this, but then he might ask her how it was that she knew he had been in Groningen, and unless she could think of some brilliant lie, poor Klaus would get the blame for speaking out of turn. She allowed several possibilities, most of them highly impractical, to flit through her head before deciding regretfully that she was a poor liar in any case, and she would not have the nerve, not with Fabian's dark, penetrating gaze bent upon her, so she discarded them all to explore other possibilities.

She could run away—a phrase she hastily changed to beating a retreat—if she did that, it would save Fabian the necessity of arranging her journey and at the same time save her pride and allow him to see that she was quite able to look after herself.

She didn't need his help, she told herself firmly, in future she would have nothing to do with him. Doubtless he would be delighted—had he not told her that she was tiresome to him? Mary Jane paced up and down the comfortable room, in a splendid rage which was almost, but not quite, strong enough to conceal her love for him. But for the time being, it served its purpose—she would write him a letter, thanking him for all he had done... She began to plot, sitting before the fire in the pleasant room.

By lunch-time she had it all worked out, she would leave that very afternoon. She wouldn't be able to take her case with her, but Klaus had said that she might go for a short walk if she had a mind to. He had told Mevrouw Hol this—it made it all very easy; she had her passport and plenty of money still, she could buy what she needed as she went, and this time she would fly—it would be quicker and she supposed that there would be several flights to London once she got to Schiphol. She ate her lunch on a wave of false excitement and over her coffee began the letter to Fabian.

Her pen was poised over the paper while she composed a few dignified sentences in her head when the door opened and he walked in. If he saw her startled jump and the guilty way she tried to hide her writing pad and pen, he said nothing.

'Young Vliet tells me you're quite recovered,' he began without preamble. 'I've arranged for you to travel home this evening.'

She gazed at him speechlessly, feeling dreadfully deflated after all her careful planning, and when she didn't speak, he went on, 'I expected you to express instant delight, instead of which you look flabbergasted and dreadfully guilty. What have you been doing?'

'Nothing—nothing at all.' Her voice came out in a protesting, earnest squeak. 'I'm surprised, that's all. I—I was—that is...' She remembered something. 'Did you have a nice time in Utrecht?'

'Yes. I see you're writing letters—leave them here and I'll see that they're posted.'

She was breathless. 'No—that is, they're not important—there's no need...' She tore the sheet across and crumpled it up very small and threw it on the fire. She had only got as far as 'Dear Fabian,' but she didn't want him to see even that. She sighed loudly without knowing it and said with a brightness born of relief, 'There, I can write all the letters I want to when I get home.'

Fabian had seated himself opposite her and was pouring himself the coffee which Mevrouw Hol had just brought in. 'Not to Mervyn, I hope?'

'Mervyn?' She stared at him, her mouth a little open. She had forgotten about Mervyn because there wasn't anyone else in the world while Fabian was there. 'Oh, Mervyn,' she said at last, 'no, of course not. I don't know where he is.' She stared at the hands in her lap. 'I don't want to know, either.'

'The temptation to say "I told you so" is very great, but I won't do that.' He put down his cup. 'The train leaves here about six o'clock—do you need anything or wish to go anywhere before you leave?'

He wanted her out of the way. She got to her feet and said coldly, 'No, thank you—I'll go and put a few things together...'

'Five minutes' work,' he was gently mocking, 'but it's as good an excuse as any, I imagine.' He went to the door and opened it for her. 'I shall be in the study if you should want anything,' he told her.

She made no attempt to pack her case when she reached her room; he was right, five minutes was more than enough time in which to cast her few things in and slam the lid. She sat down in the little bucket chair by the window and stared down into the little courtyard, not seeing it at all. It was a very good thing that she was going away, although perhaps not quite as she had planned. She should never have come in the first place, only Fabian had been so insistent. She allowed her thoughts to dwell briefly on Cousin Emma and Doctor Trouw and wondered if she would ever see them again—perhaps they would come and stay with her later on, then she would get news of Fabian. Although wasn't a clean break better? He had told her that her affairs were now in good order, anything which needed seeing to could be done by letter or through Mr North.

She got up and prowled round the room, touching its small treasures with a gentle finger—glass and porcelain and silver— Fabian had a lovely home and she would never forget it. Presently she sat down again and dozed off.

Mevrouw Hol wakened her for tea, bustling into the room, wanting to know if she felt well and was she cold, or would she like her tea in her room. Mary Jane shook her head to each question and went downstairs. There was no sign of Fabian; she ate her tea as she had always done, from a tray on the small table by the fire. He must have gone back to the hospital. She poured a second cup, wondering if he had left instructions as to how she was to get to the station.

She finished her tea and went back upstairs to ram her things into her case in a most untidy, uncaring fashion, not in the least like her usual neat ways, and, that done, went back downstairs and out to the kitchen where Mevrouw Hol was preparing dinner. Mary Jane watched her for a moment and asked in her frightful Dutch: 'People for dinner?' and when Mevrouw Hol nodded, felt a pang of pure envy and curiosity shoot through her. 'How many?' she wanted to know.

The housekeeper shot her a thoughtful glance. 'Three,' she said, 'two ladies and a gentleman.'

'Married?' asked Mary Jane before she could stop herself.

Mevrouw Hol nodded, and Mary Jane, her imagination at work again, had a vivid mental picture of some distinguished couple, and—the crux of the whole matter—a beautiful girl— blonde, and wearing couture clothes, she decided, her imagination working overtime. She would have a disdainful look and Fabian would adore her. She got down from the edge of the table where she had perched herself. 'I'll get ready,' she said in her terrible Dutch.

She went downstairs at twenty to six, because Fabian had said that the train went at six o'clock, and perhaps she should get a taxi. She was hatted and coated and ready to leave and there was no sign of anyone. Fabian came out of his study as

she reached the hall. He said briefly: 'I'll get your case,' and
when he came downstairs again she ventured, 'Should I call a
taxi—there's not much time.' She searched his tranquil face. 'I
didn't know you'd come back,' she explained.

'I've been here all the afternoon—I had some work to do. If
you're ready we'll go.'

'Oh—are you taking me to the station? I thought...'

'Never mind what you thought. Don't you agree that as your
guardian the least I can do is to see you safely on the way to
England?'

She had no answer to that but went in search of Mevrouw
Hol, who shook her by the hand and wished her *'Tot ziens,'*
adding a great deal in her own language which Mary Jane
couldn't understand in the least.

The journey to the station was short, a matter of a few
minutes, during which Mary Jane sought vainly for something
to say. She couldn't believe that she was actually going—that
perhaps she might not see Fabian again for a long time, perhaps
never, for he had no reason to see her again.

She looked sideways at his calm profile and then at his
gloved hands resting on the wheel. She loved him very much;
she had no idea that loving someone could hurt so fiercely. She
went with him silently into the station and on to the platform
and found the train already there. She watched while Fabian
spoke to the guard, took the tickets which he handed to her and
thanked him in a small voice.

'There's a seat in the dining car reserved for you,' he told
her. 'Someone will fetch you. The guard will see about a porter
for you when you reach the Hoek. Just go on board, everything
is arranged. There's a seat booked on the breakfast car from
Harwich. Have you your headache tablets with you?'

'Yes, thank you, and thank you for taking so much trouble,
Fabian.'

'You had better get in,' he advised her, and disappeared, to
reappear within a few minutes with a bundle of magazines.
'Don't read too much,' he told her.

She lingered on the steps. 'I must owe you quite a bit—for the journey—shall I send it to you?'

'Don't bother. Mr North will settle with me.' He put out a hand. 'Goodbye, Mary Jane, have a good trip.'

She shook hands and answered him in a steady voice—how useful pride could be on occasion! She even added a few meaningless phrases, the sort of thing one says when one is bidding someone goodbye at a railway station. He dismissed them with a half smile and got out of the train. She watched him getting smaller and smaller as the train gathered speed and finally went round a curve, and then he was gone.

The journey was smooth and so well organised that she had no worries at all; it was as though an unseen Fabian was there, smoothing her path. She wondered to what trouble he had gone to have made everything so easy for her. It was a pity that his thoughtfulness was partly wasted, for she spent a wretched night and no amount of make-up could help the pallor of her face or the tell-tale puffiness of her eyelids. She arrived, thoroughly dispirited, at Liverpool Street station in the cold rain of the January morning, and the first person she saw was Mrs Body.

CHAPTER NINE

LATER, LOOKING BACK on that morning, Mary Jane knew that she had reached the end of her tether by the time she had reached London, although she hadn't known it then, only felt an upsurge of relief and delight at the sight of Mrs Body in her sensible tweeds and best hat. She had almost fallen out of the train in her eagerness to get to her and fling herself at the older woman, and Mrs Body, standing foursquare amidst the hurrying passengers, had given her a motherly hug and sensibly made no remark about her miserable face, but had said merely that the dear doctor had been quite right to ask her to come to London, much though she disliked the place, for by all accounts Mary Jane had had a nasty bang on the head. She then hurried her into a taxi and on to the next train for home, and Mary Jane, exhausted by her feelings more than the rigours of the journey, slept most of the way.

She had been home for almost a week now, a week during which she had filled her days with chores around the house and long walks with a delighted Major trailing at her heels. Her evenings she spent chatting with Mrs Body, talking about the village and what had happened in it while she had been away, various household matters, and the state of the garden. Of Holland she spoke not at all, excepting to touch lightly upon the wedding and her fall, and to her relief neither Mrs Body nor Lily had displayed any curiosity as to what she had done while she was there, nor, after that one remark Mrs Body had made on Liverpool Street station, had Fabian been mentioned. It should have made it all the easier to erase him from her mind, but it did no such thing; she found herself thinking of him constantly, his face, with its remote expression and the little smile which so disconcerted her, floated before her eyes last thing at night, and was there waiting for her when she wakened in the morning; it was really very vexing.

She tried inviting a few of her grandfather's old friends in for drinks one evening and realised too late that they were deeply interested in her visits to Holland, and wanted to know all about that country, and what was more, about her guardian too. They discussed him at some length—very much to his advantage, she was quick to note—and old Mr North, when asked to add his opinion to those of the other elderly gentlemen present, observed that, in his judgement, Jonkheer van der Blocq was a man of integrity, very much to be trusted and the right man to solve any problem. 'That episode with Mr Mervyn Pettigrew, for example,' he began, and then coughed dryly. 'I beg your pardon, Mary Jane, I should not have mentioned him; doubtless your feelings on the matter are still painful.'

He smiled kindly at her, as did his companions, and she smiled gently back, happily conscious that her feelings weren't painful at all, at least not about Mervyn. 'It doesn't matter,' she assured them, 'I got over that some time ago.' She realised as she said it that it was only a few weeks since her heart had been broken and had mended itself so quickly. 'I made a mistake,' she said calmly. 'Luckily it was discovered in time.'

'Indeed yes, and solely due to your guardian's efforts. To travel to Canada when everyone was enjoying their Christmas showed great determination on his part. I feel that your future is in safe hands, my dear.'

The other gentlemen murmured agreement, and Mary Jane, busy playing hostess, wished with all her heart that what Mr North had said was true; there was nothing she would have liked better than to have had a safe future with Fabian, not quite such a one as her companions envisaged perhaps, but infinitely more interesting.

The next morning, urged on by a desire to do something, no matter what, she took the Mini to Carlisle and bought clothes. She really didn't need them; she had plenty of sensible tweeds and jersey dresses and several evening outfits which, as far as she could see, she couldn't hope to wear out, let alone wear.

She had bought them when Mervyn had come to visit her. Now, speeding towards the shops, she decided that she loathed the sight of them; she would give them all away and buy something new.

Once having made this resolve, she found that nothing could stop her; several dresses she bought for the very good reason that they were pretty and she looked nice in them, even though she could think of no occasion when she might wear them. She balanced this foolishness by purchasing a couple of outfits which she could wear each day, and, her conscience salved, bought several pairs of shoes, expensive ones, quite unsuitable for the life she led, and undies, all colours of the rainbow.

She bought a red dressing gown for Mrs Body too, and more glamorous undies for Lily, who was going steady with the postman and was making vague plans for a wedding in the distant future.

She and Mrs Body and Lily spent an absorbing evening, inspecting her purchases, but later, when she was alone in her room, she hung the gay dresses away, wondering wistfully if she would ever wear them. It seemed unlikely, but it wasn't much good brooding over it. She closed the closet door upon them and got into bed, where she lay, composing a letter to Fabian, reminding him that she still hadn't got a horse to ride. The exercise kept her mind occupied for some time and although she knew that she would never write it, and certainly not send it, it gave her a kind of satisfaction. She should have said something about it in the short, stiff letter she had written to him when she arrived home, a conventional enough missive, thanking him for his thoughtful arrangement of her journey and his care of her while she had been in hospital. It had taken her a long time to write and she had wasted several sheets of notepaper before the composition had satisfied her. He hadn't answered it.

The weather, which had been almost springlike for a few days, worsened the next morning, with cold grey clouds covering the sky, a harsh wind whistling through the bare trees and a light powdering of snow covering the ground. A beastly day, thought Mary Jane, looking out of the window while she pulled on her slacks and two sweaters. She had promised Mrs Body and Lily most of the day off too, to attend a wedding in the village, and heaven knew what time they would get back; weddings were something of an event in their quiet community and the occasion of lengthy hospitality. With an eye to the worsening weather, Mary Jane saw them off after an early lunch and went back to the kitchen to wash up and set the tea tray. This done, she wandered into the sitting room. It looked inviting with a bright fire burning and Major snoozing before it, but there was a lot of the day to get through still; she decided on a walk, a long one down to the lake and along its shore for a few miles and then back over the hills, and if the weather got too bad she could always take to the road. It would get rid of the restlessness she felt, she told herself firmly, and went to put on an old mackintosh and gumboots.

They set off, she and Major, ten minutes later—it was no day for a walk, but she was content to plod along in the teeth of the wind, thinking about Fabian, and Major was content to plod with her.

They got back home at the end of a prematurely darkened afternoon—the snow had settled a little, despite the wind, and the daylight had almost gone. The cold had become pitiless. Mary Jane and Major, tired and longing for tea and the fire, turned in at the gate and hurried up the short drive. The house looked as cold as its surroundings; she wished she had left a lamp burning as a welcome, then she remembered as she reached the door that she hadn't locked it behind her—not that that mattered, she had Major with her. But Major had other ideas; he had left her to go round the side of the house to the back door; years of training having fixed in his doggy mind that on wet days he had to go in through the garden porch.

She went in alone, pulling off her outdoor things as she went and casting them down anyhow. The hall was almost in darkness and she shivered, not from cold but because she was lonely and unhappy. She said quite loudly in a miserable voice: 'Oh,

Fabian!' and came to a sudden shocked halt when he said from the dimness, 'Hullo, Mary Jane.'

She turned to stare at him dimly outlined against the sitting room door and heard his voice, very matter-of-fact, again. 'You left the door open.'

She nodded into the gloom, temporarily speechless, but presently she managed, 'Have you come about my horse?'

'No.'

She waited, but that seemed to be all that he was going to say, and suddenly unable to bear it any longer, she said in a voice a little too loud: 'Please will you go?'

'If you will give me a good reason—yes.'

She didn't feel quite herself. She supposed it was the shock of finding him there, but she seemed to have lost all control over her tongue.

'I've been very silly,' her voice was still too loud, but she didn't care. 'It's you I love. I think I've always loved you, but I didn't know—Mervyn was you, if you see what I mean.' She added, quite distraught: 'So please will you go away—now.' Her voice shook a little, her mouth felt dry. She urged: 'Please, Fabian.'

He made no movement. 'What a girl you are for missing the obvious,' he observed pleasantly. 'Why do you suppose I've come?'

She wasn't really listening, being completely taken up with the appalling realisation of her foolish and impetuous speech, but she supposed he expected an answer so she said, 'Oh, the horse—no, you said it wasn't, didn't you. Have I spent too much money? You could have written about that, there was no need for you to have come...'

He crossed the hall and took her in his arms. 'You're a silly girl,' he told her, and his voice was very tender. 'Of course there is a need. Only perhaps I have been silly too—you see, my darling, you are so young and I—I am forty.'

'Oh, what has that got to do with it?' she demanded quite crossly. 'You could be twenty or ninety; you'd still be Fabian, can't you see that?'

His arms tightened around her. 'I'll remember that,' he told her softly, 'my adorable Miss Pettigrew,' and when she would have spoken he drew her a little closer. 'Hush, my love—my darling love. I'm not sure when I fell in love with you, perhaps when we first met, although I wasn't aware of it—that came later, the night Uncle Georgius died and I opened the sitting-room door and you were on the stairs looking lost and unhappy. But after that you were never there, always disappearing when I came. I waited and waited, hoping that you would love me too, and then Mervyn turned up. I have never been so worried...'

'You didn't look worried,' Mary Jane pointed out.

'Perhaps I'm not very good at showing my feelings,' he told her, 'but I'll try now.' She was wrapped in his arms as though he would never let her go again—a state, she thought dreamily, to which she was happily resigned, and when he kissed her she had no more thoughts at all. Presently she said into his shoulder, 'I was going to run away, but you came back. I thought you didn't like me being in your house—that you wanted me to come back here.'

He loosed his hold a little so that he could see her face. 'My dearest darling, there was nothing I wanted more than to have you in my home, but you were my ward...'

'You let me go.' She frowned a little, staring up into his dark eyes. 'You arranged for me to go.'

'Because I knew that you would run away if I didn't—you see, my love, I know you better than you know yourself.' He pulled her quite roughly to him and kissed her thoroughly. 'I haven't been the best of guardians, but I shall be a very good husband,' he promised her, and kissed her again, very gently this time.

It was quite dark in the hall by now, and Major, fed up with waiting at the back door, pattered in and came to sit down beside them, thumping his tail on the floor. 'He wants his supper,' said Mary Jane in a dreamy voice.

'So do I, my darling girl.'

She wasn't dreamy any more. 'Oh, my darling Fabian, you're

hungry! I'll cook something.' But when she would have slipped from his arms he held her fast. 'Not just yet...'

'We can't stay here all night—Mrs Body and Lily won't be back for ages—they've gone to a wedding.' She smiled up at him, quite content to stay where she was for ever.

'They shall come to ours, my darling.'

'Oh, Fabian!' She could hardly see his face although it was so close to her own, but that didn't matter, nothing mattered any more. Life had become blissfully perfect, stretching out before them for ever. She clasped her hands behind his neck and because she couldn't put her happiness into words, she said again, 'Oh, Fabian!' and kissed him.

A WINTER LOVE STORY

by

Betty Neels

CHAPTER ONE

CLAUDIA leaned up, took another armful of books from the shelves lining the little room, put them on the table beside her and sneezed as a cloud of mummified dust rose from them. What had possessed her, she wondered, to take on the task of dusting her great-uncle William's library when she could have been enjoying these few weeks at home doing as she pleased?

She picked up her duster, sneezed again, and bent to her task, a tall, slim but shapely girl with a lovely face and shining copper hair, which was piled untidily on top of her head and half covered by another duster, secured by a piece of string. Her shapely person was shrouded in a large print pinny several sizes too big, her face had a dusty smear on one cheek and her nose shone. Nevertheless she looked beautiful, and the man watching her from the half-open door smiled his appreciation before giving a little cough.

Claudia looked over her shoulder at him. There was nothing about him to make her feel uneasy—indeed, he was the epitome of understated elegance, with an air of assurance which was in itself reassuring. He was a big man, very tall and powerfully built, not so very young but with the kind of good looks which could only improve with age. His hair was pepper and salt, cut short. He might be in his late thirties. Claudia wondered who he was.

'Have you come to see Great-Uncle William or my mother? You came in through the wrong door—but of course you weren't to know that.' She smiled at him kindly, not wishing him to feel awkward.

He showed no signs of discomfort. 'Colonel Ramsay.' His commanding nose twisted at the dust. 'Should you not open a window? The dust...'

'Oh, they don't open. They're frightfully old—the original

ones from when the house was built. Why do you want to see Colonel Ramsay?'

He looked at her before he answered. 'He asked me to call.'

'None of my business?' She clapped two aged tomes together and sent another cloud of dust across the room. 'Go back the way you came,' she told him, 'out of the side door and ring the front doorbell. Tombs will admit you.'

She gave him a nod and turned back to the shelves. Probably someone from Great-Uncle William's solicitor.

'I don't think I like him much,' said Claudia to the silent room. All the same she had to admit that she would have liked to know more about him.

She saw him again, not half an hour later, when, the duster removed from her head and her hands washed, she went along to the kitchen for coffee.

The house was large and rambling, and now, on the edge of winter, with an antiquated heating system, several of its rooms were decidedly chilly. Only the kitchen was cosy, with the Aga warming it, and since there were only her mother, Mrs Pratt the housekeeper, Jennie the maid and, of course, Tombs, who seemed to Claudia to be as old as the house, if not older, it was here that they had their morning coffee.

If there were visitors Mrs Ramsay sat in chilly state in the drawing room and dispensed coffee from a Sèvres coffee pot arranged on a silver tray, but in the kitchen they all had their individual mugs. However, despite this democratic behaviour, no one would have dreamt of sitting down or drinking their coffee until Mrs Ramsay had taken her place at the head of the table and lifted her own special mug to her lips.

Claudia breezed into the kitchen with Rob the Labrador at her heels. Her mother was already there, and sitting beside her, looking as though it was something he had been doing all his life, was the strange man. He got to his feet as she went in, and so did Tombs, and Claudia stopped halfway to the table.

She didn't speak for a moment, but raised eloquent eyebrows at her mother. Mrs Ramsay said comfortably, 'Yes, I know, dear, we ought to be in the drawing room. But there's been a fall of soot so the fire can't be lighted. And Dr Tait-Bullen likes kitchens.'

She smiled round the table, gathering murmured agreements while the doctor looked amused.

'Come and drink your coffee, Claudia,' went on Mrs Ramsay. 'This is Dr Tait-Bullen who came to see Uncle William. My daughter, Claudia.'

Claudia inclined her head, and said, 'How do you do?' in a rather frosty manner. He could have told her, she thought, instead of just walking away as he had done. 'Uncle William isn't ill?' she asked.

The doctor glanced at her mother before replying. 'Colonel Ramsay has a heart condition which I believe may benefit from surgery.'

'He's ill? But Dr Willis saw him last week—he didn't say anything. Are you sure?'

Dr Tait-Bullen, a surgeon of some fame within his profession, assured her gravely that he was sure. 'Dr Willis very wisely said nothing until he had a second opinion.'

'Then why isn't he here now?' demanded Claudia. 'You could be wrong, whatever you say.'

'Of course. Dr Willis was to have met me here this morning, but I understand that a last-minute emergency prevented him. I have been called in as consultant, but the decision concerning the Colonel's further treatment rests with his doctor and himself.' He added gently, 'I was asked my opinion, nothing more.'

Mrs Ramsay cast a look at Claudia. Sometimes a daughter with red hair could be a problem. She said carefully, 'You may depend upon Dr Willis getting the very best advice darling.'

Claudia stared across the table at him, and he met her look with an impassive face. If he was annoyed he showed no sign of it.

'What do you advise?' she asked him.

'Dr Willis will come presently. I think we should wait until he is here. He and I will need to talk.'

'But is Great Uncle William ill? I mean, really ill?'

Her mother interrupted. 'Claudia, we mustn't badger Dr Tait-Bullen.' She looked round the table. 'More coffee for anyone?'

Claudia pushed back her chair. 'No, thank you, Mother. I'll go and get on with the books. Tombs knows where I am if I'm wanted.'

She smiled at the butler and whisked herself out of the room, allowing the smile to embrace everyone there.

Back in the library, she set about clearing the shelves, banging books together in clouds of dust, wielding her duster with quite unnecessary vigour. She had behaved very badly and she was sorry about it—and a bit puzzled too, for she liked him. What had possessed her to be so rude? She had behaved like a self-conscious teenager. She ought to apologise. Tombs, she knew, would come and tell her what was happening from time to time, so when the doctor was about to leave she would say something polite...

She spent a few minutes making up suitable speeches—a dignified apology, brief and matter-of-fact. She tried out several versions, anxious to get it right. She was halfway through her final choice when she was interrupted.

'If those gracious words were meant for me,' said Dr Tait-Bullen, 'I am flattered.'

He was leaning against the door behind her, smiling at her, and she smiled back without meaning to. 'Well, they were. I was rude. I was going to apologise to you before you left.'

'Quite unnecessary, Miss Ramsay. One must make allowances for red hair and unpleasant news.'

'Now you're being rude,' she muttered, but went on anxiously. 'You really meant that? Great Uncle William is seriously ill? I can see no reason why I shouldn't be told. I'm not a child.'

He studied her briefly. 'No, you are not a child, but Dr Willis and I must talk first.' He came into the room, moved a pile of books and sat down on the table. 'This is a delightful house, but surely rather large for the three of you?'

He spoke idly and she answered him readily. 'Well, yes, but it's been in the family for a long time. Most of the rooms are shut up, so it's easy enough to run. Tombs has been here for ever, and Mrs Pratt and Jennie have been here for years and years. The gardens have got a bit out of hand, but old Stokes from the village comes up to help me.'

'You have a job?'

'I did have. Path Lab assistant—not trained, of course, just general dogsbody. But London's too far off. I've applied for several jobs which aren't so far away so that I can come home often.'

He said casually, 'Ah, yes of course. Salisbury, Southampton, Exeter—they are all within reasonable distance.'

'And there are several private hospitals too. I didn't much like London.' She added chattily, 'Do you live there?'

'Most of my work is done there.'

She supposed that he hadn't added to that because Tombs had joined them.

'Dr Willis has arrived, sir.' He looked at Claudia. 'Mrs Ramsay is in the morning room, Miss Claudia. Jennie has lighted the fire there for the convenience of the doctors.'

'Thank you, Tombs.' She glanced at the doctor. 'You'll want to go with Tombs. I'll come presently—I must just tidy myself.'

Left to herself, she took off her pinny, dragged a comb through her hair and went in search of her mother.

Mrs Ramsay was with the two men, making small talk before they began their discussion of their patient's condition. She was still a strikingly beautiful woman, wearing her fifty years lightly. Her hair, once as bright as her daughter's, was streaked with silver, but she was still slim and graceful. She was listening to something Dr Willis was saying, smiling up at him, her hand on his coat-sleeve. They were old friends; he had treated her husband before his death several years ago, and since he was a widower, living in a rather gloomy house in the village with an equally gloomy elderly housekeeper, he was a frequent visitor at the Ramsays' house.

He looked up as Claudia joined them.

'My dear, there you are. Come to keep your mother company

for a while? Are we to stay here, or would you prefer us to go
to the study?'

'No, no, stay here. There's a fire specially lighted for you.
Claudia and I will go and see to lunch.' She paused at the door.
'You will tell us exactly what is wrong?'

'Of course.'

In the dining room, helping her mother to set the lunch,
Claudia asked, 'Is Great-Uncle William really very ill, Mother?'

'Well, dear, I'm afraid so. He hasn't really been very well
for some time, but we couldn't persuade him to have a second
opinion. This Dr Tait-Bullen seems a nice man.'

'Nice?' Claudia hesitated. 'Yes, I'm sure he is.' 'Nice,' she
reflected, hardly described him; it was far too anaemic a word.
Beneath the professional polite detachment she suspected there
was a man she would very much like to know.

They were standing idly at the windows, looking out into the
wintry garden, when Tombs came to tell them that the doctors
had come downstairs from seeing their patient.

Dr Willis went straight to Mrs Ramsay and took her hand.
He was a tall, thin man, with a craggy face softened by a com-
forting smile as he looked at her. He didn't say anything.
Claudia saw her mother return his look and swallowed a sudden
surprised breath. The look had been one of trust and affection.
Don't beat about the bush, Claudia admonished herself silently.
They're in love.

There was no chance to think about it; Dr Tait-Bullen was
speaking. Great Uncle William needed a triple bypass, and
without undue loss of time. The one difficulty, he pointed out,
was that the patient had no intention of agreeing to an operation.

Claudia asked quickly, 'Would that cure him? Would he be
able to lead a normal life—be up and about again?'

'The Colonel is an old man, but he should be able to live
the life of a man of his age.'

'Yes, but...'

'Claudia, let Dr Tait-Bullen finish...'

'Sorry.' She flushed and he watched the colour creep into

her cheeks before he said, 'I quite understand your anxiety. If Dr Willis wishes, I will come again very shortly and do my best to change the Colonel's mind. I feel sure that if anyone can do that it will be he, for they have known each other for a long time. I can but advise.'

He glanced at the other man. 'We have discussed what is best to be done—there are certain drugs which will help, diet, suitable physiotherapy...'

'I'm sure you have done everything within your power, Doctor,' said Mrs Ramsay. 'We will do our best to persuade Uncle William, and if you would keep an eye on him?' She looked at Dr Willis. 'That is, if you don't mind, George?'

'I am only too glad of expert advice.'

'Oh, good. You'll stay for lunch, Dr Tait-Bullen? In half an hour or so...'

'I must return to London, Mrs Ramsay. You will forgive me if I refuse your kind invitation.'

He shook hands with her, and then with Dr Willis. 'We will be in touch.'

'Claudia, take Dr Tait-Bullen to his car, will you, dear?'

They walked through the house together, out of the door and across the neglected sweep of gravel to where a dark grey Rolls Royce stood. Claudia stared at it reflectively.

'Are you just a doctor?' she wanted to know. 'Or someone more important?' She glanced at his quiet face. 'Mother called you Doctor, so I thought you were. You're not, are you?'

'Indeed, I am a doctor. I am also a surgeon...'

'So you're *Mr* Tait-Bullen. You're not a professor or anything like that, are you?'

'I'm afraid so...'

'You might have said so.'

'Quite unnecessary. Besides, being called a professor makes me feel old.'

'You're not old.'

He answered her without rancour. 'Thirty-nine. And you?'

She had asked for that. Anyway, what did it matter? 'I'm very nearly twenty-seven,' she told him.

He said smoothly, 'I am surprised that you are not yet married, Miss Ramsay.'

'Well, I'm not,' she snapped. 'I've not met anyone I've wanted to marry.' She added pettishly, 'I have had several proposals.'

'That does not surprise me.' He smiled down at her, thinking how unusual it was to see grey eyes allied with such very red hair. He sounded suddenly brisk. 'You will do your best to persuade the Colonel to agree to surgery, will you?'

When she nodded, he got into his car and drove away. His handshake had been firm and cool and brief.

Claudia went back to the morning room and found her mother and Dr Willis deep in talk. They smiled at her as she went in, and her mother said, 'He's gone? Such a pleasant man, and not a bit stiff or pompous. Dr Willis has been telling me that he's quite an important surgeon—perhaps I shouldn't have given him coffee in the kitchen.' She frowned. 'Do you suppose Uncle will take his advice?'

'Most unlikely, Mother. I'll take his lunch up presently, and see if he'll talk about it.'

Great-Uncle William had no intention of talking to anyone on the subject. When Claudia made an attempt to broach the matter, she was told to hold her tongue and mind her own business. Advice which she took in good part, for she was used to the old man's irascible temper and had a strong affection for him.

He had been very good to her mother and to her when her father died, giving them a home, educating her, while at the same time making no bones about the fact that he would have been happier living in the house by himself, with his housekeeper and Tombs to look after him. All the same, she suspected that he had some affection for them both, and was grateful for that.

It was a pity that on his death the house would pass to a distant cousin whom she had never met. That Uncle William had made provision for her mother and herself was another reason for gratitude, for Mrs Ramsay had only a small income, and after years of living in comfort it would have been hard for her to move to some small house and count every penny.

They would miss the old house, with its large rooms and elegant shabbiness, and they would miss Tombs and Mrs Pratt and Jennie too, but Claudia supposed that she would have a job somewhere or other and make a life for herself. Somewhere she could get home easily from time to time. Her mother would miss her friends. Especially she would miss Dr Willis, always there to cope with any small crisis.

The days went unhurriedly by. Claudia finished turning out the library and turned her attention to the rather battered greenhouse at the bottom of the large garden. The mornings were frosty, and old Stokes, who came up from the village to see to the garden, tidied the beds and dug the ground in the kitchen garden, leaving her free to look after the contents of the glass house.

It contained a medley of pots and containers, filled with seedlings and cuttings, and she spent happy hours grubbing around, hopefully sowing seed trays and nursing along the hyacinths and tulips she intended for Christmas.

And every day she spent an hour or so with her great-uncle, reading him dry-as-dust articles from *The Times* or listening to him reminiscing about his military career. He still refused to speak of his illness. It seemed to her anxious eyes that he was weaker, short of breath, easily tired and with an alarming lack of appetite.

Dr Willis came to see him frequently, and it was at the end of a week in which he could detect no improvement in his patient that he told Mrs Ramsay that he had asked Mr Tait-Bullen to come again.

He came on a dreary November morning, misty and damp and cold, and Claudia, busy with her seedlings, an old sack wrapped around her topped by a jacket colourless with age, knew nothing of his arrival. True, she had been told that he was to come again, but no day had been fixed; he was an exceedingly busy man, she'd been told, and his out of town visits had to be fitted in whenever possible.

He had spent some time with the Colonel, and even longer with Dr Willis, before talking to Mrs Ramsay, and when that lady observed that she would send Tombs to fetch Claudia to join them, volunteered to fetch her himself.

Studying the sack and the old jacket as he entered the greenhouse, he wondered if he was ever to have the pleasure of seeing Claudia looking like the other young women of his acquaintance—fashionably clad, hair immaculate, expertly made up—and decided that she looked very nice as she was. The thought made him smile.

She had looked round as he opened the door and her smile was welcoming.

'Hello—does Mother know you're here?' And then, 'Great Uncle isn't worse?'

'I've seen the Colonel and talked to your mother and Dr Willis. I've been here for some time. Your mother would like you to join us at the house.'

She put down the tray of seedlings slowly. 'Great Uncle William won't let you operate—I tried to talk him into it but he wouldn't listen…'

He said gently, 'I'm afraid so. And the delay has made an operation questionable.'

'You mean it's too late? But it's only a little more than a week since you saw him.'

'If I could have operated immediately he would have had a fair chance of recovering and leading a normal quiet life.'

'And now he has no chance at all?'

He said gravely, 'We shall continue to do all that we can.'

She nodded. 'Yes, I know that you will. I'll come. Is Mother upset? Does she know?'

'Yes.' He watched while she took off the deplorable jacket and untied the sack and went to wash her hands at the stone sink. The water was icy and her hands were grimy. She saw his look. 'You can't handle seedlings in gloves,' she told him. 'They are too small and delicate.'

'You prefer them to dusting books?' he asked as they started for the house.

'Yes, though books are something I couldn't possibly manage without. I'd rather buy a book than a hat.'

He reflected that it would be a pity to hide that glorious hair under a hat, however becoming, but he didn't say so.

Her mother and Dr Willis were in the morning room again, and Mrs Ramsay said in a relieved voice, 'Oh, there you are, dear. I expect Mr Tait-Bullen has explained...'

'Yes, Mother. Do you want me to go and sit with Great-Uncle?'

'He told us all to go away, so I expect you'd better wait a while. Mr Tait-Bullen is going to see him again presently, but he doesn't want anyone else there.' She turned as Tombs came in with the coffee tray. 'But you'll have coffee first, won't you?'

They drank their coffee while the two men sustained the kind of small talk which needed very little reply, and presently Mr Tait-Bullen went back upstairs.

He was gone for some time and Claudia, getting impatient, got up and prowled round the room. 'I don't suppose he'll come again,' she said at length.

'There is no need for him to do so, but the Colonel has taken quite a fancy to him. Mr Tait-Bullen calls a spade a spade when necessary, but in the nicest possible way. What is more, his patients aren't just patients; they are men and women with feelings and wishes which he respects. Your great-uncle knows that.'

Mr Tait-Bullen, driving along the narrow roads which would take him from the village of Little Planting to the M3 and thence to London, allowed his thoughts to wander. He and the Colonel had talked about many things, none of which had anything to do with his condition. The Colonel had made it clear that he intended to die in his own bed, and while conceding that Mr Tait-Bullen was undoubtedly a splendid surgeon and cardiologist, he wished to have no truck with surgery, which he considered, at his time of life, to be quite worthless.

Mr Tait-Bullen had made no effort to change his mind for

him. True, he could have prolonged his patient's life and allowed him to live for a period at least in moderate health, but he considered that if he had overridden the Colonel's wishes, the old man would have died of frustration at having his wishes ignored. They had parted good friends, and on the mutual understanding that if and when Mr Tait-Bullen had a few hours of leisure he would pay another visit as a friend.

Something he intended to do, for he wanted to see Claudia again.

He went straight to the hospital when he reached London; he had an afternoon clinic which lasted longer than usual. He had no lunch, merely swallowed a cup of tea between patients. It was with a sigh of relief that he stopped the car outside his front door in a small tree-lined street tucked away behind Harley Street, where he had his consulting rooms.

It was a narrow Regency house in a row of similar houses, three storeys high with bow windows and a beautiful front door with a handsome pediment, reached by three steps bordered by delicate iron railings. He let himself in quietly and was met in the hall by a middle-aged man with a craggy face and a fringe of hair. He looked like a dignified church warden, and ran Mr Tait-Bullen's house to perfection. He greeted him now with a touch of severity.

'There's that Miss Thompson on the phone, reminding you that she expects to see you this evening. I told her that you were still at the hospital and there was no knowing when you'd be home.' Cork lowered his eyes deferentially. 'I trust I did right, sir.'

Mr Tait-Bullen was looking through the post on the hall table. 'You did exactly right, Cork. I don't know what I would do without you.' He glanced up. 'Did I say I would take her somewhere this evening? It has quite slipped my mind.'

Cork drew a deep breath through pinched nostrils. In anyone less dignified it would have been a sniff. 'You were invited to attend the new play. The opening night, I believe.'

'Did I say I'd go? I can't remember writing it down in my diary.'

'You prevaricated, sir. Said if you were free you'd be glad to accept.'

Mr Tait-Bullen picked up his case and opened his study door. 'I'm not free, Cork, and I'm famished!'

'Dinner will be served in fifteen minutes, sir. The young lady's phone number is on your desk.'

Mr Tait-Bullen sat down at his desk and picked up the receiver. Honor Thompson's rather shrill voice, sounding peevish, answered.

'And about time, too. Why are you never at home? It's so late; I'll go on to the theatre and meet you there. The Pickerings are picking me up in ten minutes.'

Mr Tait-Bullen said smoothly, 'Honor, I'm so sorry, but there is absolutely no chance of me getting away until late this evening. I did tell you that I might not be free; will you make my excuses to the Pickerings?'

They talked for a few minutes, until she said, 'Oh, well, you're not much use as an escort, are you, Thomas?' She gave a little laugh. 'I might as well give you up.'

'There must be any number of men queueing up to take you out. I'm not reliable, Honor.'

'You'll end up a crusty old bachelor, Thomas, unless you take time off to fall in love.'

'I'll have to think about that.'

'Well, let me know when you've made up your mind.' She rang off, and he put the phone down and forgot all about her. He had a teaching round the next morning and he needed to prepare a few notes for that.

He ate the dinner Cork set before him and went back to his study to work. He was going to his bed when he had a sudden memory of Claudia, her fiery hair in a mess, enveloped in that old jacket and a sack. He found himself smiling, thinking of her.

The first few days of November, with their frosty mornings and chilly pale skies, had turned dull and damp, and as they faded towards winter Great-Uncle William faded with them. But although he was physically weaker there was nothing weak about his mental state. He was as peppery as he always had been, defying anyone to show sympathy towards him, demanding that Claudia should read *The Times* to him each morning, never mind that he dozed off every now and then.

His faithful housekeeper's endless efforts to prepare tasty morsels for his meals met with no success at all. And no amount of coaxing would persuade him to allow a nurse to attend to his wants. Between them, Claudia, her mother and Tombs did as much as he would allow them to. Dr Willis, inured to his patient's caustic tongue, came daily, but it was less than a week after Mr Tait-Bullen's visit when Great-Uncle William, glaring at him from his bed, observed in an echo of his former commanding tones, 'I shall die within the next day or so. Tell Tait-Bullen to come and see me.'

'He's a busy man...'

'I know that; I'm not a fool.' The Colonel looked suddenly exhausted. 'He said that he would come.' He turned his head to look at Claudia, standing at the window, lingering after she had brought Dr Willis upstairs.

'You—Claudia, go and telephone him. Now, girl!'

She glanced at Dr Willis, and at his nod went down to the hall and dialled Mr Tait-Bullen's number. Cork's dignified voice regretted that Mr Tait-Bullen was not at home.

'It's urgent. Do you know where I can get him?' She added, so as to make things clear, 'I'm not a friend or anything. My great-uncle is a patient of Mr Tait-Bullen's and he wants to see him. He's very ill.'

'In that case, miss, I will give you the number of his consulting rooms.'

She thanked him and dialled again, and this time Mrs Truelove, Mr Tait-Bullen's receptionist, answered.

'Colonel Ramsay? You are his niece? Mr Tait-Bullen has mentioned him. He's with a patient at the moment. Ring off, my dear; I'll call you the moment he's free.'

Claudia waited, wondering if Mr Tait-Bullen would have time to visit Great-Uncle William or even to phone him. She supposed that he was a very busy man; he could hardly be blamed if he hadn't the time to leave London and his patients to obey the whim of an old man who had refused his services. Then the phone rang, and she picked it up.

'Yes,' said a voice in her ear. 'Tait-Bullen speaking.'

This was no time for polite chit-chat. 'Great-Uncle William wants to see you. He says he's going to die in a day or two. He told me to phone you, so I am, because he asked me to, but you don't have to.'

She wasn't sure if she had made herself clear, but apparently she had. Mr Tait-Bullen disentangled the muddle with a twitching lip and answered her with exactly the right amount of impersonal friendliness.

'It is very possible that your great-uncle is quite right. I'm free this evening; I will be with you at about seven o'clock.'

He heard her relieved sigh.

'Thank you very much. I'm sorry if I've disturbed your work.'

'I'm glad you phoned me.'

She could hear the faint impatience in his voice. 'Goodbye, then.' She rang off smartly, and then wondered if she'd been rather too abrupt.

He arrived punctually, unfussed and unhurried. No one looking at his immaculate person would have guessed that he had been up since six o'clock, had missed his lunch and stopped only for the tea and bun his faithful Mrs Truelove had pressed upon him. Dr Willis was waiting for him, and they spent a few minutes talking together before they went up to the Colonel's room. Dr Willis came down presently. 'They're discussing the merits of pyrenaicum aureum as opposed to tenuifolium pumilum...'

Mrs Ramsay looked puzzled. 'Is that some new symptom? It sounds alarming. Poor Uncle William.'

'Lilies,' said Claudia. 'Two varieties of lily, Mother.'

Dr Willis patted her mother's arm. 'Don't alarm yourself, my dear. Your uncle is enjoying his little chat. It was good of Mr Tait-Bullen to come.'

'But he's not doing anything to help Uncle…'

But that was exactly what he *was* doing, reflected Claudia, although she didn't say so. Instead she asked, 'Do you suppose he will stay for supper? Mrs Pratt can grill a couple more chops.'

But when he joined them presently, he declined Mrs Ramsay's offer of supper, saying that he must return to London.

'I hope we haven't spoilt your evening for you—caused you to cancel a date?'

Claudia noticed that he didn't answer that, merely thanked her mother for her invitation. 'If I might have a word with Dr Willis?'

They left the two men, returning when they heard them in the hall.

Mrs. Ramsay shook hands. 'We're so grateful to you. Uncle did so wish to see you again—although I'm sure you are a very busy man.'

He said gravely, 'The Colonel is going to die very soon now, Mrs Ramsay; he is content, and in no pain, and in Dr Willis's good hands.'

He turned to Claudia. 'I was bidden to tell you to read the editorial in *The Times* before he has his supper.' His hand was firm and cool and comforting. 'He's fond of you, you know.'

He left then, getting into his car and driving back to his house to eat the meal Cork had ready for him and then go to his study and concentrate on the notes of the patients upon whom he would be operating in the morning. Before that, he paused to think about the Colonel. A courageous old man hidden behind that crusty manner. He hoped that he would die quietly in his sleep.

Great-Uncle William died while Claudia was still reading the editorial. So quietly and peacefully that it wasn't until she had finished it that she realised.

She said softly, 'You had a happy talk about lilies, didn't you, Uncle William? I'm glad he came.'

She bent to kiss the craggy old face and went downstairs to tell her mother.

CHAPTER TWO

THE Colonel had been respected in the village; he had had no use for a social life or mere acquaintances, although he had lifelong friends.

Claudia had very little time to grieve. Her mother saw the callers when they came, arranged things with the undertaker and planned the flowers and the gathering of friends and family after the funeral, but it was left to Claudia to carry out her wishes, answer the telephone and make a tidy pile of the letters which would have to be answered later.

Dr Willis was a tower of strength, of course, but he was more concerned with her mother than anything else, and Mrs Ramsay leaned on him heavily for comfort and support. She needed both when, on the day before the funeral, the cousin who was to inherit the house arrived.

He was a middle-aged man, with austere good looks and cold eyes. He treated them with cool courtesy, expressed a token regret at the death of the Colonel and went away to see the colonel's solicitor. When he returned he requested that Mrs Ramsay and Claudia should join him in the morning room.

He stood with his back to the fire and begged them to sit down. Already master of the house, thought Claudia, and wondered what was coming.

He spoke loudly, as though he thought that they were deaf. 'Everything seems to be in order. The will is not yet read, of course, but I gather that there are no surprises in it. I must return to York after the funeral, but I intend to return within two or three days. Monica—my wife—will accompany me and we will take up residence then. My house there is already on the market. You will, of course, wish to leave here as soon as possible.'

Claudia heard her mother's quick breath. 'Are you interested as to where we are going?'

'It is hardly my concern.' He eyed Claudia coldly. 'You must have been aware for some time that the house would become my property and have some plans of your own.'

'Well,' said Claudia slowly, 'whatever plans we may have had didn't include being thrown out lock, stock and barrel at a moment's notice.' When he started to speak, she added, 'No, let me finish. Let us know when you and your wife will arrive and we will be gone in good time. What about Tombs and Mrs Pratt and Jennie? I understand that they have been remembered in Uncle William's will.'

'I shall, of course, give them a month's wages.' He considered the matter for a moment. 'It might be convenient if Mrs Pratt remained, and the girl. It will save Monica a good deal of trouble if the servants remain.'

'And Tombs?'

'Oh! He's past an honest day's work. He will have his state pension.'

'Have you any children?'

He looked surprised. 'No. Why do you ask?'

She didn't answer that, merely said in a matter-of-fact voice, 'Well, that's a blessing, isn't it?' Then she added, 'I'm glad you're only a distant cousin.'

He said loftily, 'I cannot understand you...'

'Well, of course you can't. But never mind that. Is that all? We'll see you at dinner presently.'

She saw him go red in the face as she got up and urged her mother out of the room.

In the hall, her mother said, 'Darling, you were awfully rude.'

'Mother, he's going to throw Tombs out, not to mention us. He's the most awful man I've ever met. And I'm sure Mrs Pratt and Jennie won't want to stay. I'm going to see them now.'

She gave her mother a reassuring pat on the shoulder. 'Why don't you go and phone Dr Willis and see what he says?'

Over a mug of powerfully brewed tea, she told Tombs and Mrs Pratt and Jennie what her cousin had said. They listened in growing unrest.

'You'll not catch me staying with the likes of him,' said Mrs Pratt. She looked at Jennie. 'And what about you, Jennie, girl?'

'Me neither.' They both looked at Tombs.

Claudia hadn't repeated all her cousin had said about Tombs, but he had read between the lines.

'I'll never get another place at my age,' he told them. 'But I wouldn't stay for all the tea in China.'

He turned a worried old face towards Claudia. 'Where will you and madam go, Miss Claudia? It's a scandal, turning you out of house and home.'

'We'll think of something, Tombs. We've several days to plan something.'

'And Rob?'

'He'll come with us. I don't know about Stokes…'

'I'll see that he gives in his notice,' said Tombs. 'What a mercy that the Colonel isn't here; he would never have allowed these goings on.'

'No, but you see this cousin of his has every right to do what he likes. If you intend to leave when we do, have you somewhere to go? Mother's on the phone to Dr Willis, who may be able to help. If not then we will all put up at the Duck and Thistle in the village.'

'I could go home,' ventured Jennie. 'Me mum'll give me a bed for a bit.' She sounded doubtful, and Claudia said, 'Well, perhaps Dr Willis will know of someone local who needs help in the house. I think we'd all better start packing our things as soon as the funeral is over.'

She found her mother in the morning room. It was cold there, for the fire hadn't been lighted, and Mrs Ramsay was walking up and down in a flurried way.

'Mother, it's too cold for you here, and you're upset.'

'No, dear, there's nothing wrong—in fact quite the reverse. Only I'm not sure how to talk to you about it.'

Claudia sat her parent down on the sofa and settled beside her.

'You talked to Dr Willis? He had some suggestions? Some advice?'

'Well, yes...'

'Mother, dear, does he want to marry you? I know you're fond of each other...'

'Oh, yes we are, love, but how can I possibly marry him and leave you and the others in the lurch? At least...'

'Yes?' Claudia had taken her mother's hand. 'Do tell. I'm sure it's something helpful. He's such a dear; I'll love having him for a stepfather.'

Mrs Ramsay gave a shaky little laugh. 'Oh, darling, will you really? But I haven't said I'd marry him.'

'But you will. Now, what else does he suggest?'

'Well, it's coincidental, but his housekeeper has given him notice—wants to go back to her family somewhere in Lancashire—so Mrs Pratt could take over if she would like the job. And he knows everyone here, doesn't he? He says it should be easy to find a place for Jennie.'

'And Tombs?'

'George said he's always wanted a butler. His house is quite small, but there would be plenty for Tombs to do. And he'd love to have Rob... Only there's you, darling.'

'But, Mother dear, I'll be getting a job. I've already applied for several, you know, and none of them are too far from here. I can come for holidays and weekends, if George will have me.'

'You're not just saying that to make it easy for the rest of us?'

'Of course not. You know that was the plan, wasn't it? That I should come here for a week or two while I looked for something nearer than London?'

She didn't mention that she had had two answers that morning from her applications, and both posts had been filled. There was still another one to come...

'Well, Claudia, if you think that's the right thing to do. We shall go and tell Tombs and the others.'

'Yes, but no one had better say a word to Mr Ramsay. When do you see Dr Willis—no, I shall call him George if he doesn't mind?'

'After the funeral. He thought it best not to come here.'

'Quite right too. We don't want Cousin Ramsay smelling a rat. Mother, you go to the kitchen; I'll hang around the house in case he comes looking for us.'

Later at dinner, Mr Ramsay made no mention of their plans; he had a good deal to say about the various alterations he intended making in the house. Monica, he told them, was a woman of excellent taste. She would have the shabby upholstery covered and the thick velvet curtains in the drawing room and dining room torn down and replaced by something more up-to-date.

'The curtains were chosen by Great-Uncle William's mother,' observed Mrs Ramsay, 'when she came here as a bride.'

'Then it's high time that they were removed. They are probably full of dust and germs.'

'Most unlikely,' said Claudia quickly. 'Everything in the house has been beautifully cared for.'

He gave her an annoyed look. He didn't like this girl, with the fiery hair and the too ready tongue. He decided not to answer her, but instead addressed Mrs Ramsay with some query about the following day.

It was after the last of the Colonel's friends and acquaintances had taken their leave, after returning to the house for tea and Mrs Pratt's delicious sandwiches and cakes, that Mr Potter, the Colonel's solicitor, led the way across the hall to the morning room. He had been a friend of the family for years, and his feelings had been hurt when Mr Ramsay had told him that he would no longer require his services.

His father and his father before him had looked after the Ramsays' modest estate, but he was old himself and he supposed that Mr Ramsay's own lawyer would be perfectly capable. He said now, 'If someone would ask Tombs and Mrs Pratt and Jennie to come in here.' He beamed across at Dr Willis. 'I had already asked you to be present, George.'

He took no notice of Mr Ramsay's frown, but waited patiently until everyone was there.

The will was simple and short. The house and estate were to go to Cousin Ramsay, and afterwards to his heirs. Mrs Ramsay was to receive shares in a company, sufficient to maintain her lifestyle, and Claudia was to receive the same amount, but neither of them could use the capital. Tombs received five thousand pounds, Mrs Pratt the same amount, and Jennie one thousand pounds. Claudia heard Cousin Ramsay draw in a disapproving breath at that.

Mr Potter put the will back in his briefcase and said, suddenly grave, 'If I might have a word with you, Mrs Ramsay, and Claudia, and you, Mr Ramsay?'

When the others had gone, he said, 'I am afraid that I have bad news for you; the company in which the shares were invested and destined for you Mrs Ramsay, and you, Claudia, has gone bankrupt. I ascertained this the day before the Colonel died, and I intended to visit him on that very day. There is nothing to be done about the terms of the will, but perhaps you, Mr Ramsay, will wish to make some adjustment so that Mrs Ramsay and Claudia are not left penniless.'

He saw no sign of encouragement in Mr Ramsay's stern features. Nevertheless he persisted. 'Their incomes would have been small, but adequate. I can advise you as to the amount they would have been. One wouldn't expect you to make good the full amount, but I'm sure that a small allowance for each of them...' His voice faded away under Mr Ramsay's icy stare.

Claudia saw the painful colour in her mother's face. 'That is very thoughtful of you, Mr Potter, but I think that neither mother nor I would wish to accept anything from Mr Ramsay.'

Mr Ramsay looked above their heads and cleared his throat. 'I have many commitments,' he observed. 'Any such arrangement would be quite beyond my means.'

Mr Potter opened his mouth to protest, but Claudia caught his eye and shook her head. And, although the old man looked bewildered, he closed it again.

It was Mrs Ramsay who said, in a voice which gave away

none of her feelings, 'You'll stay for supper, Mr Potter? I remember Uncle William promised you that little painting on the stairs, which you always admired. Will you fetch it, Claudia?'

She smiled at Mr. Ramsay. 'It is of no value, and one must keep one's promises, must one not?'

Mr Potter refused supper and, clutching the picture, was escorted to his car by Claudia. 'It is all most unsatisfactory,' he told her. 'Your great-uncle would never have allowed it to happen. How will you manage? Surely even a small allowance—'

Claudia popped him into the car and kissed his cheek. 'I'll tell you a secret. Mother is going to marry Dr Willis and I've my eye on a good job. We haven't told Mr Ramsay and we don't intend to. And Tombs and Mrs Pratt and Jennie are all fixed up. So don't worry about us.'

He cheered up then. 'In that case I feel very relieved. You will keep in touch?'

'Of course.'

She waved and smiled as he drove off, then went back into the house. Despite her cheerful words she would hate leaving the old house, although she told herself sensibly that she would have hated staying on there with Mr Ramsay and his wife, who would doubtless alter the whole place so much that she would never recognise it again.

Later, in her mother's bedroom she said, 'You'll have to marry George now, because I told Mr Potter you were going to.'

'But, Claudia, there's nothing arranged...'

'Then arrange it, Mother dear, as quickly as you can. There's something called a special licence, and the vicar's an old friend. Now, what's to happen when we leave? Is George giving us beds, or shall we go to the Duck and Thistle?'

'George wants me to go and see him tomorrow morning. I think he has something planned. Will you stay here, in case Mr Ramsay wants to talk to us about something?'

'Not likely. But I'll be here. Take Rob with you, Mother; *he* doesn't like dogs.'

Mr Ramsay spent the next morning going from room to

room, taking careful note of his new possessions. The kitchen and its occupants he ignored; they could be dealt with when he was satisfied with his arrangements. He kept Claudia busy answering his questions about the furniture and pictures, all of which he valued.

'We shall sell a good deal,' he told her loftily. 'There are several pieces which I think may be of real value. But these...' He waved an arm at a pair of Regency terrestrial and celestial globes in one corner of the morning room. 'I doubt if they'd fetch more than a few pounds in a junk shop.'

Claudia, who happened to know that they were worth in the region of twenty thousand pounds and had been in the family for well over a hundred years, agreed politely.

'And this clock—Monica has no liking for such old-fashioned stuff; that can go.' He pointed to a William the Fourth bracket clock, very plain and worth at least two thousand pounds.

He brushed aside a stool. 'And there are all these around. I have never seen such a collection of out-of-date furniture.'

The stool was early Victorian, covered with petit-point tapestry. Claudia didn't mention its value, instead she said politely, 'There is a very good firm at Ringwood, I believe—a branch of one of the London antiques dealers. But I expect that you would prefer to go to someone you know in York.'

'Certainly not. I am more likely to get good prices from a firm which has some knowledge of this area.'

Claudia cast down her eyes and murmured. If and when he sold Great-Uncle William's family treasures, and she could find out who had bought them, she might be able to buy one or two of them back. She had no idea how she would do this, but that was something she would worry about later.

She knew the elder son of the antiques dealer at Ringwood; he might let her buy things back with instalments. Which reminded her of the letter she had stuffed in her pocket that morning. The post mark was Southampton, and it was the last reply from the batch of applications she had sent. Perhaps she would be lucky...

She was roused from her thoughts by Mr Ramsay's sharp, 'Where is your mother?'

She looked at him for a moment before replying. She wondered if she dared to tell him to mind his own business, but decided against it.

'Well, she will have gone upstairs to check the linen cupboard with Mrs Pratt—a long job—then she told me that she would be taking Rob for his walk and doing some necessary shopping in the village. She should be back by lunchtime. I don't know what she will be doing this afternoon.'

He gave her a suspicious glance. 'I wish to inform her of my final plans for moving here.'

'Well, I am going to the kitchen now to see about lunch.'

But first she went into the hall and out of the side door at its end, taking an old coat off a hook as she went and making for the glass house.

The letter was a reply to her application for the post of general helper at a geriatric hospital on the outskirts of Southampton. She had applied for it for the simple reason that there had been nothing else advertised, and she hadn't expected a reply.

Providing that her references were satisfactory, the job was hers. Her duties were vague, and the money was less than she had hoped for, but on the other hand she could start as soon as her references had been checked. It would solve the problem of her immediate future, set her mother's mind at rest and put a little money into her pocket.

She didn't see her mother until the three of them were sitting down to lunch, but she deduced from the faintly smug look on that lady's face that her talk with Dr Willis had been entirely satisfactory. It wasn't until they left the house together to take Rob for another walk that they were able to talk.

'When's the wedding?' asked Claudia as soon as they had left the house.

Her mother laughed. 'Darling, I'm not sure. I won't marry George until you're settled...'

'Then he'd better get a licence as soon as he can. I've got a job—in Southampton at one of the hospitals. I had the letter this morning.'

Mrs Ramsay beamed at her. 'Oh, Claudia, really? I mean, it's something you want to do, not just any old job you're taking to make things easy for us?'

To tell a lie was sometimes necessary, reflected Claudia, if it was to a good purpose, and surely this was. 'It's exactly what I'm looking for—quite good money and I can come back here for weekends and holidays, if George will have me?'

'Of course we'll have you.' Her mother squeezed her arm. 'Isn't it strange how everything is coming right despite Uncle William's horrid cousin? And George has found a place for Jennie—they were looking for someone up at the Manor, so she will still keep her friends in the village and see Mrs Pratt and Tombs if she wants to.'

'Good. Now, when will you marry?'

'Well, as soon as George can get a licence.'

'You'll stay with him, of course?'

'Mrs Pratt and Tombs will be with me.'

'Mr Ramsay wants to talk to you about his plans. He didn't say anything at lunch...'

'Perhaps this evening.'

He was waiting for them when they got back. 'Be good enough to come to my study?' he asked Mrs Ramsay. 'I dare say Claudia has things to do.'

Dismissed, she went to her room; there were clothes to pack and small, treasured ornaments she had been given since childhood to be wrapped and stowed in boxes. As soon as Mr Ramsay went back to York Dr Willis would come and load up his car and stow everything they didn't want in his attics.

She hoped that the new owner of the house would stay away for several days, for they all intended to be gone, the house empty of people, by the time he and his wife arrived. He had said nothing to Tombs or Mrs Pratt, nor to Jennie; perhaps he expected them to stay on until he saw fit to discharge Tombs. He was arrogant enough to suppose that Mrs Pratt and Jennie would be only too thankful to remain in his service.

Since it was teatime, she went downstairs and found her
mother in the morning room. There was no sign of Mr Ramsay,
and at her questioning look Mrs Ramsay said, 'He's gone to
see the vicar. He's going to York tomorrow afternoon and returning with Monica in two days' time. I am to tell Mrs Pratt
and Jennie that they are to stay on in his employment—he
hasn't bothered to ask them if they want to—and I'm to dismiss
Tombs.'

'Why doesn't he do his own dirty work?' demanded Claudia.
'What else?'

'He avoided asking me where you and I were going; he made
some remark about us having friends and he was sure we had
sufficient funds to tide us over until we had settled somewhere.'

'Mother, he's despicable. Does he know about you and
George?'

'No, I'm sure he doesn't, for he made a great thing of offering to send on our belongings once we had left.'

'Have you had a chance to tell Tombs?'

'No, I'd better go now; if he comes back, come and let me
know.'

Not a word was said about their departure during dinner, and
the following day Mr Ramsay got into his car and drove himself
back to York.

'You may, of course, remain until the day following our return,' he told Mrs Ramsay. 'Monica will wish to be shown
round the house.' He looked over her head, avoiding her eyes.
'Kindly see that Tombs has gone by the time we return.'

He turned back at the door. 'It will probably be late afternoon
by the time we get here. Tell Mrs Pratt to have a meal ready
and see that the maid has the rooms warm.'

Mrs Ramsay lowered her eyes and said, 'Yes,' meekly. She
looked very like her daughter. 'I'm sure that if you think of
anything else you will phone as soon as you get home.'

They waited a prudent hour before starting on their packing
up. He was, observed Claudia, the kind of man who would
sneak back to make sure that they weren't making off with the
spoons. They collected their belongings, taking only what was

theirs, and presently, when Dr Willis drove up, loaded his car. Mr Ramsay had said two days before he returned, but to be on the safe side they had decided to move out on the following day.

Dr Willis would have taken them all to his house for supper, but they refused and, while Mrs Pratt got a meal for them, began on the business of leaving the house in perfect condition. Tombs was set to polish the silver, Jennie saw to the bedrooms, and Claudia and her mother hoovered and dusted downstairs. After supper, tired but happy, they all went to bed.

They were up early in the morning, making sure that there was nothing with which the new owner could find fault, and as soon as the morning surgery was over Dr Willis came to fetch them to his house. He had to make two journeys, and Claudia left last of all, wheeling her bike and leading Rob on his lead. Mr Ramsay had a key—he had taken care to have all of the keys in his possession—but she had a key to the garden door which she had kept. She wasn't sure why and she didn't intend to tell anyone.

Dr Willis's housekeeper had already left, and Mrs Pratt slipped into the kitchen as though she had been there all her life, taking Tombs and Jennie with her.

'There are an awful lot of us,' worried Mrs Ramsay as they ate the lunch the unflappable Mrs Pratt had produced.

'The house is large enough, my dear, and Jennie goes to her new job tomorrow.'

'And I go to mine in a day or two,' said Claudia.

'You're quite happy about it?' he asked her kindly. 'There's no hurry, you know.'

'It sounds just what I'm looking for. When will you marry? I'd like to come to the wedding.'

'Darling, we wouldn't dream of getting married unless you were there.'

'Within the week, I hope,' said George. 'Very quiet, of course, just us and a few friends here at the church. I've put a notice in the *Telegraph*.'

Everyone in the village knew by now that there was a new

owner at Colonel Ramsay's house. Those that had met him didn't like him overmuch. The postman, who had been spoken to sharply by Mr Ramsay because he whistled too loudly as he delivered the letters and had been discovered drinking tea in the kitchen, had promised that any letters would be delivered to the doctor's house. The village considered Mr Ramsay an outsider, for he had made no effort to be pleasant. Even the vicar, a mild and godly man, pursed his lips when his name was mentioned.

There was a letter for Claudia the next morning. Her references had been accepted for the post of general assistant and she should present herself without delay to take up her duties. The list enclosed was vague about these, but the off duty seemed fair enough. She was to have two days a week free and the money was adequate. There was accommodation for her within the hospital.

She wrote back at once, accepting the post, and saying that she would present herself for duty in the early evening of the following day. Feeling pleased that things were turning out so well, she went away to unpack and repack what she would need to take with her.

Dr Willis drove her to Southampton after lunch the following day, and that same afternoon, as dusk was gathering, Mr Ramsay came back to take possession of his new home. An arrogant man, and insensitive to other people's feelings, he had taken it for granted that he would be received suitably—the house lighted and warm, a meal waiting to be put on the table, Mrs Ramsay there to show his wife round, Jennie to see to the luggage. He got out of the car and surveyed the dark, silent house with a frown before unlocking the door.

It was obvious that there was no one there. Monica pushed past him, switched on the lights and looked around her. She saw the letter on the side table and opened it. Mrs Ramsay wrote politely that as Mr Ramsay had requested they had left the house. And, since neither Mrs Pratt or Jennie wished to work for him, they had also left. There was food in the fridge, the fires were laid ready to light and the beds were aired and made up.

Monica laughed. 'You told them you wanted them out, and they've gone. I wonder where they went?'

'It's of no consequence. We can get help from the village easily enough, and I had nothing in common with either Mrs Ramsay or that daughter of hers.'

'A pity about the servants...'

'Easily come by in a small place like this—they'll be only too glad to have the work.'

'There was a butler, you said.'

'Oh, he was too old to work. I dare say he has found himself a room or gone to live with someone. He'd have his pension.'

His wife gave him a long look. 'You're a heartless man, aren't you? You'd better bring in the luggage while I find the kitchen and see what there is to eat.'

Dr Willis left Claudia at the door of the hospital with some reluctance. The place looked gloomy and down at heel, and he was sorry that he hadn't found out about it before. True, geriatric hospitals were usually the last ones to get face lifts— probably inside it was bright and cheerful enough, and she had wished him goodbye very happily, with the promise that she would be at the wedding. She poked her head through the open window of the car.

'I know that you and Mother will be happy. You really are a very nice man, George.'

She picked up her case and went into the hospital.

She knew she wasn't going to like it before she had gone ten yards from the door, but she ignored that. A tired-looking porter asked her what she wanted, told her to leave her case and follow him and led her down a long passage. He knocked on the door at the end of it. The label on the door said 'Hospital Manager,' and when the porter opened the door in answer to the voice inside, she went past him into a small austere room.

It was furnished sparsely, with a desk and chair, two other chairs along one wall, and a great many shelves stuffed with paper files. The woman behind the desk had a narrow, pale face, a straight haircut in an unbecoming bob and small dark eyes. She looked up as Claudia went in, pursing her mouth and frowning a little.

'Miss Ramsay? It's too late for you to do much for the rest of the day. I'll get someone to show you your room and take you to where you will be working. But if you will draw up a chair I will explain your schedule to you.'

Not a very good start, reflected Claudia, but perhaps the poor soul was tired.

Her duties were many and varied and rather vague. She would work from seven o'clock until three in the afternoon three days a week, and her free day would follow that duty, and for the other three days the hours would be three o'clock in the afternoon until ten o'clock at night.

'The off duty is arranged so that you are free from three o'clock before your day off, and not on duty until three o'clock on the day following.'

Two nights at home, thought Claudia, and felt cheered by the thought.

She asked politely, 'Am I to call you Matron?'

'Miss Norton,' she was told, in a manner which implied that she should have known that without being told. She was dismissed into the care of a small woman with a kind face and a bright smile, who told her that her name was Nurse Symes.

'You're on duty in the morning,' she told her. 'Ward B—that's on the other wing. First floor, thirty beds. Sister Clark is in charge there.'

She paused, and Claudia said encouragingly, 'And...?'

'She's terribly overworked, you know—we can't get the staff. She doesn't mean half she says.'

'Tell me, what exactly do I do? General assistant covers a lot of ground, and Miss Norton was a bit vague.'

'Well, dear, there aren't many trained nurses, so you do anything that's needed.'

They got into the lift at the back of the hall and stepped out

on the top floor, went through a door with 'Private' on it and
started down another corridor lined with doors.

'Here we are,' said Nurse Symes. 'Quite a nice room, and
the bathrooms are at the end. There's a little kitchen too, if you
want to make tea.'

The room was small, with a bed, a small easy chair, a bedside
table and a clothes cupboard. It was very clean and there was
a view of chimneypots from its window. There was a washbasin
on one corner, and a small mirror over the wide shelf which
served as a dressing table. A few cushions and photos and a
vase of flowers, thought Claudia with resolute cheerfulness, and
it would be quite pretty.

'We'll go to the linen room and get you some dresses. You'll
get three, but of course you'll wear a plastic apron when you're
on duty.'

The dresses—a useful mud-brown—duly chosen and taken
to her room, they began a tour of the hospital. It was surpris-
ingly large, with old-fashioned wards with beds on either side
and tables with pot plants down the centre. The wards were
full, and most of the patients were sitting in chairs by their
beds, watching television if they were near enough to the two
sets at either end of the wards.

Most of them appeared to be asleep; one or two had visitors.
Claudia could see only one or two nurses, but there were several
young women shrouded in plastic pinnys, carrying trays, mops
and buckets and helping those patients who chose to trundle
around with their walking aids.

It wasn't quite what she had expected, but it was too early
to have an opinion, and first impressions weren't always the
right ones.

It was Cork who folded the *Telegraph* at the appropriate page
and silently pointed out the notice of the forthcoming marriage
between George Willis and Doreen Ramsay to Professor Tait-
Bullen as he ate his breakfast.

He read it in an absent-minded fashion, and then read it
again.

'Interesting,' he observed, and then, 'I wonder what will happen to the daughter? Staying on at the Colonel's house, I suppose.'

He thought no more about it until that evening when, urged by some niggling doubt at the back of his mind, he phoned Dr Willis. His congratulations were sincere. 'You will be marrying shortly?'

'In four days' time. Mrs Ramsay is here with me, so are Mrs Pratt and Tombs. Jennie, their maid, went to the Manor to a new job this morning.' George added drily, 'They were turned out by the new owner.'

The professor asked sharply, 'And the daughter—Claudia?'

'Fortunately she found a job at Southampton, in a hospital there—geriatrics. Didn't like the look of the place, but they wanted someone at once.'

'You mean to tell me that this man turned them all out? Is he no relation?'

'A cousin of sorts.'

'Extraordinary.' The professor had a fleeting memory of a lovely girl with red hair and decided that he wanted to know more. 'I'm going to Bristol in a couple of days. May I call in and wish you both well?'

'We'd be delighted. And if you can come to the wedding we should very much like that.'

Mr Tait-Bullen put down the receiver and sat back in his chair. With a little careful planning there was no reason why he shouldn't go to the wedding.

CHAPTER THREE

By THE end of her first day at the hospital Claudia knew exactly what a general assistant was: a maker of beds, carrier of trays, bedpans, and bags of bed linen. And when she wasn't doing this she was getting the old and infirm in and out of bed, finding slippers, spectacles, dentures, feeding those who were no longer able to help themselves and trotting the more spry of the ladies to the loo.

It was non-stop work, and, going off duty soon after three o'clock, she was thankful that she was free until seven o'clock the next morning and that by some miracle she would have her day off on the day following that. The whole day, she thoughtful joyfully, and not on duty until the afternoon after that. She got into her outdoor clothes and hurried out to the nearest phone box.

Her mother and George were to be married in three days' time; she would be able to go to the wedding, although she would have to leave Little Planting directly after the ceremony. The bus service between Romsey and Southampton was frequent; it was just a question of getting from Romsey to Little Planting and back again.

She would be met, declared her mother; any of their friends in the village would be glad to collect her. 'Phone me tomorrow and let me know what time the bus gets to Romsey. And don't worry about getting back to Southampton, there'll be someone to give you a lift. You're happy there, Claudia?'

'Yes,' said Claudia, 'I'm sure I shall be happy.' She was so convincing that her mother observed happily to George that Claudia sounded perfectly content, and wasn't it lucky that she should be free for the wedding?

Claudia went back to the hospital and had a cup of tea with some of the other girls, then went to her room, kicked off her shoes and curled up on the bed. Her feet ached and she was tired. It had been a hard day's work, but it wasn't only that; she felt sad and lonely and uncertain of the future. She was prepared to stay in this job for as long as it took to save enough money for her to train in something which would allow her more freedom. Enough money for her to have nice clothes, and a holiday. A career girl.

It would have to be something to do with computers, shorthand and typing and a knowledge of the business world. A receptionist, mused Claudia, a nine-to-five job with free weekends so that she could go and stay with her mother and George from time to time. And, of course, a nicely furnished flat, and friends to entertain and to be entertained by. She might even meet a man who would fall in love with her and marry her...

Mr Tait-Bullen's handsome features imposed themselves upon her wishful thinking, but she brushed them away. One didn't cry for the moon, and she was never likely to meet him again. Even if she did, she wasn't sure if he had noticed her as a woman. She wondered what he was really like behind that impersonal, impassive face. Probably quite nice...

A thump on the door brought her back to reality, and when she called, 'Come in,' a girl opened the door. One of those on the afternoon shift.

'Oh, good, you're here. The other two are out and Sister sent me. Mrs Legge—that's the one with the Zimmer walker—fell over and she's broken a leg and an arm. She'll have to go to the City General with a nurse, and that only leaves Sister and me and we're up to our eyes. Could you come back on duty for an hour or two, just until someone can be found to take over?'

Claudia crammed her feet back into her shoes. It would be, after all, a way of passing the empty evening.

She stayed on the ward for more than two hours, and was sent off at last with the promise of extra time off when it was convenient. She ate supper with several of the other girls, watched television for half an hour and then went to bed. She was too tired to think much. Someone had to look after those old ladies…she would be an old lady herself one day, but hopefully loved and cherished by a husband. Someone like Mr Tait-Bullen, she decided, half asleep.

By the end of the following day she had realised that—never mind what Miss Norton had told her—the off duty was very much in the hands of the ward sister. It was possible, one of the other assistants told her, to have five days in a row of seven o'clock duty, or several days of afternoon shift with no more than an hour or two's notice.

So she wasn't altogether surprised when she was told that she would have an afternoon shift before her day off. That meant she wouldn't be able to go home until the following morning. Still, that would give her all the day before the wedding, and she had already told her mother that she would have to leave directly after the ceremony. She caught the first bus in the morning, after phoning her mother, and found Tombs waiting for her at Romsey. He was driving the doctor's car—a battered old Ford, long ago pensioned off in one corner of the garage, but used in emergencies. It wasn't a long drive, and Tombs filled it with gossip about Mrs Ramsay, the wedding and how well they had settled in at the doctor's house. Indeed, he seemed to have shed several years; Claudia hadn't seen him as happy for some time, and she was glad of that; she had known him all her life and he was part of it. They talked about the wedding at some length, and he said, 'It is a great pity that you have to return so soon, Miss Claudia. Mrs Ramsay tells me that you have a very good job.'

She enlarged upon that, drawing upon her imagination rather more than was truthful, and was rewarded by his satisfied, 'We all want you to be happy, Miss Claudia.'

At the doctor's house she was greeted by her mother and borne away to inspect the wedding hat, give her opinion of the outfit to go with it and listen while her parent told her of the plans for the wedding.

'Very quiet, of course, but that's how we want it. George can't get away for a week or two, but then we're going down to Cornwall. He has a cottage at St Anthony—that's a bit further on from Falmouth. But we'll be back for Christmas, of course. Will you be able to come home?'

'I don't know, Mother. The off duty is made out a week or two at a time, and it has to be altered from time to time. I'll certainly do my best.'

Christmas was still five weeks or more away; anything could happen...

The wedding was to be at eleven o'clock in the morning. A fellow doctor had come over from a neighbouring village to keep an eye on the practice until the evening, and Mrs Pratt had arranged luncheon for the few friends who had been invited. Tombs, to his tremendous delight, was to give the bride away, and Miss Tremble, who had played the organ for more years than anyone could remember, had insisted on playing for the service.

Claudia, in the grey suit she had had for rather longer than she would have wished, perched a velvet beret on her bright hair and took herself off to the church, leaving her mother and Tombs to follow in George's car.

The handful of friends who had been invited were completely swallowed up by the villagers, who had turned out to a man and woman to see the doctor they respected and liked marry Mrs Ramsay. Claudia, sitting in the front pew greeting those she knew, turned round, craning her neck to see who was there. Almost everyone, except of course Mr and Mrs Ramsay, but they wouldn't have been welcome anyway. She turned round again and looked at George's upright elderly back, and then turned her head once more, this time with everyone else, to watch her mother coming down the aisle, her hand on Tombs' arm.

It was a short, simple service, but what it lacked in grandeur it made up for in warmth and friendliness as the congregation surged down the aisle after the happy pair. Claudia, hemmed in by well-wishers and friends she hadn't seen for some time, looked around her as she waited patiently to leave the church.

At the back of the church Mr Tait-Bullen, towering over those around him, was looking at her. He wasn't smiling, but that didn't prevent her from feeling pleasure at the sight of him. She made her way towards him and held out a hand.

'Hello, how nice to see you here. Did George invite you?'

He took her hand, shook it briskly and gave it back to her. 'I invited myself. I saw the notice in the *Telegraph* and, since I am on my way to Bristol, George kindly suggested that I might like to come to the church.'

They were outside now, everyone getting into cars or walking back to the doctor's house.

'You're coming to the house?'

'Yes.' Without asking her, he opened the car door and popped her in. 'Are you still at the Colonel's house? George said something about you leaving...'

He didn't sound very interested, so all she said was, 'Yes, we have all left.'

'And you?'

'Oh, I've got a job at Southampton. I'm going back this afternoon.'

They had reached the doctor's house, and Mr Tait-Bullen parked the car, opened her door and followed her inside. They were separated almost at once by other guests, and, feeling let down that he had evinced so little interest in her, Claudia wormed her way to where her mother and George were standing.

She kissed them both. 'I know you're going to be happy,' she told them. 'And this is a lovely wedding; everyone here wants you to be happy too.'

Her mother beamed at her. 'Darling, it's such a wonderful day. Must you go back so soon?'

'I'm afraid so. I'm on duty at three o'clock. I must get to Romsey in time to catch the bus, it goes at a quarter past the hour. Could Tombs take me?'

'Of course he can. And if he can't there are plenty of people here who wouldn't mind running you over to Romsey.' Her mother frowned. 'I meant to have fixed something up, but there was so much to do and think about...'

'Don't worry, Mother. And it will be a pity to take Tombs

away; he's being so useful here. I'll get Tom Hicks from the garage to run me over.'

It was ten minutes or so later when she went back to the buffet with the plate of canapés she had been handing round, that she found Mr Tait-Bullen beside her. He took the plate from her, put it back on the table and handed her a glass of champagne. He said pleasantly, 'I'll drive you to Southampton. When do you want to leave?'

'But you're not going to Southampton; you're going to Bristol. You said so.'

'Indeed I am, but I have ample time to take you back on my way. At what time do you need to leave here?'

'I'm on duty at three o'clock. I was going to catch a bus from Romsey. There's really no need—it's very kind of you, but you'll miss the rest of the reception.'

Looking at him, she could see that he was taking no notice of what she was saying. He said now, 'If we leave at half past one that should give us ample time. Presumably you will need time to get ready for whatever job you are in.'

'I'm a general assistant at a geriatric hospital. It's near the docks.'

She spoke defiantly, as though she expected him to argue with her, but all he said was, 'You'll have to guide me. Do you like your work?'

'Yes. I've only been there for a short while. It's—it's very interesting.'

The vicar joined them then, and presently she excused herself and went to talk to Mr Potter, who asked her worriedly if she was managing.

'I hear you have work at Southampton. Providential, my dear, providential. I have been worried about you and your mother, and can only be thankful that things have turned out so well for you both.'

'Oh, everything is splendid,' said Claudia. 'And Dr Willis has been so kind and thoughtful to all of us.'

'You have not seen Mr and Mrs Ramsay since they returned to the house?'

'No, and I don't want to.' She patted his arm. 'We don't need to worry about them any more, Mr Potter. We hated leaving the house, but we couldn't have stayed even if he had suggested it.'

She wandered round the room then, talking to other guests, most of them old friends who had known her for years. But she kept her eye on the clock, and when she saw that it had just struck one, she went in search of her mother and George, wished them goodbye, assured them that Mr Tait-Bullen was driving her back, and promised to come again just as soon as she had a free day.

Then she got her case and went into the hall. Tombs was there, talking to Mr Tait-Bullen as he shrugged himself into his coat.

'Ah, there you are, Miss Claudia. I was just saying you'd be here dead on time, and so you are.'

'Tombs, it's been a lovely wedding, and I'm sure you did a great deal to make it so. I'll be back when I get a day off. Take care of yourself, won't you? I've seen Mrs Pratt and Jennie.'

'Bless you, miss,' said Tombs, and opened the door for them. 'A safe journey.'

Claudia settled herself in the comfortable seat. 'Do you know how to get onto the Romsey road? Through the village and keep straight on, then turn left at the crossroads. Then it's a right-hand fork. The roads are narrow.'

He said thank you so meekly that she was emboldened to say chattily, 'We're so glad that George gave Tombs a job. He'd been with my great-uncle for years and years. I don't suppose there are many like him...'

Mr Tait-Bullen, not a man for small talk, gave a grunt. And, since he had nothing to say, Claudia observed, 'Are you one of those people who don't like to talk while they are driving? I dare say it takes quite a lot of concentration, especially in a car like this one.'

Mr Tait-Bullen, whose work demanded powers of concentration well beyond the average, gave another grunt.

Claudia, not one to give up easily, took a look at his profile.

It looked severe. 'Oh, well, if you don't want to talk...' She turned her head to look out of the window. 'Probably you're tired.'

'No, I am not in the least tired. Claudia, tell me your off duty for next week...'

'Whatever for?' When he didn't answer, she said, 'Oh, well...' and told him. 'But it gets changed at the last minute very often. There don't seem to be enough staff...'

'It is not, I believe, the most popular form of nursing.'

'Oh, I can quite see that, and I'm not even a nurse.'

'You say that you will be free at three o'clock on Friday? I shall call for you shortly after that and we will spend the rest of the day together.'

'Oh, will we? Have I been asked?'

'Ah, forgive me. I presumed that you would like to see me again, just as I would like to see you.'

'Well!' exclaimed Claudia. 'Whatever next...?'

'Just so. That is what I wish to find out.'

A remark which needed to be thought about and still remained puzzling.

'Well, thank you,' said Claudia, deciding to ignore his remark for the moment. 'But don't be annoyed if my off duty's been changed.'

'I don't think you need worry about that.'

They were threading their way through the outskirts of Southampton. 'Tell me where I should turn off?' he said.

It was half past two when he stopped before the hospital entrance. He got out to open her door and walked with her into the entrance hall. He handed her case over, and when she put out a hand shook it briefly.

'Thank you for the lift.' She smiled up at him and he smiled in return, a slow, gentle smile so that he looked quite different from the rather silent reserved man she had thought him to be. And the smile warmed her loneliness, making the future full of unexpected hope. It wasn't until then that she realised how much she needed a friend.

When she had gone, Mr Tait-Bullen strolled over to the old-fashioned porter's lodge. He was there for several minutes, until its elderly occupant led him away down a long, dreary corridor, knocked on a door and ushered him inside.

Claudia didn't exactly forget him for the rest of the day; he was there at the back of her mind, almost smothered in her non-stop chores. The old ladies were such a cruel contrast to the pleasures of the morning she could have wept with pity for them. Not that weeping would have helped in any way: cups of tea, endless trundles to the loo, mopping up after the inevitable accidents, making beds and the back-breaking task of getting elderly frail bodies back into bed... By ten o'clock, when she went off duty, her mother's wedding seemed part of a dream.

She fell into bed and was instantly asleep. In the morning, after a quick shower, she got into the brown dress and went down to her breakfast, her spirits fully restored. And they stayed that way all day, despite the hundred and one setbacks and Sister's sharp tongue. Claudia forgave her that, for coping with forty old ladies, keeping them clean and tidy and well fed, was no easy task. Claudia, putting clean sheets on a bed for the umpteenth time, considered Sister a splendid woman, even if she had no time to waste on being friendly.

All the same, it was difficult not to feel hard done by when that lady told her that her Friday off duty would be altered; she was to go on the afternoon shift instead of the morning. She wouldn't be able to go out with Mr Tait-Bullen after all, and there was no way of letting him know. She hoped that he wouldn't be too annoyed about it; not to annoy him was suddenly important. Not that it mattered any more. He would go away and not bother to see her again. That thought left her feeling sad.

She was going off duty the next day when Sister called her into the office.

'You'll take your original off duty on Friday.' She sounded cross. 'There will be an extra nurse here for a couple of days, so there will be no need for you to change.'

'I shall be free at three o'clock on Friday?' asked Claudia, just to make sure.

'I've just said so, haven't I? You young girls are all alike, never listening to a word that is said to them.'

Claudia begged her pardon in a suitably humble voice, and once out of the office did a few dance steps along the corridor. Maybe the future wasn't going to be so bad, after all.

Friday dawned wet and cold. Claudia, deep in her morning chores, found the time to look out of the windows in the hope that the weather would improve. It did no such thing. Indeed a nasty wind had sprung up. It would have to be the grey suit and a raincoat—both suitable for the conditions out of doors, but hardly likely to inspire Mr Tait-Bullen to take her anywhere fashionable for tea.

She thought that three o'clock would never come, and even if it did, would she get off duty punctually? She did, hurrying through the hospital to her room, in a panic that she would be called back at the last moment.

Once there, she didn't waste a second—tearing out of the brown uniform, racing to the shower room before someone else got there, dressing with the speed of light. He had said shortly after three o'clock, but if she didn't show up within fifteen minutes of that time she hardly hoped that he would wait much longer. It was already five minutes over time as she gained the entrance hall, out of breath, and with her hair bundled up underneath the velvet beret. There had been no time to do more than powder her nose and put on some lipstick. She didn't look her best, she worried. He would take one look at her and decide that he was wasting his time...

Mr Tait-Bullen, leaning his length against a marble bust of a bewhiskered Victorian dignitary, entertained no such thought. He watched her slither to a dignified walk as she crossed the hall and reflected that she was the most beautiful girl that he had ever set eyes on. Even in the unbecoming garment in which she was swathed. But then she would look mouthwatering in a tablecloth with a hole cut for her head.

None of these interesting thoughts showed on his face as he went to meet her.

'Hello,' said Claudia, her smile so enchanting that he had difficulty in keeping his hands to himself. 'I haven't kept you waiting? I was so afraid that you might think I wasn't coming.' She plucked a bright lock of hair which had escaped her brush and tucked it behind an ear. 'I haven't done my hair properly.' She searched his calm face. 'I'm not dressed up either. You don't mind?'

'No, I don't mind. You look very nice.'

A tepid compliment which satisfied her; he had smiled at her when he had made it, which gave her a comfortable feeling that he had meant exactly what he had said.

'Shall we have tea first? I thought we might drive into the country for dinner later.'

'That would be lovely. Nowhere grand—I'm not dressed for it. I mean, I didn't know if we would be going out this evening—I was in a hurry so's not to miss you...' She paused, aware that she was babbling.

He said gently, 'There's a nice quiet hotel at Wickham. But tea first.'

He drove into the heart of Southampton and took her to a small quiet tea room tucked away in a side-road where he was able to park the car. The place was half-full, warm and pleasantly lighted, and they sat down at a table in the window curtained against the gathering dark of the late afternoon.

They ate hot buttered teacakes, and Claudia, urged to do so, sampled the creamy confections the waitress brought, and all the while Mr Tait-Bullen kept up an undemanding flow of small talk, calculated to put her at her ease so that presently, warm and nicely full, she answered his carefully put questions with less caution than she might have done.

Yes, it was hard work, she admitted, but the other girls were friendly and most of the old ladies were dears. 'Although there are one or two who are a bit difficult...'

'In what way?'

'Oh, they don't mean to be. They get cross, but I'd get cross if I had to sit in a chair because I couldn't do anything for myself. You see, they don't seem to have anyone to look after them—if they had daughters or someone, or sons or husbands who could look after them…'

'That might be difficult in a household with children, or where everyone goes out to work.'

'Yes, I know. Only it would be nice.'

Her hand was lying on the table, and he saw that it was rough and rather red. He said lightly, 'I dare say you have a lot of mopping up to do.'

'Oh, yes. All the time.' She smiled suddenly. 'It's not the cool hand on the brow kind of work—more like a char-woman—plastic pinnys and mops and buckets.'

'You intend to stay there?'

'When I've saved up enough money I shall train for something…' She saw his raised eyebrows. 'Well, I don't know what yet.' She paused. 'I'm talking too much. Will you tell me about you?'

'I live and work in London. I have a house there, and Cork, who has been with me for a long time, looks after me. I have patients in several hospitals and hold clinics in each of them. I have a private practice, and I operate twice a week—sometimes three times. I travel round the country from time to time if I'm wanted for a consultation or to operate.'

'You have lots of friends?'

'I have a few old friends and acquaintances, yes. I'm not married, Claudia.'

She went pink. 'I should have asked you that ages ago, shouldn't I? I did want to, but I—well, I don't know you well enough…'

'We must do something about that. At what time do you have to be back?' And when she told him he said, 'Good, we'll drive to Evershot for dinner. It's a pleasant drive, even in the dark, and we have no need to hurry.'

At her uncertain look, he added, 'Don't worry, it's a quite small hotel. At this time of the year it will be half-empty, and it isn't somewhere where one needs to dress up.'

They went back to the car then, and he drove through the heavy evening traffic until they had left the city behind, taking the secondary roads through the New Forest. Mr Tait-Bullen drove slowly, stopping from time to time to allow the ponies to cross the road ahead of him, and a badger to amble along, refusing to be hurried. He drove for the most part in silence, an easy, undemanding silence in which there was no need to talk for the sake of uttering.

Claudia sat cocooned in warmth and comfort and watched the road unwind ahead of them in the car's headlights. She hadn't felt so quietly happy for a long time.

Evershot was a sizeable village, and even on a dark, wintry night looked charming. The hotel was charming too—not large, but delightfully furnished, warm and welcoming. They went to the bar and sat over drinks, then dined on crab ravioli with ginger, breast of duck with potato straws and tiny brussels sprouts, and pear tatin with cinnamon ice cream. Claudia ate it all with a splendid appetite, sharpened by the wholesome, rather stodgy fare offered at the hospital.

She sat back, savouring the last mouthful of ice cream. 'That was lovely—and do you know it was just luck that I was free this afternoon? Sister changed my duty to the afternoon shift, and then she changed her mind. It was a miracle...'

Mr Tait-Bullen, who had engineered the miracle, agreed that indeed it was.

They sat over their coffee and Claudia, gently encouraged by her companion, talked. There was not much time to talk at the hospital—really talk. On duty conversations were confined to cheerful chat with those of the patients who welcomed it, and only that when there were a few minutes to spare. And off duty, although she got on well with the other girls, the inclination was either to go out or to sit in front of the television. But now she allowed her tongue full rein, vaguely aware that later on she would regret it but happy now, saying whatever came into her head. She paused briefly.

'Am I boring you?'

'No. I do not think that you will ever bore me, Claudia. I

have to go away for a couple of days. When I return I should like to take you out again.'

'Oh, would you? I'd like that too.' She beamed at him. 'We get on well together, don't we? I didn't think I would like you when we met, but I've changed my mind.'

'I hoped that you would. As you say, we get on well together.'

He drove her back presently, saw her into the hospital and, under the porter's interested eye, bent to kiss her cheek. It wasn't until she was in her room that she realised that he hadn't said anything more about seeing her again.

Claudia, brushing her fiery locks, stopped to stare into the small mirror above the little dressing table.

'You're a fool,' she told her reflection. 'Whatever he said, he must have been bored out of his mind. I must have sounded like a garrulous old maid. No wonder he didn't say when he would want to see me again.' She put down the brush and got into bed, suddenly sad; she liked him and felt at ease in his company. If only she hadn't behaved like an idiot. Living in London, obviously a successful man in his profession, and presumably comfortably off, she thought gloomily, he would have his pick of elegant women who had a fund of witty and amusing talk and knew when to hold their tongues...

Two days later she was on the afternoon shift. It was drizzling outside, with a mean wind, and the thought of a morning doing nothing by the gas fire in the recreation room was tempting. Then Claudia thought of the long hours on the ward until the late evening, buttoned herself into her mac, tied a scarf over her hair, found her gloves and sensible shoes and made her way to the side door the hospital staff used. A brisk walk would do her good...

She was crossing the back of the hall when the porter called after her.

'I've been ringing round for you,' he grumbled. 'You're to go to the visitors' room.'

'Me? Why?'

'How should I know? That's the message I got and I'm telling it to you.'

'Yes—well, thank you!'

She turned round and went the other way along the wide corridor from which the boardroom, the manager's office and the consultants' room opened.

'Mother,' she said, suddenly afraid of bad news, and opened the door.

The room didn't encourage visitors. It was a dark brown, with shiny lino on the floor and a hideous glass lantern housing a stark white bulb glaring down onto the solid table beneath it. Chairs were arranged stiffly around the walls, and, half lost in the massive fireplace, there was a very small gas fire. Watching her from the other side of the table was Mr Tait-Bullen.

Claudia slithered to a halt. 'Oh, it's you.' And then, aware that perhaps that had sounded rude, added, 'What I meant is, I didn't expect you.' He smiled then, and she smiled back. 'I was just going out for a walk.'

When he didn't speak, she asked, 'Are you on your way somewhere or are you on holiday?'

'I'm on my way back to London.'

'Well, what luck I'm on afternoon duty.' She flushed. 'What I mean is, you could have called in and I would have been working.' She hurried on, because it sounded as though she expected him to take her out. 'I expect you're anxious to get back home...'

'In which case I should have driven straight back to London...'

'But you didn't know if I was free...'

'Yes, I did. I phoned up first to find out. I have to go away again for a couple of days, and I wanted to see you before I go.'

'Me? Why? Mother's not ill, or George? Did they ask you to come?'

'No, they are both, as far as I know, in the best of middle-aged health.'

He smiled at her, a slow, warm smile. 'Claudia, before I say anything more, will you answer me truthfully? Are you happy here? Are you content to be, eventually, a career girl and, if not, will you tell me what you really wish for?'

'Why do you want to know?' she asked, and, when he didn't answer, went on, 'Well, all right—no, I'm not happy here. I'm truly sorry for the old ladies, but I miss the garden and the village and being out of doors. We're well looked after, you know, but I feel trapped.' She had lost herself in her own thoughts. 'And I suppose I wish for what every woman wants— a home and a husband and children.'

'Not love?'

'That too, but I think that isn't granted to everyone—I mean, the kind of love that doesn't mind being poor or neglected or kept hidden, and will love and cherish despite that.' She stopped suddenly. 'Why did you make me say all that?'

He didn't answer her at once, but stared at her across the table, seeing a rather untidy figure, her bright hair escaping from the scarf, enveloped in her sensible mac.

'Will you marry me, Claudia?' he asked quietly.

At her astonished look, he said, 'No, don't say anything for a moment or two. You see, I think we might have a successful and happy marriage. I need a wife and you long for freedom. We could help each other in many ways; I have no doubt that you will be an excellent housewife and hostess, and a companion I shall always enjoy, and you could be free to spread your wings in whichever direction you wish to fly.

'I haven't said that I love you, nor do I expect you to tell me that. There's time enough for us to get to know each other. And I shan't hurry you. But it seems to me that to marry as soon as possible would be the sensible thing to do. You will need to give a week's notice at the hospital, but there is no reason why we shouldn't marry before Christmas.'

Claudia opened her mouth to speak, and shut it again, reflecting on what he had said. It all sounded so sensible, so calmly thought out. And he didn't love her. On the other hand he must like her, if he intended to marry her, and she would enjoy having a household of her own—meeting people, making friends, being there when he wanted a companion. And she liked him; she liked him very much.

Mr Tait-Bullen asked quietly, 'You would like to think about it? I shall quite understand if you dislike the idea, but I shall be disappointed. You see, Claudia, I have been honest with you. I have not promised love and endless devotion, but I have offered you what I hope will be a happy and contented life together. We like the same things, don't we? And laugh at the same jokes. We would be good companions and friends. That, I think, is more important than a sudden and uncertain infatuation.'

He was right, of course. It was, she told herself, a sensible and sincere offer of marriage made by one of the handsomest men she had ever met, and a man she liked wholeheartedly. She didn't know much about him, but, as he had said, getting to know each other was something they could do in their own good time. She would be a good wife, just as she was instinctively aware that he would be a good husband.

She looked across the table at him, standing there with no sign of impatience.

'Yes, thank you, I should like to marry you.' She laughed suddenly. 'I don't know your name...'

He came round the table and put gentle hands on her shoulders. 'Thomas,' he said, and bent to kiss her. 'Thank you, Claudia.'

CHAPTER FOUR

CLAUDIA looked up into his quiet face. 'What do we do next?'

Mr Tait-Bullen suppressed a smile. A girl after his own heart; no coy smiles and fluttering of the eyelashes, no girlish whispers. Claudia obviously liked to meet a situation, when she encountered it, head-on.

'If you will give in your notice today? Phone me this evening—I'll be in Edinburgh; I'll give you my number—let me know the soonest you can leave and I'll fetch you.'

'Where will I go?'

'To George Willis. We'll marry there if you would like that. I'll get a special licence—remind me to ask you for some particulars when you phone. Your mother?'

'I'll phone her.'

'A pity that I have to go back to town this morning; I could have called in at Little Planting. I'll telephone her this evening.'

He was holding her hands in his. 'This must be the most unlikely place in the world in which to receive a proposal of marriage.'

'I don't think that matters at all. I mean, moonlight and roses wouldn't have been suitable, would they? Not for us.'

He frowned a little. 'You will be happy, Claudia? I am a good deal older than you...'

'I like you just as you are, Thomas. Please don't change any of you. We shall be happy together.'

'I must go. Forgive me, there isn't even time to give you a cup of coffee.'

She went with him to the hospital entrance and he kissed her again, a light kiss which meant nothing, although she hadn't expected it to, got into his car and drove away.

It was a few moments before she moved—back into the hospital, intent on doing what Thomas had suggested, not noticing the porter's interested stare. She must compose a suitable letter and then take it to Miss Norton, and she must do it at once, so that when Thomas phoned that evening she could tell him when she could leave. And she must phone her mother...

She wrote her letter of resignation and presented herself at Miss Norton's office, inwardly quaking; could she be prevented from leaving? She hadn't signed a contract, and she was paid weekly, all the same she wasn't absolutely sure...

Fifteen minutes later she closed the office door behind her with a sigh of relief. Miss Norton hadn't been very pleased. Indeed, she had read Claudia a lecture on young women who were irresponsible and said she hoped that she had given marriage serious thought, but she hadn't refused to let Claudia go. She was, she had pointed out, scrupulously fair in such matters; if a girl wasn't happy in her work then she was entitled to leave. Normally, said Miss Norton severely, after a reasonable period. Claudia had hardly given herself time to settle down, but in the circumstances she could, of course, leave.

Claudia had thanked her and asked if she could leave two days earlier, since she would have her week's days off due. Miss Norton had looked affronted but she had agreed.

Claudia got into her mac again and went to telephone her mother; there was a phone in the hospital, but it was in a passage and in constant use; to discuss anything other than the weather was impossible.

Her mother was delighted, surprised as well. 'Darling, I didn't know that you and Mr Tait-Bullen—Thomas—were so close. I'm delighted, and I'm sure George will be too when I tell him. What are your plans?'

Claudia inserted all the money she had, and explained. 'And we want to have a very quiet wedding, Mother. Thomas is getting a special licence and we'd like to marry at Little Planting. I'm leaving in five days; Thomas will fetch me. May I stay with you and George until the wedding? It'll only be for a day or two.'

'Of course, darling. And we must do something about clothes...'

Claudia, with an inward eye on her scanty wardrobe, agreed.

The rest of the day passed in a dream; since she was happy, she wanted everyone else to be happy too, coaxing smiles from even the most cantankerous of the old ladies, clearing up unmentionable messes, changing sheets, trundling round the ward with the tea trolley, the supper trolley and at the end of the day having to listen to a lecture from Sister, who, apprised of her leaving, took it as a personal affront.

It was after ten o'clock by the time she left the ward—too late to go to the phone box at the end of the road. Besides, the passage where the hospital phone was was empty so late in the evening. She rang the number Thomas had given her and waited, half afraid that he wouldn't answer.

His voice sounded strangely businesslike.

'It's me,' said Claudia, heedless of grammar. And she added quite unnecessarily, 'You told me to ring you up, but I haven't kept you up, have I?'

Mr Tait-Bullen, studying the notes of a patient he was to operate on the next day, assured her that she hadn't.

'You saw Miss Norton?'

'Yes, I may leave in five days' time—actually, it's four days now. That's a Friday.'

'In the morning? You're actually free to leave after duty on Thursday?'

'Yes, but I must pack my things and give my uniform back...'

'I'll come for you at nine o'clock on Friday morning, Claudia.'

'Thank you, but don't you have to work?'

He said gently, 'Oh, yes, but not until the afternoon, I'll drop you off at Little Planting on my way back. Now, tell me— where were you born, how old are you, have you any other names besides Claudia, and are you British by birth?'

She told him in a matter-of-fact voice, sensing that he hadn't time to waste on idle talk. She hesitated before she said, 'My other name is Eliza...' and waited for him to laugh.

But he didn't. All he said was, 'That's a nice old-fashioned name. You must be tired, my dear. Get to bed and sleep well. I'll see you on Friday.'

'Good night, then,' Claudia said, and hung up. It would have been nice if he had said something like, I miss you, or, I'm looking forward to seeing you. But he wouldn't pretend to feelings he didn't feel; she quite understood that. Theirs would be a sensible marriage, she reflected, undressing and falling into bed, there would be no false sentiment.

The following afternoon she took herself off to the shops; she hadn't much money, but it was essential that she had something suitable in which to be married. Luck was on her side; she found a small dress shop going out of business and selling up at half price. Claudia thrust aside a wish to wear white chiffon and a gauzy veil and tried on a plainly cut dress and jacket in fine wool. It was in a misty blue, with a grey velvet collar and cuffs, and fastened with a row of velvet buttons. And when the saleslady found a charming hat in matching velvet, Claudia decided that she need look no further.

'It's for a special occasion?' enquired the sales lady.

'Well, yes—my wedding.'

Which prompted the sales lady, who had a sentimental heart under her smart black dress, to make a special price. And that meant that there was enough money left to buy gloves and shoes—and some essential underpinnings from Marks and Spencer.

Well pleased with her purchases, Claudia went back to the hospital—too late for tea and too early for supper, but that didn't matter. She tried everything on once more and spent a long time trying out various new hairstyles, none of which pleased her. Perhaps once she was married she would be able to go to a good London hairdresser and have it expertly cut.

The days dragged; Friday was never coming, and she had ample time to wonder if she was about to make the mistake of a lifetime. A letter or a phone call from Thomas would have cleared up her uncertainty, but there was nothing. He had told her that he would see her on Friday and with that she had to be content. She had phoned her mother again, and that lady, agog with maternal delight, had told her that she was to go with her to Salisbury and get a few clothes. 'Our wedding present to you, darling. Have you bought anything yet?'

Claudia described the dress and jacket.

'They sound just right. Aren't you excited? And will you have a honeymoon?'

'No. Thomas can only take a day off—we'll go later.'

On the Thursday she bade the old ladies goodbye, leaving a vase filled with chrysanthemums on one of the tables, wishing she could have done more to brighten the ward. Sister wished her goodbye in an ill-humoured way, and then surprised her by saying, 'A pity you are leaving; the old ladies liked you.'

And the other girls were friendly—laughing and joking and asking her to send photos of the wedding.

'Well, it's not that kind of wedding,' she explained. 'Just us and a few family and no one else...'

'Who'd want anyone else but him, anyway?' declared one of the girls, who had seen Mr Tait-Bullen leaving the hospital. Everyone laughed and Claudia got out a bottle of sherry and a packet of biscuits. It seemed the right moment for a farewell party.

She was ready and waiting long before nine o'clock the next morning. Supposing Thomas had changed his mind? Had a breakdown, an accident, been called away to an emergency? She sat, as still as a mouse, wrapped in the mac, since it was raining again, her hair glowing in the gloomy entrance hall.

Mr Tait-Bullen knew exactly how she felt the moment he set eyes on her.

He nodded to the porter and reached her before she could get to her feet, his eyes searching her face. What he saw there reassured him, and he smiled.

'I can see that I am marrying a treasure. Do you know that the one virtue a medical man longs for in a wife is punctuality? You see, he is never punctual himself...'

'I was a bit early. I wasn't sure—that is, I thought that perhaps...' She met his steady gaze. 'No, that's not quite true—I knew you'd come.'

'Of course. Do you have to see anyone? You've said your goodbyes?'

And, when she nodded, he picked up her case and together they left the hospital.

They were clear of Southampton, driving through a dripping countryside, before he said, 'If you will agree, we can be married on Monday. I'll come down to Little Planting on Sunday evening, and we can marry in the morning and drive back in the afternoon.'

He had a list on Tuesday, but there would be Monday evening in which to show Claudia her new home. Cork had confided plans for a splendid supper, and Mr Tait-Bullen had left his devoted servant icing a cake for tea. It wasn't the kind of wedding that Cork would have liked for his master, but he was determined to make it as bridal an occasion as possible.

And that reminded him of something. He brought the car to a gentle halt and fished around in a pocket.

'Ours must be one of the briefest engagements ever known,' he observed, and opened the little velvet box in his hand. The ring it contained was a sapphire, a rich, sparkling blue surrounded by diamonds and mounted in gold. He picked up Claudia's left hand, resting in her lap, took off her glove and slipped the ring on her finger.

'Oh, it's beautiful—and it fits.' Claudia's sigh was one of pure delight. 'Thank you, Thomas.' She stared at it, incongruous on her roughened hand with its short, clipped nails. She would have to do something about that before the wedding.

She looked at him and saw that he was studying her hand. She said quite awkwardly, 'We did wear gloves whenever we could, but sometimes it just wasn't possible.'

His smile was kind. 'It was my grandmother's engagement ring. She left it to me with the wish that I would give it to the girl I married.'

'She was fond of you?'

'Indeed, she was; we were the best of friends.'

'You miss her?'

'Yes, we all do—my mother and father, my two sisters and younger brother. You will meet them all at Christmas...'

Claudia said faintly, 'Oh, shall I? Do they all live in London?'

'No, Mother and Father live in Cumbria, a small village called Finsthwaite, at the southern end of lake Windermere. It is rather remote but very beautiful, close to the heart of Grizedale Forest but not too far from Kendal. My sisters are married. Ann—she's the elder—lives in York; her husband's a solicitor. Amy and her husband live near Melton Mowbray; he's a farmer. James is at Birmingham Children's hospital—a junior registrar.'

'They won't be coming to our wedding?'

'Mother and Father—the rest of the family you'll meet at Christmas. We shall spend it at Finsthwaite.' He added casually, 'They'll be delighted to welcome you into the family.'

'They don't know me. They might not like me...'

'You will be my wife,' said Thomas.

A fact which she could not dispute.

Tombs, beaming widely, opened the door to them when they reached George's house. He shook Claudia by the hand, and then Mr Tait-Bullen, wished them happy and led them across the hall to the sitting room. Her mother was there and embraced Claudia warmly before offering a cheek for her future son-in-law.

'Such a surprise,' she told them. 'We're all so excited. George is in his surgery but Tombs has gone to fetch him. We had no idea...'

Nor had I, thought Claudia, but she didn't say so. 'We thought we'd be married on Monday...'

'Darling—but you haven't any clothes, and I must have a new hat at least, and who is to be invited? Such short notice...'

'Thomas would like his parents to come, Mother.' Claudia looked at him and felt a touch of peevishness at the sight of him standing there, looking faintly amused.

'May they do that, Mrs Willis? We both want a quiet wedding, and I can't spare more than a day. We would like to marry in the morning, then drive back to London, which would give us the rest of the day together.'

'Of course, you poor dears—scarcely more than a few hours to be together.'

'We shall make up for that later on,' said Mr Tait-Bullen soothingly.

He turned as George came into the room. 'We do hope we haven't spoilt any plans you and Mrs Willis may have made...'

Dr Willis kissed Claudia and shook hands with him. 'We don't go away until the end of next week, and even if we had plans we would be delighted to upset them for such a happy occasion. Staying for lunch, I hope?'

Tombs had brought in the coffee tray, and Mrs Willis poured while Claudia, glad of something to do, handed around cups and saucers and biscuits.

'I must get back. I've a clinic this afternoon and patients to see this evening.'

Claudia, sitting beside her mother, watched Thomas, perfectly at ease, everything arranged as he had wished, calm and self-assured, listening to George explaining the difficulties of being a GP's wife. He made no attempt to mention his own work; she guessed that it was just as time-consuming and demanding.

She went out with him to his car presently, and he stood for a minute, looking down at her. 'I'll see you on Sunday evening. My mother and father will be with me in their own car. We'll put up at the Duck and Thistle.'

He took her two hands in his. 'Quite sure, Claudia?'

She said steadily, 'Yes, Thomas. It's a bit unusual, isn't it? Getting married like this. But if we're sure, and it's what we want, there's no point in mulling it over for months, is there? And I don't suppose that if we were engaged for a long time we'd see much of each other—I mean, get to know each other better—for you would be working and I'd be bogged down in plans for the wedding.'

'What a sensible girl you are, Claudia.' He bent and kissed

her, a brief, friendly kiss, before getting into his car and driving away.

Back in the sitting room, her mother said, 'Darling, we're all so happy for you. He's just right for you and so handsome. You'll have a delightful life together. I can hardly believe it— there we were a few weeks ago, with not a penny piece between us and no roof over our heads, and look at us now. I'm here with George, and so very happy, and you'll be happy too with Thomas.' She paused to look at Claudia. 'Clothes—you must have some new things...'

'I've told you about the dress and jacket, and the hat, and I've bought one or two other things. Enough to go on with. I expect I'll get some new clothes when we're in London. There hasn't been time, and Thomas knows that.' She added carefully, 'You see, there didn't seem much point in waiting—my job in the hospital wasn't quite what I thought it would be, and Thomas wanted me to leave as soon as possible.' She smiled suddenly. 'So did I.'

Mrs Willis started to say something, and then stopped. Instead she observed, 'I expect Thomas fell in love with you the first time you met...'

'It happens all the time,' said Claudia. 'Look at you and George.'

'Well, dear, for George, yes. But it took me a long time to discover that I loved him. And I dare say if it hadn't been for that awful Ramsay cousin, and us being turned out of the house, I might never have discovered how I felt.'

'What a good thing it happened that way, then. Though it was horrid, wasn't it? Do you hear or see anything of him and his wife?'

'No, dear. They keep themselves very much to themselves, and the village isn't friendly towards them.' Mrs Willis sighed happily. 'How nice that we don't have to think about them any more. Now, on Monday I thought that we would have a buffet lunch. Mrs Pratt is longing to prepare a feast for you. A pity that it is to be such a quiet wedding.' She glanced at Claudia. 'You don't mind?'

'No, Mother, I'm happy to do whatever Thomas wants. If we had decided to marry later on, we wouldn't have seen much of each other—he's busy all day most days. At least I shall see him when he comes home in the evenings.'

A remark which satisfied her mother, just as Claudia had meant it to.

Claudia woke early on Monday morning. It was still dark outside as she got out of bed, wrapped herself in her dressing gown and crept downstairs. The light was on in the kitchen and Mrs Pratt was there, carefully lifting tiny vol-au-vents from a baking sheet onto one of Dr Willis's best china dishes. Tombs was there too, sitting by the Aga, polishing wine glasses.

'No, no. Don't move,' said Claudia as he started to get up. 'I thought I'd make a cup of tea.'

Mrs Pratt beamed at her. 'You should still be in your bed, Miss Claudia. I dare say you're excited. It isn't every day a girl marries. The kettle's boiling, if you'd like to make tea...'

'We'll all have a cup. You're both coming to the church, aren't you?'

'Wouldn't miss it for all the tea in China, Miss Claudia,' said Tombs. 'Me and Mrs Pratt are that pleased. Took to the doctor the moment we set eyes on him, didn't we?'

Mrs Pratt, whipping something delicious in a bowl, agreed. 'A handsome pair you'll be—though it's to be hoped you won't let him see that old dressing gown, Miss Claudia. Warm and cosy it may have been at one time, but it's past its best...'

Claudia warmed the teapot and had a sudden moment of doubt. Surely Thomas would have realised that she had had no time to buy a lot of clothes? And would he mind anyway? She had gained the impression that her appearance wasn't something he found important. True, he had told her that she looked nice...

'I shall go shopping in London.' She turned to smile at Mrs Pratt. 'I'll leave this dressing gown behind!'

The three of them drank their tea in a friendly silence, and Rob, rousing from sleep in his basket, came to join them.

'I'll let him out and take the tea up as I go,' said Claudia.

'Begging your pardon, Miss Claudia,' said Tombs, at his most stately. 'You will do no such thing. That is a morning task for myself.'

'Oh, Tombs,' cried Claudia. 'I'm going to miss you and Mrs Pratt.'

She finished her tea and went to the garden door with Rob, who lumbered out into the garden. She stood watching him and looked at the sky, beginning to lighten. It had been a frosty night, and her breath drifted away in soft swirls. It was going to be a lovely winter's day. A good omen? She hoped so.

Rob came in then, making for the warmth of the Aga, and she went back to her room.

It was growing lighter by the minute. She went to the window, opened it wide and leaned out, breathing the cold air. At the other end of the village Thomas was sleeping—his parents too. They had come at teatime—Thomas in his Rolls Royce, his father driving a Daimler. She had seen them arrive from her bedroom window and hurried downstairs, her hair very tidy for once, wearing a dark green jersey dress which she had had for so long it had become quite fashionable again.

It was essential to make a good impression; Thomas's parents might live miles away, but they were bound to meet occasionally. She hadn't allowed herself to speculate about them, she'd only hoped that they would like her.

Thomas's mother had come in first, pausing to smile at Tombs, but before she reached Claudia, Thomas had been there, bending to kiss her cheek, putting an arm round her shoulder.

'This is Claudia, Mother—Father.' And they had both shaken her hand and kissed her warmly, so that her vague doubts had vanished.

Thomas's father was an elderly edition of his son, still very upright, grey-haired and handsome. His mother was almost as tall as Claudia, and still a beautiful woman, with a beauty she had allowed to age gradually, without excess make-up or tinted hair. Her face wrinkled in all the right places, and her hair was grey and simply dressed. But her eyes were still young—vivid blue and smiling. She was well dressed too, in an understated and slightly old-fashioned way. Claudia had liked her at once.

It had been easy after that first meeting. Her mother and George had joined them, and the evening had been pleasant. Neither of the Tait-Bullens had badgered her with questions; they had talked about the wedding in a soothing manner, remarked upon the charm of the village and told her something— but not much—of their own home. And she had had no chance to talk for more than a few moments to Thomas. Only as they had been leaving to go to the Duck and Thistle had he asked her kindly, 'Cold feet, Claudia?'

'Certainly not,' she had answered him indignantly, and then, looking into his face, seeing the casual friendliness in it, had added softly, 'No, I promise you, Thomas.'

Someone was coming down the lane from the village. She withdrew her head and then poked it out again; in the dim light of dawn Thomas was coming through the open gate and up the short drive. He stopped under her window.

'Come for a walk?' he invited.

How could he have known that that was the very thing she most wanted to do?

'Five minutes,' said Claudia, and closed the window.

There were trousers and an old sweater in the cupboard; she put them on over her nightie, tied back her hair, cleaned her teeth and went down to the kitchen; her wellies were there, with socks stuffed inside them. Under Tombs's and Mrs Pratt's astonished gaze, she put them on, bundled on one of the coats hanging behind the kitchen door, blew them a kiss and went out into the garden round the house to where Thomas was waiting.

He took her arm and walked her briskly along the lane, away from the village. 'No gloves?' he asked, and took his own off and put them onto her cold hands. 'This isn't quite the usual behaviour of the bride and groom on their wedding day...'

'But it isn't a usual kind of wedding, is it?'

The lane petered out into a rough track, its rutted surface frost-bound, and as they walked Thomas began to talk—a nicely calculated jumble of odds and ends about his work, and information about his home, his friends... 'I hope you will like them—most of them are married...'

'Have you had any girlfriends? I'm not being nosy, but if I were to meet them I'd have to know who they are, wouldn't I?'

Mr Tait-Bullen didn't pause in his stride. He said briskly, 'Naturally I have been out and about with several woman acquaintances, but they have never been more than that, Claudia.'

'Have I annoyed you by asking? I don't expect to know about your life, but I don't want to be taken unawares. Anyway, I don't suppose you've had much time to fall in love.'

'I'm not sure if time is needed when one falls in love. I imagine it happens in the blink of an eye. I can promise you that I have had neither the inclination or the time. I have always been too busy. But I shall enjoy being married to you; we shall be good friends and companions and above all we like each other. Liking the person you marry is as important as loving them.'

'I'm sure you're right,' said Claudia, 'although we can't be quite certain, can we? I mean, you'd have to be married to someone you loved and didn't like...'

They had been walking uphill; now they paused to watch the first rays of a wintry sun creep over the countryside. They stood and watched for a moment, and Claudia said, 'Nice, isn't it?' She added slowly, 'That's the only thing. I expect I'll miss this for a bit.'

'Yes, I can understand that. I thought we might look around for a small house not too far from here, where we can spend weekends. It's an easy run up to town.'

He had flung an arm round her, and she turned within its comfort so that she could see his face. 'Oh, Thomas, that would be lovely. But would you like that, too?'

'Very much. We will wait till after Christmas and then go house-hunting. There are plenty of villages between here and the M3.'

The sun was above the horizon now, and Claudia said reluctantly, 'We'd better go back. We're not dressed for the wedding, are we?'

Mr Tait-Bullen took a good look at her. 'No. I like the hair, but you look all the wrong shape...'

'Well, I didn't stop to dress—only an old sweater and trousers over my nightie. And I don't know whose coat this is—I took it from the back door.'

'And you still contrive to look beautiful,' he told her, and then turned her round smartly and marched her back.

He left her at the kitchen door, bending to kiss her quickly. 'Don't be late,' he said, and walked away as she opened the door.

'Your ma is in a fine state,' said Mrs Pratt. 'Miss Claudia, whatever possessed you to go gallivanting off like that? Looking like a scarecrow, too.'

Claudia flung her arms round her old friend's neck. 'It was lovely—a kind of ending and a beginning, if you see what I mean.' She skipped to the door and flew upstairs to shower, then put on her dressing gown again and went down to breakfast.

Mrs Willis submitted to her hug. 'Darling, you shouldn't have gone off like that—you and Thomas aren't supposed to see each other until you meet in church, and Mrs Pratt says you looked like a bag lady...'

Claudia helped herself to toast. 'It was lovely. We watched the sun come up. Mother, I'm so happy!'

And Mrs Willis, happy herself, leaned across the table and patted her daughter's arm. 'Oh, love, I do understand. So does George. He was called out just before you came downstairs— old Mrs Parson's grandson cut his arm on a bottle.'

'George will be back in time for the wedding?'

'Don't worry, dear, he will. It's only a matter of a few stitches.'

Claudia, casting a critical eye over her reflection, wished for a brief moment that it was white chiffon and yards of veiling and not the blue outfit she was looking at. She had dressed with care, taken pains with her face and her hair, and arranged the hat at the most becoming angle. She supposed that for a quiet wedding she looked all right.

Supposing it didn't work out well? Thomas was so sure that it would, and so was she, but that hadn't prevented last-minute doubts creeping in. Did all brides feel as she did? she wondered. Wondering if they were making the biggest mistake of their lives? Or was that because she was marrying Thomas after such a short time in which to know him?

She turned away from the mirror and went to look out of the window; she couldn't even see the Duck and Thistle from it, but it was only a few minutes' walk away. Was Thomas standing at his window as full of doubts as she was, perhaps wishing that he had never set eyes on her?

Her mother, coming into the room, broke into her thoughts. 'Darling, just look at this—Thomas doesn't know what you're wearing, so the flowers are white—isn't it gorgeous?'

The bouquet she was offering Claudia was truly bridal; white roses very faintly tinged with pink, lilies of the valley, hyacinth pips, orange blossom, little white tulips and miniature white narcissi nestling in a circle of green leaves. It made up for the lack of white chiffon; just looking at it made her feel like a bride.

A very quiet wedding, Thomas had said, but that hadn't prevented everyone in the village who could get to the church from going to see Claudia married. But they understood, sitting at the back of the church quietly so that Claudia and Thomas were unaware of them, knowing that they wanted a quiet wedding. Only as they left the church did she become aware of smiling faces and voices wishing them luck and happiness.

Back at George's house, they drank the champagne which Mr Tait-Bullen had thoughtfully provided, and presently sat down to an early lunch, waited upon by Tombs at his most majestic. Mrs Pratt, refusing to be discouraged by the brief notice she had had of the wedding, had sat up late and got up early in order to provide a feast worthy of the occasion.

Cheese soufflés, each in their own small ramekin, followed

by salmon *en croûte*, watercress salad and potato straws, and, following that, Tombs carried in the wedding cake. Not quite in the traditional manner, perhaps—Mrs Pratt hadn't had time for that—but she had iced a fruit cake and ornamented it with silver leaves, searched for at length in the village shop, and arranged it on one of George's much prized Coalport plates, which he kept under lock and key.

'Nothing but the best for Miss Claudia,' Mrs Pratt had told him, standing over him while he took the plate from the glass cabinet where it was displayed.

It was a pleasant meal. No one made a speech, although they did drink the bride and groom's health, with Tombs and Mrs Pratt summoned from the kitchen, well pleased with their efforts, beaming at them from the door.

It was Thomas, refilling their glasses, who said, 'My wife and I thank you both for giving us such a delightful lunch; it has made our happy day even happier.'

They had coffee in the drawing room, and presently Thomas said, 'I think we should be going, Claudia.' He looked at George. 'We both thank you for making our wedding such a happy occasion. Once we are settled in we do hope that you will come and visit us.' He turned to his mother and said, 'And of course you and Father. But we shall be seeing you at Christmas.'

'We look forward to that, Thomas.'

It took quite a while saying goodbye to everyone. Thomas put the luggage in the car and then waited with no sign of impatience while Claudia went from one to the other. Tombs and Mrs Pratt had to be bidden goodbye, messages left for Jennie, and Rob hugged. But finally there were no more goodbyes to be said, and she went out to the car with Thomas and got in beside him. It wasn't until they had driven for a mile or two that she said in a small voice, 'It has all been so sudden...'

He touched her hand briefly. 'Don't worry, Claudia, I shan't hurry you. Think of us as being engaged, if that makes you feel happier...'

'Well, I dare say it would, but I won't. We're married, aren't we? Once I get used to that everything will be fine.' She added quickly, 'Don't think I'm regretting it; I'm not. I'm very happy—only a bit out of my depth.'

'You may have all the time in the world to find your feet. I have to work tomorrow, but on Wednesday I shall be home in the morning—time for us to talk.'

He was on the motorway now, driving fast through the already fading light.

'Cork will have tea for us and we shall have this evening together. I enjoyed our wedding, Claudia, and I hope you did too?'

'Oh, yes, I did. And the flowers—they were glorious. They made me forget that I was wearing an ordinary outfit. I felt as though I was in white chiffon and a veil—a real bride.'

'But you were a real bride, my dear. You looked beautiful...'

A remark which lifted her spirits, so that for the rest of the journey she was utterly happy.

CHAPTER FIVE

THOMAS'S description of his home in London had been vague; Claudia had gathered that he lived near his consulting rooms in a terraced house, and she had pictured a typical London house—solid, mid-Victorian, with rather a lot of red brickwork. And, since she knew very little of London, her visits having been confined to brief shopping expeditions and the occasional visit to a theatre, she'd visualised a busy road, noisy with traffic and not a tree in sight.

When Thomas stopped before his home, got out and opened her door, she got out too and stared around her. It was quite dark by now, but the street lighting was shining onto the elegant houses standing back from the tree-lined pavement. He took her arm and led her up the three steps to the door being held open, giving a glimpse of a softly lighted hall.

'Ah, Cork,' said Mr Tait-Bullen. 'Claudia, this is Cork, who looks after me so well and will doubtless do the same for you.' He put a hand on the other man's shoulder. 'My wife, Cork.'

Claudia offered a hand and smiled into the craggy face, and Cork allowed himself a pleased and relieved smile in return. A nice young lady, he saw at once, just right for his master.

'May I wish you both every happiness?' he observed solemnly. 'And I shall hope to give you as much satisfaction, madam, as the master.'

'Very nicely put,' said Mr Tait-Bullen, busy taking Claudia's coat and gloves and tossing them and his own coat onto one of the chairs flanking the side table.

Cork allowed himself another smile. 'Tea will be brought to the drawing room in five minutes, sir.'

He melted away, and Thomas took Claudia's arm and led her through a door—one of three leading from the hall.

The room was large, with its windows overlooking the quiet

street. There was an Adam fireplace, with two sofas and a maple and rosewood library table arranged before it, a Regency writing table under the window and a magnificent Chinese lacquer display cabinet facing the window. There were comfortable chairs too, upholstered in the same burgundy velvet as the curtains draping the window. And small lamp tables here and there, too, piled with books and magazines. A lovely room, restful and lived in.

Claudia felt instantly at home in it—a good augur for the future? she wondered, smiling at Cork, coming in with the tea tray. He didn't return the smile. She appeared to be a nice young lady, at first sight a suitable wife for his master, but time would tell, and he was a man who did nothing hastily. She might want to interfere in his kitchen...

Claudia had seen the prim set of his mouth. If Cork was anything like Tombs then she would need to tread carefully for a while. It had taken her quite a time to win over Tombs, but once she had he had become her firm friend and ally. She sat down in the chair Thomas had offered her and composedly poured their tea, as though she had been doing it for years.

Mr Tait-Bullen, leafing through his post, observed her from under his lids. He had known instinctively that she was the right wife for him: taking things in her stride, accepting each new challenge as it arose, fitting into his life without fuss. And he liked her; he liked her very much.

He considered himself beyond the age of falling in love, and he had no intention of doing so. His work was all-engrossing. The way of life that he had chosen suited him very well; he had no doubt that Claudia would accept that. They had similar tastes. She would be free to make her own friends, and whenever they had the time they would spend a day or so in the country. He must remember to do something about that...

Cork came back presently, removed the tea things and ushered her upstairs. The staircase was narrow, and curved against the end wall of the hall, and Claudia stopped to admire it. She ran a hand over its mahogany banisters, gleaming with polish.

'Lots of elbow grease,' she reflected out loud, and Cork gave her a respectful look.

'Nothing beats it, madam.' He allowed himself the ghost of a smile.

Her room was at the back of the house, overlooking a long, narrow garden. Even in winter it looked charming, with a tracery of leafless trees grouped here and there. Doubtless in the spring there would be crocuses and daffodils around them, and bright flowers in the summer.

She turned from the window and found Cork still standing at the door. 'The bathroom is through the door on the right, madam, and beyond that is the Professor's room. Tomorrow, if you wish, I will conduct you round the house.'

'Oh, please, Cork. And if you will tell me anything that I should know—advise me. You will know exactly how the—the Professor likes things done.'

'I trust so, madam.'

When she was alone she took stock of the room and could find no fault with it. The bed was a satinwood four-poster, curtained and covered with a gossamer-fine ivory silk patterned with forget-me-nots, and the bow-fronted chest was of the same wood. There was a satinwood and mahogany mirror on the mahogany sofa table under the two windows, and a tallboy in exquisite marquetry. On either side of the bed were delicate little side tables, each with a china figure bearing a rose-coloured lamp. There was a wall cupboard too, she discovered, and beyond the further door a bathroom to be drooled over. She peeped round the door in the bathroom too: another bedroom, furnished more plainly, but with the same beautiful old pieces.

It was something she hadn't thought about; that Thomas had comfortable means had always been apparent, but this house of his was full of treasures. Had he inherited them? she wondered. Or did he collect old and valuable furniture as a hobby?

She went downstairs presently, determined to find out.

Thomas looked up from his letters as she went into the room. 'Is your room all right? Most of the furniture here was left to me by my grandmother, who had it from her husband's family—they had an enormous old house in Berkshire. I loved it when I went to stay with her as a boy, and I still do.'

'So do I, and it's just right for this house, isn't it?'

'I think so, and I'm glad you agree. This place isn't large but the period's right.'

'I was wondering—you know, while I was upstairs—if you collected old furniture or something like that?'

'No, but when we have found the house we like in the country we will spend time finding exactly the right furniture for it. I'm seldom free for any length of time, so it may take months.'

Lying in the four-poster, nicely drowsy, Claudia reviewed her wedding day. They had spent a happy evening together, talking like an old married couple, disagreeing pleasantly from time to time, discovering that they agreed about most things which mattered. Cork had served them with a splendid dinner—watercress soup, roast pheasant with all its trimmings, a dessert of his own devising—a concoction of ground almonds and whipped cream, angelica and crystallised fruit—and finally coffee in a very beautiful silver coffee pot, poured into paper-thin cups. They had drunk champagne, too, with Cork toasting them gravely and wishing them long life and happiness.

She had gone to bed quite happily. Wasn't there a song 'Getting to Know You'? That was what they were doing, wasn't it? Taking their time like two sensible people, but instead of getting engaged for a time before they married, they had married first.

'Let us give ourselves time to get to know and understand each other,' Thomas had said, and she had agreed. Life spread before her, undemanding and rather exciting. Tomorrow, she thought sleepily, she would go over the house with Cork, taking care not to encroach on his orderly life. She would wait for him to make the first suggestions as to what she should or should not do; later on, when he had accepted her, it would be for her to make suggestions...

Breakfast was at half past seven. When Thomas had suggested that she might like hers in bed, or later in the morning, she had told him that, no, she liked getting up early and would breakfast with him. She had seen his faint frown and hastened to add, 'Don't worry, I won't talk!'

In the morning she was as good as her word. Beyond a cheerful good morning she stayed silent, eating the scrambled eggs Cork put before her and following that with toast and marmalade. Thomas left before she had finished, dropping a hand on her shoulder as he went past her chair.

'I may be late home...'

'How late is late? Does Cork have a meal ready for you whatever time it is?'

'Yes. But I'll do my best to be here by eight o'clock. If I'm held up I'll phone, or get someone to do it for me.'

He had gone. She heard him speak to Cork in the hall before he went out to his car. She had finished breakfast when Cork came to clear the table.

'You will wish to see over the house, madam?'

'Yes, please, Cork. When it's convenient to you. I'm sure you have your day organised. I'd like to telephone my mother and write a letter or two, so will you let me know when you are ready? Does someone come in to give you a hand?'

'Mrs Rumbold comes each morning except Saturday and Sunday. A reliable, hardworking person, and entirely trustworthy. If it suits you, I will bring you coffee at ten o'clock, after which I shall be free to take you round the house.'

'Thank you, Cork. Ought I to meet Mrs Rumbold?'

'Certainly, if you wish, madam. I will bring her to you—she comes at nine o'clock.'

Claudia had a long and satisfying conversation with her mother, declaring herself to be entirely happy and promising a full description of the house later. She put the phone down as Cork came in with Mrs Rumbold—a stout lady with small dark eyes in a round face, a great deal of hair, in a most unlikely shade of ebony, and a wide smile.

Claudia got up and shook hands, and murmured suitably, and Mrs Rumbold's vast person quivered with cheerful laughter.

'Lor' bless me, ma'am, it's a great treat to see another female in the house. A bit of a surprise, but Mr Cork tells me as 'ow you and the Professor 'as known each other a while.'

Claudia smiled and said that, yes, indeed that was so. Cork coughed, a signal for Mrs Rumbold to take her departure, declaring that she'd do her best, same as always, and had never given Mr Cork cause to complain...

'I'm sure you haven't, Mrs Rumbold...'

She had her coffee presently, this time from a small silver coffee pot and a much larger cup, delicately patterned with roses. It looked so fragile that Claudia was in two minds as to whether to drink from it. But she did.

She went for a walk after lunch, finding her way round the quiet streets, lined by similar houses, going to the nearest main road to study the bus timetables. There were no large stores close by, although she did find a row of small shops tucked away behind an elegant row of houses. The kind of shops she was used to—selling wools and knitting needles and high-class green-groceries, an antiquarian bookshop, a tiny tea shop—very elegant—and at the end a dusty, rather shabby little place selling small antiques and a variety of odds and ends.

She spent some time looking in its window, and then walked back, thinking about her morning. Cork had been very helpful, but she felt he was still suspicious of her. He had shown her every nook and cranny of the house, every cupboard... The house was bigger than she had thought at first: three storeys high and every room charmingly furnished. Cork had a room and bathroom behind the kitchen in the semi-basement, and she had no doubt that it was comfortably furnished too.

The kitchen was very much to her own taste; a cheerful red Aga, a vast old-fashioned dresser along one wall, filled with plates and dishes, a square wooden table in the centre of the room, around which were an assortment of comfortable, rather shabby chairs, and pots and saucepans neatly stacked on the shelves on the walls. There were checked curtains at the window and a thick rug before the Aga. It reminded her of Great-Uncle William's kitchen... She reached the front door and rang the bell, reminding herself that she must ask Thomas for a key.

Thomas didn't get home until almost eight o'clock. She saw that he was tired and, beyond answering his queries as to how she had spent her day, she forebore from chattering. They dined in a companionable silence, and, since it was by then getting late in the evening, she said that she was tired and would go to bed if he didn't mind. It had been the right thing to say, but she tried not to mind when she saw the relief on his face.

Still, he bade her goodnight and kissed her cheek, then reminded her that he was free in the morning and they would go shopping. 'I shall open an account for you at Harrods and Harvey Nichols, and arrange for an allowance to be paid into your bank. But tomorrow we will shop together.'

He took her first to Harrods the next morning, accompanying her to the fashion floor, telling her to buy whatever she liked and making himself comfortable in one of the easy chairs scattered around.

'You mean a dress and coat, and things like that?' asked Claudia. 'How much may I spend?'

'One dress will hardly do. Buy several—and certainly a winter coat and anything else you like. Don't look at the price tags, Claudia.' He smiled at her. 'Buy all you need for the next few weeks; we shall be going out a good deal, I have no doubt...'

'Dinner dresses,' breathed Claudia, and her eyes sparkled.

'Certainly, and a couple of dresses for dancing—the hospital ball and so on. And something tweedy for the lakes. I shall take you walking.'

'You don't mind waiting here?'

'Not in the least. Come and show me what you buy from time to time, if you like.'

So Claudia, guided by a majestic saleslady in black crêpe, went shopping in earnest. She had had nothing new for some time, and her present wardrobe was sparse in the extreme, but that didn't prevent her from knowing exactly what she needed to buy.

A beautifully tailored winter coat in dark green, a tweed skirt with a matching soft leather jacket, a twinset in cashmere, peatbrown, a jersey dress in soft blue and another in dove-grey, and, at the sales lady's suggestion, a handful of silk blouses and another cardigan. She had shown most of these to a patient Mr Tait-Bullen, then gone with him to the restaurant for a cup of coffee before embarking on the choosing of a crêpe dress in old gold, and another in a green patterned silk jersey. She would have bought a little black dress, but when she mentioned her intention to Thomas he begged her not to. 'They're not for you,' he told her. 'Get something with a waist and a wide skirt.'

Which wasn't much to go by. Anxious to please him, she spent some time looking for such a garment and found it at last. Blue again—a smoky blue—with long sleeves and a modest neckline, and a tucked bodice cinched in at the waist by an embroidered belt, the skirt was several layers of chiffon, and it showed off her splendid figure. She paraded before him in it and saw that he approved.

'Would you like me to stop now?' she asked him.

'No. No. Let us by all means get the basics. What else do you need?'

'Well, evening dresses. I won't be long...'

She knew what suited her and she didn't dither, although there was a magnificent black taffeta she longed to own... She chose instead a russet taffeta with a tucked bodice, shoestring shoulder straps and a wide skirt which rustled delightfully as she walked. And a honey-coloured crêpe, very simple in cut.

'I've bought masses of clothes,' she told Thomas finally. 'I do hope....'

'We'll have lunch, and, if you haven't made me bankrupt, we will go to Harvey Nichols.'

'But I've bought masses of stuff.'

'Undies, dressing gowns, shoes, boots, a Burberry—a hat for church on Christmas Day?'

She stared up at him with wide eyes. 'You think of everything.'

'No, my dear, but you forget I have sisters, and I have from time to time accompanied them on shopping expeditions.'

'Oh, well, if you don't mind.'

'No, I don't mind,' said Mr Tait-Bullen, and thought how very pretty she looked.

They lunched at Harvey Nichols, in the basement bar-restaurant because Claudia declared that she was too full of excitement to eat much. All the same, gently urged on by Thomas, she managed grilled salmon and a salad, and apple tart, and, thus fortified, spent the next hour or so adding to her wardrobe. Having approved of the Burberry, boots, and shoes, Thomas left her in the undies department.

'I'll look around for presents for the family,' he told her, 'on the ground floor.' He glanced at his watch. 'An hour? I'll be waiting by the main entrance.' He smiled down at her happy face. 'Don't hurry.'

She lost herself in the delights of the lingerie department, but she remembered that he had said an hour. Laden with carrier bags, she went punctually to the ground floor and found him waiting.

He looked at the bags. 'They can be delivered with the other things,' he suggested.

She shook her head. 'I can't bear to part with them,' she told him seriously. 'You have no idea how lovely...'

'Shall we go home for tea?' he asked in a matter-of-fact way, which stopped her short.

They had their tea, and then an hour or so sitting together talking about nothing in particular. There would be more Christmas presents to buy, he warned her. And would she like to go to Little Planting before Christmas?

'I can spare a Sunday, if you would like that. And don't forget the hospital ball next week. You will be bound to get any number of invitations for us both from the people we meet there. I rely on you to deal with them. There is a certain amount of hospital social life, and you will probably be roped in for some charity or other. Don't take on too much...'

They were halfway through dinner when he was called away. He went quickly, warning her that he might be late back.

As he went he dropped a kiss on her cheek. 'I enjoyed our day together,' he told her.

'Me too. Only I've spent an awful lot of your money…'

'Our money,' he said quietly. 'It was a great pleasure.'

She sat in the drawing room that evening, leafing through magazines, thinking about her delightful day. Thomas had been a splendid companion too. Patient, and interested in what she had bought. Of course, she quite understood that as the wife of a well-known cardiologist she needed to be well turned out— he wouldn't want her to meet any of his friends and colleagues wearing the shabby tweeds and woollies she had always worn at Little Planting.

She got up and took a look at herself in the Georgian gilt-wood mirror. Perhaps she should have her hair cut and styled? Go to a beauty parlour and learn how to apply make-up? She tended to forget anything but lipstick; there had seemed no point in it when she lived with Great-Uncle William. On the sparse occasions when she'd gone out to dinner she had dashed powder over her nose, added lipstick and done her best with her hands, so often grubby from gardening. She would remedy this, she promised herself, so that Thomas need never feel ashamed of her.

The long case clock in the hall had struck eleven, and he still wasn't back. She went to the kitchen and found Cork sitting there, reading the evening paper.

She said quickly, 'No, no. Don't get up, Cork. I think I'll go to bed. Do you wait up or does the Professor let himself in? And does he need anything? A drink? Or sandwiches?'

'I wait up, madam. There is coffee, and there are sandwiches if he should require them. I'm sure he would wish you to take your normal rest.'

'Yes, well…I'll go to bed, then. Thank you, Cork.'

'Thank you, madam, and goodnight.'

He held the door for her and didn't return her smile. She went up to her room, still not sure if he approved of her or not. She must have been a surprise to him, and doubtless he wondered if she was going to interfere. She didn't intend to; perhaps she'd do the flowers, discuss the food with him and then later on, when he had accepted her, he might allow her into the kitchen.

Thomas was already at breakfast when she went down in the morning. He looked as he always did, immaculate in his sober grey suit and silk tie, but there were lines in his face...

She wished him good morning. 'When did you get home?' she asked.

'Round about one o'clock. I didn't disturb you?'

'No, no. Do you often get called out? I thought specialists and consultants could more or less please themselves.'

Mr Tait-Bullen looked surprised. 'We're just the same as any other medical man. We go when and where we're needed.'

'And you are going to the hospital this morning?'

'No, first to one of the private hospitals. I operated there a couple of days ago, and I must visit my patient there first. Then to the hospital, and a clinic after lunch, and then private patients at my consulting rooms.'

'Will you come home for lunch?'

He shook his head. 'I'm afraid not. I may be back in time for tea, though.' He glanced at her. 'You'll be all right?'

'Yes...'

'I should have warned you that I'm away a good deal.'

He left the house presently, and, since Cork informed her that it was Mrs Rumbold's day for turning out the drawing room, she guessed quite rightly, that they would like her out of the house.

'I thought I'd explore a bit,' she told him. 'Hyde Park and perhaps Kensington Gardens...'

'A pleasant walk, madam. Lunch at one o'clock?'

'Yes, please. Something on a tray will do.'

She had put on the tweed skirt and one of the silk shirts, and, since it was drizzling with a chilly wind, she donned the Burberry and the boots. The Burberry had a little matching hat, which she crammed onto her hair with no regard to her appearance, so that copper strands escaped. She took her new shoulder bag, her expensive leather gloves, bade Cork goodbye and left the house.

There weren't many people about as she made her way to Marble Arch. Cork, that paragon of servants, had thoughtfully provided her with a small street map, and it wasn't until she reached Marble Arch that there was much traffic and the first sight of Christmas shoppers.

She crossed the road into the park, following the Serpentine, enjoying the quiet emptiness, for there was scarcely anyone else to be seen. She was halfway to Rennie's Bridge, which would lead her to Kensington Gardens, when she saw a very small dog sitting under the bushes some yards from the path. He didn't bark, nor did he take any notice of her, and she walked on, supposing that its owner was somewhere nearby. But an hour later, as she came back the same way, he was still there.

There was no one in sight; she crossed the grass and bent down to take a closer look.

It was a very small dog indeed—a puppy, pitifully thin and shivering with cold. It made no sound as Claudia touched his matted coat with a gentle hand; it only looked at her with terrified eyes, cringing away from her. He was tied by a thin rope to a thicket behind him, and she could see that the rope was tight around his throat. If he'd tried to run away he would have choked.

She opened her bag, found the small folded scissors she always carried with her and began to saw through the rope. It took time, but the puppy didn't move, and when at last he was free she scooped him up and tucked him into the front of her Burberry, where he shivered and shook but made no effort to escape.

'You poor little scrap,' said Claudia. 'You're coming home with me, and I'll make sure that you're never frightened nor hungry again.'

It was only as she reached the house that she wondered what Thomas would say—or Cork!

He had seen her coming along the street and had the door open before she had a chance to get out her key.

She didn't beat about the bush. 'Cork, I found this tiny dog tied to a tree in Hyde Park. He's starving and cold...'

Cork peered at the small creature. 'The Professor has said on various occasions that he intended to get a dog, madam. Perhaps, a box with an old blanket by the Aga?'

'Oh, Cork, may he stay just until he's warm? And I thought a little warm milk… I'll have him as soon as I've got my things off.'

'If I might suggest, madam, you allow him to rest quietly for a period while you have lunch. By then we shall be able to see if he is recovering.'

So the puppy was settled in a cardboard box and covered warmly, and Claudia fed him with warm milk. Although he cringed still, he looked less terrified.

He was asleep when she went to fetch him after lunch.

'Thank you for having him in the kitchen, Cork, I won't let him bother you.'

'I have no doubt that when he is feeling more himself he will be a nice little dog. I'm partial to dogs, madam.'

Claudia beamed at him. 'Oh, are you, Cork? So am I.'

She took the little beast with her to the sitting room beside Thomas's study—a charming little room, where she chose to sit and have her meals when Thomas was away from home—and he fell asleep by the warmth of the fire, twitching and whimpering in his sleep. And when Cork brought her tea tray he handed her a small jug. 'Egg and milk, madam,' he explained. 'Perhaps a few spoonfuls from time to time…'

They inspected the sleeping puppy and decided that he looked a little better.

'As soon as I dare, I'll clean him up a bit,' said Claudia. 'He's stopped shivering…'

She went to her room presently, and changed her blouse and skirt for one of the jersey dresses, not bothering overmuch about her face and hair. She was feeding the puppy, kneeling by the box, rather untidy about the head, when Thomas came quietly to join her.

She scrambled to her feet when she saw him. 'Thomas, I'm so glad you're home. Come and see what I found this morning…' She paused while Cork placed a tea tray on the rent table by the easy chair where Mr Tait-Bullen often sat. 'I'll pour your tea. Have you had a busy day?'

He could see that for the moment his day would have to take second place to whatever it was in the box which had given her eyes such a sparkle and her cheeks such a fine colour.

'And what did you find?' He went over to the box and got down on his hunkers to take a better look.

'Cork says you always wanted a dog...'

Mr Tait-Bullen choked back a laugh. 'Oh, indeed I have.' He put a gentle finger on the skinny little body. 'Lost? Starved? Probably ill-treated. Where did you find him?'

'Sit down and drink your tea and I'll tell you. Then you can examine him, can't you?'

He drank his tea and ate the toast she offered him, and listened without interrupting. 'And Cork has been marvellous. I thought he would mind—I mean, a grubby little dog in this lovely house—'

'Our house,' he interrupted her gently.

'Well, of course it is, but you know what I mean, don't you? Please may we keep him? I don't know what kind of a dog he is, but I dare say he'll be handsome when he's older.'

Mr Tait-Bullen studied the puppy thoughtfully. 'There is always that possibility,' he agreed. 'Let's have a look at him.'

Claudia was surprised to see that the puppy accepted Thomas's gentle hands feeling his poor, bony frame, with no more than the whisper of a whine.

'Starved and kicked around, but I can't feel any broken bones. I'm on nodding terms with the local vet; I'll get him to come round and take a look.'

'May we keep him? You don't mind?'

'No, I don't mind. Cork was right. I have often said that I would like a dog.' He didn't add that the dog he had had in mind was a thoroughbred Labrador.

They dined presently, and tended to the puppy's needs, and later that evening the vet came. He was a youngish, thickset man, with a great deal of black hair and a face one could trust.

'Thomas, what's all this about a dog? Where did you get it?'

'Come and meet my wife. It was she who found the creature.'

The two men crossed the hall to the sitting room, where Claudia had gone to feed the puppy.

The vet shook hands. He had heard about Tait-Bullen's unexpected marriage, and, glancing at Claudia, he considered him to be a lucky fellow. Beautiful and charming—nice voice too.

He said out loud, 'I must get Alice—my wife—to call on you. Now, where's this dog?'

He took his time going over the puppy's small frame. 'No bones broken. Several swellings, though—he's been kicked. And just look at these paws—he's been tied up somewhere and tried to escape. Poor little beast.'

'Any idea what breed?' said Mr Tait-Bullen.

'Take your pick. He'll never be a large dog, nor perhaps a handsome one, but I guarantee he'll be a faithful companion to you both. I'll give him a couple of jabs while I'm here. As to food and exercise...'

He outlined suitable treatment. 'And a run in the garden is all he'll need for several weeks—that and frequent small meals.' He looked at Claudia. 'You will be busy, Mrs Tait-Bullen.'

'I've time enough to look after him, and I shall enjoy it. You'll have a cup of coffee?'

He stayed for a while, idly chatting, and presently Thomas went with him to the door. 'You've a charming wife, Thomas. You must come to dinner one evening.'

'We'll be delighted.'

He went back to the sitting room, where Claudia was kneeling by the puppy's box. She looked up as he went in. 'Thomas, thank you. Perhaps he's not the kind of dog you wanted, but he'll be such fun to have.'

Mr Tait-Bullen contemplated the skinny creature, sitting up now and no longer cowering, knowing that he was among friends. Under the dirt and mud his coat was black. His ears were far too large for his small foxy face, and he had a long, thin tail of which any rat would have been proud.

'I have no doubt that he will grow into the most unusual type,' he observed gravely.

'That's what I thought,' said Claudia happily. 'I like the vet. Are all your friends as nice?'

'I hope you will think so. You will meet a good many of them at the ball.' He went to sit in his chair, stretching his long legs to the fire. 'I'm sure you have a grand gown to wear among your purchases, or would you like to look for something else?'

'I have a gown. It's not grand, but I think it's suitable for your wife, if you see what I mean?'

'I trust your judgement, Claudia. You have excellent taste.'

Claudia went to bed with the pleasant feeling that it had been a happy day; they got on so well together, she reflected, and there was so much to talk about, so much that they intended to do together. Every day, she was discovering, she was finding out something else about Thomas that she liked; she hoped that he felt the same about her. She curled up and closed her eyes. Tomorrow was another day; she wondered what it would bring.

Fortunately for her peace of mind she wasn't to know *who* it would bring!

CHAPTER SIX

THE day began well. Thomas had no need to leave the house until nine o'clock, so they had leisure to clean up the puppy, anoint his battered little paws and brush his coat while he lay on Claudia's lap.

'What shall we call him?' she asked. 'A nice English name, since I found him in Hyde Park.'

'Since you found him you must choose his name.'

'Yes, well...' She thought for a moment. 'Harvey—that's easy to say, isn't it?'

Harvey cocked an ungainly ear; he was beginning to look more like a dog every minute.

Mr Tait-Bullen went presently, promising that he would be back for tea unless some emergency turned up.

'Oh, good,' said Claudia, with such transparent pleasure that he turned to look at her. She met his gaze with a look of faint enquiry. 'You look surprised. But teatime is one of the nicest parts of the day, isn't it? You can tell me what you've been doing and I'll listen...'

Mr Tait-Bullen discovered to his surprise that the idea appealed to him.

At four o'clock Cork arranged the tea things on a small table in the drawing room, and, since Mr Tait-Bullen had phoned to say that he would be home shortly after half past four, Claudia carried Harvey in his box from the sitting room and set it near the open fire. She had been out walking again, and was still in the tweed skirt and a blouse, but she had tidied her hair and powdered her nose and put on a pair of elegant kid slippers. She was sitting admiring them when Thomas came in.

He crossed the room and dropped a quick kiss on her cheek. 'How very cosy it is here. Cork's bringing the tea.'

He sat down opposite her. 'You have had a happy day? Harvey is doing well?'

'He's better. Look at him, Thomas. He's almost like a normal puppy.'

Harvey took this as a compliment and waved his tail.

'You don't mind him being in here? I don't think he'll get out of his box.'

'I don't imagine he could do much harm even if he did. He certainly looks more like a dog.' Thomas stretched an arm and tickled Harvey behind one ear. 'I must let John know how he's getting on. I dare say he'll want to see him again.'

Cork brought in the tea then, and buttered muffins in a dish, a fruit cake and a plate of paper-thin sandwiches. He arranged everything just so, and stood back to admire his handiwork.

Claudia said, 'Thank you, Cork, it all looks delicious. I hope you're going to have your own tea now?'

'Thank you, madam, yes. Dinner at the usual hour? You won't be going out again, sir?'

'I hope not, Cork.' And, as Cork slid through the door, Thomas added, 'I've a mass of paperwork to sort out. A quiet evening at home to get that done will be delightful.'

Claudia, pouring tea, agreed placidly. If she had been looking forward to an evening in his company, she didn't utter the thought aloud.

They were inspecting the fruit cake when the front doorbell was rung. And, before either of them had time to speak, Cork opened the door and stood aside to let someone in.

Mr Tait-Bullen got to his feet, his face expressionless, and his pleasant, 'Why, Honor, how nice to see you,' giving nothing away of his feelings.

Claudia stood up too, recognising in an instant that here was someone she wasn't going to like and who wasn't going to like her. But she smiled, a bright social smile, and then looked enquiringly at Thomas.

'My dear, let me introduce Honor Thompson. Honor, my wife, Claudia.'

Claudia offered a hand. 'Do sit down and have a cup of tea. I'll get Cork to bring a fresh pot...'

Honor sat on the sofa facing the fire, throwing off her coat to reveal a black dress—very short, very smart and undoubtedly very expensive. It showed off her long legs and her very slim body.

No shape at all, thought Claudia, and wondered if Thomas admired women who looked like beanpoles. She was suddenly aware of her own curves, and busied herself with the fresh tea Cork had brought in, listening with half an ear to Honor's rather loud voice complaining that she had had no idea that Thomas was getting married and why hadn't he told her. 'You must have known what a shock it would be to me.'

She glanced at Claudia, who handed her a cup and saucer. 'I expect you and Thomas are very old friends,' Claudia remarked. 'But, you see, we didn't tell anyone except our families. It was a very quiet wedding.'

'Well, I for one shan't forgive you easily, Thomas,' said Honor, and she leaned forward to lay a hand on his arm.

Mr Tait-Bullen got up and put his cup and saucer on the table without answering her, and she flushed angrily.

'Of course, I don't suppose you know much about Thomas. You can't have known each other long.' She gave Claudia a sly look.

'Long enough to know that we wanted to be married,' said Claudia, in a matter-of-fact voice which robbed the question of drama. 'You live in London?'

'Of course. Where else is there?'

'You don't care to travel?' asked Claudia guilelessly. 'I mean, around England? Perhaps all your friends live here?'

'I hate the country. I adore the theatre and dining out and dancing.' She gave a little trill of laughter. 'I can see that Thomas will have to change his ways now that he is a married man.'

'I expect most men do,' said Claudia cheerfully. 'And I don't suppose they mind or they wouldn't marry, would they?' She smiled at Thomas. 'Don't you agree, Thomas?'

'Wholeheartedly. Honor, take a look at our addition to the household.'

He bent and picked up Harvey, tucked him under an arm and went over to where Honor was sitting.

She eyed Harvey with dislike. 'You aren't serious? It's a horrid little stray. He must be filthy, and he's hideously ugly...'

'He's a brave little dog. We call him Harvey—he'll probably grow into something quite splendid. He's still rather grubby, but he's been ill-treated—look at this sore on his shoulder, and under his paws...'

Honor shrank back. 'Don't come any nearer with the nasty little brute...' She stood up. 'I must go. I'm going out this evening.' She turned a cold eye on Claudia. 'Nice meeting you, Claudia. I dare say we shall see each other around—that is, if you go out much socially.'

She didn't shake hands, and she didn't shake hands with Thomas either, since he was still holding Harvey. She reached the door as Cork, summoned by the bell-push by the fireplace, opened it and ushered her out.

It wasn't until he had returned and carried away the tea tray that Claudia said, 'I hope you're grateful that I married you. She would have eaten you alive in a couple of years. Are all your girl friends like that?'

Mr Tait-Bullen had gone back to his chair with Harvey curled up on his knee. He had expected a reproachful comment, or at least coolness and hurt looks, and he was taken aback by Claudia's cheerful question. Taken aback and, he had to admit, amused.

'I only now begin to realise what a treasure I have married. I am indeed grateful that you are my wife; calm, good sense and not a single sulky look. I can assure you that I have never had any intention of marrying Honor, although I suspect that she had the intention of marrying me. And I have had no girl-friends. Oh, I have taken Honor out from time to time, and other women too, but on a strictly platonic basis. I have not been in love for a very long time. If that were so, I would have told you.'

'Oh, my goodness, I didn't mean to pry. It's none of my business. All the same, I'm glad that it's me you married.'

'And so am I. Now, let us forget the woman and talk about other things which matter. I can be free next Sunday; shall we go down to Little Planting? Will your mother and George be home?'

'Yes, they only went away for a few days because they want to spend Christmas at home, and Mother enjoys all the preparations, you know—the tree and paper chains and holly and presents. She always managed to make it a lovely time when we lived with Great-Uncle William.'

'Then we will go, and take Harvey with us. Do you want to shop for presents?'

'I could go tomorrow...and what about your family? Should we not buy more presents for them?'

'I can't spare the time; if I give you a list, will you do your best for us both?'

It was the kind of question that required nothing more than a meek answer.

She went shopping the next morning; Thomas had left the house early, and she found no one when she went down to breakfast, but by her plate was a list of names scrawled in his unreadable writing. A long list, starting with his mother and ending with someone called Maggie, with brackets beside her name requesting warm slippers, size six! His father wasn't mentioned—presumably he bought that present himself. She added Cork's name, and Mrs Rumbold's. Probably Thomas gave them money, but a personal gift was always nice to have...

She found a cashmere stole for her mother-in-law, silk scarves for his sisters, and a small leather case containing razor, hairbrush and a variety of small necessities which a man might need when travelling. And then she decided that scarves weren't enough for his sisters; she added a small silver photo frame and a little enamelled box. There were nephews and nieces too; she spent a happy hour in the toy department of Harrods.

Thomas got home in the early evening, and she saw at once that for the moment at least he had no wish to look at what she had bought. He had greeted her in his usual manner, given her a drink, poured one for himself and gone to sit in his chair. Harvey had climbed out of his box and wriggled his way on to his knee, and Thomas now stroked the small creature gently.

'You have had a pleasant day?' he asked presently.

'Yes, thank you. But you don't want to hear about it for the moment, do you? Do you want to talk about your day? I dare say I won't understand the half of it, but I'll be a pair of ears.'

He laughed then. 'Claudia, you are so understanding. It is as if we had been married for years—you are such a comfortable woman to come home to. And at the end of the day sometimes a pair of ears is what I most want.'

He began to talk: a difficult diagnosis, a long list in Theatre, a post-operative patient who wasn't progressing as well as he should, and always a backlog of patients who needed his skill.

Claudia listened to every word. There was quite a bit she didn't understand, but that didn't matter; she was intelligent enough to have a good idea as to his working day.

Presently she asked, 'Do you have a team working with you?'

'Yes, a splendid one. My senior registrar is a most dependable man, and I have two junior registrars and a couple of young surgeons—you'll meet them all at the ball. And a splendid theatre sister too.'

Claudia felt a faint flicker of something which she didn't recognise as jealousy. All she knew was that she felt regret that *she* couldn't be his theatre sister, working beside him.

Thomas smiled across at her. 'Have I bored you? You must tell me if I do.'

'No, I like to know something of your work. I'm really interested.'

Cork came to tell them then that dinner was on the table and Thomas said, 'You must tell me what you have bought...'

She spent the next day shopping for her mother and George, and Tombs, Mrs Pratt and Jennie. It was nice having enough money to choose presents without having to bother too much about their price. Thomas had given her a very generous allowance, and told her carelessly not to worry if she spent too much, but she reminded herself that she hadn't married him for his money. Indeed, she admitted, she would have married him if he were penniless. The thought surprised her, and left her feeling disquieted.

The day after that was the hospital ball. Anxious to present as pleasing a picture as possible, Claudia spent most of the afternoon doing her nails, washing her hair, and experimenting with make-up. But by teatime she had decided that her usual dash of powder and lipstick would do. As for her hair, after a tiring hour pinning it into a variety of elaborate styles, she decided to twist it into a chignon—a simple style which suited her lovely face and which required no fuss. She suspected that Thomas would dislike it if she were to fidget about her appearance.

He had expected to be home early, but Cork had carried away the tea things and there was no sign of him. They had planned to have a light meal before going to the ball, and when she heard the clock strike seven she went along to the kitchen with Harvey trotting beside her.

'Cork, what is best to be done? We are to leave here by half past eight, and the Professor will want time to change. Would it be a good idea if you served a meal in the sitting room? We were going to have grilled soles, weren't we? Could they be saved for tomorrow? And could you give us soup and an omelette? Then whatever time he comes in we could eat when he is ready?'

'I have been thinking along those lines, madam: a plain omelette with a small salad, and I have prepared a sustaining soup with fresh-baked rolls.'

'Cork, that will be simply splendid. I'm going up to dress...'

Thomas came home half an hour later and Claudia, fresh from her bath and ready save for getting into her dress, wrapped her dressing gown round her and went down to meet him.

He looked tired after his long day, but he said cheerfully, 'Hello—did you begin to think I wasn't coming home?'

'Well, we were getting a bit anxious.' He hadn't kissed her, but she told herself that it didn't matter a bit. 'Would you like a meal at once, or do you want to change first?'

'I see that you aren't dressed yet.' He eyed her pretty pink quilted dressing gown. 'Shall we eat now?'

'Cork has a meal ready for us; we're having it in the sitting room. How well he looks after you, Thomas.'

He looked at her sharply. 'And you, too?'

'Heavens, yes! He's a treasure.' She led the way into the sitting room, scooping up Harvey as they went. He was still a somewhat battered little animal, but now that he found himself among friends, he was full of a desire to please.

Cork offered the soup, and presently the omelette, looking gratified when Thomas observed that it was exactly the meal he needed. Cork, having overheard Claudia's praise of him, murmured that it was madam who had suggested it. It was an unusually generous remark on his part, but he was becoming aware that Claudia had no intention of ousting him from his position in the household. In fact, he was beginning to like her.

The meal eaten, they went away to dress, and half an hour later met again in the drawing room. Claudia, in the cream chiffon, wasn't sure if Thomas would find it grand enough, but she need not have worried.

He watched her cross the room. 'Delightful, Claudia. Exactly right. You look charming.' He took a box from the table beside him. 'Will you wear these?' he asked. 'I think they will go very well with the dress.'

He offered pearls, a double row with a diamond clasp, and to go with them earrings, pearl drops set in a delicate network of diamonds.

'My goodness,' said Claudia, 'they're magnificent, Thomas.' She touched the pearls with a gentle finger. 'I'm almost afraid to wear them.' She smiled at him. 'Thank you very much.'

She stretched up and kissed his cheek, and he took the necklace from her and fastened it round her throat.

'My grandmother left them to me with the advice that they should be given to my wife when I married.'

'She must have loved you,' said Claudia, and swallowed disappointment; they weren't a present from Thomas—not something he had wanted to buy for her, to give her as a present; he was merely carrying out his grandmother's wishes.

She said rather too brightly, 'I'm ready if you want to leave now.'

He gave her a thoughtful look, which she met with an equally bright smile. He looked distinguished in his black tie; the formal suit, cut by a master tailor, emphasised his height and size. He was a handsome man, she reflected, who ignored his good looks and had not an ounce of conceit. He was high-handed at times, perhaps, and capable of a fine rage, she suspected, but, like so many large men, gentle.

Cork, with Harvey tucked under an arm, saw them from the house, and it was only when they were driving through the quiet streets towards the busy heart of the city that Claudia felt the first pangs of nervousness.

'I don't know anyone...'

She felt his large, comforting hand on her knee for a moment. 'Don't worry, my dear, you will soon have more friends and acquaintances than you can imagine.'

'Oh—are you very well known, Thomas?'

'Well, I do visit a number of hospitals, and have done for some years now.'

He turned the car into the hospital forecourt, parked and helped her out.

He nodded to one of the porters standing at the entrance, and one of them got into the car and drove it away as they went in.

After that Claudia found herself in a sort of dream world. Thomas led her from one hospital dignitary to the other, a hand under her elbow guiding her, and when the formalities were over he took her onto the dance floor. He danced well, in an unspectacular way, guiding her effortlessly through the crowded hall, talking casually from time to time, putting her at her ease so that presently she found herself dancing with a variety of partners and enjoying herself.

From time to time she glimpsed him dancing, partnering his colleagues' wives, she supposed, slightly older women, well

dressed and self-assured, but once or twice she saw that he was
dancing with pretty girls, who laughed up into his face as
though they had known him for years...

She was about to take to the floor with a stout, bearded man,
whom she vaguely remembered having been introduced to,
when Thomas slipped a hand under her elbow.

'The supper dance,' he observed mildly. 'You don't mind,
Harry, if I claim my wife?'

The bearded man laughed. 'It wouldn't make a scrap of difference if I did, Thomas, but I shall lie in wait for you, Mrs
Tait-Bullen!'

'Who was that?' asked Claudia, accepting a plate of vol-au-
vents and a glass of wine. 'I've met him, haven't I?'

'Yes, he's the consultant pathologist and an old friend.' He
smiled. 'You're enjoying yourself? I've been showered with
compliments about my bride.'

She went pink. 'Oh, have you? People are very kind.'

'I have been told how beautiful you are—and you are,
Claudia, that dress is exactly right.'

Somehow that last bit spoilt the compliment.

'You have been dancing with some very pretty girls. Of
course, you must know all the nurses.'

He fetched her a little dish of ice cream before he replied.

'Not quite all. You see, I meet only ward sisters and staff
nurses, and then our conversation is purely professional, but
once a year at this ball the senior staff dance with those of the
nursing staff they work with on the wards or in Theatre or the
clinics. I don't know who started the idea, but the custom is
handed down from one generation of doctors to the next.'

A remark which she found reassuring.

It was well past midnight when they got back home. Cork
had left hot chocolate on the Aga, and they sat drinking it while
Harvey snoozed in his basket.

'A very pleasant evening,' observed Mr Tait-Bullen, 'and
you have won all hearts, Claudia.'

'It's nice of you to say so, but it's only because I'm a nine-
days wonder.'

He laughed. 'What a matter-of-fact girl you are.' He took her mug from her. 'And a sleepy one, too. I must leave the house by seven o'clock, so don't get up until you have had your sleep. I should be home for tea.'

'Oh, good.' She yawned, and rubbed her eyes like a child. 'It was a lovely evening, and it was lovely to dance.'

He got up and hauled her gently from her chair. 'Indeed it was.'

He opened the door and gave her a gentle shove. 'Off to bed, and sleep well.'

She hesitated a moment, but he held the door open, smiling a little, so she wished him goodnight and took herself off to bed, feeling vaguely unhappy.

She woke late, and when she went downstairs Cork was waiting for her with Harvey scampering at his heels.

'You slept well, madam? I have set breakfast in the sitting room by the fire. A most inclement day, I'm afraid. I am to tell you from the Professor not to venture too far in this weather.'

Claudia peeped out of the window. Indeed, it looked horrid outside—dull and grey with an unremitting drizzle.

'It looks awful, Cork, but Harvey must have his run...'

'Perhaps a brisk turn in the garden, madam. There is always the chance that the weather will improve.'

'Well, I hope it does, for we are going to Little Planting on Sunday. We'll take Harvey with us.' She poured her coffee. 'Cork, you do have a day off each week, don't you?'

'I have two half-days, madam, and such free time as I can arrange without upset to the running of the house.'

He sounded cagey, and she added hastily, 'I'm sure you have it all worked out, Cork. But I just thought that it would be a chance for you to have a day to yourself while we are out.'

'Thank you, madam. I shall avail myself of your offer...'

'I expect that you have family and friends to visit?'

'Indeed, I have. At what time will you be leaving on Sunday, madam?'

'Quite early, I believe, and we shan't be back here until after tea.'

She finished her breakfast and spent the morning tying up presents, considerably hampered by Harvey. When, after lunch, the drizzle ceased, she got into her mac, tied Harvey into his waterproof jacket, and led him out for a quick walk. On the way home she stopped to look in the windows of the little shops she had found. The wool shop had a pretty knitting pattern in the window, with a basket of wools every colour of the rainbow. She already had a present for her mother, but there was no reason why she shouldn't give her another one. She scooped up Harvey, tucked him under her arm and went into the shop.

In the end shop, in amongst the glass and silver bits and pieces, she found a small porcelain model of a dog, the spitting image of Harvey, just right for Thomas's desk. She went home well pleased with her finds, and found Thomas sitting by the drawing room fire reading the papers.

'Oh, how lovely; you're home. No, don't get up. I'll tell Cork I'm back and we'll have tea.'

When she had poured the tea and offered him sandwiches she asked, 'Have you had a busy day?'

Mr Tait-Bullen bit into a buttered scone. 'Much as usual.' He offered Harvey a bit of scone, and didn't see the disappointment on her face. He seemed to shut her out of his working life sometimes. Perhaps he thought that she was not really interested. He added, 'You have created quite a sensation, you know...'

'Me? Didn't I behave like a consultant's wife? Shouldn't I have danced so much?'

'You behaved beautifully, my dear, and everyone is enchanted by you. I was inundated with invitations. I can see that we have a busy social winter ahead of us.'

'Do you mind that? If you do, I'll make excuses.'

'No, you mustn't do that. I rely on you to organise our leisure, and several of the invitations will be for you alone, I imagine—coffee mornings and tea parties.'

He finished his tea, and, with the remark that he had work to do, went to his study. Harvey went with him and she was left sitting alone. She had declared rather too quickly that she had letters to write, and he had nodded casually with the remark that they would meet at dinner.

He had told her before they married that he wanted a companion. It seemed to her that he had forgotten that—or was it that she bored him? She told herself not to be silly, allowing imagination—and, it must be admitted, a modicum of self-pity—to take over.

But she forgot all that when at dinner he suggested that they leave early on Sunday morning so that they might take a look at some likely villages not too far from Little Planting.

'Is there any particular village you fancy? We might at least look around us, so that after Christmas we can house-hunt in earnest.'

'Would we spend the weekends there?'

'Whenever possible, and any free days that I can manage. Somewhere not too far from a good road back to town.'

'Well, there's a lovely little village—Child Okeford—south of Shaftesbury, close to Blandford, and only a mile or so from the main roads. Years ago I used to go there with Mother, she had an old schoolfriend living there, but she moved away. I dare say it's changed. I must have been nine or ten years old.'

'Then we will have a look at it before we go to Little Planting. If we leave really early we should have plenty of time to look around.'

They left at eight o'clock. It still wasn't full daylight, and the streets were Sunday morning quiet. The presents were packed in the boot, and Harvey, wrapped in an old shawl, slept peacefully on the back seat. Claudia felt her spirits soar as she got into the car. She was wearing the leather jacket over a silk shirt and a tweed skirt, and leather boots which had cost so much that she felt quite faint when she thought about it. But they were worth every penny—as supple as velvet and exactly matching the colour of her jacket.

She would have liked to draw Thomas's attention to them, but he seldom noticed what she wore, although he never failed to tell her that she looked nice. But he didn't *look*, she reflected, not at her, not to see her in detail, as it were. She dismissed the thought as unworthy; he was a kind and thoughtful husband and they got on famously.

They reached Child Okeford an hour and a half later. There was a pale watery sun now, and the village still slept under it. In another hour there would be church, and people setting off in their cars or going for a country walk, but for the moment they had the place to themselves.

'Could we park and look around?' asked Claudia.

They left the car in the centre of the village and, with Harvey on his lead, began to explore.

'It hasn't changed much,' said Claudia. 'The village shop's still there, and the pub.' They paused to admire the church and walked the length of the main street, stopping to explore the narrow side turnings. It was a charming place; its cottages well kept, with one or two bigger houses standing back from the road. They had gone its length when Claudia saw a narrow lane leading away from it, half hidden by high hedges.

'Let's take a look, Thomas...'

The lane curved, and they passed two cottages with their doors opening directly onto the lane, and then round the next curve they saw another cottage, quite large, standing behind hedges. There was a 'For Sale' board beside its old-fashioned wrought iron gate.

It must have been empty for some time, for the windows were uncurtained and the garden was woefully overgrown.

Claudia looked at Thomas, and he opened the gate and they walked up the brick path to the solid door under the thatched porch. There were windows on either side, and small windows above, tucked away under the thatch.

Claudia went to peer through one of the windows. 'The kitchen,' she said. 'There's another window at the side, and two doors. Come and look, Thomas.'

She went round the side of the cottage and found a door, and, at the back, more windows. A quite large room and next to it a room which took up the whole of the other side of the cottage. She bent to peer through the letterbox. 'There's a staircase,' she told Thomas, but when she turned round he wasn't there. He was by the gate, writing down the address of the house agents.

'Oh, Thomas, do you like it? I mean, well enough to want to see inside?'

Mr Tait-Bullen put away his notebook and walked up the path to join her.

'Yes, I like it, too. The agent is a local man—Blandford—supposing we go and see him? I'll phone him from the car—he might even come here to us.'

'Now? This morning? Oh, Thomas...'

He looked at her, smiling a little. Her cheeks were flushed and her eyes shone with excitement. He had the sudden urge to wrap her in his arms and kiss her. The thought took him by surprise; it was as though he was seeing her for the first time.

'Now, this morning,' he assured her, and nothing in his level voice showed his feelings.

They went back to the car and he phoned from there. The agent was willing to drive to meet them at the cottage. He would be with them in half an hour, he assured them.

'Shall we phone your mother?' suggested Thomas. 'Tell her that we may be a little later than we intended?'

That done, they went back to the cottage, and while they were waiting poked round the garden. It was quite large, and there was a rough track at the side of it which led to a sizeable barn.

'The garage?' asked Claudia hopefully. 'And, look, there was a greenhouse there and a summer house...' She clutched his arm. 'Oh, Thomas.'

The agent was middle-aged and fatherly, wearing comfortable country tweeds and carrying a bunch of large keys. When Mr Tait-Bullen apologised for disturbing his Sunday, he made light of it. 'Come inside,' he invited. 'It's solid enough, roof was thatched a couple of years ago, brick and cob walls, the usual mod cons; the old lady who lived here went into a nursing home six months ago, but she kept the place in good order.'

He opened the door with a flourish and stood aside to let them in.

The hall was narrow, with a staircase along one wall. There were three doors, and Claudia opened the first one. The room was large, with windows both at the front and the back of the house, an inglenook and open beams. Claudia rotated slowly, seeing the room in her mind's eye just how it would look—an open fire, comfortable chairs, little tables with lamps on them, bookshelves. She crossed the hall, taking Thomas with her. The room on the other side of the hall was smaller, with cupboards on either side of an old-fashioned grate and more open beams.

'The dining room,' she breathed happily, and went into the kitchen. A quite large room, with an old-fashioned dresser and windows on either side of a door to the garden. And upstairs, leading off the small landing, were three rooms, two of them small but the third of an ample size. There was a bathroom too, rather old-fashioned, but the plumbing, the agent assured them, was up-to-date.

Claudia wandered round on her own while the two men talked quietly in the hall, and presently Thomas went in search of her. She was hanging out of a bedroom window, planning the garden in her mind's eye.

'You like it? I've made an offer; he'll let me know tomorrow when he's contacted the owner.'

Claudia flung her arms round his neck. 'Thomas, oh, Thomas!' And she kissed him. She hadn't kissed him like that before, and she drew back at once, rather red in the face. 'Sorry—I got carried away.'

Mr Tait-Bullen didn't allow the normally calm expression on his face to alter. The kiss had stirred him, but all he said was, 'Let us hope that we are able to buy the place.'

She reminded herself that he was not a man to be easily aroused from his habitual calm. But he liked the little place; she could see that. They would furnish it together and spend happy weekends there and get to know each other.

CHAPTER SEVEN

CLAUDIA'S mother came to meet them as they stopped before George's door.

'Darling, what kept you? You haven't had an accident?' She looked anxiously at Thomas. 'All you said was that you were unexpectedly delayed... But come in, do, there's coffee and mince pies...'

It had been a happy day, reflected Claudia, sitting beside Thomas as he drove back to London in the early evening. Such a lot of cheerful talk, presents to exchange, Tombs and Mrs Pratt to visit, a walk after lunch with Rob and Harvey, and, of course, the cottage to be discussed while the men exchanged views on medical matters.

Claudia, with her mother's enthusiastic help had had the place metaphorically furnished, the curtains hung and the garden dug and in full bloom by the time they got into the car. She'd still been thinking about it as Thomas began the journey home.

'Blue and white checked curtains in the kitchen, and that white china with blue rings round it—you know the kind I mean?'

'I can't say that I do, but I shall leave such matters to you—if and when the cottage is ours.'

She felt a stab of disappointment. Furnishing the little place together would have been fun. She reminded herself that he was a busy man, and that any free time he had he would want to spend in a way to please himself. She said, 'It was a lovely day, Thomas, thank you for bringing me. Harvey enjoyed himself too.'

They didn't talk much more on the way back. Thomas replied cheerfully enough to her remarks, but she sensed indifference. A polite indifference, but all the same it was there, like an invisible wall between them. It was a relief to get home and find Cork waiting for them in the warm, well lighted hall.

He led Harvey away to the kitchen for his supper, and Claudia, casting off her jacket, followed him.

'Have you had a pleasant day, Cork?'

'Yes, thank you, madam. I trust that you had an enjoyable trip?'

'Yes, yes, we did.' She would have liked to tell him about the cottage, but perhaps Thomas might not like that.

Cork, spooning Harvey's supper into a dish, said civilly, 'Would supper in half an hour suit you, madam?'

She said that yes, that would be fine, and wandered away out of the kitchen and up to her room to tidy herself. When she went downstairs presently there was no sign of Thomas.

Cork met her in the hall. 'The Professor has been called away—an emergency—he will phone you as soon as he is able. He had no time to say more, madam.'

Claudia stood in the hall looking at him, saying nothing, so he added, 'I'll serve you supper at once—there's no knowing when he will be back, madam.'

'All right, Cork. Let's hope it's nothing that will keep him away for too long.'

She ate her solitary meal and then went to sit in the drawing room, with Harvey for company. The evening was well advanced by now, and there had been no message. She sat there, pretending to read, her ears stretched to hear the sound of his return or a phone call, but there was neither. At midnight she took Harvey to his bed in the kitchen, and bade Cork goodnight after being told that he would wait up— 'The Professor wouldn't want you to lose your sleep, madam,' he said, and was interrupted by the phone.

He answered it, and then handed it to Claudia

'Go to bed, Claudia. I shall probably be here for most of the night. Sleep well—I'll have a word with Cork.'

She handed the phone to Cork, who listened with an expressionless face. His 'Very well, sir' was uttered in a disapproving voice, and when he rang off he said, 'I am not to wait up, madam. I'll lock up as soon as you are upstairs.'

There was nothing else to do but wish him goodnight, give Harvey a quick cuddle and go to her room.

She had expected to stay awake, waiting for Thomas's return, but she fell asleep almost at once to wake hours later, not knowing why she had wakened. The house was quiet, but all the same she got up, peered at her clock and saw that it was almost four o'clock. She got into her dressing gown and slippers and crept downstairs, and as she reached the hall, the front door opened very quietly and Thomas came in.

He closed the door equally quietly before he spoke. 'Shouldn't you be in bed?'

Disappointment at his terse greeting turned her pleasure at seeing him to peevishness. 'Of course I should,' she snapped. 'I'm not in the habit of wandering round the house at this hour. I woke up—I don't know why...'

She started towards the kitchen. 'I'll get you a drink; you're tired.'

'Nothing to drink, thank you, but I am tired. Go back to bed. I'll go to bed myself as soon as I've put my bag away.'

She felt a childish wish to burst into tears. He was behaving as though he wished she wasn't there. She turned to go upstairs again, and then paused.

'At what time will you want breakfast?'

He was already at his study door. 'The usual time.'

'But it's after four o'clock!'

He didn't answer, but went in and shut the door. Now that there was no one to see, she allowed unhappy tears to trickle down her cheeks as she went upstairs.

As for Mr Tait-Bullen, he sat down at his desk and allowed all kinds of thoughts to fill his head. The sight of Claudia, standing in the hall in her pink gown, her hair in glorious wildness with that look on her face, had disturbed him deeply. When he had envisaged being married to her he hadn't imagined anything like that. She was Claudia, a girl he admired and liked, a perfect companion and a wife whose company he would enjoy without any of the hazards of being in love with her.

Being in love was something he had lost faith in years ago, when he had given his heart to a woman and it had been thrown back to him. Not that his heart had been broken, not even cracked—indeed, he had remained happily heart-whole ever since. But, since then, falling in love had been something in which he didn't believe.

And now, suddenly, he had discovered that that wasn't true.

Claudia, crying her eyes out in the comfort of her bed, fell asleep at last, and woke a few hours later looking much the worse for wear. She still looked beautiful, but her eyelids were pink and so was the tip of her delightful nose; she disguised the pinkness with expensive cream and powder guaranteed to work miracles, happily unaware that they made no difference at all, and went down to breakfast, rehearsing a few polite remarks about the weather as she went, just to let Thomas see that their unfortunate conversation earlier that morning was to be ignored.

He was already at the table, the post scattered around his plate. He got up as she went to the table and wished her good morning in a brisk voice which warned her that he didn't wish to talk, so she discarded the weather and replied even more briskly. Cork, offering coffee, buttered eggs and fresh toast, returned to the kitchen quite worried, for he had allowed himself to approve of his mistress after a doubtful start. She didn't interfere, but at the same time she had made it her business to know exactly how the house was run—without interfering. She was looking unhappy, and he was uneasy.

'If it was anyone else but the Professor,' he told Harvey, 'I'd have said it was a tiff, but he's not one to waste his time on anything as silly. Very polite he is this morning, too—in a rage, no doubt. And she's been crying...'

Harvey looked sympathetic and allowed his ears to droop, so that Cork felt constrained to offer him a couple of nicely crisped bacon rinds.

Mr Tait-Bullen studied Claudia from beneath lowered lids; she had been crying, but it seemed best not to mention that, for she wore a haughty expression which warned him off. It was hardly the moment to tell her that he had fallen in love with her. Claudia, being Claudia, would probably turn on him and tell him not to talk nonsense.

He said mildly, 'I hope to be home for tea today.'

Claudia said, 'Very well, Thomas,' and, since she was anxious to be friends, even though they weren't on the best of terms at the moment, added, 'Is there any shopping you need? Have we all the presents for your family?'

'If you would check the list? Have we remembered Mrs Rumbold?'

'Yes—a cardigan. Would you mind if I added a box of chocolates? A big box tied with ribbon...'

'By all means.' He got to his feet. 'I'll see you later. Enjoy your day.'

It was her last chance to find a present for Thomas. It was a pity that he had everything. She had the little figure of the dog like Harvey, but that wasn't enough. She spent an anxious morning peering into shop windows; a tie wasn't enough, besides, he might not like it—all the same she bought one in a rich silk—dark, glowing colours in a subdued pattern.

Looking at a display of photo frames gave her an idea. She chose a small one in silver and took it back home, found one of the photos which Tombs had taken at their wedding and inserted it. It wasn't a very good photo, but they had both been laughing—perhaps it would remind him that they had declared their intention of making their sensible marriage a success!

She was in the drawing room, bent over a piece of tapestry she had bought, of roses on a creamy background which, when finished, would become a cushion cover, when Thomas came home. She saw with relief that he was his usual calm self, and they had tea together, talking casually—Christmas, his work, Harvey's progress, Christmas again—and later, after dinner, they sat together in the drawing room, she with her tapestry, he with the evening papers and his medical journals. Just like an old married couple, thought Claudia contentedly. She must remember not to bother him when he had had a hard day.

It was almost dark when she took Harvey for his evening trot the next day. It was cold, but dry, and a brisk run in the park would do him good. There were few people about—most were shopping frenziedly for Christmas. She kept to the main paths and decided to keep Harvey on his lead. He was an obedient little beast, but if he were frightened by something he might run off in a panic. She had turned back towards the road when two youths passed her, and then turned and followed her. She didn't dare look round, but she picked up Harvey and quickened her pace. The road wasn't more than a few minutes' walk away, and there would be other people...

Only there weren't—there was no one in sight!

She could feel they were close to her now. Should she run for it, scream, or turn and confront them? She spun round and found them within inches of her.

Mr Tait-Bullen, arriving home earlier than he had expected, found the sitting room and drawing room empty. Cork, coming to meet him in the hall, wished him good evening, adding that Mrs Tait-Bullen had taken Harvey for a run in Hyde Park.

'I did suggest that it was a bit dark, sir, but she said that they both needed a breath of fresh air. She usually goes there from the Bayswater Road.'

'Then I'll go and meet her,' said Mr Tait-Bullen, and got into his overcoat again. 'Explain to her if she gets back first, Cork.'

The streets were almost empty and he walked fast, which was a good thing, for he had no sooner got to the park than he heard Harvey's shrill bark.

It was quite dark now, but he could see Claudia and the two youths. As he reached them she landed a nicely placed kick on one of the youth's shins and he yelped with pain.

'Let's 'ave the dog and break 'is neck for him...'

Thomas didn't waste time in talk. He knocked the pair off

their feet, begged them in a terrifyingly quiet voice to be off before he called the police, and turned his attention to Claudia.

The youths scrambled to their feet and ran off, and Claudia said in a rather shaky voice, 'Oh, thank you, Thomas. They were going to hurt Harvey.'

Thomas's quiet voice was harsh. 'They were going to hurt you, too. It was foolish of you to come here at this time of day; you have only yourself to blame.'

He had turned her round and was marching her back, out of the park, into the lighted respectable streets with their sedate houses and infrequent passers-by.

She hadn't expected that; she had expected sympathy, kindly concern, enquiries as to whether she had been frightened or hurt. The fact that he had only uttered the truth made no difference. Rage and delayed fright made her shiver. He was an inhuman monster! Scathing remarks she would have liked to make in reply remained unuttered, for they were walking too fast for her to talk; his hand on her arm urged her forward, but it didn't feel friendly.

Mr Tait-Bullen, aware of her thoughts, remained silent. The wish to sweep her into his arms, Harvey and all, was strong, but if he did that, and kissed her, things might get out of hand. Rather, let her dislike him for the moment than be frightened off by a love she hadn't expected or asked for.

Indoors once more, he took Harvey from her, took off her coat and gloves, sat her down in the drawing room and put a glass in her hand.

'Drink this; it will make you feel better.' He sounded like a friendly family doctor.

'What is it?'

'Brandy. You don't like it, but drink it—there's a good girl.'

She tossed it back, caught her breath, whooped, was slapped gently on the back and burst into tears.

'I'm not crying,' said Claudia fiercely. 'It's this beastly brandy.'

He forebore from comment, only smiled a little and went

away to take off his own coat. Cork was hovering in the hall.
'Madam isn't hurt? An accident?'

'Thugs. No, she isn't hurt—only frightened and shocked.'

'I'll bring in the tea at once.'

'Splendid, and give Harvey a biscuit or a bone. He's been
frightened, too.'

Cork, quite shaken, glided away, to return within a few
minutes with the tea tray and Harvey.

He arranged the tea things on a table convenient to Claudia,
murmured his regrets at her unpleasant adventure, assured her
that the crumpets were freshly toasted and took himself off. His
mistress certainly didn't look quite the thing; she was usually
as neat as a new pin, but now her hair was decidedly untidy
and she was crying. He hoped that the master would comfort
her in the proper fashion.

Claudia, in a haze of brandy, took the handkerchief which
Thomas offered and mopped her face and blew her nose.

'I'll go and tidy myself,' she muttered, and started to get out
of her chair.

'No need. You look very nice as you are.' Thomas's voice
was soothing, and at the same time matter-of-fact. 'I'll pour the
tea; the brandy will wear off if you eat something.'

He was regretting his harshness in the park; he had been
afraid for her when he had first caught sight of her with the
youths and fear had made him angry. He must repair the dam-
age as quickly as possible.

He gave her tea, and put a crumpet on a plate and set it on
the small table by her chair. He said cheerfully, 'You know,
you had me scared for a moment—those boys can be so rough.
Will you promise me not to go into the parks—any of them—
once it is dusk?'

'All right—you were so angry...'

'Yes, but it was anger which spilled over from those thugs,
and I had no right to blame you. Life at Little Planting is free
from such unpleasant encounters—you weren't to know...'

It was going to be all right again, thought Claudia. They were back on their friendly footing once more. She bit into her crumpet. 'I should have used my head,' she conceded.

They didn't hurry over their tea; Thomas led the talk round to Christmas, and their journey north. 'There are some splendid walks,' he told her, 'and there is a special beauty in winter. I'm looking forward to showing you something of the countryside.'

'I'll bring my boots...'

'And something warm to wear. Have you had time to tie up all the presents?'

She nodded. 'Yes, and I've put in one or two extra things— some chocolates and a scarf and some scent, just in case we've missed someone out, or someone turns up who isn't expected.'

Nothing had changed, reflected Claudia, going to bed after a quiet evening with Thomas. True, he hadn't said much, but just having him there, sitting opposite her, was nice...

They were to drive up to Finsthwaite on Christmas Eve. A long drive but, as Thomas pointed out, they would be on a motorway for almost the whole distance: the M1 as far as Birmingham, then the M6 until they left it, just before Kendal, and took the road to the lower end of Lake Windermere and, a few miles further on, Finsthwaite—a matter of just under three hundred miles. He would go to the hospital in the morning, and they should be able to leave London by mid-afternoon—a little over four hours' driving; once out of town and on the motorway, it would be a straightforward run.

Claudia packed carefully, made sure that the presents were stowed in the big box Cork found for her, and collected Harvey's basket, tins of food and his favourite bone. She would travel in the leather jacket, with a tweed skirt and a cashmere sweater—suitable garments if they were to go walking. She took her winter coat, too, for she was sure they would go to church, and added a little velvet hat, one of the jersey dresses, the green patterned dress, silk shirts and cardigans, sensible shoes—her boots she would wear—and a pair of elegant slippers. She wanted Thomas to be proud of her...

They left at three o'clock. The afternoon was already turning into a raw, cold evening, but the shops were lighted, there were Christmas trees and coloured lights and, as they drove out of the city, pavements packed with last-minute shoppers.

'I love Christmas,' said Claudia happily. 'And people look so happy... I hope Cork will have a good time.'

'I fancy he will. His widowed sister comes for Christmas Day, and on Boxing Day some old friends of his come to lunch and stay until the evening.'

'Oh, good.'

She stayed silent then, while he threaded his way through the streets until they were on the M1.

'We'll stop this side of Birmingham for a cup of tea and allow Harvey a breath of air. There's a service station.'

After that he was mostly silent, but it was a friendly silence, and Claudia had a good deal to think about. His family—she had met his parents, but only briefly at the wedding. Supposing his mother had decided that she didn't like her? And his sisters... She began to compose a series of suitable topics of conversation.

The Rolls swept with silent speed towards Birmingham. There wasn't much traffic going north, and nothing impeded its progress. The service station lights loomed ahead of them and they parked and got out, glad of a few minutes to stretch their legs while Harvey aired his tail and then, tucked under Claudia's arm, went with them to the restaurant.

Thomas found a table, told her to sit down and went away to fetch their tea. Watching him coming back, with a tray of tea things and a plate of buttered teacakes, Claudia thought that Cork would have a fit if he could see his master now.

They didn't waste time, but drank the strong hot tea, ate the teacakes and, since there was no one to see for the moment, Claudia gave Harvey a saucer of milk, tucked a paper napkin under his small chin and fed him the last of the teacakes.

'Are we going to stop again?' she asked.

'If necessary. I'd like to get off the motorway before we do, but if you need to stop say so.'

'I was thinking of Harvey,' said Claudia primly.

Mr Tait-Bullen suppressed a chuckle. 'Of course. But with luck he'll sleep for a few hours.'

They were bypassing Liverpool in just over an hour; in another hour they were off the motorway and through Kendal. There the road was still good, but narrow in places, with long stretches of dark countryside and few villages—Grigghall, Croathwaite, Bowland Bridge, and then nothing until they rounded the end of the lake at Staveley. Now the road had become a narrow lane, running between trees.

Finsthwaite was a small village: farms, a cluster of cottages, a village store and post office, the church, and a village school lower down a gentle slope. A short walk away there was Grizedale Forest. It was a little paradise, but now shrouded in darkness, save for a few lighted windows, and then, unexpectedly, a lighted Christmas tree by the church.

Thomas drove through the village, turned into an open gateway and stopped before the house where he had been born; it was a nice old house, built of grey stone, with light streaming from its windows and its solid door flung open before they were out of the car.

Claudia need not have worried about her welcome. She was drawn at once into the family circle, kissed and hugged, helped out of her coat, then carried away by Ann and Amy to warm herself by the log fire in the drawing room and be plied with delicious coffee.

'Just to warm you up,' said Ann. 'Dinner will be in about half an hour. Don't change.' She hesitated. 'Well, perhaps you'd rather. Did you have a good trip here? Thomas is such a good driver. A pity it was dark, but I don't suppose you could come any earlier?'

When Claudia had finished her coffee they took her up the wide staircase at the back of the hall and along the gallery above it. 'You're here, Thomas's dressing room is next to it, and there's a bathroom. I expect he'll be up presently. Come down as soon as you can; we've still got to put the presents round the tree.'

They left her then, in the high-ceilinged big room. The furniture was big too: a vast brass bed, a tallboy and a mighty wardrobe in mahogany, and an old-fashioned dressing table with a great many little drawers and a triple mirror standing in the window. Despite the heavy furniture the room was charming, with its sprigged wallpaper, thick cream carpet and chintz curtains and bedcover, and two bedside tables, each with a rose-shaded lamp.

Claudia opened the door in the further wall and saw the bathroom beyond, and another door on its opposite side which she opened too. The dressing room.

She went back then, unpacked her case, which someone had brought to the room, and changed into the patterned jersey. She did her hair and her face and then sat down on the bed. She was suddenly nervous of going downstairs. Thomas had no right to leave her alone...

There was a tap on the door and Thomas came in. He took one look at her and sat down beside her on the bed. 'Feeling a bit overpowered?' he asked, and put an arm round her shoulders. 'Don't—they are all so delighted to see you. Come down; Father's waiting to open the champagne and James wants to kiss you under the mistletoe!'

They went down to the drawing room together, and Claudia stifled a wish that Thomas had been the one who wanted to kiss her. A silly wish, she reflected. He wasn't a demonstrative man... Hadn't he told her that before they married? That he had no interest in being in love, that he had loved once, but never again? And she had accepted that.

Everyone was in the drawing room—a square room with two windows overlooking the front garden. It had panelled walls, and chairs that were roomy and very slightly shabby, but the furniture was solid and beautifully kept, the chairs covered in a dark red damask which matched the curtains, and a vast sofa before the stone fireplace, which housed a roaring log fire. The room was warm—warm with content and happiness and love; there was no doubting the affection Thomas's family had for each other, although it wasn't on display.

They drank their champagne and presently crossed the hall

to the dining room. It was panelled, like the drawing room, and had a vast mahogany table surrounded by Victorian balloon back chairs, a William the Fourth pedestal sideboard, which took up almost all of one wall, and a magnificent giltwood side table. There were a number of paintings on the walls—Claudia supposed that they were family portraits—dimly lit by wall sconces.

The table had been decked for Christmas, with a centrepiece of holly and Christmas roses, a white damask cloth and napkins, and heavy silverware. When the soup was served Claudia recognised Coalport china.

She was hungry and dinner was excellent: game soup, roast pheasant and a chocolate and almond pudding. She wasn't sure what she was drinking; all she knew was that she was very happy and enjoying herself. And Thomas, sitting beside her, had once or twice put his hand over hers, which gave her a warm glow inside.

They arranged the presents round the tree after dinner.

'We all go to church in the morning,' Amy told her. 'But perhaps you and Thomas would like to go to the midnight service? It's only a short walk to the church and it's a lovely service. We always went, but now we have the children we stay at home. They still wake in the night sometimes, and we like to be there.'

'How many have you?'

'Two, and another one in the spring. Ann has one so far.' She smiled. 'They're such fun, but an awful lot of work.'

Claudia went to sit by her mother-in-law then, until that lady declared that it was time they all went to bed. 'You still have the children's stockings to fill,' she reminded them. 'Breakfast at eight o'clock. Church at half-ten.'

'I'm taking Claudia to the midnight service,' said Thomas quietly, and smiled across the room at her.

'Then we'll leave the side door unlocked. I'll tell Maggie to leave coffee on the Aga, and there are sandwiches in the fridge if you feel hungry.'

There was a leisurely round of goodnights as the party broke up, leaving Claudia and Thomas sitting by the fire.

'Well?' he asked. 'Are you going to like my family?'

'Yes, very much. I've never had more than Mother—and Father, of course, but he died several years ago. I think it must be wonderful to be one of a large family.'

'Indeed, it is. We don't see a great deal of each other, but we make a point of meeting for important occasions. Amy and Ann are happily married—Jake and Will are sound men—and I suppose James will marry in due course.'

'Your mother and father aren't lonely so far from you all?'

'No. They are happy to be together. Mother has her garden, Father sits on various committees, and they both enjoy walking. Besides, there is quite a social life here, even in the winter.'

He glanced at the walnut long case clock. 'Would you like to walk to church? It's only a question of five or ten minutes.'

'I'll go and get a coat.'

It would be cold outside. She put on her winter coat and the little velvet hat, found gloves and sensible shoes, and went back downstairs to where Thomas was waiting for her in the hall.

He took her to a door beyond the staircase and opened it onto the night. There was a clear sky, alight with stars and a dying moon, and he walked her along a path leading from the side door of the house to a small gate which led onto the lane.

'The church is below the village,' he told her, and took her arm. And round a bend she saw its squat tower close by. There were other people making their way there, too, and when they reached the church she saw that it was already almost full. Thomas made his unhurried way to a pew in the front, stopping to greet people he knew and introduce her, but presently she had time to glance around her. The church was small, rather cold, but scented with the evergreens and holly and Christmas flowers which decorated it. She liked it, and she enjoyed the service, simple and peaceful.

They walked home later, and Claudia said, 'It's Christmas Day...'

Thomas stopped. 'Ah, yes, and we have no need to wait for

the mistletoe.' He hugged her close and kissed her, and then let her go rather abruptly. He had very nearly lost his self-control.

Claudia had enjoyed the kiss very much; if she hadn't been taken by surprise she would have kissed him back, but he had released her before she had the chance. Perhaps later...

The house was in darkness as they went quietly through the side door and into the kitchen. It was a thoroughly old-fashioned one, with a huge dresser along one wall, a big scrubbed table with ash and elm Windsor chairs around it, and two elbow chairs on either side of the Aga. The floor was of flagstones and there was a rag rug before the Aga. Harvey was fast asleep in his basket, and curled up on one of the chairs was a large tabby cat.

Thomas fetched two mugs and poured their coffee. 'Maggie has been with us for a lifetime,' he told her. 'She's a really marvellous cook. We all love her, and the children can't be kept away from her when they come to stay. She has plenty of help, of course, but both maids have gone home for Christmas Eve. They'll be here in the morning, and go again after lunch. There's an ancient man who does the heavy work in the garden; he should have been pensioned off years ago, but the people round here don't retire.'

'Would you rather live here than in London?'

'This is my home, and I love it, but my work is in London and that is my life. I am fortunate enough to be able to have both.' He glanced at her. 'You like living in London, Claudia?'

'Oh, yes, you have a lovely home, and the parks are close by.'

'I've bought the cottage at Child Okeford. We'll go down to see it in the New Year. It seems pretty sound, but it will need painting and some small alterations.'

'You've bought it? Oh, Thomas, how splendid. Did you forget to tell me?'

'I didn't know myself until this morning, when the agent phoned. You're pleased?'

'Yes. Oh, yes. You're pleased, too?'

'Yes!' He got up and took her mug. 'It's very late. Go to bed, my dear, you have had a long day.'

'And a very happy one.' She leaned up and kissed his cheek. 'This is such a lovely Christmas.'

For a second time that evening Thomas very nearly lost his self-imposed restraint.

Claudia went down to breakfast in the morning to a chorus of greetings and good wishes. The children were there too. Ann's small son was in a high chair, but Amy's two—little girls— were sitting at table. There was a lot of noise and laughing while they ate, and afterwards, before they all went to church.

Claudia could see that Thomas was on excellent terms with his nephew and nieces. He would be a splendid father, only it seemed that he had no desire to be one. Perhaps in a few years' time, when they had grown closer to each other... She shut the thought away; he had married her for companionship and because he wanted a wife to order his household and entertain his friends. Their marriage was a sensible one, based on friendship and compatibility, and a genuine liking for each other.

The church was warmer now, and there were even more people there. She stood between Thomas and his mother and sang the carols, and told herself that she was the luckiest girl on earth.

CHAPTER EIGHT

CHRISTMAS dinner was at midday, so that the children could share it—turkey and Brussels sprouts, roasted potatoes, braised celery, cranberry sauce—nothing had been overlooked. Then the Christmas pudding, set alight with great ceremony, and last of all mince pies. They drank champagne again, and then coffee before going to the drawing room to open their presents. The children first, of course, before they went for their afternoon naps, and for a while the room was awash with coloured paper, ribbon and toys.

Presently it was the grown-ups' turn. Everyone was there, including Maggie, the two maids and the gardener, and they collected their gifts first, drank a glass of sherry and went off to the kitchen to enjoy a splendid high tea.

Mr Tait-Bullen Senior handed out the presents, and very soon the room was just as untidy as when the children had been there. Claudia, looking round her, thought how delightful the room looked, with the lighted tree and the gaily covered presents, the roaring fire and the soft lamplight. She wished that her mother and George could have been there, too, although when she had phoned her mother that morning that lady had sounded in the best of good spirits. She caught Thomas's eye and smiled—a wobbly smile, for she was on the verge of tears—and he came to sit by her, taking her hand in his large, cool one and giving it a friendly squeeze.

'You haven't opened all your presents...'

'No. There are so many and they're all so lovely.' She picked up a small box and tore away the paper. A jeweller's box, blue velvet and quite small. She looked at the tag then, and said, 'Oh, Thomas, it's from you....' She opened it and looked at the earrings bedded in white satin—sapphires in a network of gold and diamonds.

'Oh, Thomas…'

'Go on, kiss him,' said Amy, who had been watching. 'You're in the family now.' They had all turned to look, smiling and nodding, so she kissed him, very pink in the cheeks, feeling shy.

Thomas didn't kiss her back. She thought he might have done, with everyone watching, but he took the earrings out of the box and fitted the hooks neatly into her ears. She got up then, and went to admire the earrings in the gilt mirror opposite the fireplace, and that gave her time to let the blush die down and regain her composure.

She still had more presents to open, so she went back and sat down again on the massive sofa beside Thomas and started to open them. A gorgeous silk scarf from Harvey, who was sitting at her feet and muttered sleepily when she thanked him. A leather writing case from her in-laws—red leather with her initials. Gloves and scent and a jewel case from Thomas's sisters and brother. She went round thanking everyone, and being thanked, and when she sat down again Thomas was opening his presents. He had a great many, but he saved hers till the last, quietly approving of the tie. When he unwrapped the photo frame he said nothing for a few moments.

'It's a kind of reminder,' said Claudia quickly. Perhaps he didn't like it; perhaps he thought it was a silly, sentimental thing to have done.

'I shall put it on my desk at my consulting room,' he told her quietly, 'so that everyone can see what a beautiful wife I have.'

'That wasn't why I did it,' she told him. 'I thought it would remind you…' She paused to get it right. 'It's difficult to explain…'

'Then don't try, Claudia. I think I understand and I shall treasure it.'

The presents had all been opened by now, and everyone was sitting round, content to do nothing for the moment.

'Shall we go for a quick walk?' Thomas pulled her to her feet.

'Yes, dear, take Claudia towards the forest,' his mother said. 'Tea will be a little later because of the children. Be back by five o'clock.'

So Claudia fetched her coat, tied her new scarf over her head, got into her boots and went down to the hall where Thomas, coated but bare-headed, was waiting.

They went out of the side door again, and along the lane towards the church, and then turned away along a rough track which took them almost at once into the forest. It was a perfect late afternoon, the sky in the west a blaze of red and yellow, the rest of the heavens already darkening, lights from the village and outlying farms twinkling.

'It's been such a lovely day,' said Claudia as they walked along arm in arm. 'I feel happy, don't you, Thomas?'

He didn't answer that, but observed, 'It would be hard to be unhappy here. Some places are meant to be happy in—I think the cottage at Child Okeford will be such a place.' He looked down at her face, rosy with the cold. 'What are we going to call it?'

'Why, Christmas Cottage, of course.' She went on happily. 'We'll have a cat—at least, he'll have to live with us in London and go to and fro like Harvey... Should we have brought Harvey out with us?'

'Harvey is sleeping off a much too large dinner. I'll give him a run after tea.'

'Your parents haven't got a dog? I know Maggie has a cat...'

'Jasper, our Labrador, died a month or so ago. He was old and a devoted friend. In a while, when they are over his death, I've arranged for a puppy—another Labrador—to join the family.'

'Oh, Thomas, how kind. They must miss him terribly.' She stopped to stare into his face in the gathering dusk. 'You think of everything, don't you?'

'I do my best.' He reflected that he hadn't thought of falling in love...

They walked back presently, to eat Christmas cake and drink tea from delicate porcelain tea cups round the fire while the

children sat at a small table eating an early supper. They had
had an exciting day and were inclined to be peevish. Amy and
Claudia went to sit with them, coaxing them to eat their peanut
butter sandwiches, the little fairy cakes Maggie had made for
them, which followed the Marmite toast, and to drink their
milk.

When they were borne off to bed there were plaintive re-
quests for Daddy to tuck them up and read them a story. They
were taken upstairs then, and presently Amy and Ann came
down again. 'Now it's your turn,' Amy told the men, and as
they went away she said laughingly to Thomas, 'Just you wait;
it'll be your turn next. I don't know why fathers read bedtime
stories better than mothers, but be prepared for it!'

Thomas said mildly, 'What do you suggest? That I start re-
reading Hans Anderson? A bit out of date, I dare say. How
about the *Wind in the Willows*? My favourite when I was a
small boy.'

The conversation became general then, and Claudia joined
in, avoiding Thomas's eye. She supposed that there would be
a good many such remarks, but, since they didn't seem to dis-
concert Thomas, she must learn to treat them in a light-hearted
manner.

She had married him so quickly there hadn't been time to
foresee the small pitfalls, but as long as he didn't mind, she
wouldn't allow it to bother her.

Everyone went away to dress presently, and when she came
downstairs there were guests, invited for a drink—local people
who, it seemed, had known Thomas and his family for years.
They accepted her as one of the family at once, but the talk
inevitably turned to reminiscences, so that she felt an outsider
despite everyone's efforts to include her in their talk. But she
did her best, and Thomas's hand on her arm reassured her.

When the last guest had gone, they went in to supper. A
buffet—the vast sideboard laden with bowls and dishes filled
with Maggie's delicious food: smoked salmon, salads of every
kind, a ham on the bone, stuffed eggs, chicken pie, miniature

hot rolls. Claudia allowed Thomas to fill her plate and found herself sitting by James.

'Pity you have to go back tomorrow. I suppose Thomas can't be away for more than a few days. Time he took a holiday. He doesn't need to work quite so hard, you know.'

'Yes, I do know, but he loves his work, doesn't he? It's important to him.'

'He's good, of course, you know that. You should see him in Theatre...'

'And people like him, I think. He came to see my great-uncle, you know—that's how we met...' She paused, remembering that she hadn't much liked him then. 'They got on awfully well together. People do things for him, too, don't they?'

James chuckled. 'Well, he can be a bit hoity-toity if he can't get what he wants—in the nicest possible way, mind you. And in no time they are all doing exactly what he wants!'

But it was something Ann said which made her vaguely uneasy.

'You're so right for Thomas. We've all hoped he would marry, but for years and years—ever since he had that miserable love affair with that girl who went off with a tycoon from South America—he's been considered a splendid catch. Not that he's bothered about that. I don't suppose you've met a woman called Honor Thompson? She'll be livid when she hears that he's married...'

'I've met her,' said Claudia in a carefully level voice.

'You have? I expect Thomas told you about her. She's one of the persistent ones. Don't let her worry you, though. He doesn't care tuppence for any of them. He's always known what he wanted from life and now he's got you.'

Was that why Thomas had married her? she wondered. To be a barrier against wishful partners? Someone who wouldn't spoil the even tenor of his life by demanding undying love? Really, it was a sound idea! An undemanding relationship, the tolerance of good friends towards each other, shared pleasures—and they did like the same things. He could have married Honor, or any other of his women acquaintances if he had wished, but he had chosen her. Well, she was quite prepared to be the wife he wanted. And just let Honor try any of her tricks, Claudia thought waspishly.

They didn't leave until after lunch on the following day. In the morning they had gone for another walk, taking one of the paths which led into the heart of the forest. They had talked about Christmas, and plans to come again, perhaps for Easter, or perhaps he could persuade his parents to visit them.

'The cottage should be quite ready by then, and I'm sure they would enjoy it. We will go down there as soon as possible and see what needs doing. I'm sure you have some ideas, and the place will need painting and decorating.'

'And furnishing.' Claudia's eyes sparkled. 'Curtains and things.'

It had been a most satisfactory morning, she reflected, and began a leisurely round of goodbyes. Christmas had been two wonderful days; she liked Thomas's family, and she loved the countryside around his home and the comfortable old house. She hoped that they would come again, but she doubted if Thomas could spare the time to drive up frequently. She got into the car with real regret, made sure that Harvey was comfortable on his blanket on the back seat, and turned to give a final wave.

It was still light, although the day was fading. She looked around her at the country as Thomas drove back to join the motorway, and, since he didn't speak other than to ask her if she was comfortable, she stayed silent.

They were approaching the motorway when he said, 'We'll stop for tea just before Birmingham, but do tell me if you want to stop before then.'

Her, 'Yes, Thomas,' was the epitome of wifely obedience.

It was quite some time before he said, 'You're very quiet?'

'Well, I thought that's what you wanted. I'm sure you have a great deal to think about...'

'For instance?' He sounded amused.

'Your work and your patients, and perhaps you are wishing

you were back with your family and that Christmas was just beginning and not over.'

He didn't comment on that. 'You enjoyed your Christmas?'

'Oh, I did. I loved every minute of it, and I like your parents and your sisters and brother.'

'They like you, Claudia.'

They stopped for tea at a service station, took Harvey for a brisk walk around the car park and resumed their journey, speeding along the motorway, talking of this and that. And Claudia had the feeling that even while he talked Thomas's mind was on something else.

'Are you worried about something?' she asked. 'You don't have to talk if you don't want to. I shan't take umbrage.'

He laughed then. 'I'm not worried, Claudia.' He began to talk about plans for Christmas Cottage, and she felt as though she had been snubbed. It had been nicely done, but whatever it was, she wasn't to be told about it.

London was empty of traffic; Boxing Day was a family visiting day and many people were indoors. Later they would return to their own homes, but just now it was quiet.

Cork opened the door and they went in to a welcoming warmth and a faint but delicious smell from the kitchen. He welcomed them with grave pleasure, fetched the cases and then announced that dinner would be in half an hour if that suited them.

'Excellent,' said Thomas. 'I'll take Harvey for a run.' Which left Claudia to go to her room and tidy herself and unpack before going down to the drawing room. Thomas wasn't there, but Harvey was sitting before the fire looking drowsy.

'I gave Harvey his supper, madam,' said Cork, coming silently into the room. 'The master's in his study; he will be joining you presently.'

'Thank you, Cork. Have you had a happy Christmas?'

'Very pleasant, madam. I trust that you enjoyed yourself?'

'Very much. The country was beautiful.'

Cork went away, and she fetched her tapestry and began to stitch. It was a bit of an anticlimax after the cheerful racket that had been such fun. Only yesterday, she thought, and it seems like weeks ago already.

Mr Tait-Bullen, coming into the drawing room some minutes later, paused for a moment in the doorway. Claudia looked delightful, sitting there working away at her embroidery. It seemed to him that she had always been there; it was hard to think of the house without her in it. He wondered what she would say if he were to tell her that he had fallen in love with her, but he thrust the temptation aside. He thought she was happy and content, and he must have patience; in time she might come to love him, but until then they must stay good friends. It was lucky that he had more than enough work to keep him busy.

He sat down opposite her and observed mildly, 'I've a good deal of work on my hands for the next week or so, but we might go down to Child Okeford next Sunday and take a good look round. You might like to spend an hour or two with your mother.'

'Yes, I would, and I'm longing to see the cottage again. You don't have to go away, do you?'

'In a couple of weeks I have a seminar in Liverpool—two days or so.' He gave her a thoughtful look. 'I'm afraid you will be on your own a good deal, Claudia.'

'Oh, I don't mind that,' she said cheerfully. 'I've all those coffee mornings and tea parties to go to—with people I met at the hospital ball—and plans for the cottage.'

'Ah, yes. You must decide how you want it furnished...'

'Well, you must decide too, for you'll be living there as well, whenever we get the chance.'

They spent the rest of the evening together. 'Like an old married couple,' said Cork to himself. 'They ought to be out dancing or whatever. It isn't right.'

Such an idea hadn't entered Claudia's head. She was perfectly content, sitting there, making heavy weather of the tapestry while Thomas immersed himself in a pile of medical journals. It was nice, she reflected, that they enjoyed each other's company but made no demands on each other.

Soon after ten o'clock she folded her work, declared that she was tired and took herself off to bed, after giving Harvey a hug and bestowing a friendly goodnight on Thomas as he got up to open the door for her. His manners were beautiful, she reflected as she went upstairs, and he was unfailingly kind. She heaved a sigh, not knowing quite why.

She didn't see a great deal of him for the next few days. He was away early in the mornings and didn't get home until early evening; there was a good deal of flu, he told her, and his registrar was off sick.

'Take care!' said Claudia. 'Are there many off sick at the hospital?'

'Amongst the nursing staff, yes—quite a few of the medical staff, too. And, of course, the wards are all full...'

There was nothing she could do to help, but she took care to see that a meal was ready when he got home, with welcoming warmth and no disturbances if he wanted to work. As for herself, her days were nicely filled. Walks with Harvey, such shopping as Cork allowed her to do, coffee with various of the ladies she had met at the ball and most afternoons spent reading though not always understanding some of the medical books in Thomas's study. But it was necessary that she had some idea of his work, and now was no time to bother him with any questions. If ever he chose to talk to her about work, at least she would have some idea of what he was talking about.

There was also the New Year to look forward to—only a day away—and all being well they were to go out to dinner tonight, and dance the New Year in. Claudia washed her hair, did her nails and massaged in a cream guaranteed to improve the complexion. That she had no need of it was quite beside the point.

She took Harvey for a long walk in the afternoon and returned home, thankful to be out of the damp cold, looking forward to tea round the fire. She let herself in, dried Harvey and took off her outdoor things, then went to sit down in the small sitting room. It was already past the usual teatime, but she supposed that Cork had forgotten the time. After half an hour she went to the kitchen, vaguely uneasy. Cork ran the house like clockwork. Perhaps he had had to go out for some reason...

He was huddled in a chair by the Aga, with a white face and shivering.

'Cork, you're ill.' She put a hand on his forehead and felt its heat. 'You must go to bed at once.' When he protested feebly, she added, 'No, please do as I say.' She saw that the effort to get out of the chair was too much for him, so she heaved him up and helped him to his room, sat him on the bed, took off his shoes and pulled the bedclothes over him. 'Now, lie still, there's a good man. I'm going to get you a drink.'

There was bottled water in the fridge; she filled a jug, found a glass and took them to his room, gave him a drink and tucked the bedclothes round him.

'Your tea, madam,' croaked Cork. He closed his eyes.

'Don't give it a thought. Go to sleep if you can. I'm going to find a warm water bottle for you. As soon as the Professor gets home he'll come and see you. I expect it's the flu.' She cast a worried glance at him. He really looked ill; thank heaven Thomas would be home early.

She went to the kitchen and made a pot of tea. Cork wouldn't have any, although he drank some more of the water, so she went back to the kitchen and drank her own tea. She ate some of the sandwiches on the tray, fed Harvey, and, since they wouldn't be going out to spend the evening, peered into the fridge and the cupboards, collecting the makings of a meal.

She was still there when Thomas came home. Harvey ran into the hall to greet him, and as the dog came into the kitchen, with Thomas behind him, she dropped the potato she was peeling and ran to him, quite forgetting to be calm and sensible.

'Thomas, I'm so glad to see you. Cork's ill. I've put him to bed but he's so hot and shivery.' She tugged at his sleeve. 'Do come and see what's wrong.'

Mr Tait-Bullen's features displayed nothing but calm assurance. He said in an unhurried manner, 'This wretched flu, I expect. I'll take a look.' He paused on his way. 'You didn't take his temperature?'

'Well, no. His teeth were chattering so much I was afraid he would break the thermometer.'

He nodded and went out of the kitchen and into Cork's room, and Claudia peeled the last of the potatoes. There was plenty of food in the fridge; she had chosen salmon steaks to go with the potatoes, frozen petit pois and there was a cabbage in the sink to clean and cook. Dull fare for Old Year's Night, but with Cork ill, food didn't seem very important.

'It will have to be cheese and biscuits afterwards,' she told Harvey, 'and I just hope he likes it.'

'He'll like it,' said Thomas, from somewhere behind her. 'Cork has the flu, but he's not too bad. I've given him paracetamol and I'll go back presently and settle him down. We've plenty of orange juice and cold drinks, I presume? That's all he'll need for a while...'

'Poor man. Now, just you sit down and I'll make a pot of tea. Supper won't be very exciting, but it'll be food...'

Mr Tait-Bullen sat, watching his wife trot to and fro, her glorious hair getting very untidy, her lovely face flushed. She might look a bit disorganised, he reflected, but she was efficient and quick. A pot of tea was placed before him, with the sandwiches, now rather dry, and a dish of the little cakes Cork was so clever at baking.

'If you don't mind waiting for dinner, I'll go and see to Cork.'

'My dear girl, he would rather die. He needs to be undressed and put to bed—washed and so on.'

'Oh, well, I'm quite able to do that, you know.'

'Of course you are. All the same, I think it is better if I see to him while you get our dinner. By all means see to his drinks and any food that may take his fancy.'

He got to his feet. 'I'll check the post and be back very shortly.'

He was as good as his word. 'We'll eat here, shall we?' he asked, taking off his jacket. 'I'll see to the table presently.' He didn't wait for an answer, but went to Cork's room and shut the door.

Claudia drank another cup of cooling tea, offered Harvey a biscuit, because he was being such a good boy, and turned her attention to the salmon. She was a good cook; if she had known that she was to cook the meal that evening she would have thought out a dinner worthy of the occasion, but it would have to be a simple meal. She thought with regret of the pretty dress she had laid out ready to wear this evening, the delicious supper they would have had, the excitement of toasting the New Year. What could they have for a pudding? she wondered, and began to squeeze oranges for poor Cork.

Thomas came back presently, put on his jacket and then started to lay the table. It took some time, since he had to search for everything in drawers and cupboards, but the end result was as elegant as if Cork had done it himself. He took a bowl of hyacinths from the windowsill and put it at the centre of the table, arranged silver and glass just so, and went to look in the fridge. Cork, that admirable man, had put a couple of bottles of champagne in it earlier that day. Thomas opened one, filled a glass and took it to Claudia.

'I'm sorry—you must be disappointed that we can't go dining and dancing with the rest of the world,' he told her. 'We'll make up for it later on.'

Claudia took a good drink of champagne. 'I don't mind a bit; I'm so sorry for Cork.' She wrinkled her nose. 'Why does champagne make you feel so uplifted?'

'A good question.' He topped up her glass. 'Something smells good.'

Claudia drained the cabbage, chopped it fine, added nutmeg and a squeeze of lemon and put it on the dish Thomas had got from the dresser. She had creamed the potatoes with plenty of butter and milk and dished up the peas; now she laid the salmon on two warmed plates and took it to the table.

'Not very exciting, I'm afraid,' she said. 'But there's a nice piece of Stilton for pudding!'

Mr Tait-Bullen, who had snatched a sandwich for his lunch, cleared the plate. 'You're a good cook,' he told her. 'What a treasure I have married.'

Claudia went pink. 'Well, I can't cook anything fancy. Great-Uncle William didn't hold with spending a great deal of money on what he called "elaborate food" so I became good at fancying up sausages and things.'

'Tell me more about your great-uncle,' suggested Thomas and filled her glass again.

And Claudia, nothing loath, her tongue nicely loosened by the champagne, told—until she stopped suddenly. 'I'm being boring. It's all the champagne—you should have stopped me...'

Mr Tait-Bullen, enjoying himself, made haste to assure her that he hadn't been in the least bored. 'After all, we know very little about each other even now.'

While she made coffee he went to look at Cork.

'Sleeping like a baby. Now, let us discuss the cottage. As soon as Cork is better, we will spend a day at Child Okeford, see what is to be done and get hold of a builder. We had better find a gardener too, to get the place into some shape before we can take over. I'll get hold of the estate agent—he may be able to recommend someone. We will try not to alter the place too much, but the barn will need a secure door and a firm run-in for the car. Had you thought of anything you wanted changed or added to?'

Claudia shook her head. 'I loved it as it was. Will it take long, the necessary repairs and the garden?'

'It shouldn't do. We can choose carpets and furniture once we have all the measurements. A local firm, I think, don't you? Sherborne or Shaftesbury.'

'Carpets and curtains,' said Claudia happily, 'and comfortable furniture. Thomas, it will cost an awful lot of money...'

'Probably, but it will be our second home, won't it? We mustn't spoil the ship for ha'porth of tar.'

They washed the dishes together then, and in no time at all, it seemed, it was five minutes to midnight.

Cork was still asleep. Thomas came back into the kitchen, filled their glasses and went to stand by her. As the clock struck midnight they toasted the New Year, and then he took the glass from her hand, put it with his on the table and bent to kiss her.

An unhurried, gentle kiss, quite different from his usual rather brisk salute, it stirred something inside Claudia's person, and she stared up into his face, vaguely puzzled.

He was as calm as he always was. 'A Happy New Year, my dear.'

'You too, Thomas.' She paused. 'You're quite happy, aren't you? I mean, with us being married? We're good friends, aren't we? And I promise I'll not get in your way—with your work, you know. When we married I hadn't thought of all the things which could go wrong.'

He had seen the puzzled look; his Sleeping Beauty was beginning to wake up. He said in a matter-of-fact manner, 'I'm very happy, Claudia. Getting married was something I should have done years ago—to you, of course!'

'Well, you didn't know me, did you? Do you have to go to the hospital tomorrow—no, today?'

'No, unless I'm needed. Supposing we go down to the cottage?'

'But we can't leave Cork.'

He took the phone out of his pocket and dialled.

'A male nurse will be along at eight o'clock; he'll stay with Cork until we get back. He's a good man—kind and trustworthy.'

'But won't he be on duty?'

'No, he has days off, and he'll be glad of the fee.'

'Oh, won't anyone mind?'

He smiled and shook his head, and she said, 'Are you so important that you can do things like that?'

'I must admit to having a certain amount of clout.'

'Well, it would be marvellous. All day? We must take a notebook and pen and a tape measure. But only if Cork feels better...'

'Of course. Now, go to bed, Claudia. If we're to leave early you'll need your beauty sleep.' He added, 'You don't need any beauty sleep, actually. You're already as beautiful as it is possible to be.'

A remark so unlike Thomas that she stopped to stare at him.

Then, 'It's all that champagne,' she told him. 'You're looking at me through rose-coloured spectacles.'

Thomas only smiled, and he didn't kiss her as she went past him. She was quite disappointed.

Mr Tait-Bullen saw to Cork, locked up and took himself off to his study. He still had reports to read, patients' notes to examine, his workload to be checked. Harvey went with him, to snooze on his shoes until Thomas went to his bed after a last visit to Cork, who, while still very much under the weather, was prepared to stay alive after all.

Claudia woke soon after six o'clock and went down to the kitchen to make tea. She peeped at Cork, made him another jug of lemonade, laid the table and went back to dress. A day at the cottage meant sensible clothes: the leather jacket, a sensible tweed skirt and a pullover. She made short work of her hair, did almost nothing to her face, and went back downstairs. She could hear the murmur of voices from Cork's room as she set about frying bacon and eggs and making toast, and presently Thomas came in with a short, middle-aged man.

He wished her good morning and added, 'This is Sam Peverell, my dear. Sam, my wife. We'll have breakfast as soon as it's ready. You know what to do for Cork, and you can reach me on my mobile, of course, if you need me. We should be back in the early evening.'

Claudia piled plates with bacon and eggs and made more toast. 'I'll put your lunch ready for you, Mr Peverell, and a tray for tea. There are oranges and lemons in the fridge, and milk and yoghurt. So will you help yourself?'

'Certainly, Mrs Tait-Bullen.' He turned to Thomas. 'Phone calls, sir?'

'I'll put on the answering machine. But get hold of someone at the hospital if you're worried.'

'It's very kind of you to come, Mr Peverell,' said Claudia. 'On your day off, too. We're awfully grateful.'

'No problem, Mrs Tait-Bullen. My wife's gone to her mother's, and the girls are spending the day with friends.'

'You have daughters?'

'Two, fourteen and sixteen, and you wouldn't believe what a worry they are...'

Mr Tait-Bullen sat back, listening to Claudia charming Sam—a martinet on the ward, a splendid nurse and reputed not to have much of an opinion of young women. *His* Claudia, he reminded himself, who was a delight to the eye and the ear and whom he loved.

They left well before nine o'clock, and, since the streets were almost empty after the night's celebrations, they were on the motorway in no time at all. They stopped at a service station after more than an hour's driving, had coffee and allowed Harvey a brief stroll before resuming their journey. Claudia felt a little thrill of excitement as Thomas turned the Rolls into the network of small lanes which would lead them to Child Okeford. Supposing they didn't like the cottage now that they had the leisure to look it over?

'Where's the key?' asked Claudia, a bit late in the day.

'I'm to fetch it from the end cottage as we pass.'

The village was quiet, its inhabitants no doubt sleeping off the excesses of the previous night, but when Thomas knocked on the cottage door he was soon given the key; several keys, in fact.

The cottage looked a bit forlorn, for it was a dull morning with the hint of rain, but Claudia, seeing it in her mind's eye with roses round the door, curtains at the open windows, the garden full of flowers, skipped inside the moment Thomas had the door open.

They went slowly from room to room, checking them with the particulars which the estate agent had sent. The cottage was in good heart, its small windows secure and solid, large cupboards, the stairs sound. The kitchen would need cupboards and shelves, and an Aga, and its flagstone floor cleaned, but the vast stone sink was something Claudia wanted to keep.

They went round a second time while Claudia argued the merits of porridge-coloured carpeting against different colours in each room. Thomas listened patiently, told her to have whatever she liked and suggested that they went and looked round the garden. It was larger than they had first thought, and there were apple trees forming a screen between the garden and the open fields beyond.

'We can grow vegetables,' said Claudia, quite carried away, 'and there's space for a little greenhouse, and we could have a small summer house in that corner, so that you could have somewhere quiet to go.'

Thomas agreed gravely, waiting to see if she would suggest a swimming pool, but she didn't. She did suggest a rockery, and a little pool where frogs might live.

They went to the village pub presently, and ate a ploughman's lunch and emptied a pot of coffee between them. The cottage was every bit as delightful as they remembered it—better, even, for now they had explored it from bottom to roof.

'I'll get on to the agent tomorrow,' said Thomas, 'and get things started.'

He glanced at his watch. 'Do you want to see your mother and George as we go back?'

'May I? Is there time? And what about Cork?'

'I'll check when we go back to the cottage. We must lock up properly.'

Claudia beamed at him across the pub table. 'Oh, Thomas, I'm so happy...'

CHAPTER NINE

CLAUDIA'S glow of happiness lasted until they were back home. They had called at George's house, had tea with him and her mother, and stayed for a while. Claudia and her mother had a lot to say to each other, but, mindful of Cork, she'd got up at once when Thomas suggested mildly that they should go. It wasn't for a while that she'd realised Thomas was rather silent. She'd stopped talking then, sitting quietly beside him, still happy, her thoughts busily occupied with the cottage.

It wasn't until they were home again, and Sam Peverell had given his report, pocketed his fee and gone home, and she had been to see Cork and gone to the kitchen to get a meal, that she realised that Thomas, after seeing Sam Peverell off home and spending a short time with Cork, had gone to his study and shut the door.

It was as if he had erected an invisible barrier between them. She told herself that he was probably tired or had work to do, and that the faint air of reserve would have disappeared by the time their supper was ready.

Lamb chops, sprouts, potatoes and mint sauce. Plain fare indeed, but it was already after seven o'clock and she still had to cook... She rummaged around in the cupboards, found what she wanted, made an apple pie and popped it in the oven and then made an egg custard for Cork. He was feeling more himself, assuring her that he would be on his feet in another day or so, adding, with a touch of suspicion, that he hoped she could find everything she wanted in the kitchen.

'Oh, indeed I could, Cork, and I've been careful to put everything back where it belongs.' She gave him a motherly smile. 'We do miss your lovely cooking.'

Cork, still pale and poorly, nevertheless looked smug at that. The first few days of January went swiftly by; Claudia enjoyed them, for she was kept busy shopping and cooking, and although Mrs Rumbold came each day there was always something to be done: the flowers to arrange, the phone to answer, bills to pay. She was careful to ask Cork's advice about most things, and in a few days, when he was feeling better, he sat by the Aga, warmly wrapped, and advised her about the best methods to cook their meals.

She found this rather tiresome, since she was a capable cook, but she knew that he meant it kindly and nothing would have induced her to snub him. And Cork, for his part, acknowledged the fact that she was an ideal mistress, never encroaching on his preserves while asserting a gentle authority. The master was a lucky man.

The master was a busy man too, away early in the morning and for the most part not back again until the early evening. He made time, though, to visit Cork, and spent what leisure he had in Claudia's company, although she sensed his reserve towards her. She tried to remember if she had said or done something to annoy him and wondered if she had disappointed him in some way. One day, she promised herself, when he wasn't away from home so much, she would ask him.

Cork, back on his feet once more, took over his normal duties again. He made her a little speech of thanks with the voice and manner of a benevolent person, making it quite clear that, much though he had appreciated her help, he no longer required it. Claudia, thrown back onto her own resources, took long walks with Harvey, drank coffee with various of the wives she had met at the ball, and ploughed her way through the books in Thomas's study, not understanding them by half but feeling that by doing so she was bridging the gap which she felt was between them.

It was something of a relief when he told her that he had to go to Liverpool for two or three days, and would she like to visit her mother?

'I can drop you off on my way, and then why not bring your mother back here for a day or so? There's the possibility that I may go on to Leeds and have to spend the night there.'

'I'd like that, Thomas. I'll phone Mother; I'm sure she'd love to come, and we might do some shopping.'

'Yes, well, take her to Harrods or Harvey Nichols and use our account.'

He looked so kind when he said it that she was tempted to ask him if there was anything wrong, but she didn't; he had come home later than usual and he looked tired.

Harvey was to stay with Cork, for she intended to stay only one night at George's house; she and her mother could return by train and they would spend two days together. Her mother hadn't seen Thomas's home, and Claudia was longing to show it to her. They could have a good gossip and shop. She got into the car two days later, on a still dark morning, and Thomas drove out of town, leaving Cork and a protesting Harvey behind.

'I hope Harvey won't pine,' said Claudia, 'and that Cork will take care of himself...all alone,' she added doubtfully.

'I should imagine that he is pleased to see the back of us. He now has the opportunity to take a nap when he feels like it, and rearrange everything around the house to his satisfaction. He will spoil Harvey, bully Mrs Rumbold, and probably drink my port.'

She laughed. 'He'd never do that; he's your devoted slave.'

'And yours, I fancy. I'll phone you this evening, but don't worry if you don't hear from me after that. I'll let you know when I'm coming home.'

They didn't talk much, just casual remarks from time to time, and although Thomas was friendly it was as though the real Thomas was hidden behind this pleasant man sitting beside her. She could say something about that now, she supposed, but then changed her mind. He wouldn't want to be bothered when he had the seminar ahead of him to think about.

They reached George's house by mid-morning and, despite her mother's pleas that he should stay for lunch, he was on his way again after a cup of coffee. Claudia went with him to the car and he kissed her lightly as he got in. She poked her head through the window as he was about to drive off.

'Do be careful, Thomas, and I hope everything is successful.'

Her face was very close to his, and he drew back with a jerk, an action which sent a cold shiver down her spine. She stood back, fighting sudden tears. It was as though he couldn't bear her near him. When he got home again they would have to talk...

She enjoyed her day with her mother and George. That they were quietly happy together was evident, and Mrs Pratt and Tombs were, in their own way, just as happy. George drove them over to Child Okeford one evening, and they looked round the cottage. She hadn't got the key, but the builders had already started on the repairs and they peered through the windows and explored the garden. George pronounced it a nice little property, and her mother could find no fault with it.

She bore her mother off to London the next day. Thomas had phoned on the previous evening, expressed the hope that she was enjoying herself and warned her that he might not phone her for a couple of days. He had sounded friendly, but even over the telephone she'd imagined she could hear the constraint in his voice.

Her mother was delighted with the London house. She professed herself overwhelmed with its comfort and luxury, and Cork's perfections. Claudia took her walking in the park with Harvey, and the next day went shopping with her. George had given her money with which to buy herself something she liked, and Claudia, mindful of Thomas's suggestion, persuaded her mother to accept a cashmere twinset, and the wool skirt which went so well with it...

Thomas had told her not to expect to hear from him for a day or so, but all the same she was disappointed that there was no word from him. She had to explain this to her mother, who said roundly, 'The poor man; it's time he slowed down. After all, he's a married man now; his work is important, but so is his married life.'

Claudia said cheerfully, 'He loves his work, Mother, but once the cottage is ready we shall be able to spend weekends there, away from his patients.'

She took her mother to the station the following morning and saw her onto the train. Feeling suddenly lonely, Claudia lingered at the station entrance, trying to decide whether she would join the taxi queue or walk home. She could cross the road and go through Hyde Park—quite a long walk, but it would fill in her morning.

She had left the park, crossed Park Lane and was walking along Brook Street when she came face to face with Honor.

She summoned a social smile and a hello, and went on walking, but Honor put out a hand so that she was forced to stop.

'Claudia—it is Claudia, isn't it? How delightful to meet you again. I've been away; I can't stand London at this time of year. I phoned Thomas at his rooms before I left, and he told me that you were very occupied getting ready for Christmas. Such a bore, having to go all that way to the Lakes just for a couple of days.'

'I enjoyed it,' said Claudia. 'Nice to see you again. I really must get on...'

Honor didn't let go of her arm. 'My dear, you can spare half an hour, surely? Let's have a cup of coffee...?'

Against her will, Claudia agreed. Perhaps Honor really was an old friend of Thomas's, in which case she shouldn't be rude—besides, Honor was making herself pleasant.

Over coffee, after a witty account of her holiday in Italy, Honor began asking questions put so casually it was difficult to ignore them.

'Thomas is away?' she asked. 'Off on one of his jaunts?'

'Well, it's not a jaunt. He's in Liverpool, and probably going on to Leeds.'

'Has he taken Emma with him?' Honor gave Claudia a sly glance. 'His secretary goes everywhere with him. A beautiful creature—very efficient and very sexy. Of course, now he's a married man, I expect he's more discreet.'

'I haven't the least idea what you're talking about.'

Honor said quickly, 'Oh, my dear, I'm sorry. I quite thought you knew. After all, it isn't as if you and Thomas are desperately in love—anyone could see with their eyes that neither of you are...' She paused as Claudia got to her feet.

'You're talking rubbish, and spiteful rubbish at that,' said Claudia. 'If making mischief is all you know how to do, I pity you.'

'You're upset,' said Honor. 'Naturally. You don't have to believe me, but if you ring Thomas's rooms I'm quite sure that Emma won't be there.'

'I'll do no such thing,' said Claudia. 'Goodbye, Honor, I hope we don't need to meet again.'

Honor had a parting shot. 'You wouldn't dare find out for yourself,' she laughed. 'But I shouldn't be surprised to hear that Thomas won't be home for a few more days.'

Claudia didn't answer that, but walked out of the elegant café where they had been sitting and then walked all the way home.

This gave her time to remember every word Honor had said, and to assure herself over and over again that nothing would induce her to phone his rooms—a nasty, low-down action not to be contemplated.

She hardly touched the lunch Cork had ready for her; she took Harvey for his afternoon walk, and the moment she got back picked up the phone.

Mrs Truelove answered. After an exchange of pleasantries, she said that, no, Emma wasn't there. 'She doesn't come in when the Professor is on one of his trips. A most efficient girl,' enthused Mrs Truelove, 'quite indispensable.'

Claudia chatted for a few minutes before putting down the phone. Mrs Truelove hadn't asked her why she had rung, and she hoped that she wouldn't wonder about it later. She felt mean and wicked and disloyal, but no more so than Thomas...

'I hate him,' said Claudia to Harvey, and burst into tears. She didn't hate him, she loved him, and what a time to discover it.

Before she'd made that shattering discovery it wouldn't have mattered about Emma—after all, he had never said that he loved her or was likely to do so. Theirs was to be a sensible marriage, wasn't it? So he was free to do what he liked, wasn't he? She knew that he would never be unkind to her, would always be a friend, even be a little fond of her and share at least some of her life, but now, with the discovery that she loved him, that wouldn't do.

This was something they would have to talk about. She would never tell him that she had fallen in love with him, but she would make sure that he wasn't having second thoughts about their marriage. And he would be home the next day.

She had pecked at her dinner and was poking her needle in and out of her tapestry when Thomas phoned. He would be delayed for another day, perhaps two, he told her. 'I'm in Leeds; I'll come home as soon as possible.'

She said, 'Yes, Thomas. Goodnight,' and hung up on him. If she had said more she would have burst into tears.

The next day seemed endless. She filled it with walks and arranging the flowers and trying to eat the delicious little meals Cork had set before her, but by the evening she was restless, and at ten o'clock she decided to go to bed. The day had been long enough, and there was all tomorrow to get through before Thomas got home.

'Bed,' she told Harvey, and started towards the kitchen with him, but in the hall he stopped and rushed to the door, barking furiously, and a moment later Thomas came in.

He closed the door gently behind him, bent to fondle Harvey and looked at Claudia, standing speechless. She had rehearsed all the things she was going to say to him but she couldn't remember a word of them. She said, 'Hello,' and then, 'You said you'd be home tomorrow.'

'I'm home today because something's wrong, isn't it? You were upset when I phoned last night.'

He was taking off his coat as he spoke, and Cork, coming into the hall, greeted him with grave pleasure, took the coat, enquired if he would like a meal or drinks and then went away, taking Harvey with him.

'Cut the air with a knife, I could,' Cork told the little dog. 'What's up, I'd like to know. Well, we'll have to leave them to it, won't we? And hope it comes out in the wash.'

Harvey, accepting a biscuit, wagged his ridiculous tail.

Claudia found her voice. 'Would you like a meal, or something to drink?'

Thomas smiled briefly. 'Cork just asked me; you couldn't have been listening. And, no, I don't need anything. What I do need is to know why you sounded as you did last evening?'

Claudia, playing for time, asked, 'How did I sound?'

'Don't waste time, Claudia. You were upset, angry—too angry to speak to me. Why?'

He took her by the arm, marched her into the drawing room and shut the door. 'Let us sit down...'

He sounded friendly, and reassuringly calm, and she longed to fling herself at him, feel his arms around her, but first she must know about this secretary of his. She wouldn't mention Honor, for he might dismiss her as a malicious gossip bent on making mischief, and perhaps she was, but Mrs Truelove was quite another kettle of fish.

'Where do you go when you aren't at a hospital? I mean, do you have friends or stay at a hotel—in the evenings when you're free.'

If she had been looking at him she would have seen the sudden stern set of his mouth and his cool stare, but she wasn't, so she plunged on, getting muddled and resenting his calm silence. 'Don't you meet people you know? Or—or have a meal out, or something?'

She did look up then, and sat up straight at the sight of his cold anger.

He said in a quiet, icy voice, 'Are you accusing me of something, Claudia? Perhaps you should be more explicit.'

She had gone too far now to stop. Besides, she had to know... She steeled herself to look at his expressionless face. 'Your secretary, Emma—she wasn't at your rooms. Mrs Truelove said that she was never there when you were away...'

Mr Tait-Bullen crossed one long leg over the other. He said mildly, 'You wish to know where she was for some reason?'

'Yes, well, I think you should have been honest about it. I

know it doesn't matter, because we—we don't love each other, but I am your wife.'

'Let me get this quite clear. You have been told by someone that when I go away Emma goes with me, so when I'm not working we can—er—live it up together.'

He spoke quietly, but Claudia flinched at the contempt in his voice. 'And who told you this?' He smiled thinly. 'I'll give you credit for not imagining it for yourself.'

'Of course I didn't imagine it,' said Claudia hotly. 'It never entered my head. I met Honor...'

'And you believed her?'

She peeped at his face. He was in a splendid rage, but he was controlling it with an iron will. She said recklessly now, knowing that she had cooked her goose with a vengeance, 'Not quite. I tried not to think about what she had said, but she told me Emma wasn't at your rooms—she laughed and said I didn't dare to find out for myself... So I did. I phoned Mrs Truelove and she told me that Emma wasn't there.'

'I see.' He got to his feet. 'Our marriage may not be quite as other marriages, Claudia, but I thought that we shared a mutual trust, and I hoped that our liking might have turned into something deeper in time. It seems as if I was wrong. This is something which must be put right as soon as possible. If you are unhappy, and I think you are, you must make up your mind what you want to do. Take your time, and we'll talk again later.'

He walked to the door. 'And now I must do some work. Goodnight, Claudia.'

She said in a squeaky voice, 'Thomas, are you very angry?'

He smiled then. 'Yes, my dear.' It was a bitter smile.

She heard him whistle to Harvey and then shut his study door, and she went up to her room, reflecting that he still hadn't told her if Emma had been with him.

The night seemed endless, and by the end of it she hadn't had a single sensible thought. She would never be able to tell Thomas that she loved him now. Not that she would have done, she contradicted herself, but they would have made something of their marriage, because loving him, even secretly, would have made it worthwhile. Something would have to be done, but she had no idea what.

She went down to breakfast, her pale face carefully made up. It didn't conceal her puffy eyelids or her pinkened nose, and Thomas, bidding her good morning in his usual voice, had difficulty in restraining himself from picking her out of her chair and carrying her off somewhere quiet, where he could tell her how much he loved her. But of course that wasn't possible; she had demonstrated only too clearly last night that her feeling for him wasn't strong enough to overcome her doubts.

He said in his usual calm way, 'I shall be away all day. Could dinner be a little later? I've a meeting at the hospital, and I'm not sure how long it may last.'

He finished his breakfast, wished her a pleasant day and went away, leaving her to feed Harvey with her neglected toast.

She was trying to decide what to do when the phone rang, and she went to answer it.

'Mrs Tait-Bullen? This is Emma, the Professor's secretary. Mrs Truelove told me that you had asked for me. I'm sorry I wasn't here; when the Professor goes away he allows me to go home—I live in Norfolk—at least, my parents do. I'm getting married in the summer, and there's such a lot of planning to do; was there something I could do for you?'

Claudia, astonished at herself, heard her own voice saying the first thing which came into her head. 'Emma, how nice of you to phone. I just wondered if you had any ideas about a wedding present? I've seen some lovely china... The Professor says I should make it a surprise, but perhaps there's something you would like to choose? A dinner set, or something for the house? Will you think about it and let me know?'

She rang off presently, Emma's thanks ringing in her ears. But she forgot that immediately. What a fool she had been; with her stupid outburst yesterday evening she had destroyed any chance of Thomas ever falling in love with her. He must despise her. They would have to go on living together, outwardly friendly, while she ate her heart out for him, and he would treat her with a distant courtesy which would chill her to the bone.

She suddenly couldn't bear it any longer. Thomas would be at his consulting rooms until ten o'clock; she picked up the phone and dialled.

Mrs Truelove answered her. The Professor had just seen a patient. If Mrs Tait-Bullen would wait a second, she would get him to come to the phone before she ushered in the next one. She came back to the phone very quickly.

'I'm so sorry, the Professor asked me to say that he is unable to talk to you at the moment. I was also to tell you that he would be late home this evening and that you weren't to wait up for him.'

The dear soul sounded worried, and Claudia hastened to say that it wasn't important and that she had expected him not to be home early. 'It was nothing important,' she added, 'really, it wasn't.' As though repeating it would convince her, as well as Mrs Truelove.

Her normal common sense had been taken over by a kind of recklessness. To stay quietly at home waiting for his return and then probably be met by his cold stare and refusal to talk was impossible. She swept upstairs, changed into a tweed skirt, a sweater and the leather jacket, pulled on boots, found scarf, gloves and a handbag and went in search of Cork.

'I'd like to go for a drive in the Mini,' she told him. 'Would you fetch it round from the garage for me, Cork, while I take Harvey for a quick walk?'

Cork put down the silver he was polishing. The Mini lived in the garage in the mews behind the house, for his use and as a second car if it was needed. It was kept in good order, ready for the road at a moment's notice, and there was no reason why Claudia shouldn't drive it. All the same, he felt doubtful.

'I could drive you, madam. The traffic's very heavy...'

'I've been driving for years,' Claudia told him, which wasn't true; she had used Great-Uncle William's old car from time to time, driving him to friends, before he took to his bed, and her mother to the nearest supermarket, but now fright and rage and bitter unhappiness had made her pot valiant. 'I won't take Harvey. I've had a message to say that the Professor won't be back until very late this evening, so something on a tray will suit me. I'll be out to lunch.'

She fastened Harvey's lead, gave Cork a reassuring smile and went for a brisk walk, going over in her mind the route she must take to get her onto the motorway. It was still early, and the morning rush was at its height, but it was coming into the city; traffic going out of it would be much lighter.

When she got back Cork had the Mini at the door. He was still uneasy, but he received Harvey, begged her to take care as she drove away and went indoors. He wasn't a man to say much, but he voiced his doubts to Mrs Rumbold.

'Don't you worry, Mr Cork,' said that lady comfortably. 'You just said she'd had a message about him not being home early. Like as not she told him where she was going.'

Cork took comfort from that. At least Claudia had looked confident as she had driven away.

She might have looked confident, but several times during the next hour she wished herself anywhere but behind the wheel of the Mini. She was a good driver, but London traffic was something she hadn't had to deal with, and it was daunting. Only the despairing urge to get away from Thomas as far as possible kept her going.

She followed the route Thomas had taken, driving steadily, thankful at last to turn into the country roads from the motorway. It was after midday when she turned the little car from Child Okeford's main street and down the lane to Christmas Cottage.

The dry morning had clouded over, and it was drizzling. The cottage looked forlorn, although she could hear voices from within. She got out of the car and opened the front door.

There were several men working there and she stood, forgetful of her worries for a moment, marvelling at the amount of work which had been done. The walls were plastered and the woodwork painted, and two men were laying an oak floor in the sitting room.

She wished them good afternoon, told them who she was and asked if she would be in the way if she looked round.

No one minded, and one of the men led her from room to room, pointing out what had been done and what was still needed.

The plumbing was done, he pointed out, but none of the bathroom fitments had arrived yet. 'Nor yet the stuff your husband ordered for the kitchen.'

'You've been so quick....'

'Well, seeing as how there's not much work around at this time of year, and us being paid on the nail, we got started right away. Staying in the village, are you, missus?' She crossed her fingers and fibbed. 'No, I just came down to have a look on the way to visit my mother. I expect my husband and I will be coming down at the weekend if he's free.'

'Busy man, isn't he? The house agent told us he is a famous doctor.'

'Yes, he is.' She couldn't bear to think of Thomas. 'Look, I'm going to the pub for lunch, and then I want to look round the village. What time do you go?'

'We'll pack up as soon as the flooring's down—can't do much outside with this rain. About three o'clock, I should say.'

'Well, if I'm not back before you go, thank you for letting me see round. I've a key, but you'll lock up, won't you? The car won't be in the way if I leave it there? I'd like to have a walk.'

'Right you are, missus.'

They parted the best of friends, and Claudia went back to the village main street and went into the pub. It was almost two o'clock, but the landlord found coffee and sandwiches for her and, when she told him who she was, came and sat at the table while she ate, giving her a friendly insight into the village and the people who lived there. By the time she had finished her leisurely meal it was already dusk, and almost three o'clock.

She made her way back to the cottage and found the men loading their van, ready to leave. It was obvious they expected her to leave too, so she got into the Mini, reversed it into the lane so that the van could pass and waved them on. She stayed where she was, though, until they had been gone for a few minutes, then drove back and parked the car at the side of the cottage, found the key and went in.

The electricity had been turned on, but there was only one naked bulb in the kitchen. Someone had left an old wooden chair there and she sat down. Her sudden spurt of recklessness had worn itself out. She had been a fool to come, but she had wanted to see the place where she had hoped that they were going to be happy. She hadn't thought beyond that. 'I'll sit here for a bit,' she said out loud, 'and presently I'll drive back. Perhaps Thomas will let me explain.'

Mr Tait-Bullen saw the last of his private patients out, got into his car and went to the hospital, where he had a clinic and ward round waiting for him. He would be finished by teatime, and then he would go home and he and Claudia could talk. There was a great deal to be talked about. Their sensible marriage wasn't working out; after only a few short weeks she had let him see that she didn't trust him. All the same, he was going to tell her that he loved her...

The ward round went smoothly, and the clinic wasn't quite as busy as usual. He saw his new patients, giving them his meticulous attention, and then, waiting for the first of his old patients, he phoned Cork.

'Is Mrs Tait-Bullen home, Cork?'

'Sir—a good thing you called. I was getting that worried. She took the Mini early this morning, and said she wouldn't be back for lunch. Didn't say where she was going.'

'Took the Mini? Did she seem upset, Cork?'

'Worked up, as it were, sir. Left Harvey with me, said you wouldn't be home until late, and that she'd have something on a tray.'

'I see, Cork. I'll be home as soon as I can. She may have decided to go and see her mother. Phone Mrs Willis, will you, and find out? Don't ring me here as I shall leave as soon as I can.'

He put the phone down, deliberately dismissing Claudia from his mind while he looked through the patients' notes to see if there was anyone whom he should see. There wasn't; he could safely leave them to the registrar.

It was too early for the evening rush hour, and he took short cuts.

Cork was hovering in the hall when he went in, and said at once, 'She's not at Mrs Willis's. I shouldn't have let her go.'

Thomas gave him a reassuring pat on the shoulder. 'Nonsense, Cork. You weren't to know that she would be gone for so long. Besides, I think I know where she is.'

Cork brightened. 'You do, sir? I'll get your tea…'

'Later, Cork. I'll bring her back in the car. The Mini can be fetched later.'

Mr Tait-Bullen drove out of London a good deal faster than Claudia had done, and once on the motorway put his large, well-shod foot down, sliding past traffic, a sleek, dark shadow, there one minute, miles away the next. He had taken time to go to Claudia's room before he left the house, and had seen with satisfaction that she had taken no clothes with her. Indeed, all the usual things a girl would put carefully into her handbag before a day out were strewn on the dressing table. Her driving licence was there too. He had smiled when he saw it. His Claudia had left the house without her usual common sense.

He was forced to slow down once he left the motorway; all the same he made the journey in record time. He slid the car slowly up the lane and its lights showed him the Mini. He turned off his own lights and got out of the car, and saw the faint glow of light from the kitchen. He had brought Harvey with him; now he tucked the little beast under one arm, one hand over his muzzle to muffle his bark, and went into the house.

Claudia was still on the wooden chair. She was sitting very untidily and she was fast asleep, her head at an awkward angle. She would be stiff and cramped when she woke.

He stood looking at her, loving her very much and Harvey,

suddenly realising who it was sitting there, gave a small, pleased yelp. Claudia opened her eyes.

She stared up at Thomas for a few moments, eased her stiff neck away from the chair and said in a wondering voice, 'Thomas, dear Thomas. I thought I'd never see you again.'

He put Harvey down then, and stooped and swept her into his arms. He was tired, and he had been very worried, but now that didn't matter. He said slowly, 'You said "dear Thomas"...'

'Well, you are. Only I didn't know, and now it's all such an awful muddle...'

'No, it's not, my darling. You see, I love you. I've loved you for quite a while now. Just when I have despaired of you ever loving me, you called me dear Thomas.'

'Oh, you are, you are. I must have been blind or something. I think I've loved you for a long time too, only we both thought the other one didn't, didn't we?'

Mr Tait-Bullen listened to this muddled speech with delight. 'Dear love, you couldn't have put it more clearly.'

He bent and kissed her in a way which proved how right she was. 'Were you running away?' he asked, and bent to kiss her again. 'Because if you try to do so again, remember to take your driving licence with you.'

'I'll never do it again, Thomas. Thomas, you do love me? Really love me?'

'My dearest love, I would not wish to live without you.'

Claudia kissed him. 'We have the rest of our lives together,' she said, 'and we'll come here whenever we can, won't we? And be happy together—with Harvey, of course.'

'And a handful of sons and daughters, my darling. Harvey will need young company...'

'He has us.'

'Yes, and I have you too, Claudia.'

She peered up into his face. The bland calm wasn't there any more; she saw the man she loved, the man who had been there all the time.

'We're going home now,' said Mr Tait-Bullen.

Modern Romance™
...seduction and
passion guaranteed

Tender Romance™
...love affairs that
last a lifetime

Sensual Romance™
...sassy, sexy and
seductive

Blaze Romance™
...the temperature's
rising

Medical Romance™
...medical drama on
the pulse

Historical Romance™
...rich, vivid and
passionate

27 new titles every month.

With all kinds of Romance for
every kind of mood...

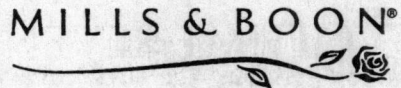

MILLS & BOON®

Yours to WIN!

We have **SIGNED COPIES** of
BETTY NEELS novels
PLUS
Weekends in beautiful
AMSTERDAM[*]...

*Yours to WIN –
absolutely FREE!*

To enter, simply send a postcard with
your name and address to:
'Betty Neels Ultimate Collection Prize
Draw', Harlequin Mills & Boon Ltd.,
U.K.: PO Box 236, Croydon, CR9 3RU.
R.O.I.: PO Box 4546, Kilcock, County Kildare.

Closing date for entries: 31st July 2003

NO PURCHASE NECESSARY
Terms and conditions apply.
Please see next page for details.

Betty Neels Ultimate Collection
Official Prize Draw Rules

NO PURCHASE NECESSARY

Each book in the Betty Neels Ultimate Collection will contain details for entry into the following prize draw: 4 prizes of a signed Betty Neels book and a weekend break to Amsterdam and 10 prizes of a signed Betty Neels book. No purchase necessary.

To enter the draw, hand print the words "Betty Neels Ultimate Collection Prize Draw", plus your name and address on a postcard. For UK residents please send your postcard entries to: Betty Neels Ultimate Collection Prize Draw, PO Box 236, Croydon, CR9 3RU. For ROI residents please send your postcard to Betty Neels Ultimate Collection Prize Draw, PO Box 4546, Kilcock, County Kildare.

To be eligible all entries must be received by July 31st 2003. No responsibility can be accepted for entries that are lost, delayed or damaged in the post. Proof of postage cannot be accepted as proof of delivery. No correspondence can be entered into and no entry returned. Winners will be determined in a random draw from all eligible entries received. Judges decision is final. One mailed entry per person, per household.

Amsterdam break includes return flights for two, 2 nights accommodation at a 4 star hotel, airport/hotel transfers, insurance and £150 spending money. Holiday must be taken between 1/8/03 and 1/08/04 excluding Bank holidays, Easter and Christmas periods. (Winner has the option of accepting £500 cash in lieu of holiday option.)

All travellers must sign and return a Release of Liability prior to travel and must have a valid 10 year passport. Accommodation and flights are subject to schedule and availability. The Prize Draw is open to residents of the UK and ROI, 18 years of age or older. Employees and immediate family members of Harlequin Mills & Boon Ltd., its affiliates, subsidiaries and all other agencies, entities and persons connected with the use, marketing or conduct of this Prize Draw are not eligible.

Prize winner notification will be made by letter no later than 14 days after the deadline for entry. Limit: one prize per an individual, family or organisation. All applicable laws and regulations apply. If any prize or prize notification is returned as undeliverable, an alternative winner will be drawn from eligible entries. By acceptance of a prize, winner consents to use of his/her name, photograph or other likeness for purpose of advertising, trade and promotion on behalf of Harlequin Mills & Boon Ltd., without further compensation, unless prohibited by law.

For the names of prize winners (available after 31/08/03), send a self-addressed stamped envelope to: For UK residents, Betty Neels Ultimate Collection Prize Draw Winners List, PO Box 236, Croydon, CR9 3RU. For ROI residents, Betty Neels Ultimate Collection Prize Draw Winners List, PO Box 4546, Kilcock, County Kildare.